I0655616

Praise Among Literary Reviewers for the
First Edition of "The Seeker in Forever"

" 'The Seeker in Forever' is an entertaining book that is a great read for
anyone who enjoys a fast-paced, well-written political satire."
—Cherie Fisher, *Reader Views*

"Highly recommended . . . to be given high praise for an originality and
cleverness that is as entertaining as it is thought-provoking."
—Small Press Bookwatch, *Midwest Book Review*

"A mind-bending world . . . This flight through the imagination requires
a full and complete appreciation for the raw, elemental beauty of the human experience."
—Miranda Orso, *The Electric Review*

"This book will take you on a wild ride . . . A definite read for anyone
looking for a rare adventure of violence, insanity, and power struggles."
—Adreann Stephens, *SLUG Magazine*

"An interesting read with a powerful message."
—Jasmine Greene, *Static Multimedia*

"The reader should be forewarned that this is not your mother's political
satire, but instead a whole new animal altogether. . . . Prepare yourself
for a bit of joyride the open-minded will undertake with gusto."
—Sylvia Cochran, *Roundtable Reviews*

ALAN FOX

Alan Fox has been featured as an expert source on the business uses of storytelling and showmanship by "The Chicago Tribune"/Tribune Media Services; "Entrepreneur Magazine"; "Chief Learning Officer Magazine"; and other leading print media. He has also appeared on numerous radio stations across the country to discuss effective presentation techniques and the high art, craft, and principles of great showmanship.

He has been studying and practicing story-driven 'showmanship,' in its many forms—ranging from film to theater, industry to politics—for more than twenty years.

In addition, Mr. Fox has operated a thriving practice as a respected business communications counsel and director in both Los Angeles and New York for more than fifteen years.

Presented in this volume, is the newly revised second editon of his first novel, "The Seeker in Forever."

For more information, please visit:
www.storyfocus.com

The Seeker in Forever

Revised Second Edition

Alan Fox

StoryFocus™ Communications
New York
www.storyfocus.com

The Seeker in Forever (Revised Second Edition)
Copyright © 2009 by Alan Sean Fox
First Edition Copyright © 2004-2008 by Alan Sean Fox
All rights reserved.

Based on the screenplays "Throwing Sketches at the Wind" and
"The Sidewinder" by Alan Sean Fox
Adapted from text copyrighted 2004: LOC Reg. No. TXu1-153-193
And book text copyrighted 2006: LOC Reg. No. TX 6-352-541
Publisher's Reference:
Text Import 2008_1002--50_Master
Output 2008_1015--54_Master

This book, or parts thereof, may not be reproduced in any form without permission from
the publisher; exceptions are made for brief excerpts used in published reviews.

Published by:
StoryFocus™ Communications
New York
Tel (718) 775-5540
www.storyfocus.com

Printed in The United States of America

ISBN-13: 978-0-9762276-1-8 (trade paperback)
ISBN-10: 0-9762276-1-4 (trade paperback)

Acknowledgements

Pop culture frames our world. We all go down our own road, but we start where the old roads leave off. I'd like to thank the following for expanding the realms and reaches of our pop culture, for myself and for us all.

Patricia Barber—One of the truly greatest of singers/pianists/songwriters
Jack Bruce/Pete Brown—Songwriting team
Stanley Handelman—Comedian
James Douglas Morrison—Cryptic poet of some intensity
Dorothy Parker—Writer of some repute and literary renown
Don Richardson—Master director and author
George Shdanoff—Acting teacher

Also:

Muhammad Ali
Raymond Chandler
Madonna Ciccone
Vinicius de Moraes
Dick Gregory
Frank Herbert
Robert A. Heinlein
Bill Hicks
Michael Hutchence
Peggy Lee
Ricardo Montalban
Roland Orzabal
Cole Porter
Bonnie Raitt
Ayn Rand
Socrates
Pete Townshend
Stevie Ray Vaughan
H.G. Wells
And Many Others

This book is dedicated to you

And I hope it makes you happy to know,
My love goes with you, wherever you go

The Seeker in Forever

Her Scorching Beauty
and
His Wicked, Wicked Sidewinding Ways

ONCE UPON A TIME in a dark corner of the All, there was a world that *peopled.*

It emerged from fires.

And its motions rippled outward, upward, onward, roundward. And conspired an armor.

The ripples turned and spread within themselves.

The motions, once started, did not stop. There was only the moving forward—motions leading on to motions.

The world rippled, and the ripples *peopled.*

The people, found that time stretched out before them and called them to journey.

Reckless and hungered, they coursed. Murders by the roadside, spoke of their progress, as they sowed a brave new world. As they peopled a brave, strange flowing world.

And found themselves flowing in mighty currents.

The people, struggled and strove, and broke each other.

The motions rippled.

Creating—while the world was young—a he-being, *Miles Roark,* and a she-being named *Daphne Fox,* a woman who swam in mystery.

Her mystery groped out at he-beings and drove them to grow hot. And bothered. And to long achingly for her motions.

In the course of the timeline, in the slipstream of the now, in a tavern, her mystery groped out at two He-Men—the team of *Mahoney and McSmithers*—who had emerged from a duststorm on the horizon and retreated into the establishment's dark shades for a round of drinks.

Outside, the sun was fled and gone.

Nightfall covered the realm.

The ground rhythm rippled onward, outward and upward.

Wildfire, ran wild in the wilderness.

The motions suggested the he-being, *Miles Roark.* He, that would one day encounter the she-being, *Daphne Fox,* that swam in mystery.

He, was a seething burning fire.

She, was a princess, queen of the byways.

They were in a strange night of stone.

She, was steeped in mirth. He, seething.

Their motions would extend into the furthermore.

Into the recesses and reaches of forever.

But first, there would be great barriers, which were quite a consideration. What difficulties lay before the onward motion? What was there to halt the forwarding?

The world, and its gold. A force red, and its might.

But, these lay in the storms of the futureflow. Out there. In the looming moving storms of the futureflow.

In the here and now . . . which when you get down to it, is all we ever have, had or will have . . . there is a region . . .

And in the region of the now, there lies *the tavern*—and within the hollow tavern's recessed dark shades sit the two He-Men—the team of Mahoney and McSmithers—applying themselves seriously to getting rotten, stinking drunk. And warming themselves on a feeling . . . of the embrace of her warm, wet mystery. Or more particularly by visions of her warm, wet inner being.

The thought trails spreading out into the tavern, speak of the team at work, rendering, forming the philosophical stylings of Mahoney and McSmithers.

A Tavern, "The Caveman's Grotto & Grill"

IT WAS A DANGEROUS WORLD filled with overrated treasures and underrated pleasures. Mainly to be gotten through hunting, murdering, destroying and devouring. And this tavern was a retreat, but it had a kind of calm that verged on violence.

A dark center gave out dark motions, which streamed outward to a shore of walls that buffeted them back. The walls were made of granite and stone, of bedrock and boulders.

Lying on the shorewalls—adorning them, lending them dignity— were wooden deathclubs; dark face masks; flaked flint arms; and ground stone weapons. The place had the look and charm of the good old days, of the Stone Age! . . . and the outdoor life. It was filled with the haunting remnants of happy days spent under the sun hunting, struggling, fielding, dying and murdering.

This was the backdrop.

And in the spotlight, the team was at work.

Mahoney drank his whiskey.

"In books . . . the hero's a superstar," said Mahoney. "The hero is a firebrand. In books, the hero is a freaking firestorm running wild. He's a secret service agent. He's a swashuckler, buccaneer, you know what I mean? A 'firestorm cocktail'—burning with feeling, baby. You following me?—"

"Oh aye, that's correct," said McSmithers.

"He's outside the field," said Mahoney, "outside the grid—The hero is a big burning question and we have to hang in for the answer—see that's the hook, that's what pulls us, the audience, into it . . ."

"That's the fantastic thing always," McSmithers said.

"And he's in a big game—Secret service double agent, maybe," said Mahoney. "Commander turning a war, maybe. Commando being chased, maybe. That kind of shit. That level of frickin' cosmic happening, okay."

"That's right, a proper game," said McSmithers.

"The hero is a mystery and he's in a mysterious game. That's what I'm getting at there. Okay, now."

"Yes, that's fantastic," McSmithers said. "Tells you a bit of something it does."

"Fantastic," said Mahoney, "that's right it's always fantastic—If not a commando, then a former commando. If not on Her Majesty's Secret Service, then formerly with Her service. Can speak any langage, true? Expert with any weapon. Can chop his hand through a wooden trunk the size of an elephant."

"Oh aye, that's a marvelous thing," said McSmithers.

"His hands are weapons. More dangerous than my mouth. You know the kind of guy I mean?"

McSmithers saw the profit in being a hero: "That's for sure. Very cool—Has all these magnificent women around."

The man drank his whiskey. "Yuhp, and he's always in the game, always a player. Never looks around—wait a goddamn minute—Goddamn hell, what am I doing here? Like any normal person.

"Well . . ." the man swung around to the trail he had been carving, "this girl is just like that . . . *Daphne Fox* . . . Oh . . . Fashionably lean.

And, ah! . . . no drag on her. You watch the way she walks—no fears. Wild with the power. Wild as can be."

The man drank his whiskey.

This was the straight shoot, the hard hit, and the knowing sit of the team of Mahoney and McSmithers.

Outside, a siren blared and it began to rain in the deep forest.

Scorching Beauty

DAPHNE FOX LAUGHED.

She was moving through crackling rains. Crystal teardrops drenched her. She was floating on water and air, and wind and sky.

She walked naked, in her clothing. This was the feeling she always gave people. Particularly he-beings.

She laughed, at what had been and what was to come. At life. At the explosive sky above.

She knew this was a moment between battles. She was on an island floating on nothing, nothing more than her life force, which was a force like a whirlwind.

The earth opened wide as she soared. She rose and left it all behind.

The drops drenched her body, making love to it.

She did not know that she was in enormous danger, and might be murdered in a few minutes.

Yet, it was there. Much was being given unto her. She was about to have a chance to die.

She approached her front door.

On the other side a man waited, in a chair, sleepy-eyed probably just having taken a nap, holding a gun.

Daphne entered, unaware of the man concealed further in the room.

Daphne spun to slam the door with her leg. As she turned, she spotted the man with the gun. She froze with her leg raised in the air.

She looked at the intruder. He was huge. Nearly seven feet tall. *And, she thought, he has the coiled killer look.*

"Hello," she said.

"How are you?" the giant said.

"Fair to middlin'. How are you?"

"Better and better," the giant said.

She brought her leg down. "Are you looking for me? I wasn't expecting anyone with a gun."

"Yes, you and a guy that was very rude to some friends of mine a few days ago. When do you expect the gentleman?"

She swept her gaze across the room. "Are you here by yourself?"

"I have some friends nearby. When do you expect the gentleman?"

"Should we invite them in? Will they be carrying pistols? Can they bring cocktails?"

The giant was courteous as he moved toward her. "You want to play some games? Let's play some games. What the hell, you want to try a little of this?"

Pow! He punched her. She tumbled.

"How is that?" he said. Now, his objective was to be popular. He felt you should do your best to be popular with your victim. This was what he was about. This meant for her to think that he was wonderful and terrific and entertaining. And also to be popular when he went home and solved the case for the boss. To be popular . . . okay . . . And now he was feeling it, giving this thing an emotion that suited him. *Hey, isn't this fun?* he thought. *I mean waiting for these things is a pain in the ass but when they turn up . . . then you get to play! Okay . . . okay . . .*

"Was that a good thing?" he said. "Did you like that?"

"Very solid," Daphne said. "I can see why you would be proud of it." She rose to her feet. "I'd like to study that when we have the time."

"Why don't we make the time?"

"Let's," she said. And smiled.

Now he hit her in the head. He belted her. With enormous feeling and conviction. He felt that it would have to be a hit that threw her head, that threw her head so hard that she would fly across the room. Bam! Her head went flying across the room. And as this thing was happening what he needed from her, in order to feel his full manhood, was he had to hear a yell of pain that was unbelievable; he listened to her scream, and concluded that her yell was that of a tortured woman being brutally beaten by a man—It was a good scream.

Now she was writhing on the floor, her face buried.

Once the agony subsided, she came up laughing. It was as though he played a terrible joke on her by belting her.

"Okay," she said, "you won that one."

She crawled over and tapped his foot.

"Ahh, tag, you're it," she said.

He kicked her hard. She screamed with the pain. Then started laughing.

She pulled herself up by using the table. She was in bad shape. She grabbed a thing off the table.

The giant aimed his gun at her.

She revealed that the thing she was holding was an army knife, the kind you fit in your pocket. The blade was in its case.

Daphne winked at him.

She held herself in place and spoke to him. "I knew a loan shark," she said, "who knew people better than any psychiatrist. A woman came to him to borrow money . . ."

The giant held his gun completely still. He held it in the air. With a bead on her. His hand was steady. He didn't move a muscle except to breath.

"This loan shark asked this woman how much she needed," Daphne said, "and she told him. The man took the money out, without counting it—this loan shark knew how much money he had—and he put the stack on the table. 'Shall I wrap it for you?' he asked.

" 'No,' she said taking the stack and putting it in her bag.

"She thanked him and started for the door—He stopped her.

" 'Give me the money back!' he said.

" 'But why?' she said.

" 'Because you don't intend to repay the loan—you didn't count the money.' "

The giant was fascinated. "You didn't count the money, huh. Hah! I like that! That's hot!"

"You're not here to use the gun," Daphne said.

"One never knows, do one?"

"You're here to do some damage but not to kill anyone."

She started using her femininity to enthrall him.

"What if I fought back?" she said. She raised the army knife in an ineffectual, harmless way. She pulled open the blade. She turned her eyes from the blade to him. She smiled with great sexuality. "What if I fought back? Would you like that?"

"You're a marvelous girl. Listen little girl, don't you know I'm dangerous?"

"Why are you dangerous?" she said. And if you heard only what she was saying, you could have sworn she had no idea why anybody would consider him dangerous.

"Because I have a gun," he explained. "Because I'm paid to beat people. If your boyfriend walks in, I'll beat him worse than you."

"Nah-nah na-na-na. I'm a killer too. I can be just as dangerous as you."

"Is that so?" he said.

She smiled. And proved herself very sexy.

"Would you like me to fight back?" she asked.

"What could you do little girl?"

Now holding the blade out, she began to move toward him. She stumbled. She could barely walk.

The giant brought his eyes to the blade. It was a slim, and slender thing, not much of a blade at all. She was charming, he thought. Nobody, that he ever came to beat the hell out of, ever did a thing like this. There had been other beautiful women he had beaten and normally the women cried, some tried to defend themselves; but no woman ever came at him with nothing. This blade she was brandishing was nothing.

"You're going to stab me with the knife?" he said. "You'd never make it. And what could you make of it?"

He showed her how he would knock her back. As he extended his gun hand, she flew at him.

She bit his wrist while stabbing the knife into his abdomen. You never saw a woman stab anything harder. But it was really a feint. What she was really doing was what she did next. She quickly got the gun from him, backed out of his reach, and fired into his chest.

He tumbled back. Then began to rise toward her.

"Enough little girl," he said, "now you shot me, are you happy?"

And now he was on his feet. He was coming at her, shrugging off the bullet wound.

She took hold of the gun by the barrel and attacked him. Bam! Her blow sent him to the floor. And now what she did was to beat him, hard. It was a little of this, and a little of that, and before long she was finished beating him with the gun.

She pulled herself up. She was bruised and bloody from what this man did to her.

Now she jumped up into the air. "Wwhheeeee!" she yelled. And as she came down, she landed on his ribs.

She stepped to the floor.

Then she sat on the giant.

Instead of crying with relief, she was laughing.

"I won the game," she said softly and studied him for a reaction.

She took hold of his nose in her fist. The whole nose, and gave it a good hard twist. His lights seemed to be out. He didn't seem to be feeling a whole hell of a lot at the moment. Or was he? Did she see a trace of something?

Now she grabbed his ears. She twisted both of his ears as hard as she could.

Pull.

Pull.

She fell back laughing.

House Crimson

IN THE SAVAGE FOREST CITY there was a center, and in that center, a skyscraper, and within—a charged core, where a group was rallying.

At the flare point, of the large gathering, stood their leader—*Cinjun Khan S'mythe!*

He stood on a stage, firing up his people.

The audience was a crowd of young people. The faces—pretty and handsome. The bodies—supple, strong, and sexy.

Many had only now joined *his people.*

And what these young people saw in Cinjun Smythe was an enormous thing. It began with his very look. Cinjun Smythe had the look of a great being. His features seemed to be the work of a master sculptor. His eyes blazed with rapid and deep energies. His body ran wide in frame and seemed built of only lean, sinewy muscle. As these young people looked at him, they imagined him leading men onto a battlefield. This would be his proper setting. They imagined him aiming a gun. This would be his proper setting. They imagined him directing forces from a command chamber. They imagined him leading a troop of horseback riders into a rugged mountain wilderness. They imagined him living within an enormous estate. Living within a command mansion. These things were his proper setting.

This man was barrel-chested, and when he spoke, his voice rose like a thundering boom from some great depth of emotion and power.

As they gazed at him now, he was taking control of the atmosphere and producing enormous charges of feeling. He was creating, with his presence, one of those times when every little movement stood in significance; where every movement became distinct and vastly important; where every movement seemed to ring into an eternity of emotional feeling.

Now Cinjun drew in the charged moment he was producing and hurled its energies, like some big generator, back into and across the reaches of the chamber.

"I," Cinjun said, *"am the greatest mind on the planet!"*

That was all.

Now lying within this hovered the understanding that your mind is not as it is felt by us. Your mind does not live in your body, your body lives in your mind. Your mind is the *All*—all of nature, and all of the cosmos—as it is focused at the point you call here and now.

He left it there, holding the moment in a state of extreme charge with the force of his will. He produced a hell of an effect on the audience. His confidence seized their attention entirely.

The interesting thing in all this was that he had never said this thing before—but he could see it now—*He was the greatest mind on the planet.* Of course, that's what he was.

The moment he spoke a thing, it became entirely true to him; he could see it, touch it, believe in it with every part of his being.

Cinjun had made the jump, in his mind, from leader to *god emperor.* He saw it now, he was their *god emperor.* His only difficulty was: Would they go along with him?

They must cheer him. He forced them; he willed them to cheer him.

The silence thickened.

Cinjun attacked it with his will; he directed his will into the mass of young people. He hurled his life force at them. They must bend to his will, or he will break them, destroy them, punish each man and woman in the place.

Could they possibly accept that he was the greatest mind on the planet?

Now the answer came.

Cheers!

He must force them further. Could he press them into a more extreme state? Where was too far in this journey? Where would they fight back, fight him to the death? Because to go on would mean surrendering their inner being to him, Cinjun Khan S'mythe.

"I am the greatest mind on the planet!" He must have their power. To do with as he wished.

Cinjun held the moment in the air. He would not allow it to be reduced in any way. Because it could fall from the mark here and now, but Cinjun would not accept the possibility. He would not allow failure to enter his operation.

How far could he push this, Cinjun thought, before they would oppose his will? He must be ready for it, when it comes.

There must be no relenting, no stopping, this was how Cinjun operated. He moved forcefully, spoke forcefully. He must press his way through all barriers. He must be certain of everything. No one can be allowed to perceive weakness in him. *You will not see weakness in me.* No weakness, anywhere . . . Because Cinjun knew he had none.

Each step forward was a test of Cinjun's being. But he was no mere human being, he was a *god emperor,* as he was coming to realize, the more and more he thought about it.

Now he stood there, holding himself still, feeding the silence.

The energy in the place quickened.

A follower howled, detonating a round of cheers.

This ignited more clapping.

Cinjun was setting the night on fire. This was the way it was meant to be. This was the energy you needed to change lives.

"I bring us out of the darkness! I bring us into the light!" Cinjun said, riding the waves of the people ocean.

The waves rippled to the outward reaches of the hall.

Now he spoke in simple, heartfelt human tones.

"I bring a journey song. I bring *The Promise of Great Journey.* I bring you the ship of unity. I bring you the craft of unity. I bring you *The Craft of State.* I will bend the shape of our existence into *The ForceSong of Bold Union.* I bring the *ForceSong of a People Boldly United.*"

This sent them into a roar.

"I take you into the air now!" Cinjun said.

They pounded. Stomped. Beat the floor. The firestorm ran wild in the wilderness.

"We will set sail in *The Craft of State.* To cross the ranges and seas of *Big Sky Country.*

"We must take the helm. I intend to take the helm of the command deck," Cinjun said.

"Tonight we turn our light and features upward. And we defy gravity to bring us down. We move into the air now. We must steady the controls. We must set a course. We must fly with steely resolve. We must travel. We must make our bold voyage. Oh, we must journey, my friends. The furies cry. Dear hearts burn with it. We must reach our glide path. We must fly our craft as steady as she goes. Our destination is *The Whyte House Under the Big Sky.* And the command deck at the bridge of *Big Sky Country.*

"We must be ambitious for the hard choices of government!

"We are up in the air now!"

They roared. And he stood before them, the lion tamer with the enormous bullwhip.

"I bring you from out of the cold. I bring you from out of the dark. Tonight we shine. Tonight we move the tides. We ride the air currents.

"We are up in the air now!

"Gravity will yield. Gravity will not conspire to bring us down.

"We are up in the air now!

"We all have wings now. We rise over walls. We form bold union. We form a perfect design.

"We are up in the air now!

"We will not fall into darkness. The air will not thin. Plane up and farewell. Farewell to those who will not risk. Farewell to those who will not use their fist.

"We are up in the air now!

"We will make the shape of reality. We will push into great risks.

"We are up in the air now!

"The color of our purpose will begin to sing and play. The color of our mission will carry. We will take our purpose, we will take our journey . . . to all the frontiers of our country. This world will bend to our will.

"We are up in the air now!"

They grew wild. The place exploded. They were on the verge of leaping into the air.

They applauded with all the force of their being.

The place filled with bone-shattering noise.

"Well done. Well done," Cinjun said. "Settle down now.

"Let us get to matters. I hear your thoughts.

"Let us speak tonight of the color of our mighty purpose."

Now he sang softly.

His words began to weigh.

With great concentration and effort of will he forged his next thought into being.

"You're fortunate to have me," Cinjun told them.

Having made it through to the other side, he set a different rhythm.

"I will lead you through the wilderness to *Eden Estates,* to *The Whyte House Under the Big Sky.*"

Now he pounded the beat. And made the rhythm dance.

And brought them deeper and deeper into temptation.

He built the road with simple stones.

They will not be able to resist this journey, Cinjun thought. *Now I will take them into the moment.*

"The Federation is about blue, the blue of the sea. It's about white, the white of the true pure open. But it is also about—*Red!*

"And we cannot forget that. We cannot forget what red is, what it stands for.

"This 'Foundation House' we stand in—now for twenty years, it was vastly important, moving the people's business, standing for the nation, for the red, white and blue of the Federation.

"This was a very important place for twenty years. But now it is time to move to the next stage of thinking.

"Yes—this Foundation House—this place, its ways—this was a good start, *but can you picture what now will be? From here, we cross to a realm of joy; we cross the range to a realm of light.*

"When I came into this place, I saw our difficulty. We were strong in the blue and white, but we were weak *in the red.*

"I focused in on the red. And strengthened the red, heightened it.

"We must make it a deep, rich red. A healing red."

Now he took them into the moment:

"Tonight, we launch House Crimson!"

Red flags went up.

The flag of House Crimson was a stark splash of red.

It was nothing but pure, bright red.

Now, red flags went up everywhere in House Crimson. Blood red.

"There is the blue and white of peace, but there must also be the red of war. The red of a united front. Raise the red lifeglow!"

These people filled the place with cheers! Now these aroused men and women were feeling the possibilities. All the *possibilities.*

No one in the place would see any sleep tonight.

The Sidewinder

IN THIS FOREST SOCIETY—there was a cocktail party, held at night; and within, there was a woman—a Daphne Fox being—who strode and shimmered and lit up the night.

She was a rip current that drew in all full-blooded men. That pulled all full-blooded men toward her gravitational center. They came at her from all directions—men in suits.

Alone and apart, stood: *He.*

Now, he was *Miles Roark.* At this party, he brought a touch of madness into the mix.

He, stood on the far side of the room, swimming in mystery.

There was something about him that appealed to some of the room's beautiful young ladies. For some of the young ladies, he sparked thoughts of soft warm bedrooms; lingering touches, bodies confused—swims in satin silks and strange senses. He, was sexual imagination and a cure for unhappy girls locked in prisons of solitaire—He tore traps away, he broke through barriers, and flew fast away—He swam in mystery.

He stood, in a long upward surge. He was wild-eyed with tousled hair. There was something savage about him. He had the look of a young lion.

A friend appeared before him, saying:

"How would you like to meet a woman—who is *wild with the power, wild as can be?* Everybody loves this baby."

It was this, that lured Miles into action—

And Miles moved in the way winter springs into summer, and summer falls into winter. He was a living force, moving forward, a set of changes making changes go round.

It was as if he were a man stepping out of a whirlwind. This was the way he moved. He emerged from a storm. Around Miles's features you imagined the tempest, and the savage wildman.

He, had the thing! The charm of the insane. The jungle was his setting, the wilderness—He was realization—He emerged from a thunder.

A thundering Earth.

A savage night.

A brooding sky.

And in this way, . . . he moved, . . . a tempest, moving with gentle mood.

And in this gentle way, Miles gently entered Daphne's awareness.

"Hello Daphne," he said, and she turned to him. "My name is Miles," he said, as if she was asking.

She looked at him. Her eyes, a frontier swirl.

"Miles, . . . Miles, . . . Miles, . . ." she said, binding him in coils. "Miles, . . . do you like to travel?"

"I do . . ."

She smiled teasingly.

"Do you like to have sex?"

"I do . . ."

"Then why don't you go fuck off?"

He looked at her. He liked her. She had gotten him to say, "I do!" Twice. Within a moment of meeting—Suddenly, they were taking marriage vows. Well, how do you like that?—He recognized this, this was a love storm.

He was enthralled by the nature of her feminity. She revealed many dimensions in every aspect of her being; she produced an amazing presence. She was a woman who was not afraid to use the language of adulthood, to use industrial-grade language—to open her show with "Fuck off." He sensed that in her cursing, she was saying there is nothing wrong with the language. She felt free to use the entire language. Even words that some people separated off—because they were normal, and filled with nasty inhibitions that she did not have. A lot of people escaped direct language. To her this was a source of great sadness. There was nothing more useful in communications, than making your point and getting to it. It showed a high regard for Miles when she said to him, "Fuck off." She placed them immediately on a level of direct communication. She was making a human-to-human connection. She was forging a lovely bond—and now she continued.

"Why are you squinting?" she said. "Do you think it makes you look sexy?"

She locked eyes with him. Her eyes, were shimmering . . . On a whim, she adopted his squint. And made some improvements on it—It made her look sexy as all hell.

Miles grinned.

"I'm in love with you," he said.

She raised her lovely face high and looked at him.

"There's a beautiful sunset out there," she said, "in case you'd like to go ride off into it." Now she lowered her face. And now *Tygers* crouched in jungles in her shimmering dark green blue eyes.

He looked at her. He was meeting another of his own species.

She relented. They stood a long moment staring into each other.

She drew a breath.

"How well can you kiss a woman?" she asked.

She parted her lips, sending a phantom kiss floating on the air out to him. In this way, she drew his attention to her lips. And once she had him there, she spoke.

"I need perfection," she said softly to him.

And now with a deliberate upward sweep of her head—that threw back her hair in soft waves, revealing a fuller beauty in her features—she drew his attention to her eyes and what lay in them.

And she said, sofly, ever so softly:

"I need perfect intent, perfectly cast. I need wicked perfection. Some twisted heart that can entangle me. To keep me alive."

Now he was looking into her eyes. *So many twists and turns in those eyes,* he thought, *those twisted, twisted eyes.* Dark green and blue, and filled with dangerous turns. He felt himself assailed by huge grips of emotions that came flooding out of her eyes. *Tygers* of feeling, raging. Abruptly, she became turbulent waves of feeling moving into everything. He saw her moving about him, heaving with violent disturbances, and yet staying perfectly still. She made him see misty streets of blue. And an immense feeling for him among other feelings. Now, bolts of feeling crackling and surging through the all of her. She said this thing and many things softly but he felt himself torn by the immense feelings bursting out of her. She was shattering his world and yet the only physical signs of the great emotions she was displaying to him were—the *Tygers* springing wildly from those mad eyes of hers; those mad, mad eyes.

"Hmmm," she said eyeing him through those mad, mad eyes.

"Mystify me," she said. And her eyes held him.

"I dare you, Miles," she said. *"Mystify me,"* she said again; this time in a haunting way—that would stay with him forever, she knew.

Now she had him bound firmly in the mighty grip of her gaze. She held herself and him in silence.

The silken moment went on forever.

And now she moved away from him. She walked away, carving through these people with no effort only the force of her emotions, she walked away, into streets, true and blue, . . . she, was rise and fall. She, was delirium, promises, . . . ways to try, and ways to fly.

Miles stood there a moment, holding his gaze outward. She was slipping in and out of sight on the far side of the room.

Miles rejoined his friend. "She is, wild with the power, wild as can be."

"That, she is," the friend said.

Wild!—Miles thought—*Wild with the power to make every moment come alive.*

"How do I get hold of her?" Miles said.

"She's beyond your reach," the friend said.

"Don't be so sure. I'm growing every day," Miles said.

Miles watched from afar, as *Skyler Larkin Malloy,* a businessman, strode over to Daphne. Skyler molded himself into a stance, and placed his arm around her waist. Miles saw that they were together . . . but he didn't see it lasting.

She had instinct, she had class, she would drop that Skyler boy on his ass—She was a derangement of the senses, taking him deeper and deeper, into life.

None has her beauty! Miles thought.

Fascination with no limits, deeper and deeper it went.

Scorching beauty bearing a name—Daphne.

In this night, . . . white light everywhere, but he couldn't see a thing. She filled his night, with blinding light. And everything that she was. Everything was broken up in dances, . . . dancing rhythm. And all that she was.

Style and rhythm. Substance and purpose. Force and sway.

He was losing his mind, she was causing the world to vanish around him. Leaving only her, and eternity.

Leaving only a bright eternity! and her.

Her glaring sun streaks . . .

Her glare and glory . . .

All this, as he gazed on her sun-streaked looks.

She, was her orchestration and her precision. And here and there, she was a glimpse of her thigh. She was a cool wind in a hot summer.

Outside, the night was laughing.

At the ebb and flow, of her.

At her form and spell. It felt the ebb and flow, of her.

She was doing it to the night as well. Maybe this night, was a man. Or a woman, admiring. The night felt itself carried. It felt the ebb and flow, of her.

She was doing to the night, what she did to men—the stars cried for her kisses.

"I Am the Sky God"

IN THE GATHERING HALL, Cinjun was taking his people to a feverish high.

"There are two forces out there," Cinjun said to the audience. "One is good, godly, righteous! . . . The other is evil, sick, vicious!"

There was a truth that spoke of what Cinjun was doing. There was a truth that had expressed itself over the years and fields of humankind. It was an expression that said, 'The world is divided into two kinds of people: those who divide the world into two kinds of people, and those who don't.'

Cinjun was now taking them deep into a very ancient, primitive scene. One that had repeated many times along the corridors of ancient galleries.

He had now become the great, ancient leader. He was prying something open for them. Something important. Something incredibly deep and wide. He was bringing them to a great, big whalloping, secret from the ancient gallery. Now they could touch it for themselves:

There are good people and there are bad people. Cinjun was helping them sort out which they were.

What Cinjun was doing was all too plain to see. Yet it was appealing. He spoke in simple words. From which, he illuminated something for them. Something elusive. Some huge thing.

The people, of bold union, adored him. He illuminated something for them. Something very important. It was this great, big thing.

He was giving them something fleeting—that they desperately needed.

'We are good. They are bad.' 'We will win. They will lose.' 'You are with us. Or you are against us' . . . He was singing a very popular song. A song of cheer, 'All Will Be Well.' Quite a classic. And what a hell of a rendition. Ferocious.

No more complicated order to tear at certainty and confidence, and to weaken you in the night. He willed them into a raw, cheerful state.

They were good, others were bad.

Ah, now it all made sense at last. And Cinjun continued to make sense for them.

They would no longer feel cold in the night.

"The forces shaping our world must be brought under our control," Cinjun said.

"Only strength can make us whole. Only strength can control the forces shaping our world. Only absolute standards will function toward our purpose."

They ate every moment of his slow moving.

They were desperate to come into power. And he was bringing them into raw primitive forces that could move the times.

He was writing history, standing on his feet.

This was an extreme sense of showmanship.

"We will know clear rules of behavior. We will know the difference between right and wrong.

"Our task is to restore stability. We will put the just back in charge of affairs.

"We will set simple tests.

"What we have imagined for so long, now will be. This is our time.

"We move up in the air now!"

"Today, we must wield discipline. We must learn control. And use it to destroy. So that we may *build*.

"Certainty can be used. To rid oneself of inner conflict. To lift those less certain.

"We don't need black and white thinking but we need to see the black and the white.

"We don't need an all or nothing point of view, but we need to see the all and the nothing.

"Our standards must be visible. We must see the two sides. Of right, wrong; good, bad; and sinner, saint.

"We must see the color of our purpose.

"The demand is purity. The just must judge themselves. And others.

"I'm going to *The Whyte House Under the Big Sky*. I'm there already, it's just a matter of time. I know the shots, I have mastered the shots, and I breathe victory.

"I'm going to be the President and take *The Whyte House*.

"I'm going to be the Commander-in-Chief, here in *Big Sky Country*.

"There's nobody who can stop me. And I'm taking all of you with me!

"We are up in the air now!"

Fists flew into the air. It was a promising beginning. They were off to another planet.

Nothing

NOTHING HAPPENED . . . for a while . . .

And then change sprang from the void.

The Stone Cold Attack

MILES WAS MEETING with the stone man-being who was his stone boss-being—commander of his field and realm.

And the stone boss-being was forcing into the world a scene, from the ancient gallery, the ancient order of business—He was seizing upon the midnight day and explaining to Miles how now seemed it rich to die.

He commanded Miles: To seize upon the midnight! and die with no pain!—He was to do this for his career. Miles had a big round, fulsome difficulty here; he was not the dying type.

The boss-being and Miles were met in a high office within a mighty skyscraper in the great forest city.

The boss-being was *Mister Dean Deacon.* He had many sides to his being. He had many missions, many things to do. Much to put proper. And with life so short—he had little time to do his great works.

They sat in this place, both men clad in mighty business suits.

"God damn it!" said Deacon. "I've just about had it with you. All you have to do is follow some basic rules. Repeat some basic messages. You follow some basic principles, and you follow some basic thoughts, and that's all you do—Can you understand that?"

Miles felt the wind shout like a drum, it had come. The black thing was risen here.

"I do things my way," Miles said. "I work clean. And I work . . . smart . . . Maybe it's good that I do things my way."

"You're a fucking kid—Some people around here think you're ar-rogant." Deacon breathed deeply.

"Some of the people here," Deacon said, "feel that you talk like a *Sound Chaser.*" He looked at Miles, and paused for a reaction. "That's what they say about you." Miles gave him no reaction. "Now they treat you the way they do because they feel *you're insane!*" Deacon paused. Received no reaction. "Do you understand where we are? They look at you and they see a person who is totally insane!—"

"All the best people are," Miles said.

"I," Deacon said, "don't have room in my life for this sort of thing. We do not have room in our lives for this sort of thing. *You* do not have room in *your* life for this sort of thing. Do you understand? So I'm going to help you become a better person. You will correct yourself, right now. You will fix your entire being, right now. You will no longer act like some goddamned *Sound Chaser.* Do you understand? Are we clear?"

He got no reaction.

"Are we clear!" demanded Deacon.

"Not all who wander are lost," Miles said.

"What a thing to say." Deacon came out of his chair. "I think it's very interesting. Who said that, *Scofield Morefield?* That damn *Sound Chaser.*

You're going to feed me lines from that maniac?" He was moving slowly but this was indeed the risen Deacon, a big, burly bear—on his hind legs. And now when he hovered over Miles, it was to use his size for intimidation. "You're going to talk like this when I'm doing my darndest to help you become a better person?" On this dark street the sun was black. Time had died; the wind had died. Deacon had set them wheeling across this landscape. They were on the way . . . The street was cold; it's trees were gone . . . He assaulted Miles, slowly with iron determination.

"I have never been talked to like this." Deacon held still. "You have right now to straighten out. Show me that you can fall in line. And show it to me now."

There was something here Deacon did not like seeing, he would break this man! It was necessary. And for his own damn good. He would teach Miles. Make him obedient. Crush him, and stamp out the menace in this young madman.

Not all who wander are lost? Deacon raged! He was a night without day. He was about to crush a life, a lesser form of life. Deacon was a superior man dealing with a young man of an inferior race.

Deacon was king of the highway.

Miles would fall on this road.

Miles stayed very even and spoke simply:

"A man doesn't borrow other people's arms and legs," Miles said, "so why should he borrow other people's brains? I think my way, and I say what I think."

Deacon harumphed.

Deacon leaned forward and said something very clearly and distinctly, "You're free to pick any color you want, as long as you pick red."

"I understand," Miles said.

"Pick a color." Deacon said.

Miles held his look firmly on Deacon.

Deacon held his position, and kept his eyes locked on Miles. "I want you to pick your favorite color for me now."

And now Deacon smiled charmingly; he was ready to be Miles's friend. "I hear red is your favorite color."

Deacon's smile became marvelously warm; everything was going to be all right; they were going to live in the same world and be friends; and it was going to be a beautiful world filled with happy trails. "Red is a marvelous color. Isn't red your favorite color? Go ahead. Tell me—What is your favorite color?"

"Green." Miles said.

"You're fired," Deacon said.

Miles had answered plainly; green happened to be his favorite color; truly it was, and some things were forever.

There, Miles thought, *it had to be.* Here on this stage, the time had come. They were going to drive a while . . . down into the scenic drive of the below . . . and spend a while observing the black all around, counting the hours to a rendezvous . . . Dark cool waters of pain dying beneath a sky without stars would pass their long while before time would see life move into the song. For now, there was annihilation, and a black thickening cloud.

The moment would cost Miles many things, things extremely dear to him. A heavy price, but the moment had a rightness—and a great goodness—to it. The darkness could not be helped—there was no avoiding it; Miles dove into the dangers to be found below, before him, and all around him.

The danger loomed, a horrible menace, describing itself as a reflection in Miles's eyes. Miles took his heart and let the melody of his heart play his song. Miles's song was dark and rich and deep; and, there was a tenderness, that lay there; and found emergence; tumbling up, a bursting, exploding fiery light that took on startling shapes. And there was something else—*Tygers* crouched in jungles in Miles's dark eyes.

Miles loosened his tie. It was such a pleasure to have it sit askew that he did not want to forego the pleasure for an instant longer.

He would drive a long while into distance . . . lonely distance, away from bitter time.

Dark winds crying. He would find the sun at the rendezvous.

Into the Wild Blue Yonder

IT WAS A MOMENT OF GREAT ACTIVITY in Miles's office, within the high office company, within the high skyscraper.

Skyler Larkin Malloy—the he-being that had been a shadow beneath the light of the she-being Daphne Fox—he, . . . that lucky, lucky Skyler Larkin Malloy, he was here.

Skyler and Miles worked in the same place, *The Agency.*

Skyler was skilled and mighty in the stone cold way.

He was a stone friend being, practiced in the stone cold way. Hollow eyed, but burning with black fire. Black flashes of darkness. He moved in his way. Of raised slow eyelids, and beautiful curly mouth. He was lucky—lucky in fortune—and lucky in love . . . the beautiful women many a time being upon his bed. Skyler took his luck as his due. And his stone-cold thoughts, he presented as mighty works from on high, lavishments from his high and abutted place. He loved watching them descend upon the day.

"Miles, you're the darndest bastard in the world!" Skyler said. "Why would you blow a good time like this! Are you a fool, boy, or are you just doing a damn good job of looking the part!"

Miles turned to Skyler. "I do things my way."

"Why should anybody let you do things your way!" Skyler said.

"Sometimes I bring a better way—"

"Well, you're a fool, boy! That's my professional opinion. I hope that clears things up for you."

"Not all who wander are lost," Miles said.

"Ah, wow, is that a *Scofield Morefield* line!" Skyler said. "What the hell is it with you? Are you another *Scofield Morefield?"*

"No," Miles said.

"A goddamn *Sound Chaser,"* Skyler said. "You're going to give me the talk of some goddamn *Sound Chaser?"* Skyler turned to Miles. "Why would you build a ship and then when it's ready, sink it?"

"I'm going to study with him," Miles said. Miles wasn't looking at Skyler.

"With who?" Skyler said.

"Scofield Morefield," Miles said.

"You can't. He's dead," Skyler said.

"Not yet," Miles said.

"Too bad. He's insane," Skyler said.

"That's the best way to be. You can see farther that way."

"For a talented guy," Skyler said, "you've got to be the lousiest fool I ever met. You heard what he did with his career? You get involved with him and you're finished. What could you possibly hope to get from that lunatic?"

"To see a few things," Miles said.

Tearing Away From . . .
The Stone Cold Black Hold

HE WAS HURTLING out of the place. Not fleeing into sadness.

He was rising into the wild blue yonder.

Here on the stage, the time had come. Under the strains of horrible rumblings and cold surroundings.

The song was going to be played—*Or he would die attempting it.*

Miles would never rest, never tire, never stop. He would pick up honesty, the best of himself, and then let it go, into time and space.

Come what may. Let stone cold attacks come.

Many there had been, many there would be. Growing in force and menace.

Threatening colds.

Cold cold cold.

Sucking out the air, sucking out the light, sucking out warm being.

Biting biting biting.

Cold cold cold.

Let it come, he would fight.

It had come and was coming and was yet to come.

The stone cold attacks.

Here on the stage.

"You need to stop where you are! And bury this thing you've been carrying around." Voices aching, the sounds they were making were cold. So cold. Played so wrong.

Screaming, blaming.

Get some honesty, and take the best, the rest let go, Miles thought.

Not this thing they came to him with, a cage. A cold cage.

An icy future.

Pain, was their goodnight song. Played so wrong.

And they screamed so loud, so long. Blaming. Screaming so loud, so long.

"Welcome to the real world!" they said. Welcome to the *We* world! was their song. We own it, you're just staying with us for a little while.

And if you don't straighten out, it will be an extremely short while.

Cold death, in the form of friendship.

Get some honesty, take the best, and then the rest let go.

He was thrown onto the stage, thrown into this world. He would make it bright and fill it with sun streaks.

He was thrown into it, and he would make much of it, before the end came.

If he was to sing his swan song, it would be sweet and mighty and brave.

Light and flowing, soaring and easy.

The Stone Cold Players do come!

The dangerous people do come to you, here, as friends. Always, they come.

The Doom Patrol.

The Stone Cold Marauders.

Bullying you into the stone cold way of life.

They lay it all out for you. Follow the We way and you can do great things. I know you can. For surely what We do is greatness! A greatness come to the Kingdom.

They attack with presumptions.

They suppose their greatness into being, and then all must yield to it.

"We're here to help you, and you must accept our help." More—you must be grateful for our help. Show obedience and show that you like us. Show worthiness to be helped. Show that you can be guided and made in our image.

Show that you accept being pushed around.

"Here is how we need you to be." Here is how we need you to live your life. Here is how you must be.

So Beautiful, once you are become We.

Oh, so beautiful to be,

We and we and we.

Ever beautiful to see, just

We and we and we.

Welcome. To a warm world of warming We.

Oh, To See

Oh, Beautiful World

of We and we and we

　　　of we & we & we

Did you ever see anything as beautiful as we & we & we?

Blood in the streets.

When you don't go with *We,* when you bring danger to *We,* you must be removed, obliterated, stamped out, smothered, choked, killed and buried. You must vanish from the realm and be erased from the mind.

Blood in the streets in the stone cold friends.

Blood in the streets in the stone cold players.

Blood in the streets in the chilling blows.

Danger, pounding a beat.

Hideous, wretched and sad. Stone cold.

The stone cold Damners.

Cold cold cold.

Biting biting biting.

Howl howl howl.

Shriek shriek shriek.

The shrieking madness.

The shrieking musts.

Ashen ashen ashen.

Murder murder murder.

Devouring devouring devouring.

Frozen to the bone.

Sinking like a stone.

Lone lone lone.

Alone alone alone.

Nothing more, nothing more, nothing more.

Don't let your heart do anything new. Enter the prison. Enter the dead stone prison, there's a lot of joy to be found here.

Don't they know what life is worth?

What it is to rise?

"No!—You will not rise! You will not rise! You will not rise!"

Fear fear fear.

Shivering shrill sentences.

He, would not let it end there. There were fine vistas beyond. Much to be found in the beyond. Much beauty, and truth.

They break you down. Fears. Break you to pieces.

Stand Tall, Headstrong Like a World!

There is much light out there.

Dark dank cold, was a little too short on love for Miles's taste.

He liked more tropical climes.

Fresh light, fresh being. Free and strong.

Tigerish walks, and flowing struts.

Expanding ribs, extending spines, he liked growing taller and stronger. That was more his *Way*.

Let their revolution of blood eat their bones and bring them into the cold earth.

Miles was going to spread his wings, and take to the skies. He was going to find *The Wãoynde*.

No more cold sleep, no more stone cold being under stone cold bites from stone cold scavengers.

Time waits for no man. Time slipping. Creating the future. An open future.

It was there for you.

No more cold daggers,

No more icy daggers, and cold knives.

He was going to flame, and take to the skies.

The great way was out there. *The Wãoynde* that rose into the skies.

That tore free of the ground, escaped from, sailed free of gravity and tyranny.

Opened and opened and opened.

Proceeded in twisting curving motions.

A flight clothed in the colors of light.

A purpose and a might, a soaring light.

A flight.

Life.

Chew chew chew.

Go, go, go, go, go. Chew chew chew.

Stone cold dogs.

Hyenas in the form of jackals in the form of dogs, in the form of friends. Dear friends, there to help. Dear and near.

And chew chew chew.

The stone cold compassionate ones.

Laughing at the sun.

Chew chew chew.

Cold cold cold.

Abyss abyss abyss.

Nothing to be made, nothing to be seen, nothing to be known. They know all. And they will show all to you.

Chew chew chew.

Bite!

Cold cold cold.

The stone cold end.
It's beautiful, try it, you'll like it.
The stone cold end.
Death clothed in a warm sun blanket.
This was the offer.
Accept it or die!
Really, there is a lot of good in it.
Miles would have none of it. All right then, he would be damned.

Maybe there was something improper in Miles's upbringing. Some deadly flaw in his mind. A flaw in his character to bring on ruin. But Miles was on a hurtling hunt, for a sweet dream known—and known only to himself—as—*The Whirlwind Wãoynde.*

. . . This dream, . . . known only to himself.

Out in the Fields, Scofield Morefield

MILES WAS KNOCKING on the front door but not getting a response. He could hear the soft strains of music coming from the back yard.

"Scofield Morefield!"

In yelling the name, Miles stretched out every vowel.

"Scofield Morefield!"

Scofield Morefield, a handsome old man came to the door, stark naked with an apple martini in his hand.

"Hello, I'm Scofield Morefield."

"I'm Miles Roark."

"Ah, magnificent! Tell me now, who the bloody, piss-besotted hell is Miles Roark!"

He yelled this one past Miles, playing to the neighborhood—It was standard theatricality.

Miles said, "Let's put your drink down. We've got work to do."

The Big Red One

THE STREET BOARDS PROMOTING House Crimson were abstract. Big red splashes. And occasionally—you might find—filling the frame . . . an image of *Cinjun "Big Red" Smythe.* He was 'Big Red' in the sense of a big red dawn.

A *light*vision reporter was questioning Cinjun in front of one big red splash. He asked Cinjun, "Why do they call you Big Red?"—The cover of a leading magazine presently available featured—in banner writing—a fascinating story about *"The Big Red One,"* filled with every praise known to man.

Cinjun looked into the light with an iron gaze that missed nothing.

He filled his setting; his presence seemed to be a massive life force emerging from the deep, streaming background splash of red. And the life force was smiling warmly. As warm and charming as anything you ever saw in your life.

"I represent a force in the world," Cinjun said.

"And the force is red.

"I represent a force without form. Moving with savage grace. A heat, a beat, and a light. The light is red.

"It's a very, very good thing. And it's building. Nothing can stop it. No one can stop it. And do you know why?"

Cinjun did not ask the question in an arrogant manner.

He filled the question with a great humanity, a tenderness; and then said, "Because it is right. And right is might."

Start It All Over Again

A NAKED WOMAN WAS BATHING in Scofield's hot springs bath, and sipping an apple martini.

Scofield had slipped on a robe and was walking Miles through his garden—and you could not help but notice that this was the strangest garden you ever saw . . . a meadowbeauty filled with greenery and fertile flowers . . . and soaring, flowing, exploding shapes cast in marble and bronze.

Miles swept his gaze across this place, took in the entire immense expanse . . . and in a gently streaming movement lifted his gaze from the beautyscape . . . and now aimed it at Scofield.

"I'm here for training," Miles said. "I'm here to learn what you learned and pick up where you left off."

Miles's eyes were locked on Scofield. They were doing something, Scofield observed; producing and radiating beams of a joy-splashed kind of fire.

Scofield felt a wave of savage energy radiating from this young man.

Scofield had seen this before—

"I don't train sound chasers anymore," Scofield said.

Scofield was going to shift this world into its true orbit.

"Listen kid," Scofield said. "You want to get girls, to make a little cash, make people laugh, nothing wrong with that. You want what I had. I still want it myself.

"Buy yourself a little jokebook, try them out on your friends, and the ones that work, *you stick with.*

"Now let me get on with my day. I was in the middle of a very important love affair when you walked into town."

Miles held himself entirely still. His eyes were on fire.

"Let's hold it now, old man," Miles said, blazing back brightly, "we're wasting precious time. I'm going to travel over ground you've covered."

Miles continued to hold himself entirely still. His voice came softly. And now Miles again came to his terrible purpose, "You're going to train me. It's time to start it all over again."

Miles's eyes were on fire. And now Scofield saw *Tygers* crouched in jungles in Miles's dark eyes.

Scofield stood and wondered what he might make of this young man.

As the now had rolled ever further into the past, it had come to be ever known in the land, that the young self of the Scofield Morefield being had been a man of exceeding promise, who had sped along the timeline. Distances had spread out before him . . . and were covered in a great trailblazing. There were ripplings and meltings. And great exceedings that sang sweetly. Sometimes, a rare country visitor came upon Scofieldland—upon Scofield's forest city dreamscape—unexpectedly in the moonlight and stopped and wondered from what dream the vision had come. The dream was the blue bird being of Scofield Morefield. He went through the years of his fame like a projectile flying to a goal no one could guess . . . He made startling experiments . . . once in a while . . . but people expected it, and one did not need to stop him . . . they would allow it for a while . . . but something was growing in him . . . struggling, taking shape; it seemed to be rising—dangerously—to an explosion. The explosion came . . . a fire . . . a fire that broke and swept through their ordered world . . . then, came the mighty collisions—the people emerging, the people talking so loud, so long, the people bringing fighting . . . And bringing into his world: *Professionals of a high order. Threats of great beauty. Beatings of royal splendor. Endings that sang of greater endings.*

"I'm not going to help you get your skull split," Scofield said. "You can't know what you're asking for. I do . . . A world that hurts so bad. There's trouble ahead. Difficulties. You can't know. Brutal difficulties. Terrible. To be avoided. Slow down. Think with me here."

"There's a bright future for me," Miles said, "in the blood, pain and sand. Oh, if that's the trip, that's the trip. Get your saddle, let's ride!"

"They," Scofield said, "will beat you with fists, break you with planks, trample you with horses."

And, oh, there were beatings; a flowering of beatings. Such was the form of the past.

"You had it rough," Miles said, bounding along cheerfully. "No denying it. Some will slip, some will drown. Some fall down. When your chin hits the ground, you pick yourself up, dust yourself off, start all over again."

And the men and women of good cheer had been a sight. Through their light reflected, there had been the beholding of confidence and resilience.

"You can't know," Scofield said. "How do I make it clear to you? They will tear you in half. It's their world."

"You have to fall to rise again," Miles said. "Let's start it all over again. Take a deep breath. Let's start it all over again."

"Don't make the mistake I made," Scofield said. "Don't imagine there's a way to win. It's a no-win."

Now Miles thought about this. *It's a no-win.*

"From start to finish," Scofield said.

Miles thought it through . . . he drew a deep breath. His eyes—that throughout had held Scofield—now became hard, and bright.

"I only know about winning," Miles said, "you're the expert on not winning."

"By all the bastards of the deep, how important do you think you are! You're being an arrogant, presumptuous netherworld bastard!"

Miles smiled.

"No, that won't work, huh? You see through me. You're probably as good as you think you are."

Scofield held his look. "Don't be rude," Scofield said. "Will you listen to me and not answer?"

"Yes. For a minute. Speak."

"I'd be committing a crime if I kept you here. You need to recover. I would make you worse."

"Perfect."

"The path looks fine to you at your age. The air smells of spring. But I've seen where it goes."

And there was a red stream. A deep, rich red, carving through the canyons of the All.

"It's the same old story, a fight for love and glory!" Miles said—he was a living force rolling forward. "The frontier is open land—Ride in. Set up camp. When the bandits come, stand your ground, stand tall, stride the earth. Stand tall, headstrong like a world."

And the rugged individualists did settle the frontier. And shape and mold it as their vision directed.

"Let's start it all over again," Miles said.

"I don't train sound chasers anymore."

"Is that so? An interesting theory. You might want to write it down. It sounds like something to put on your gravestone," Miles said.

Scofield looked at Miles then. He wondered if he was meeting another of his own species.

"I . . . don't . . . train . . . sound chasers . . . anymore."

"If I were you, I would say it until I believe it. There's no substitute for persistence in learning a thing."

Scofield was looking at Miles now with eyes that missed nothing. The wind began to blow, Scofield noticed. Something was calling his name out loud, and knocking on his door. And he wondered who in the piss-besotted hell this was. *Danger!* Scofield thought. *This man seems nice but he's loaded to bear with danger.* Scofield liked that about him. And it made Scofield wonder about a certain thing.

"I don't teach you . . . how to be a sound chaser, anymore. But I do have a class for some of the simpler *hots* in life. How would you like to learn how to get pretty darn hot—even if it doesn't make you a sound chaser?"

Miles was determined to get where he was going—Bring him hell or high waters; bring him pain or anguish. You see, the problem was that the weather was running too low for him, he liked it right around *'Too darn hot!'* He was on his way—such a way—and the destination of his journey was *Too darn hot!* No low cycles. Only one place. A place by the name of *Too darn hot!*

Scofield, scrutinized Miles. And Scofield wondered if indeed he was meeting another of his own species.

"I teach a class," Scofield said at last. "You may join. How would you like that?"

"Yes. It'll be an honor for you to have me. I'll shake you out of your rut," Miles said.

Oh, Let it Rain!

THE MORNING PASSED into late day. Scofield stood in his garden, threw himself into a surging form, and whirled to the sky. To the blue sky.

"Oh, let it rain!"

He could not stand a life of blue sky one more day.

"Oh, let it rain!"

Take away the empty shape of the day.

He wanted mood and motion.

"Damn it all, let it rain!"

Oh, bring on the night and bring on the rain. A pelting, powerful rain, palpable, sensual. Insane.

A Liquid Flight. Of slips and slides.

The sun made him feel like a fool, it did not much his mood. Oh, let it rain.

Let the thunder crack, and the lightning snap the tension.

Washing away the times.

"C'mon, bring on the rain!"

Bring on the rain. Pelting rain, palpable, sensual. Insane.

The Wãoynde

MILES ROARK WAS ON A HUNT.

He was on a hunt. A mad hunt.

He was hunting *The Wãoynde!*

He had no trail to follow, no report of what it looked like, or even a report that it existed.

He would will it to exist. And no matter where it lay, he would hunt it down and take it up, . . . take it up, and take it on an upward ride into the heavens.

Some people called it insanity. Some called it derangement. Delusion.

Some called it: *Shadows in the Rain.*

It had killed many, ruined many, but it was the way to see far and clear.

Did it exist? Truly? Or was it derangement?

It must exist. In a state of perfect grace. He recognized it by its pattern. He caught traces of it across the path of the human timeline.

Truth is beauty, beauty is truth. It was too beautiful a thing to not exist.

And now he was on the hunt for it. *The Wãoynde!*

Her Stormy Lover

HE HAD THOUGHT much of her. Now he called her to journey.

He had reached her on the call instrument. As the signal had called out to her, Miles had gazed out his window.

Daphne had picked it up at her end and spoke politely with him. He seemed to have caught her interest. This was his hope. Miles lived on the outer edges of hope, he was used to taking it for all the ride it had.

He asked if he might see her; if he might come around to her place; and take her out to ride on a whirlwind. And his thoughts went to her eyes as he talked to her. Her eyes, and their frontier swirl.

"No," Daphne said, "I can't see you Friday. You see," Daphne now spoke softly but with great conviction, revealing a terrible predicament, "my old fiancé from years ago returned from the Peace Corps on Sunday." She drew a deep breath, and produced a sigh that shook her with great emotion. "What can I tell you?" she said. "I'm sorry. But the flame rekindled. Hotter. Than ever." She sounded sorry as all hell.

"I'll be," Miles said, "a perfect gentleman and make great dinner conversation."

"You're very sweet," she said, and then she was struck by a thought of importance. "You would make someone else a very good husband."

Now he beamed, "You're going to have a delightful time."

"Oh my," she said, with a sexy, girlish cry. And then grew alert to the enormous danger. She said softly, "What about my stormy lover from the Peace Corps?" She spoke with great concern. She was in dire straits. This was a hell of a perilous situation.

"We can talk all about him," Miles said. "We'll have a lovely, brilliant time."

"Friday night," she said, "meet me here at sunset." She said this thing almost in a whisper. She was taking a great chance.

"What should I wear?" Miles said.

"Clothing!" she explained, didn't he know.

"Where are we going?" he opened wide her imagination.

She closed it with a sexy whisper and a silky tone, "Why don't we pretend that you're the man in the relationship. You pick the place. I'm longing for a surprise. I'm longing for a man to surprise me, in the right way."

"Where's your flat?" Miles said.

"Oh now," Daphne said, "you got my call exchange. I'm sure you'll be able to track down my flat. I have enormous confidence in your abilities. And now I'll reveal nothing more." She broke off the connection.

Pure, Bright Red

HOUSE CRIMSON HELD its red flag up to the world. With its beautiful mark—of nothing but pure, bright red.

And there were red flags up everywhere in House Crimson. Blood red.

They were doing several important things for heavens' sake.

And for the heaven-sent red.

Here on 'House Crimson Lane,' there was much great activity and shining down on every stop, a heaven-sent red.

And they were feeling it now, the heaven-sent red.

They spoke in their inner beings to the red, and said, "What can I do? I've thought about you?"

And they strode about this scene with enormous conviction, the kind of conviction that comes from having thought through a great crimson purpose.

Here in House Crimson, these people were driven by great crimson purpose.

Don't—don't you dare come between them and their crimson purpose, mister.

Somewhere . . . within the inner circle . . . a member—'Smackwater Jack'—spoke:

"We are on alert," dear sweet Jack said. "Vigilant against our enemies."

Cinjun was running this place like a compassionate company, like a warm hearted, good natured business.

The inner circle was simply his board of directors. His great executive committee.

And Smackwater Jack was simply a leading official, just a marvelous spokesperson, educating the public. He was young and new to the enterprise; but demonstrated himself to be a promising young he-man who was giving worthy voice to the feelings of his fellow freedom fighters; and in the way he composed himself, breathing the beautiful mission of House Crimson, which was . . . *To save the world.*

Near him, Big Jim, sat at ease, and said with an easy charm, "We fight for redness."

These people were fighting for the color they believed in. And they didn't give a damn who knew it.

"And," now Bulldog Bill spoke, "it is the best color because it starts the spectrum." How could there be any denying its primacy? "The first color of sunrise is red, and the last shade of sunset is red." His tone became soft but firm. "We are following the natural order—red."

"It's time to take red back from the communists," Big Jim intoned. And this held great meaning for him.

Smackwater Jack nodded behind him, feeling it now in a strong way.

Bulldog Bill said, "Red has been used to deceive us." He spoke of great ordeal. "To invert the meaning of red." He spoke of great conflict. "Red has been used against us." He drew a breath. "But red is ours." And this sustained him.

"We're going to be red," Big Jim said. "We're going to feel red. We're going to breathe red."

His thoughts went to the meeting he had had with an associate in the library at House Crimson—Professor Brick Bullwinkle—who put forth the theoretical proposition that in all the ways that mattered: "It is the most forward syllable. Red."

Bulldog Bill picked it up. "We have to take red back. Put it where it belongs. In the hands of the people. On the side of liberty, justice, and the pursuit of happiness."

"Red is blood," Big Jim said. This he knew; this everyone knew. "Blood is the flow of God within us." He felt himself grow poetic. And now he felt himself inspired to a new height. "Redliness is next to Godliness," he said. And let the matter rest there, on that high promontory.

Cinjun Khan Smythe, the god emperor, might very well be feeling it now. The feeling in this room was now growing so very vast and reaching so far and rising so high, that it had to be reaching and touching others. Reaching Cinjun in his command chamber astride House Crimson. High atop this forest city.

The First Ground of Being: The Fire Attitude

SCOFIELD WAS TEACHING his class in a vast acoustic solarium. He was sitting a distance from the stage. At the moment, a student stood on the stage, and a line of students waited to file onto the stage.

"You can't make a direct appeal," Scofield said, "You can't do what everybody else does.

"If you see a guy come on the stage and the first thing he says is, 'Hello, how are you folks doing tonight?' Ask your date—'Do you want to go see a show after this?' Because this particular happening cat already proved he isn't worth watching. Say to yourself, what would everybody else do? And then don't do it. Next!"

Miles walked onto the stage. He was about to open his mouth, when he saw Scofield sigh.

Miles walked off the stage and proceeded to the rear of the solarium. Scofield and the other students watched this.

Now Miles ran down the center aisle and leapt onto the stage.

He landed gracefully, and stood poised, his legs spread wide, his weight held low, entirely still, with his back to them all.

The people in the place held their eyes on him.

Miles turned, slowly. And walked toward them, but you wouldn't really call it a walk. A prowl, is what it happened to be.

The people breathed, this was all they did.

Now Miles lunged a pace forward, drove his body into a graceful upward surge, and let loose something.

"Rrrraaarrgh!" Miles hollered, sending a terrible cry into all the reaches of the night.

He roared, his voice crackling with a bellowing rumble coming from deep in the gut. He was feeling the lion. And it affected him, he seemed taken by a madness that reached from the ground and surged through his entire being.

He produced a deep and vast reaction in the people. One young lady felt a chill travel her spine.

Miles prowled the grounds. Like a lion driven mad in a wilderness of pain.

"Aaarrrgh! Yarghhh! Yeh! Oh yeah!" He seemed overpowered by some crazy feeling.

Scofield studied him. Just studied him. Scofield revealed nothing. Nor did he show any intention of reacting any time soon. He seemed made of stone, but a stone in a state where it is fired to an extreme heat, and is casting off a red orange glow.

Now Miles—in a staccato burst—shot his gaze to the other wing of the place, catching the eye of one of the young ladies in the class. "Rargh!" he told her. She shrieked.

Now the people made noises.

"Hold it—" Scofield said, "hold it down everybody—"

The place became silent.

Miles turned to Scofield and observed that the old man was studying him with great intensity. So Miles reflected the intensity and studied Scofield with just as enormous an intensity. It didn't happen to be intense enough to produce a reaction in Scofield. Scofield was heated, burning, stone—that revealed nothing.

There was no talk, no noise, anywhere in the place.

"Now," Scofield said slowly but very deliberately, "out with what you took the stage to say!"

Miles broke away from his penetrating study of Scofield. Abruptly, Miles became laid back and exuded an easy charm. "I," Miles said, "don't have anything to say—yet."

"You mean to tell me," Scofield said, "you don't have anything at all?"

"Not yet," Miles said. "Important to get a good start though, don't you think?"

"Get the hell off my stage," Scofield said. "Next!"

Force Red

CINJUN AND ANOTHER REPORTER WERE STANDING before a big red splash. The reporter repeated the fashionable question: "Why do they call you 'The Big Red One'?"

Cinjun smiled warmly, efficiently radiating charm and energy. He seemed to radiate the big red dawn they spoke of.

"I am a force in motion. And I'm part of a force that is bigger than I, bigger than our time, Force Red.

"People name me for what they see in me. And in themselves. And all of us together are the force. You may name it what you like, I name it Force Red."

Force Red, this was in the ancient tradition of power expressed. One person in charge. Society control flowing outward from a person of power, an architect of dreams. This was the way to rise—for *all* to rise. A man has to become ruler. We need it. It's absolutely essential.

Wanted: A good man. A new strongman.

And he was here.

New strongman for sale!

A man emerging with his cousins, sons, and daughters. *His lovely daughters,* Cinjun thought. *Beautiful, sexy.* One-ruler leadership, being the subject on his mind and elsewhere regions of his bodily form.

What does your vision tell you about the future of this country?

One-person rule and immense people force.

In his mind Cinjun was firing shells at opponents. Providing comfort with air cover. Threatening them, when they left the meeting. Firing rockets, to show who was in charge.

Oh, sweet Strong Man in Charge.

This place needed it . . . It had always had a strong man to hold the country together, to guide the people force along the civilized path. It needed it now again. Oh, sweet New Strongman for Sale!

Let the poets pipe of love in their childish way—

Let the *reporter-poets* pipe of love in their childish way—

Let the *reporter-poets* pipe of *peace* in their childish way—

Let the *people* pipe of peace in their childish way—

Who's prepared to pay the price for a trip to Paradise?

New Strongman for Sale!

Who will buy? Who will sample his supply?

Let the poets pipe of love in their childish way—He knows every type of love better by far than they—New Strongman for Sale!

If you want the thrill of love, you've got to go through the mill of love.

New strongman for sale!

"Follow me, and climb the stairs." New strongman for sale!

If you want the thrill of life, you've got to go through the mill of life.

Who's prepared to pay the price for a trip to Paradise?—New Strongman for Sale!

Old life, new life, any life that is true life.

You need to pay the price of the through life, of the through strife—

"Follow me and climb the stairs"—New Strongman for Sale!

He would: Experiment in patience and money.

History seemed to him a thing that built in sweep and scope, rising to a kind of Paradise. This was the thing to come in the natural way of things.

Cinjun would move in his people force, soon. Take the battle on the wind.

Scenarios forging, beautiful options developing. This was where to find hope.

He conditioned himself and his forces to advance his works. His great, good, noble works.

He was going to make the crooked places straight, lay the mountains low, exalt and raise the valleys, . . . and melt all turmoil into gold.

Tough times demanded a sweeping style.

His armed forces—not troops—armed forces, this was the way to think of them—

Bank accounts, this was also a thing he would work further.

The funds were growing, his war chest was massive, but he would fill it further.

His arsenal would have to be overwhelming, devastating, winning.

These were the broodings of his high office.

His great deeds would be expensive.

He needed money, he always needed money.

Abundance was relative. Wealth could lose to greater wealth.

He needed the biggest gun in the world.

This was what he deserved. A man of his stature and importance, de-served the biggest gun in the world.

In this world that *peopled,* the greatest gun was *people.*

Fit, strong, ready men . . . and women. Cooperative women. His vi-sion remained on the subject of women for some time.

And then he would turn to the world. He would be hard, hitting, sav-age, but manly.

In this world that peopled, killing people was part of the natural way, and the right and proper work of a high executive confronted by tough times. He was a high executive, he was a killer. He was that or he was nothing . . . Either that or he was a pushover, and that he would not be. He would not let his enemies turn him into a pushover. He would kill them first.

It was a violent world that peopled violently. And blood was in their blood.

It was simple, so simple. And yet many didn't see it, he would make them see it. Once he showed them his weapons, they would see it fast enough.

It was just a matter of psychology, once he showed them his big people force gun, they would see it. Many of the women would enjoy it, and many men would be inspired. He was an example, this was his burden and his joy.

This was a blood-soaked city, but what a beautiful place to live, he thought.

Many women would know joy and the people force gun, and many men inspiration in its visage, its bulging looks. He loved the *he* and the *she* of it, particularly the *she* of it.

He invented a language, very similar to the age old language of bloodshed, but with a lot of improvements. *New fighting language for sale!* So much bloodshed had been senseless; he would change all that; his bloodshed would make sense. Brilliant? Cinjun knew it was. Murder! There were so many god-awful murderers out there, that it had put the practice in a foul state, but murder was natural. Wholesome when used to create. Splendidly effective sometimes. And therefore, beautiful.

Clean murder! That's a professional. That's a professional at work.

An attack, that worked wonders, was a beautiful thing to see.

And spoke of warm progress under the stars.

He was forging fearsome being. And that meant producing different sides to his character. To everything turn, turn, turn. To every season a purpose.

This season was for opening wide the promise of House Crimson.

His thoughts traveled into distance. He turned his memory lives and inner fires to the difficulties of future days. He would have to forge fearsome being; and from that being what wonders might come.

He entered a thinkstorm of wonders.

He would be absolutely wonderful, and would wield people force, sunbeams and moonbeams to great effect, to produce marvelous life change.

He was forging fearsome being.

He would ascend the imperial path and take the seat of power in the imperium through deeds, the deeds of a god emperor.

He was forging fearsome being.

Oh architect emperor.

Oh marshall emperor.

Oh Cinjun Khan S'mythe.

New strongman for sale.

Bringing form to his being of CinjunKhan who would take the imperial path, and in good season, his being KhanSmythe, who would produce fearsome wonderful life change for the people of this good world, of this goodly world.

He was setting up the dimensions of the things to come.

Large scale things.

To save the people.

New strongman gathering energies and forging the fearsome being, with violent dimensions.

Vrooom. Thrak. B'Boom. He was forging fearsome being.

He felt himself to be an architect emperor. People force could be shaped in the way an architect shaped a building.

He would shape a people dream.

He had crafted the dream. And now—to bring the dream into reality. To shape this mighty people force that stretched out before him.

Now an architect pounded and forged into being.

Vrooom. Thrak. B'Boom. He was forging fearsome being.

What mattered heavily in his high office were the challenges of the violence that needed to come. The architect was readying himself.

He will unleash the dream. He will set the dream on the world; unleash its power; and take the world into its golden designs. All would be set to order; and held rigidly in place by supporting beams that could sustain enormous force. They all had a friend in Cinjun Smythe.

He would be a friend to the just and a fearsome being to the evil ones.

Those who would not get friendly would get dead. This design remained elegantly simple. The supporting beams would have to carry great weight. They would have to prove themselves fit.

Cinjun would be gentle and compassionate in murder, as a true gentleman should be. When he killed there would be nothing personal in it; this was extremely important to him. He would never murder out of a personal struggle. You could only murder as a swordmaster, quietly feeling the mighty purposes of the dream.

Cinjun's dream was beautiful, and now he bit hard on the beauty.

Unfortunate, but you would always have the damned—*Enemies be damned.* Keep them from creature comforts. Bring them to a lesser condition. Freedoms were nice things. But you could not afford to give everybody freedoms. The price was too high.

Beauty could be made real. So that beauty could shine all throughout the land. Purple mountain majesties. And no one would stop the goddamned beauty from having its beautiful way. Don't you dare get in the way of the beauty. This was the idea. Brilliant? Of course it was.

His thoughts were ever of beauty, and brilliance, and life wonder. And paradise. And goodness all the days of his life.

Beautiful things to see, playing misty visions. Beautiful things to see. Wandering through this wonderland.

That spoke of warm progress under the stars.

Nothing

NOTHING HAPPENED.

Nothing traveled a long day's journey into night.

Now, night nighting.
Dark darkening.

The Mainspring of the All

MILES OVERCAME a hornswoggle from Scofield and wrangled him—out to a tavern, "The Caveman's Grotto and Grill," perhaps you've heard of it. The team of Mahoney and McSmithers performs here, and yes, many top flight entertainers work this room, many performers, and drunks.

Miles wanted an answer to the burning question. Sometimes, the secret is not in the mountains, it's under your feet, or across the table. *How do you do it?* Was the burning question.

He wanted to manifest the players.

The Grounds and the Ground Rhythm

The rhythm and the motion.

The grounds were the episodes.

The ground rhythm was the motion.

Ground rhythm to . . . motion.

The question was burning.

He saw the motion. Motion was rhythm. *Where does the motion meet the rhythm?* he needed to know.

I'm looking for the ground rhythm, Miles thought.

You go through it all day without thinking about it. The beat that makes the ground rhythm of life. That establishes the feeling and then changes the way you feel it.

The drum is the centerpiece, the bass walks it, and the piano accompanies it. Together they push, pull and tug, and move the band. They are: the engine, the wheels and the body—Power from the engine; roll from the wheels; and form from the body.

Roll from its strut—The strutting, creates the rhythmic feeling. Giving it shape, and 'comping, . . . accompaniment.

Then comes the loose hit!

That's what I'm looking for. That thing. The looseness. The unfit, the offbeat. The thing that gives it its tigerish strut.

The question was: "How do you get to it, *how do you do it when you know how to do it?"*

Miles drew in the mystery swirling all around him and aimed it at Scofield. He held Scofield in a steady gaze and spoke.

"How do you do it?" Miles said. He raised his head: "How? . . . How do you do it?" That was all: How do you do it?

Nothing else needed to be said.

Scofield took in a deep breath, a sigh or an expansion?—It was a movement, and a recognition.

Scofield said, "You want . . . the secret . . . of *everything."*

"Yes . . . Call it out, I'd like to have a look. I've been looking for that damn secret everywhere."

Sometimes, the secret is not in the mountains. It's at your feet, . . . or sitting across the table.

Scofield smiled, and his face was the wall of all time.

"You . . . want . . . the secret . . . of everything." Scofield said it flatly, deadpan. There was no teasing involved, no asking. It was a simple statement. Clear. And to the point. It was their heading, . . . forward.

Miles liked where they were heading. He felt it—The moving.

"Ah," Miles said, "it wouldn't be a bad way to spend the evening— Taken all in all, *Infinity* is not a bad night's work."

The Trap

It takes some time to settle into your gut, Scofield thought.

The shocking thing about it was its nothingness. At first blush, it seemed to be nothing. *Everything* in the guise of *nothing*—the cosmic operation was immense and almost entirely invisible.

It *seemed* to be nothing, . . . this was the trap.

The Haunting Truth

"Tell the truth, that's the craziest thing you can do when you get up in front of people, tell of the haunting truth that drives people insane," Scofield said.

"The madness—the forces that shape our lives."

Scofield continued. "The thing that scares you at night. The part that makes you weep; that tears your soul . . . You have to tell of the tenderness there. The eerie, willowy, haunting part attached to every truth trail under the sun. That's what most of them miss . . ." Scofield was going to say more, but paused . . . he echoed himself, ". . . yes, that's what they miss."

And then Scofield leaped—dove into it—with all he was:
He Gave Away the Show.

Scofield pulled away the curtain; ripped the curtain away and threw it aside. And Scofield showed him the changes that shape the song.

He charted the harmonies.

Charted the harmonies, laid bare the arrangement.

What he said was:

"The . . . secret . . . of . . . it . . . all . . . is . . . *Opposites.*"

He tossed it into the air, it loomed there, accelerating.

Haunting.

In its simplicity. And depth.

One sound string, one thought—and the song of one cosmic all.

It floated in the air, accelerating.

Faster and faster, it went, the secret in the air.

Wings of blue sky, form of time.

The secret that took to the air.

The song it sang was opposites and it moved in beats.

And it said: The beat goes on, the beat goes on, the beat goes on . . .

A whirlwind worldwãoynde, running into tomorrow.

Into a frontier wilderness.

At first glance, at first blush . . . he seemed to be saying only something that had been evident to all, wisdom floating in the public domain about *opposites,* and perhaps, next, he would go into some folksy advice about the element of surprise, but he went on to say far more than that.

He was going to delve deeper into the secret mechanism—To the hidden roots inside of us that reach back to the beginnings of man.

The Melody of Scofield's Heart

Let's move in visions, let's fly in pictures, let's dance in sights, to glimpses of fleeting purposes.

This was what he was saying to Miles.

He was saying it with his feelings, which flowed from him and took to the air, charging everything they touched.

In back and under Scofield were crystal ships and crystal visions and great whirling motions.

This was what he was giving Miles.

The words, they didn't matter much. Oh, they didn't matter much at all.

There were a thousand other noises Scofield could have made with his mouth. Just as rich and deep. They were just the noises he made. Ah, but the feelings! Were forever.

The notes just played and played. The song was rich and deep, set in a deep blue. It was the melody of Scofield's heart—you know—that the notes obeyed.

Scofield said, . . . some more. He said words and called them by name. What matter of it?

Ah, but the feelings.

The words, why? It had little connection to what he was doing to Miles. He was making a connection with Miles. Willing it—Mind to mind. River current. Time flow. Time slipping. Time slipping.

He was breathing a feeling, a deep and rich feeling, an insanity, a madness.

It was all set in a deep blue. Scofield continued to flow.

There were more words, words that pointed to feelings

And there were feelings, feelings Scofield would let affect the words.

And, let imaginary forces work on the words to rend them with feeling.

He was feeding Miles enough to produce a feeling. A sympathetic reaction.

Something that could build to the heights and match the intensity of Scofield's feeling.

From there, expand to fill a world, and an all.

What he was giving to Miles was a view and a feeling for the world that peopled.

"Hmm, let's see now, opposites," Miles said. "Day, night, man, woman. Light and shadow."

Scofield said, "Most people stop there. I'm talking about something that is both. Can you picture a light that's a shadow? That would get interesting, wouldn't it?"

"Those kind of opposites exist?"

Scofield said, "Everywhere."

Scofield was departing from something, and approaching something.

They moved steady, rock steady, closing down the town, leaving it behind—passing between the moon and the forest city—into the beyond, the wild blue beyond.

And on they soared.

Once the distance covered stretched the length of forever, Scofield rested, for a moment, took it all in, and continued flowing across the wall of all time.

Back to the beginnings of man.

He took it to the place where most things start—the beginning.

Back to the beginning of the world's peopling.

And there was one thing he knew—this song was deep and rich and it was set in a deep blue.

The Stone Age

"Let's come at it from another direction," Scofield said. "Let's strip away the modern world. Strip away everything that is not essential. Go back to the Stone Age. Make it stories about cave people. Let's peel away the layers. Let's get to the roots! Let's go to the pulse of it. Melt all the cells away."

They lurched forward into it. Scofield had tossed it into the air, and as it moved—away they went. He moved in great throttles forward. He ignited the turbo charge. And sailed across the sky.

Miles felt the chill, divine.

And moved into sun streaks.

Lately, he had begun to see a thing . . . and Scofield was giving it life and words.

In flares and ricochets, they progressed.

The blue sky called to seduce—and bewitch—And to give them the wings of their fate.

This was the slant of the pitch.

This was the hitch, they fastened on, and climbed onto eternity.

Lately, Miles had begun to feel things. He followed the feelings. Scofield set them in words. Together they riffed in rhythms.

The old man, and the young man, now become one, in the riffing, the mad riffing.

Bounds away! And anchors away!

Scofield climbed past the sea, onto land, and then flared into some certain sky streaks.

And flew on by! The destination, Sun Rains; the territory of Go Insane; and the Look of Love. Yes, joined below and above, a certain look, the look of love. Such was the nature of the place. Shimmering in glowing passion and all that lay beyond.

Scofield took his heart, and let the notes just play. This was the thing Scofield cared most about in the world. He rent it with feelings, hurled it, with mad passions.

It's dark sometimes, but surely this was light. And not the light of the world. This was the light of the All.

To most, it was not a fit subject.

To the wise, it was a cool wind from the edge of a cliff.

It was not something most people cared to waste their time on—And don't you waste their time on it either. That would be a nasty and ugly thing to do. And a most wicked sin. The work of an unforgivable sidewinder.

Scofield sidewound unforgivably, incorrigibly, devastatingly. Like he was doing no wrong! He was just a-sidewinding and a-sidwinding along, like he could get away with it, get away with anything he damn well pleased.

He flared.

He was a-reeling with the feeling. A-zapatoo, zapatoo, zapatoo. A-rapatoo, rapatoo, rapatoo—

Woooh! Flaring, baby, flaring!

Hurtling into the void.

He would drive this thing all over town. Hell, yes!

Don't get in his way, this was his being.

He knew what to want and where to go.

He flashed and flared.

And took them away.

Beneath him a drum kicked, a bass boomed, the whole Earth opened wide, as he soared. And exploded his being.

Miles was cool with it. This was the force of endless search. It was cool. He got into the beat. Crazy rhythm! . . . he liked it . . .

Yes, this was cool. And he swam, glided, and surfed with it, across the spaceways.

Way over yonder, that's where they were bound.

Then he "tapped" Miles.

As if to say: "Here we go, kid."

Let's run with it! Run, and not to touch the ground.

Run in waves in the stratosphere, where the air was thin, but space was near. Where you felt the touch of eternity, and the wide expanse, . . . beyond eternity. The realm of faster than light. And beyond. The realm of faster than speed.

And beyond.

They were on their way.

And moved in the way.

To way over yonder.

To the realm a few steps beyond the great beyond.

And they didn't stop there. They came upon such a grand view, that they journeyed into the further realm. Into mindbending, into reality warping. And beyond.

The distance from where they sat in the tavern to that place beyond, was roughly the size of forever.

Forever, . . . give or take a few steps.

Scofield continued, . . . making changes go round:

"There was the caveman who came to the other caveman's place and stayed too long. He made himself at home in someone else's home— We're talking—The Unwelcome Houseguest!—*Opposites* . . ."

And, images were upon the waters:

The caveman lounging with his feet on a boulder in another caveman's place . . .

. . . And the changes were going round, and round, and round, to . . .

The cave people wading across a river at night. And from the shore— The caveman wading in to help; knowing what he was doing; taking the torch from the clan; and then—oh oh, tripping; dropping it in the water. And then it was a-splooshing in the water—not much good to anyone—

Presently, colors were turning the world around again.

Too-doop, too-doop, too-doo doo-doo doo roop.

Scofield continued:

"The caveman who acted like he knew everything but actually knew nothing—The Bumbling Expert!—*Opposites* . . .

"The little kid caveman who knew more than the big adult caveman!—*Opposites* . . .

"The confidence-man-caveman who sold a sucker a cave that leaked in the winter—The Confidence Man and the Sucker!—*Opposites* . . ."

The images continued to roll across the waters.

To-do-doop, do-doop, doo-doo-doo doo roop.

Scofield—"The caveman who got the cavegirl pregnant and had to marry her to make peace with her daddy caveman—The Shotgun Wedding—*Opposites.*

"The little cave mouse who roared at the lions—Mice Behaving Like Lions—*Opposites.*

"The caveman who tells his wife, 'What are you getting upset about? All I did was rape your sister'—The Innocent Tyrant—*Opposites.*"

The images rolled across the timeflow, repeating themselves in the corridors, again and again performing the same movements.

The young blood-savage "erect" caveman hollering at his wife.

The many cave men & women. The people of the world, all the people in the whole damn world—ah, whole wide world.

Ah, the story of The World—deep and great and wide—and opening wider into rooms of strangers, and strange nights, strange days drifting in strange sins and wishes. Strangers in strange lands. And here, to this place, comes . . . The Clown! His face is a wall, the wall of all time. And the face, . . . is haunting . . . haunting . . . haunting, across the realms of lately, presently and soon, and all that you could see, feel or be.

Thumpa, thump a thumpa. Doom, doom, doomp, doompt.

Scofield continued:

"If you were giving me this talk instead of me giving it to you, we'd have another one—The Master Being Outdone by the Apprentice—*Opposites.*"

Miles said, ". . . *Opposites,* . . ."

Miles held himself still, ". . . and all the people in this whole wide world . . ."

"Opposites that attack logic," said Scofield. "The opposites have to be a violent assault on common sense. Those are the ones you want."

The Experience

Miles, he felt the wind shout like a drum.

It set his breath on fire, it had come.

Rending his heart with fire.

The waves of fire. Streets and avenues alight with flames, setting sail, catching stars, and on and on and on going so, so far.

He felt it come, it was come.

Fire. And . . .

The road to, the road to, The Road to Dreams.

Wind shouting like a Drum.

It couldn't last; it had to stop. But in the wave, time had died. There was only drowning; his heart drowning in love's dreams. Swirling eddies of love dreams; pulling him under. Mighty forces rending and throttling, down and around, whipping motions, of drowning.

Whipping tails of love dreams.

All whipping tails, it formed roads.

Roads to dreams, and dreams that went on and on.

You could build time on, you could build life on. The lovers of the stars—oh, if you would watch them go.

The winds of life!

Winds of life wiping away the cold of time that died.

His heart was drowning in love dreams, so deep, so rich, and blue.

And then . . .

He was setting sail for a dream so far. And the way, the leading, was all, it was all . . . tenderness . . . how dark had won, and the light was come.

The winds of life were coming on.

The winds of life were coming through.

Taking him:

. . . into Cool Rapidity. Cool, cool, cool; . . . rapidity . . .

The avenues cried. The winds of life swept through. On their way, to love dreams.

The seas were cold; the streets were dark, all going so far.

The winds of life swept through.

Whipping tails spinning in a dance. Dancing barefoot; some strange music drove them on; through strange fields of dreams. Whipping winds of life on dark streets.

He entered streets where time had died.

His heart was drowning in love dreams. All the scenes that had to fail because they were too far.

Suffering, difficulty, desire, . . . will to beauty—and a heart drowning in love dreams—

Oh, This Was the Experience! He was being, being:

    . . . experienced.

The Pacifica Love Dream Experience!

The shout the drum the dark street the winds of life the no retreat the way the road of dreams.

Man, this had been worth the trip! What an experience! And now coming out of it through a tumbling up, he streamed and expanded to fill the avenues of the All. All the colors of the wind that shouted like a drum.

All this was on the way to the path of dreams.

All this was on the way.

Away he went.

Way leading on to way.

This was the way. Way leading on to way. Swirling, whipping ways.

Echoing in corridors, repeating the same movements.

Way leading on to way. All is way.

No retreat. Time had died, and it was all there at once.

And the one thing Miles thought was:

How beautiful!

How Beautiful It All Was!

He had the feeling. And you don't give up the feeling when you've finally got it down—you keep it hot and squeeling when you take her on the town.

Opening wide, rending apart the time that had died, Miles said:

"*Opposites*—leading on to opposites, all is opposites."

And this was how he emerged from *The Pacifica Love Dream Experience.* Way leading on to way, all was way.

Scofield's old dream, long forgotten, whipped forward suddenly— leaped—and grabbed at Scofield.

Tygers crouched in jungles in Scofield's dark eyes.

Scofield, waited in this place.

Chains broke; sounds tumbled down. Amid falling leaves and tangling weaves; he tumbled into this place, . . . oh, hear it now, here and now. Truth seemed this day, not far away. And happiness lay, not far away.

Ah! The son of a bitch! Scofield thought.

"You're a mad old man," Miles said.

"Only the mad are wise, a young bastard once told me."

"When did I say that?"

"In one of your better moments," Scofield said.

Ground rhythm leading on to ground rhythm, all is ground rhythm.

The great all was different things at different times. You know, the All was lost inside the All, and a long line of years. It was taken by its own turning.

There is a time and a purpose for everything under the sun.

Turn, turn, turn. The All turns. Takes on the form of this here and that there.

Shifting forms. Turn, turn, turn.

Playing crazy games with itself.

You Have It!

Scofield marveled. Had he really gotten it that fast? Impossible. How could this showoff be that swift? Scofield thought.

Perhaps he has figured it out. Wouldn't that be marvelous!

No, no one could get it that fast!

And yet . . . he wondered . . .

He was looking for a glimpse.

Nothing is new under the sun.

But this was amazing, startling. A mainspring wrapped in wonder. Under the sun, there was shame and wonder—this was wonder.

Scofield was approaching the end of a long wonderful life. Painful. Torturous at times. But wonder-filled. And this was a new wonder under the sun.

What mad god had coached this man!

Scofield thought he had been at the end. Now he felt his needs just beginning. Now he found himself drifting in beginnings.

What wildfire had sprung this man on the world!

"You have it!" he said and asked, astonished.

"I know," Miles said.

Scofield was at the end of a life where he saw many things. But this beat all. He had seen it all. There was no new thing under the sun. But this . . . From what firestorm had he emerged? There was no trail behind him.

He seemed to have stepped out of a whirlwind. Hitched himself to its whipping tail, until it came to a place and then he had leaped off, knowing wherever he went was where he wanted to be.

There was no trail, no revealing from whence he emerged. The man swam in mystery.

He was a breeze that burned in knowing, and in knowing more, burned more.

"Let's give it a go, Sco"—Miles liked this—this was cool. "Let's riff on it."

Scofield said, "Now?"

"There's not a moment to lose," Miles said.

"You don't want to think about it?" Scofield said.

"I've thought about it, I'm better when I don't think. It slows me down. Throws me off my game."

Miles was raring to go. "Let's hit it!"

Let's go. Watch it, watch it.

Watch out now! In, we go!

Watch out now! We're going into it!

When you hit the dance floor, you've got to be jumping.

Skidalong bim tang,

A skidalong bim tang,

A skid om bop!

That wild swing, you just can't stop it.

Woah, watch it, watch it, you just can't stop it!

A thoom doom doomp! Oh, watch it, watch it.

Poo doo doom doomp!

A skidalong dim dãome, a skid ohm bãome!

Working to the Riff

Scofield felt the flaring sensation and continued.

Miles felt the ease of it. It had its own motion. He rode it. Balanced. Nimble. Himself. He used his imagination to start a fire, a fire that could make the changes go round.

His time had come.

No one else was there, or ever had been there, to ride the action.

This wave was all his, to ride as he may.

Like cloud working with sky, they worked in the natural way, making changes go round.

The splendor of nature all around.

Riffing

They entered an air of spring.

Riffing.

They riffed together:

"Where is the Scraper . . ." Scofield said.

". . . in the sky," Miles said

"Where is The Friend . . ." Scofield said.

". . . in the girl and the boy," Miles said.

"How is The Judge . . ."

". . . crooked."

There was wonder here, Scofield thought.

And went on.

They were near something. As near as you could go. They continued along the edge.

"What do you know about The Hero . . ." Scofield said.

". . . cowardly," Miles said.

"The Reformer?" Scofield said.

"Sinful," Miles said.

"The Prude?" Scofield said.

"Over-sexed," Miles said.

"The Identity?" Scofield said.

"Mistaken," Miles said.

"How did The Dope become a dope?" Scofield said.

"Education," Miles said.

"What do they do with The Other?" Scofield said.

"Each faults," Miles said.

"Who is the animal that Roars?" Scofield said.

"The mouse," Miles said.

Who suffers?

The wrong person.

Who is upset?

The wrong person.

Who is in charge.

The wrong person.

Who is getting the medals?

The wrong person.
Where is the wrong person?
Driving.
Who is in Charge?
The underling.
Who is outdoing the Master?
The apprentice.

He was startling! Scofield thought. He seemed on the verge of something, something on The Other Side, of reaching a place where few could ever follow. Or even understand, to put it bluntly and mildly.

Yes, he was on the verge. He was about to break thru Crystal Windows! Swim in Whirling Seas! Dance on Devouring Fires!

And have some fun!

"Where is the Sweet?" Scofield said.

"In the bitter," Miles said.

"What did the Burn lose?" Scofield said.

"The sun," Miles said.

What did the Tap lose?

The dance.

Where is the Up?

In the beat.

Where is the Home?

In the run.

Where is the Pillow?

In the talk.

And where is the Movement?

In the molecules.

Where is the Sense?

In the common.

Where is the Non—?

In the sense.

Sun Rains

Sheets of rain mixing with sunstreaks.

Sun Rains! Fell away revealing paths.

Their work was growth, and they fell away to reveal the growth.

Tonality, and tempo. Tonality moving in tempo. And echoing changes, making changes go round. Repeated in corridors. Performing the same movements.

Listen! To them and the spaces between.

Daring travelers to hold on.

Intensity! was what came next. Into sound and fury. Cruelty and suffering. Onward, they pressed the riffing.

Spurring each other.

Miles playing lead. Scofield playing rhythm.

Intensity, not easy to bear.

Difficulties, slaps, and knocks, blows.

Hammerholds and hammering death.

Troubles, . . . this was where the trip took on its full force gale. And all of the people in this world. All of the people, in this whole wide world.

And strongly, they worked. They went on some, and then ended.

It moved into the past, and then moved on to other moments. Everything in time, and everything to pass.

"Enough of this ————!" Miles said, ". . . Let's move on to the next secret of everything!"

Scofield looked at Miles, and held his look. He was starting to like this madman . . . To sense the range of this raving madman, the moments he could take.

Scofield moved with him in the flow, slightly in the lead. Or was Scofield, and the flow, slightly behind. It was hard for Scofield to tell, much was moving.

The distances were shifting back and forth too fast for Scofield to tell the nature of the moment. But he was seeing his way. This was leading to the . . . lovely. Everything that you could touch, was shifting. Stretching to forever, shrinking to nothing, whipping back and forth, to and fro. The resonation of maybe. Maybe this could happen. Maybe this could be.

Maybe there would be death.

Miles was about to have a chance to die.

Scofield thought: *Every time he found a key, he found more.*

Could Miles survive, that was what Scofield wondered. And would he last long enough to give the gift that would last forever?

There was much in this person, and much to come. If he lived long enough.

The Blue Night, the Field & From In to Out

NIGHT PASSED to darkest night.

And Miles went out into the blue night.

Into the blue field, amid the dark green, the violet earth and the astral yellow. To find the wicked, wicked sidewinding.

To find the sidewinding to meet the cold emptiness.

And, the stone cold players.

To fight the stone cold death.

That was coming for him.

Tonight was the night, Miles thought. This was the night, there was no other night.

This was his moment—from a star so warm he was going to ride across the dark.

To the people of the sky, to the people of The Way.

Tomorrow called to seduce and bewitch—to give him the wings of his fate, and lure him with her cosmic kiss.

He was leaving behind the sea of faces that told him to stop.

They said, "Stop!" The enemies of his endless search.

He defied them, one and all. The enemies of his endless search, were just dust in the wind, singing the same old song, Stop! You cannot do this! You cannot be this way!—Damn them all to hell, and damn him— yes, he would be damned, everything would be damned. All right then, everything would be damned. There was no stopping him.

No hanging on. No slipping away slowly day by day.

He was going to rend the night, and, tonight, be everything he was to be. He would will the enemies to vanish. He would destroy their song, and deliver himself, out of his sadness, out of his pain, and move into outer madness.

He would will himself into insanity.

Ramp it up.

Who is a good man does not try. The love that wants to it, well it is. Who says much that goes, does not go. As well as it does not go, does not come. Who inside of itself docs not leave, goes to die without loving nobody.

Keep it up.

His courage would be the only thing to guide him. The strength from inside would be all, all else would be forgotten.

He was pulling himself through.

He couldn't remember the sea of faces that told him to stop.

He couldn't recall all the things that had tried to stop him. All the cold things burning thru the void.

Now it was time for the people of the sun, people of the sky.

Time to get lost in a mission of outsiders and mavericks.

And maverick outside, to outer seas, outer skies, outer spaces, outer reaches, to outer madness. He was come.

The Ride, the Fire & the Wicked, Wicked Sidewinding

Ride the fire.

The fire is the ride.

The fire! Sparked, sparked to flame.

The becoming, he was making it happen.

No! No stopping, damn it Miles! This is the night! Go!

Move Into the Groove

Move! You will never, ever ever think your way there.

There is no think to there.

You will never, ever ever walk there, in the cold dawn.

There is no way to walk there from where you are, from anywhere, there is no walking there. The long line of years? Of walking. And going there. That was preparation. From here, you leap! You have to take to the skies.

There is no human way to do it. You have to imagine it.

You have to play the game; you know the game it means; a little game, called "Go insane." The falling leaf pleads, and the way up, leads.

Go! Move!

Out, to outer space, outer reaches.

Find yourself lost, inside a song.

Play crazy games, jump from the top of a tower.

And dive up, head straight up.

Take to the skies.

Damn it, take to the skies!

C'mon.

C'mon.

C'mon.
Fire fire fire.
Burn burn burn.
Run run run.
Wind blew.
And he blew in the wind.
He took to it.
He took to the wind.
C'mon, bring it on home! Hit it! . . . Bring it on, sweet baby, bring it on!
C'mon burn.
Burn burn burn.
Miles felt the fire, flaming.
It grew, until it took over his world. Until it filled his entire world.
Now ride it! Miles thought.
Ride it, and damn it all do not chart a course!
Hurtle. And boom.
That's all.

Break On Thru

His mind wanted to cry out loud—Yes, his mind wanted to cry out loud!
"I returned, and saw under the sun
    all is opposites.
"Opposites leading on to opposites,
"All is opposites.
"Enter the dream
"Enter the dreamscape
"Enter the scape
"Enter the escape
"Enter the bender
"Enter the mindbender!"
His mind cried out loud!
"Oh you crackling winds! Bring me giants!
"I feel too strong to war with mortals! Bring me giants!"
Oh you crackling winds!
Bring him giants. Mad, dangerous, cunning, ferocious giants.
Yes! He was a-reeling with the feeling! He yearned to wrestle with *Tygers* in the night!

He wanted force and sway—the Wilde Whirlwind Wãoynding Wild!
Screaming wild!

He was looking for The Wãoynde—he yearned for The Wãoynde—
she, the Wãoynde—a mighty lady of force and swirl . . . a girl that
looked quite like Daphne.

Astral Fields Come Away!

Radiate in waves. Pulse On! Keep it up.
   And a-sidewinding we will go!
   Sidewinding leading on to sidewinding, all is sidewinding.
   Travel in sunbursts.
   Travel into a sunburst, and emerge, into another sunburst.
   Way leading on to way, all is way.
   Astral fields come away!
   Wheels within wheels; circles from circles; motions from motions;
waves on to waves.
   Time slipping.
   Mind bending.
   To the heart of the sunrise; to the mainspring; to the great every-
thing—To The All! . . . He was come.
   Of mainsprings and opposites, of wheels and elementals.
   Oh elemental beauty!
   Sidewinding to sidewinding, wheeling in sidewinding
   To outer space, to extreme madness . . . He was come.

The Mindbender

Opposites jolting about.
   Shaking and forming, spheres, and, round go a-rounds.
   Wheeling, spinning; . . . emerging . . . Wheels within wheels. Motions
from motions. Escape! Surge and charge. Light and rumbling thunder.
Thundering grooves—grooving and smashing—smashing and thrash-
ing—thwarting and cavorting, rending and trending, slipping and a-
sliding, into way.

Ripple Breathing

Hit it! and let it go
   Hit it, and let it go

Ascent!
Spread out.
Take it all in.
Spread out, take more in.
Breathing.
Ripple breathing.
Filling, spreading out.
Breathing,
Breath pulse.
Brave weddings of summer mornings.
And, Gardens grinding out forms.
Elemental shapes and elemental beauty.
And he was into it . . .
Somewhere a Barker spoke . . .

The Barker

Somewhere a strange carnival barker cried: "Step right up! Step right up!
To the realm of strange riches!

"The name of the realm? Oh, you know the name. Don't you know
the name?

"It has a pretty name.

"And it has it all.

"Deliver yourself.

"Ah, there you are, and you are here. Now that you're here, have a
look, a look around."

Crystal ships sailing on the winds of life. Gems and rubies in the hold.

Mighty captains and mighty passengers. Looking to a rainbow, and
hills and streams. Following to the place beautiful.

People and passages.

Crystal visions journeying on the rainbow bridge to Asgard, Valhalla,
and the other paradises to found in the realms of mind.

To Thor, Odin, Loki, Athena, Aphrodite, sea of faces.

And shooting, burning across the void . . .

He saw a Seeker.

Hurtling and rending.

All boom.

The Thing Was . . .

The thing was a Capoeira, a dancing burning fighter hurtling across the sky.

Bathed in symphonies, hurling colors in exploding sunbursts.

Hurtling to hurtle. Burning to burn.

Burn burn burn.

Run run run.

It was a thing red and crimson, a thing green and emerald, blue and azure, indigo and violet.

Burn burn burn.

Run run run.

. . . in mad, furious motions.

Azure and forever, yellow and startling.

Hurtling across the history of human emotion.

Carving futures, haunting pasts, playing in the fields of space.

Red and fiery, green and forest, azure and forever, yellow and startling.

And it was soaring, gliding upward.

Leaving the barren land for the green yonder.

Leaving dusty spaces for dark green forests. And the emerald realms of life.

It exploded through winters, pushed through rivers, across springs, through skies, blazed through summers and forest mountains, raced through autumns and cool serenades, forming motions within motions and sending out wheels within wheels. All spiraling. Motions wheeling and wheeling motions. And all was moving upward.

The Wãoynde.

Forming motions from motions and wheels from wheels.

Becoming

It was beautiful.

And so easy.

So light and easy. It was lightness and ease, and . . .

. . . its shapes, its elemental shapes, . . .

Well, I'll be a son of a bitch! Miles thought. It had always been there.

It was in the shape of all his days that had come before and all his days that were to come.

The damn thing has been here all along. Well, old friend, here we go.

Do you know why I recognize you, old friend? You're me.

And your name is Miles Roark.

The cosmic kiss was on Miles. And he laughed. It was such a grand kiss.

It moved away from Miles.

The thing was a-reeling with a-feeling and flowing into way, Miles thought. Elusive whisp! Whispering wind! Windsprinting spring!

It had disappeared over the horizon.

Miles gave chase—Dawnlight smiled on the chase.

Then there was only exertion, and blood flooding through the channels of his being. His mind knew effort. "Ah! Argh! Yeargh!"

His mind cried out loud.

Exertion, and blood pumping. "Ah! Arrgh! Aaaaaarrrrrrgh!" Miles was racing, . . . this was the fastest he had ever gone. Oh furious race! A madman chasing his madness.

Miles chased it down. Aimed himself right for it. And hurtled into it.

Headlong into mad insanity.

The world exploded all around.

Miles, was in a state of perfect calm. A state of perfect pulsing grace. The moment went on forever.

Gentle, gentlest all. Moving in The Way, he broke on thru, to the other side.

It moved inside of Miles.

Miles moved inside of it.

Red and fire, yellow and light. He was in the heart of the sunrise.

And they moved. In one world, one place, one being.

The becoming of one, Miles was making it happen.

They were become one.

He took himself into it. He was become it.

He allowed it to take over everything, while he took it over.

The person and the force, were become one.

Miles Roark, the Seeker, hurtled into the futureflow.

It was all done lightly—oh, sure, with vast effort involved—but done lightly in his moving on. And on he went. To more fun. To fantasia.

To waking up in his clothes, to not knowing exactly where he was, it would all be part of his moving on.

He was a living force moving forward.

Dangerous

And he returned to the morning of the world.

Oh, dangerous, he was, he was dangerous now.

The notes were playing, and the melody of his heart, was what the notes obeyed. Warm and true, the heart was describing itself. It was a clear sound, rich and dark, set in a deep blue.

Now, heaven help him, he was dangerous. And to be dangerous in this world was to be in danger.

Now, he would meet opposition. Now, he would meet the things that would try to stop him—The things that always stopped people like him.

Yes, now, things would try to stop him. Things would get hot and ferocious.

He had purpose and force. And there were many people who did not like that at all, not one lick. They would stop him! They would try. In the end, they would succeed, he knew. It had never gone any other way. But Miles chuckled, he could go pretty damn far before they stopped him.

So let them do their mighty work. There was a deep menace in the world, and Miles was going to punch it in the chest. If the blow got through! Then, a fight, a battle, a deadly combat. And then what? Then what? Would he be killed?

Miles laughed, shrugged, and kept moving forward.

The Young Ladies . . . To Be Enfolded

CINJUN WAS MEETING with a group of new people. Enfolding the new young ladies.

The setting was the gymnasium, and the group had the feel of a team assembled.

"This is a place for the young," Cinjun said. "Typically, people who join us are educated young adults, not emotionally disturbed, but possessed of idealism, and seeking new meanings."

He walked through the ranks, passing one beautiful young lady after another.

"The transformation generates euphoria, power centered in moving from utter confusion to absolute certainty. The old beliefs melt and the new identity allows wonderful feelings to flow."

In an alcove of House Crimson, Amelia talked about joy to the new recruits.

Amelia was engaged to marry Cinjun's son. She was a ravishing beauty.

Amelia said, "You enter a secret laboratory. It's like crossing the border into a different universe.

"It's exciting. It's like being on another planet, it's us against the world.

"It's wonderful to be a part of history!"

In the gymnasium, Cinjun continued along the line of young recruits, moving from one red cheeked young woman to the next beaming young femme who was living in the pink and rosy.

"In the glow of rebirth, emerges sharing of insights and rules. Soon comes your time and loyalty, which you give gladly.

"We offer simple solutions. We promise an expanded consciousness, well being, and a righteous certainty.

"The 'we' feeling imparted generates a sense of belonging to a powerful and protective group within which your personal potential can at last be actuated.

"Typically, there is boundless reverence for the leader.

"I have learned to live with that."

The Fine Battle of a Him and Her

SCOFIELD WAS TEACHING.

A sexy young woman and a handsome man—Sara and Ken—were on the stage lying in a bed, playing out a scene of a married couple.

"The picture," Scofield said, "is *'The Fine Battle of a Him and Her.'* The story is about a couple who are incompatible.

"Before they get divorced they absolutely destroy each other. Not only destroy each other, wreck the entire house, break all the furniture, they destroy the property, and finally there's nothing left.

"Odd bedfellows should not be in the same bed together, that's what this is about. How do we physicalize that? Considering that you must always physicalize every conflict."

Images played across the screens of the students' minds, pouring into their awareness, with remembrances of sights they had seen in their own lives, of men and women locked in mortal combat—The fine mismatings of a him and her—The strains of the old song, ringing low in a lonely distance: ". . . The sleepless nights, the daily fights . . . I miss the kisses, and I miss the bites . . . The lovely loving, the hateful hates, the conversation with the flying plates, I wish I were in love again." Oh, to be in love . . . In the throes of love. Ah, love.

Scofield said, "The problem with these two people is they are madly in love with each other but can't get along. You could not possibly have as much passion as has to be generated for this story to work—I mean by the end they're hanging from the chandelier—if they did not have an enormous emotional response to one another.

"Well, I always say that the people who quarrel best, are the people who love each other the most. Egh, it's . . . it's, . . . ah, it's, uh . . . it's the old dictum. The opposite of love is indifference, not hatred————"

He continued:

If you really are involved with somebody, if they get under your skin, if they bother you, if they irritate you, it's *a connection,* even though it's a negative connection.

The problem with the scene as you played it is that you made them both dislike each other. That's not what the story is about.

The story is about two people who are crazy in love with each other, who just can't get along. That's where the root of the basic joke lies. The joke lies in *incompatibility.*

Now incompatibility doesn't mean two people aren't nuts about each other. They could be absolutely insane about each other but they're *incompatible!* Whatever the hell one says, causes disturbance in the other, you understand. Everything that you try to do leads to dissension. But if you weren't getting a bang out of the arguments, *they would not continue.*

So your problem is how to argue interestingly, with a lot of variety, for three acts?

And how to physicalize it all.

"Where are you in the story?" Scofield asked.

Sara said "He goes to the hospital and I never show up."

"It's the end of act one?" Scofield asked.

"Right," Sara said.

"He gets rushed to the hospital and they think it's a heart attack. It turns out it's indigestion," Scofield said. ". . . And now you go into the next part of it, you're home again."

"Right."

"Okay." Scofield held his look————

Now you're in act one. All right in act one, you haven't reached the point yet where you've been breaking furniture or hitting each other on the head, right? You've only reached the point of violence where you shove him off the bed. That's only the beginning.

Later it gets to where you throw things at each other. Where you wreck the house. Right? You threaten each other, right?

And the audience is sitting there saying, vicariously, boy would I love to do that. Would I . . . I get so pissed off at my wife that I would love to have the freedom to do that, except God knows it would cost a lot of money. I mean you could wind up with a divorce, and lawyers, . . . and big . . . trouble; and then worst of all, you could *lose* the other person, who you *need* very much. The idea being: that for there to be a murderer, you need a murderee. If you have a masochist, you need a sadist. It's got to be a partnership.

Whatever he says to you, Sara, causes you to get disturbed.

Now, if somebody could sit the two of you down and say, "How do you feel about her?" you would have to admit that you're crazy about her, Ken; you need her.

Somebody once said that *the most important thing in life is to have a worthy antagonist.*

If you don't have a worthy antagonist, you don't have spice in your life. You've got to have somebody you can't stand, it's very essential. It keeps your vibes going. If everything is all goddamn peaceful it's like death. But if you can't stand somebody . . . I have *Cinjun Khan Smythe.* As soon as I see him, he bothers me. The minute I see his picture, he irritates me. He disturbs me. Drives me crazy. So this is politically a very happy time for me. When it's all nice and groovy, there's no excitement, you understand?

Okay.

Now, for that to work you have to play the basic joke, which is . . .

Both of you are trying to get along. You are *trying . . . to . . . make it work,* you follow?

Sara, when you say I want a divorce, it's convince me to *not* get a divorce. 'You need me. Don't be such a drip.' She tries to be good to him.

Her emotion is guilt, because she has had secret longings that he were gone. But if he died, you'd grieve like crazy. You'd be the biggest mourner at the funeral. You understand what I'm getting at?

There are people you can't stand who you are terribly *involved* with. Her objective is: To not have an argument. His is: To get an explanation.

What's wrong? Why doesn't our marriage work. She can't give you an explanation. You're as much wrong with the marriage as she is.

Pick emotions that will irritate each other.

Sara, your emotion is guilt. He was in the hospital, right, and he was supposed to be deathly ill, and it turns out he only had indigestion.

But, Sara, you behaved terribly—you were awful! You were *glad* he was suffering. You have to be pleased at the thought that he was dead.

In other words, he deserves the suffering because he doesn't love you enough to forgive your faults, and to stop arguing. Okay?

And what emotion can you choose for *him?* His emotion is fear. 'If she doesn't love me, I'm lost. Because she's the one person in the world I need to have love me.' He's in constant torment.

She keeps saying to herself, *to not have a quarrel, to not have a quarrel, to not have a quarrel.* Try to get along. Put an ice pack on his head. Make it better but nothing can make it better.

They're *Odd Bedfellows.* They should not be in the same bed together. Tuck him in, put the blanket over him. Make him comfortable. Be a nurse. Adjust his pillows.

And him—You like the attention.

Now her—Switch pillows, you want the pillow for yourself. Don't hold his head, let his head fall."

Bang! His head hits the board—

"That's it," Scofield said.

"That's two people who shouldn't be together.

"Climb into bed right over him, step on him a little.

"Pull the blanket over yourself, so he's left with no blanket. That's an incompatible marriage.

"He says, 'What's going on?' Now she gets out of the bed. Pace. Be much more disturbed. Your guilt is overwhelming. You can't sleep. You can't rest. You're always on the edge of a quarrel. Pick up the chair, slam it down. Tell yourself to not quarrel. Now sit down.

"Now, Ken, watch every sign of her behavior. Does she love me, doesn't she love me? Why is she mad at me, what did I do?

"Okay, I'll give you another for instance . . . go to where you're in the bathroom . . ." Scofield said.

It's morning, they're standing at the bathroom sink, both holding their gaze on the mirror. They're brushing their teeth and fighting for the spout.

"He wants control of the sink," Scofield says. "She wants control. Shove each other a little."

They do. Then, next, he's shaving in front of the mirror. She's putting on her make-up.

"Get in her way with your shaving."

He does.

"Now be disturbed. Cut yourself shaving. No! A man who cuts his nose is not funny. Accidentally cut your throat. She enjoys that."

They turn back to the mirror.

"She can't see. Get to the mirror by climbing over his back!"

She climbs onto his back and continues putting on make-up.

He throws her off.

"He stands there. Puffs himself up. How does she like that?

"Now go to the next part where Ken is back in the bedroom . . .

"She locks him out of the bathroom, and tells him she wants a divorce through the door.

"He's thrown from fear into hysteria.

"He shouts through the door. She comes out, knocks him over, when the door swings open. She marches right over him to get dressed.

"Go to the next encounter. They both start getting dressed. They head in opposite directions. They collide. He finally lifts her up—out of his way.

They continue the arguments.

"Okay, I'll give you another for instance . . . We see, the marriage bed is right in the middle and no one's in it.

"They're speaking. She grabs a pillow off the bed. She punches the pillow. It's 'him.'

"While she talks, she punches 'him.'

"Pow! She belts the pillow." Scofield says. "Now go to where she says she wants to smash his face in."

Sara says, "When I look at you, when I see you, lately, I want to smash your face in."

Ken says, "You want to smash my face? Go ahead, smash my face in. Come on, smash my face in."

"She belts him," Scofield says.

Pow! She punches him. He goes flying. He meets the floor.

He opens his eyes. He blacked out for a second there, but he's okay now, it was nothing. He puts his jaw back on his face. And he's back in top form. He jumps up—Springs up. Boing!

He says, "How would you like to try that again—smarty pants—"

Bam! She belts him. Apparently she would.

He goes down. The carpet thuds. He dances cheek to cheek with the floor for the second time. Only this time, it's not so easy for him to get up—She made sure she meant it this time. But, up he goes.

He gets to his feet, barely but squarely. And now, they're ready to face off—'Into the next round, dear?'—What do you say, shall we dance?

"That's two people who love fighting!" Scofield said.

"Now you've shown this couple to us. That's an incompatible couple. And that's: Two people who love fighting. They're madly in love with each other. They need each other. Two people who love fighting—*The most important thing in life is to have a worthy antagonist.* That's the whole point of it. You need someone to keep your vibes going."

Miles was in the audience, watching. Observing with eyes that missed nothing.

The Lay of the Land—
The Lightvision, the Netways, the Syndicates, and
the Pulsing Newsfeeds

"CROSSING OVER IN STYLE, how do you do it?" Miles said.

He sat in The Caveman's Grotto and Grill, directing his attention to Scofield Morefield.

"A drifter, *off to the see the world*—how should he do it, my huckleberry friend?"

If a dream maker is going off to see the world, where should he go? There's an awful lot of world to see out there—to what end should the dream maker drift?

How do you get to Dreamsville? How do you get to the Pleasuredome?

In other words, he was saying, 'Hey, you Road of Dreams—I'm going you're way—where do I find you and where do you lead?'

Where should the drifter go? Where do you have to go to win it all, *the place* to stop and shout, and make love to all its perfection?

Life spoke to Miles in a haunting voice urging care. 'Many roads are ahead of us, with choices to be made.' Choices which Miles would have to make. 'Better make them good,' it said. One shot, was all he would get. And then there would be death. He would get dead. Like all who came before.

"Let's talk, about what a nice, young man has to do, to break on thru," Miles said to Scofield.

From in to out, we go; how do you step on out? . . . While summer was in the world.

How do you get past the gate to the stage? . . . While you still had the strength to do it.

The Gate of Wealth; the portal to Eden Estates. And the problem of how to break on thru.

This raging torrent was the swirl in his mind.

These swirling thoughts consumed his attention, these thoughts about ramping it up. They were about more than, "How do you get into the light?"— They were about: "How do you ramp it up?"

Miles felt the need. And all the things choking the need.

Let's get more intense! Let's stir it up! Let's hit it! What can we do? How do we disturb the routine? How do we make the changes go round? How do we blaze? But in ever-increasing steps.

How, to go? being the problem.

How to take the fight higher, and higher, and higher?

How to keep moving onto higher ground.

We may not know the reason why we're born into this world—where a man and woman only live to die—but we *can* know how to make the most of what's given us—*Know what we can take in the galloping fullness of time.*

The question hurled its threat at him.

The great all spoke, 'Don't just let life pass'—*What can we take in the breathing fullness of time?*

Where was li—, li—, life, life, life . . . in the light.

Where is the grace in the way? he wondered.

Where should he be at the close of the dance.

What were the boundaries to pass? To reach the way.

The fragments and questions swirled, and led Miles ever forward to a certain light he was seeking.

And pressed him to some forces he would have to fight, to make the changes go round, to bring swirling changes through the walls guarding the place of light. *The Garden,* where he could stop and shout and make love to all its perfection. Because he had won.

He was speaking to Scofield of the ways and byways to:

The Light of the World

Of The Light, haunting, spreading out through the canyons of this vast forest all.

Outside, across the vast realm, the people gathered.

Where did they gather but before the *light*tanks. For surely they were the light of the world. Where did they gather but before the *light*vision, for surely it was the light of the world. All the people. All the people in this whole wide world.

The image of the great society assaulted Miles. And the force shaping its contours. *The great gravitational pull of society.*

The gravitational pull of society, forced the form.

You could see it. *The force* pulled all things to the center and built a form moving outward.

The gravitational pull of society pulled all things to the center; all people to the center. All the ways, and doings, of all the people in the world that peopled, were pulled to the gravitational core, to Eden Estates, and in the core of Eden Estates, was the *light*vision.

The *light*vision cast its formlight upon the day.

Its great and mighty spotlight.

Everybody wanted to be in the center, and everybody wanted to be on the *light*vision.

Miles broke further into this dream of: The *light*vision. And turned his thoughts to the *newsfeeds* . . . Lately his thoughts had turned to the newsfeeds and the newsrooms that lay under and behind, . . . in back of the *light*vision. Rooms full of newspeople, peopling the power stations.

At Miles's side, a raging thought. A clown and a strange face, along the wall of all time . . . In the night, haunting Miles . . . Miles, wishing he were closer to the answer—He had to get there—He would wish and will his way there. Make his way there at all costs. No matter who rose to stop him.

How could he get onto the *light*vision, for surely that was the light of the world?

The *light*vision was the Pleasuredome of Eden Estates; the heart and soul of the world-striding Federation. All roads led to the *light*vision; it was the times. It was everything.

And in the center ring, standing in the spotlight, The Star of the Show—"Ladies and Gentleman, let's give him a warm welcome; please give a nice, big hand to:

"Cinjun Khan S'mythe."

Cheers!

Cheers, and people.

People and portals.

Portals and the Gates of Wealth.

Outside and all around. The Moneyflow Mountains.

Screaming winds. The Wilderness of the Moneyflow Mountain Range.

Inside . . . The Garden Party.

Spreading outside and beyond, lay the canyons of the All.

And out there the people wanting, wanting, wanting . . . Demanding in dark streets where time had died, . . . demanding raw, full existence.

Singing, 'How do I get to the Pleasuredome?' 'How do I get to the Pleasuredome?' 'How do I get to the Pleasuredome?'

The gravitational pull urged all things to the center, Miles thought. For in the center, was a great party! . . . for some special people. And it was very hard to get into the party. The special people didn't want you there; the world was their palace, and you were there to do the yard work, that was all. No partying for you.

Now, when you got to the spotlight, well, they had a champion standing there to meet you, Cinjun Khan Smythe. With a charming smile.

The look in Miles's eyes—of *Tygers* crouched in jungles—spoke of his thoughts.

The *light*vision cast the spotlight, which was the light of the world.

Cinjun stood in the spotlight, flare point of the lightank, which the *light*vision beamed to the world.

His power was great and beautiful to see, radiating, . . . people and money. And all the good works under the sun that money and people could force into *your* world.

The Moneyflow, shifted and slipped, . . . assaulted Miles, . . . it was what fueled the *light*vision and the newsfeeds.

Moneyflow, shook Miles's thoughts and took him into quick sensation.

Money was an idea, abstract—money was a great structured symbol for balancing and healing and growing closer, Miles thought.

It was the total structure that dazzled him, the idea that an entire world could be reflected in one dynamic, completely interconnected, symbol structure.

Money flowing. Money forming a mountain. Up and up, . . . the mountain would go. And then another mountain. And another. And another. Rising. Rising. Money forming shapes in the void, a landscape, and might waters, mighty rapids.

In the distant void, in the void, a Cash Flow.

In the void, the talents of gold flowed in streams. The cash and wealth of nations flowed. The soostones, the gems.

And there was a red flow. The talents of red flowed.

And there was a hunter—leading other hunters—traveling along the amber plains.

Amid the purple sage, the hunters attacked. There was a marauding and slaughter of vestal virgins under the shining blue sky.

The coin of realms, the silvered streaks of color, papers and wafers and stacks and stones, the colored, streaming talents that amounted to the wealth of the world.

And the stream flowed. The talents streamed. The stream flowed.

Like snow drifting. Like sand duning. It formed a mountain. High and mighty.

And at the peak of the mountain, stood Cinjun Khan Smythe. And he spoke to the assembled host in crimson words.

Bringing almost a sexual release.

Freeing the Moneyflow.

Allowing it to gush. To shoot. Allowing the Moneyflow to ejaculate.

Good people—coming out of his being—witness the glory of tomorrow and: A Beautiful Sermon on the Mount.

Witness, in the wild breeze . . . Moneyflow in orgasm. Moneyflow realized.

"He does wonders with his menu," Miles said. "He serves all of the classics. 'This is the promised land.' 'We are the chosen people.' 'Home, home on the range.' "

"If you watch him," Scofield said. "You see a man that knows how to hit all of the marks. He knows that the key is to get on the newfeeds. The newsfeeds fuel the news programs."

Ah, The Pulsing Newsfeeds. And *the central newsfeed.*

"The Associated Newsfeed is the pulse you want to reach," Scofield said.

It was the main line of the great all.

In the great society of the world striding Federation, the great networks all operated off the grace of their newsfeeds. Which in turn looked for enlightenment to The Great, Majestic Associated Feed. In shifts throughout the day, *The Rundowns*, transmitted from the central cores, instructed each station and outlet as to how it should wage the battles of the day, and where The Associated Feed was going with the day. It revealed what was the *'news of record'* for that day. The rest, was the filler business. Filling the patches, and holes, and open spaces around the centrally blessed and permitted 'news of the day.'

The core of cores, the great central body and central news line was *The Associated Feed.*

A channel into that, was what Miles needed.

The truth was plain to see. What Miles needed was a channel into that great body.

That was the great colossus that had to be ridden. Few had ever seen the bull in its ring. Fewer had ever made it onto the bull. And far fewer still had ever sustained a ride on the beast. And far, far fewer still had had ever mounted the bull by grabbing its tail.

Well, there was no substitute for experience for learning a thing, Miles thought. The man who grabs a bull by the tail is getting sixty to seventy times the information of the fellow who hasn't.

This was what Miles proposed doing. He thought it would be fun.

And why not. He had all the time in the world. What was there to stop him? Until his intent was discovered. Until the bull noticed him. Then the weather forecaster predicted clouds of pain, and beatings. Majestic, soaring beatings.

The Netways, assaulted Miles next, in the hour of his need, the world trembling around him.

The Netways springing outward from The Associated Feed, depending on the core.

All roads led to Rome, and this was the Rome that ruled the world.

The 'Roman' Feed. The Grand Feed.

Miles would get to it from a neighboring less sheltered newsfeed, perhaps that was the way on.

Newsfeeds, News Organizations, News Syndicates.

The Post Syndicate.

The Times Syndicate.

These were the forms and bodies that played across his mind.

And The Light of the World.

For where did they gather, but before the *light*vision.

Its sound and fury, many a times signifying nothing. Yet—here and there—emerged truth and purpose, the form and pressure of the times!

Beaming truth and purpose, and emerging there, the form and pressure of the times.

The *light*tank, surely it was the light of the world, the motion of the field.

The gravitational pull of society assaulted Miles's thoughts.

"How do I get to the *light*vision party?"—This is the question for Miles—the next secret of everything.

The gravitational pull of society—everybody wants to be in the center.

"How do you get to the center? How do you take center stage?"

Scofield drew a breath. "They go through Golden Gods"—Scofield said—"Their current golden god is Cinjun Smythe. And their current magic operation is House Crimson.

"They always have to have a flavor of the month and an enemy of the month.

"A flavor of the season, and an enemy of the season.

"The flavor this season is: Cinjun Smythe. The enemy this season: is *you and you and you*—all the people that do not go along with the Cinjun Smythe Group Thinking Machine.

"The Cinjun Smythe think tank. You have to join it; because if you don't, you reveal yourself to be an ally of the great enemy.

"The *light*vision eats; it eats waves. It always needs a *new* wave, a *new* age, a *new* thing. They call it news, right? To keep the *light*vision going properly, you always need a flavor wave and an enemy wave. The Golden God riding the flavor wave right now is Cinjun Smythe.

"They need the Star of the Season, who gives you the Flavor of the Season. And the Star—to make him interesting—is always fighting the Enemy of the Season. Presently it's Cinjun Smythe and House Crimson fighting . . . what? What is the great evil?—You and you and you, because you're not part of them."

Miles spoke, almost to himself: ". . . To get onto the newsfeeds . . . you have to be dressed for the party."

"And what do you wear?" Scofield said.

"Money." Miles stayed the course, pushing further along the path. "So the question is, what do I have that is stronger than money?—"

Miles directed his attention outward, to take in the world. To take the world into his grasp. The whole, wide world. And what he would give the world.

"Energy," Miles said.

Energy—You fire up the great engine. Step back. And listen to the engine hum. And you take it into the danger lurking all around, the danger to be found, the danger everywhere within *The Soft Parade*.

Miles was on his way.

Off Miles would go, with his energy.

Miles was on his way.

To a dark encounter. To a place . . . where waited Cinjun Smythe, . . . with his *death gift* . . . To a place where waited Cinjun Smythe, . . . ready to give Miles the gift that would absolutely last forever.

On the Air

THE GATEKEEPER.

News director Ripkin Kabob walked a young businessman around his newsroom.

"The wisdom of the common man," Ripkin said, "play to that and see where you end up!

"Two rules here—

"Write for a children's reading level!

"And a good picture wins out over substance, every time!"

This was what Ripkin was fond of saying, time and time again. "Two rules here—

"First, you write for one step below . . . a children's reading level. Second, you go for pictures, you abandon words as clumsy, bulky contraptions that are all too much bother. Restrict your use of words."

This was his approach: 'Words are just the noises we make, go for pictures, pictures sell.'

Enemies, Everywhere—Beware!

CINJUN SMYTHE WAS ON A PROGRAM.

The anchor said, "Tell us about House Crimson."

"I have a vision for our future," Cinjun said. "It doesn't rely on dissent and personalities—House Crimson. One nation, united, indivisible. We need to get there. The only question is how to shape it. This book is the answer."

The anchor held up Cinjun's book. "This is the work, 'House Crimson.' I found it fascinating. People should read it seven times."

Cinjun said, "Thank you."

With Cinjun, the response was never, "You're great, or it's good to be here . . . but rather . . . I'm here to teach you how to live."

Not, I'm happy to talk with you; I'll be happy to talk with you again. No. It was: I'm here to change your life!

"Listen the Federation is in deep trouble," Cinjun said. "Deep, deep trouble—House Crimson is a foundation. Our job is to fix the house, to water the garden, and to create growth."

" 'The Big Boom' theory in this book," the anchor said, "is fascinating."

"Thank you," Cinjun said.

"Your 'Theory of Relative Gravity' is also," the anchor said, "quite terrific."

"Listen, House Crimson is a science," Cinjun said.

"This thing about the gravitational pull of society," the anchor said, "and how we are all pulled to the center, is brilliant."

"There's a lot to know about the world," Cinjun said, "but I packed it all into this book."

Cinjun felt it! It was time to cross the Rubicon and take Rome. The Federation needed him. Emperor Cinjun Khan Smythe was a necessary step. In order for them all to grow.

This was the purpose of the foundation.

"House Crimson is," Cinjun said, "a beautification project. A scheme. A dream scheme. A beautiful architect's plan. I'm the face but the dream comes from The People that shaped this brave new world order. Time is calling us to journey. We must do it in the established way. House Crimson is the establishment scheme."

"I see, well put," the anchor said.

"It's my work, my job, and my pleasure." Cinjun smiled. "I'm glad I was able to come here. I feel I've helped you. And I think this is helping your viewers . . . I'm here to change lives. But, the first step is to get serious. We all have to get serious."

He was a dark matter, bringing the day . . . well, down.

He was a downer, a major downer.

And it worked.

People ate it up and asked him for more.

He offered mission, and purpose.

Dark, but most people were not looking for light.

They had their *light*vision, and surely that was the light of the world.

And everywhere it featured, Cinjun Khan Smythe.

And, incidentally or consequently, the will of the beast, that devoured the world that peopled.

Enemies Everywhere

Everywhere, enemies of the endless search.

Tricks, full of tricks. And bitter tears. You have to see your way.

And the way is enemies everywhere.

Push back, fight back, kill!

Kill softly, kill hard, kill quietly, and kill loudly. Kill your fears. And your bitter tears will turn sweet.

. . . with meaning and peace war.

Strike at the enemy, show him the hate that he has made. Let the hate kill the enemy through you. But don't become the hate. Kill, the right way—justly. And swiftly.

Maybe you should bomb your enemies, that might be the best for them. Get it done. Let's say they won't leave the town? Then bomb the town.

Don't let them get to you.

The bastards, they would just love that. But you're above them. You're good. That's the difference.

Cinjun was making it clear, perfectly clear for the masses.

They were too comfortable. Fat on the riches of Peace! What about the enemies? What about them? Lying in wait.

Cinjun's selfish ways had disappeared with the realization of the new age. And its promises.

Hear that sound!

Glory! But also enemies all around!

The time has come, children.

My children, my women and my men.

Perhaps he would start an army of women.

Full-bosomed women with long hair, long legs.

It was something to consider.

He would have to spend some time with some beautiful women and explore what could be done with them.

Some possibilities immediately came to mind.

Merrily, merrily, merrily, we roll along.

Life is but a dream, Cinjun thought.

What does he hear?

About war and peace.

What does he hear?

About love and sex.

He was going to reap a hex of love, and he was going to war for peace.

Ahuh-hum!

He was man enough to take it where it had to go.

A force of ripe fighting women, it was fitting for a god emperor.

Women in riot gear.

He would have to remove unnecessary clothing.

And dress them with his hand.

In a Dark Room

THREE MEN WERE STANDING on one side of the room. Cinjun was standing on the other side.

He stepped into their midst.

They surrounded him.

It was a test of Cinjun's will. He must prove to be invincible.

No assault must be allowed to get through.

Press on. Move forward. This was how Cinjun operated.

One man moved in. Cinjun dodged his blow and punched him in the jaw sending him flying.

Cinjun had no problem receiving their blows; he either blocked them or took the pain of any blows that get through.

He slowly obliterated the three men.

When he was finished, he kicked a body aside and stepped on another's chest.

Cinjun stood tall, and said, "Gentleman, tonight you have seen power. Go forth and tell the tale. Be not ashamed; what you've seen is beauty, with a fist."

Dance the Night Away

MILES WAS SITTING with Scofield in the tavern.

Miles said, "I'm going after Cinjun Smythe."

"What?"

"I'm going to fight Cinjun Smythe."

Scofield said, "We're just two guys in a bar, talking."

"You're talking, I'm scheming." Miles said "I'm looking for a worthy opponent."

They left the tavern, and walked to Scofield's house.

No more teaching, no more training—I'm ready to fight, only fight, Miles thought. Warden, warden, warden! Won't you break your lock and key. Let this poor boy be.

They came to Scofield's door. Miles stopped and gazed at Scofield with a grin.

"Sco," Miles said, "have you noticed how beautiful the summer is this year?"

"I have," Scofield said.

"Now is a good time, for me to do it!" Miles said. "Now, is the time!"

Scofield held his look. "Why, because the trees are green, and the sky is blue?"

"No," Miles said, "because now I'm young."

Do not schedule a thing for him. He was on his way, and he would arrange his own meetings. Fine meetings that would call forth finer days.

Scofield grinned.

"Hasta la vista, my friend," Scofield said.

"Hasta la vista, my friend," Miles said.

Miles leapt into the air, into the strange days, and the fortunes to be found, out over the moon, and a little beyond tomorrow.

Lovers of the stars, could watch his trails, lonely in their huts.

While Miles, well, he, was raising a smile.

While summer is in the world, you must seize it.

The Executive Committee at House Crimson

IN CINJUN'S INNER CIRCLE, he presided at a horseshoe table. He was a kind of king, and his people were knights and barons of the realm.

"We need your time and energy—" Cinjun said—"We need you to put your sword on the table."

He walked around the seated group.

"Do you each have a copy of my book?" Cinjun said. "Turn to the passage on bad energy. Where I talk about freedom—We must purge the bad energy.

"Humble yourself. Kneel down, and kiss the Earth." He turned to a tough, rugged man and looked him dead in the eye. "Rise."

Cinjun willed the man to step forward.

The man rose. Straightened himself with a great tough kind of dignity. And then proudly and gladly brought himself down to a dignified but accepting position.

"You're very distant from me."

The man was only a pace away from Cinjun. He brought himself closer.

The man said, "Cinjun Smythe is the greatest person that has ever lived or ever shall live."

Cinjun held his look. "Good. Excellent work." Cinjun turned to his other people, and said, "You all should learn from this."

Rendezvous

MILES WAS PICKING Daphne up at her flat.

"Hello stranger," she said.

"What do you do for work?" he said.

"Karate," she said. "I'm practicing to be a husband beater. Are you interested in a partnership?—Where are we going?"

"A political fundraiser," Miles said.

"Will they let me make a speech? Why are we going?"

"My nemesis will be there."

"You have a nemesis. Very cool. You'll have to point him out to me. I have about ninety-six nemeses. We'll see who has the more fashionable nemesis."

"You're eternally wild with the power," Miles said.

"I know," she said. And walked on by.

The Political Fundraiser

MILES ESCORTED Daphne to the gala. She saw Skyler, who was there with a beautiful woman, Mimi Sutton.

Skyler said, "Daphne, how are you?"

"Hello Skyler," Daphne said.

"Daphne, I'd like you to meet my *wife,* Mimi. Mimi, this is my *sister's friend* Daphne."

"Congratulations," Daphne said. "When did you marry?"

"A few days ago."

"Amazing," Daphne said.

"What have you been doing?" Skyler asked, as an accusation.

Daphne held herself still. "Same old thing. You?"

"House Crimson," Skyler said. "Very successful. "I'm sure you've heard about it on the news."

"Isn't that splendid?" Daphne said. "What is House Crimson?"

"We'd love to talk with you," Skyler said, "but we're here with Cinjun Smythe—It's business; I'm sure you understand."

Daphne held herself still. She watched Skyler and Mimi move away, and through a great effort of will, she did not hit anybody.

In the dining hall, the party attendees were gathered at tables listening to Cinjun Smythe who was astride the platform putting on a good show. A strong show. Filled with very powerful stuff.

"We are right," Cinjun said. "We are strong. We are better. And we will prevail. We must learn to trust that the path is right. Trust our leaders. Second guessing is deadly. Doubt is the danger. Let us remain strong, and united."

He fired up the mass of people, speaking at some length.

Cinjun stepped off the platform into the crowd of people.

A supporter said, "What a privilege to hear a man who will one day stand for us use words like sinner and repent."

Cinjun showed himself grateful, and moved into the thick of the crowd.

Presently, Cinjun found himself breaking into a spur-of-the-moment minor speech.

"The Federation is the country of the endless frontier," Cinjun said to a throng of listeners. "Of the big sky, . . . of manifest destiny, . . ." How inspired he sounded, Cinjun thought—madly in love with himself. And Cinjun pressed his rhythm to greater heights.

"Unlimited resources,

"Opportunity for all,

"Ragged forms—

"Turned to replete riches,

"Ascent through courage,

"Mass-production scales,

"Nothing-to-fear hearts,

"All-will-be-well minds,

"Clear-eyed people,

"With scientific know-how,

"Working men and women,
"The envy of the world.
"Gung ho—
"And can do.
"Oh, now—this is our history,
"And this is the place we form our bold vision—
"Oh, now—do you hear our history!
"We live in *Big Sky Country.*"

Yes, thought Cinjun, it was a fine finish. A high.

He held himself silent forcing what came next: applause and cheers. The people were shaking with a sonic boom.

Cinjun was an efficient door-to-door politician. Always, he played for effect, always he was precise, and always he proved winningly effective.

Cinjun Khan Smythe was a golden god to the people he encountered. And, also—you couldn't help but notice—a man heartbreakingly handsome. Always, the girls cried, *"Come to my arms. Forevermore stay in my arms."* Always, the men, drawn in by his chiseled looks, felt themselves lured into a comfortable underling existence, felt his inner violence, felt themselves moved to cheers, and felt themselves become determined to join his assault force. Always it was the same, . . . the crowd ate him up.

Cinjun would fire them up, and then all too soon, with great measured charm, walk on by, careful to leave them feeling that he wished he could linger.

Always they gazed as he walked on by. Always, they saw his royal heading, *The Great Sunset*—to which, they each, then found themselves drawn with longing hearts.

Always, in this manner, Cinjun strode through the crowd. And the look—the look set deeply in his eyes—was the look of the god emperor marching to victories soon to be blessed with names. Yes, His godhood's soaring look was come upon the land. He allowed it to work its magic and allowed it to join with his song of sweet tomorrows. Oh, how sweet the promises he gave to every man and woman in the place, particularly to every women, and how sweet the future he held, lying for them softly there, just a little ways out over the moon and past tomorrow.

They each saw it, reflected in his eyes. And each reached for his thrilling promises.

Pulses quickened. The energy in the place quickened.

Cinjun determined to make sure that everything tonight would absolutely go his way. He would make this grand party an absolute victory.

Cinjun felt certain of his powers, felt he could glad-hand everybody in the place. And he just might. He decided he would. After all, he was here to save each one of these souls. None would be allowed to escape the salvation he brought into their world. He moved rapidly. He advanced on tomorrow. He grabbed everybody's hand. Sometimes before they could even see him coming. This moment in time was a monument to the way he operated all his days.

He grabbed Miles's hand and shook it. Firmly. In so doing, he was saying, 'I control you.'

"Good of you to come," Cinjun said. "Thanks for your support."

Abruptly, Cinjun stopped. Thunderstruck. He felt something disturb his mood suddenly. What was it? he wondered. Was he catching something in *Miles's eyes?*

Cinjun paused. Time died.

Something in Miles's face, his casting, his aura, his persona, something vibrated.

Cinjun was immediately thrown into a different key. It was as if Miles was a continuation of something, and Cinjun felt it immediately.

Miles stood before Cinjun, simply, without appeal, without insolence; as if nothing but total honesty were possible to Cinjun here. This was not the beginning of something but the middle; it was like a continuation of something begun long ago.

Cinjun realized that he had to assume a different manner than his usual manner, that he could not speak as he had spoken moments ago.

This was: strange sensation. And bounding force. Cinjun went on extreme alert.

Miles said, "Cinjun, I'm Miles Roark."

He looked at Miles—*Tygers* crouched in jungles in Miles's dark eyes.

"You say it as though I know that name," Cinjun said.

Cinjun spoke to Miles, suddenly stripped of all his art, in entirely the full persona of his naked god emperor self, there was no need for disguise with such a one as Miles.

"The name is not important," Miles said. "You're selling happy endings. I'll give you something to talk about in a speech."

"Give it to me fast. I have to go," Cinjun said.

"In the whole history of mankind—and that has now included billions of lives—not one life has ended happily."

"Where do you get your research?"

Cinjun began to walk past Miles.

Miles said, "Would you be interested in looking at my research?"

"No," Cinjun said.

"People are barbarians. That's my contention. I can prove it. Give me a piece of a paper and a pen. The proof, the facts, the findings. You can check my work. Case closed."

"Talk to me again," Cinjun said, "and I'll have you thrown out." Cinjun recognized this. Here at this mighty party, amid these mighty engines, in this place of certain victory, Miles was throwing madness into the mix.

Now Miles said to Cinjun:

"People are barbarians."

Miles spoke with a look that said more than words could ever say—it was there, shimmering in his eyes, the look of love.

"People are *fun,* sometimes great, marvelous barbarians." The look of love radiated from Miles's face—and in his eyes, there was the start of something, something that seemed . . . like it could go to forever.

"But deep in our heart we know we're talking about savages. Some play against it—become noble savages. Most stay savage savages. Plain savages. This crowd, here, happens to be a bunch of plain savages, dressed in all the pretty colors of longing, wouldn't you agree?" Miles showered Cinjun with his look of love.

Miles understood there was no need for disguise between the two of them. They were primal forces aware of each other's powers, of each other's destructive powers.

"So for your next talk: People are savages. How about it?" Miles said. "I'll prove it to you. Show you my work. Then you can use it."

Wouldn't that be lovely?—Miles's look of love said.

"Talk to me again, and I'll have you thrown out—" Cinjun said simply, and without effort.

"—But what if I prove it?" Miles said. "Wouldn't you want to see the proof?—"

"Talk to me again, and I'll have you thrown out." Cinjun explained.

"Ah," Miles said, "there you go, you proved it for me. I thought you might. See you later Cinjun."

"We won't be seeing each other again," Cinjun said. "You can depend on it."

"See you later, Cinjun," Miles said. Cinjun paused. There was something shocking about this man that Cinjun couldn't place. Miles seemed to have some kind of unexpressed ability to close down the town. Cinjun held Miles with the dirtiest, most brutal look he had in stock. Miles didn't give the least bit of a damn. Miles held Cinjun with the look of love. And then, Miles, was raising the smile. All the while, looking at Cinjun, with eyes that missed nothing.

Cinjun didn't like what he was seeing—*Tygers* crouched in jungles in Miles's dark eyes. Cinjun knew it was crazy—but he was suddenly catching raging glimpses of strong forces—horrible, deadly things— standing between himself and the moon of the forest city. Forces strong enough to defeat Cinjun. They, well they, crouched in Miles's dark eyes.

It disturbed Cinjun all to hell. He was a long moment recovering.

Cinjun walked past Miles and greeted Skyler who was standing with some people.

Skyler said, "I'd like you to meet the venerable Cinjun Smythe and his son's fiancée, Amelia."

Cinjun was joined by the very striking, ravishing young woman: Amelia, his future daughter-in-law. They stood very close to each other. There was something sexual in it.

An *Old Rich Man* appeared before Cinjun, saying to him:

"Just stand there so, and let me *look* at you. Just *look* at him! Look at him! Ain't it just good to *look at him!* Ain't it now? Ain't he just a picture! Some call him a picture; I call him a *panorama!* That's what he is—an entire *panorama.*

"Oh, I am so glad to see you! Oh my soul, the sight of you is such a comfort to my eyes!"

This old man had come to this place, this evening, to line Cinjun's pockets with gold; to load Cinjun's war chest. He was one among a vast many who loved Cinjun so.

The Love Affair

MILES AND DAPHNE left the party.

He asked her about her history. "Skyler Malloy—how did you meet him?"

"Parachuting into enemy grounds, skiing on an alpine slope, then I saw him on a military trip in the desert. We got into a scrape in a bazaar."

"Skyler," Miles said. "He was—"

"A twisted selection, . . ." Daphne said, ". . . but far from perfection."

"The end?" Miles said.

"The end came suddenly," she said, "It came to him in a fist—And he knew that I had a strong pitching arm! He carried the evidence away with him. If he hadn't, I would have broken every bone in his body. You can depend on me there."

"What did he do?"

"I don't remember."

"What a strong arm on that girl!" Skyler had said. She had given him the wings of his fate, wings of departure, pained remembrances of her swinging arm.

Later, he was privileged to learn more about her swinging arm.

He soon took it upon himself to stay away from her.

"You make every moment come alive," Miles said.

"I know!" she said. And she walked on by . . . Now as she passed beyond him, she said with lips devil red, "All the stars that shine upon me, want to kiss me every night."

I don't want them, she thought, *I don't want the moon, don't want the sun . . . a little love will do.*

She wanted to turn winter into spring. Spring into summer. And keep a little summer forever. With a plain golden wedding ring.

The only thing she didn't want to let get away from her . . . was a little love.

They went to Daphne's apartment where they sat in her living room. She parted one of her veils to reveal one of the great secrets of her inner life—

"I have super strength!" she said.

"What?" asked Miles.

"It's true," Daphne said.

She cleared the table, put her arm in an arm-wrestling position. Miles grasped her arm and they wrestled.

They struggled mightily. Miles prevailed. Daphne walked away.

"I prove my point!" she said.

"You lost?"

"Oh, you're a sore loser," Daphne said.

"We arm-wrestled, I brought your arm down. I won. I brought your arm down. I won. I did."

"You can't; I have super strength. I'll prove it again."

And, . . . presently . . .

They grasped arms over the table and again locked wills. It was a ferocious battle. They started sweating.

Miles brought her arm down and won again. She walked away.

Daphne said, "I won again."

Miles looked at her. "Are you out of your mind? I brought your arm down. I won."

"You can't; I have super strength."

Miles demonstrated on the table. "When I take this arm, grab your arm, overcome your arm, and bring it down to the table, I win. How can you deny it?"

"It's true," Daphne said. "If you could do something like that you would win. If you had anywhere near my strength you could."

She grabbed Miles's arm. "Go ahead prove it."

They battled again. They struggled like demons.

Daphne said, "See you can't bring me down."

Miles said, "You can't bring me down either."

She said, "Maybe I don't need to show off my super strength."

"Are you insane?"

Miles relaxed his grip just a bit. Daphne slammed his arm into the table, knocking him out of his chair. She looked down at him on the floor. "You're going to tell me again that you won?"

The night passed into darkest night. And they moved into her bedroom.

Now Miles was lying on top of Daphne. He kissed her.

He was passionate, she was curious. She observed him. That was all. Observed him.

He stopped. Gave her a rueful grin. He only did duets.

Miles and Daphne stepped out of the bedroom.

Miles said, "Thanks for the evening."

"I'm glad you enjoyed it."

"Tell me supergirl, what turns you on? What charges you up?"

"You're not my type. I like talking with you."

"What makes a guy your type?"

"Danger."

"Couldn't I be dangerous? You don't know me."

Daphne stood in the center of the room.

She told him, "Slap me!"

Miles stared at her.

She insisted, "Come on. Slap me!"

Miles stared at her.

"No. You're not dangerous." She had his full measure now.

She slapped Miles—Whoosh! Slap!

She was wild with the power, to make every moment come alive.

Wild with the power, she was young, and looking for a worthy opponent.

To make every moment come alive. Her specialty: explosions of feeling.

He did not move. She told him, "Go ahead slap me."

He grabbed one of her wrists, then the other. Brought them around to her back, while keeping her face to him.

He brought both wrists into one hand. He leaned her up against the wall. His mouth was practically touching her lips.

She felt his breath on her face, his body close to her.

Wild color lit up her face.

The silken moment went on forever.

Miles said, "I'll slap you on our second date.

"If I slapped you on our first date, we'd have nowhere to go.

"I'm neat, clean, shaved and sober, and I don't care who knows it.

"I'm everything that a well-dressed young man should be. I'm dating you. Good night Daphne."

He left.

The gift he would give her, would last forever! But that change, would come further down the river.

Seasonflow

SEASONFLOW.

Seasonflow produced the waves of nothing that were the setting. And the movements of nature that emerged from the setting.

And the flowing of the world that peopled.

The actions of nature.

The duning, the sand duning. The mountains mountaining. The light lighting. The sky skying. The ocean oceaning. The stars shining on the world that peopled. And the people feeling the way.

Violent flow. Violenceflow.

Murderflow, moved across the face of the world.

And suddenly—abruptly—out of nowhere and out of nothing—posing great and sudden menace to the world order—what rose into eruption? *A Peace Craze.* Yikes!

Killing.

Murder.

Blood in the streets.

And now all might lose to *Peace.* The Peace Craze threatened the natural flow.

It was haunting. Who knew where the Peace might lead; what kind of chaos it might sow in a world that peopled. Hell, it might stop everything. It might stop absolutely everything. That was always the danger with Peace. It stilled the mighty rivers. Peaceflow was still and Peaceflow was deep.

The people girded up their loins and called for a savior. Who would save the world?

Peace might settle on the works of man—and then what? Who wanted to live in a world so troubled by Peace, so different, so horribly changed, so altered and warped from this world that peopled?

And there was more—the still more dangerous threat was the force that Peace brought into the world—beware the shadow of the craze—its shadow cast itself deep and wide—its shadow fell so soft—it produced the dark hellish shadow—the ancient evil seducer known only as *Love.* Now the people could allow much into the world but Love was out of the question. It was very hard to do business when you were suffering from love for your enemy.

The night fell upon the land.

Nightfall covered the realm. Night fell upon the realm, making all things vulnerable to Love. Softening hearts, lighting candles, opening bottles of wine, whispering sweet nothings. Love descended on the helpless world.

Help! they screamed. Help! We're drowning in love dreams!

The Love Storm tossed the tiny ship of the world that peopled. If not for the courage of the fearless few, the tiny ship would have been lost. All hope would have been abandoned to—Love Hell . . . But now hope sang its cry.

The people girded up their loins—and cried out—into—the night—they searched out—they searched out—a strongman—Night so dark—where are you—come back—so dark—so dark—come back—oh strongman and let us feel the ease of strong empire.

Life was easy in a strong empire. In a world that empired.

Oh, strongman—return now to the people of the fair and strong.

And Cinjun Khan Smythe came upon the land. Bringing the Song of Unity . . . to lead them to a House Crimson.

The god emperor savior. *Be not afraid, for I am with you*—he used this thought and shaped it into words; this being his greatest appeal. A sexy and strong appeal it was.

Peace

THERE WAS A PEACE CRAZE in the nation. A love craze in the nation. And other such deadly dangers.

There were rogues and scoundrels who were deliberately taking steps toward Peace. And they didn't care who knew it.

Peace . . . and Love . . .

THE PEACE CRAZE WAS STRONG. The Love Craze was strong. Cinjun felt it assaulting the nation. Who knew where such a craze might lead.

He girded his loins.

The people were sore afraid. They needed a god emperor.

Cinjun looked all through the country, and tried to find a man who was more of a god emperor than himself. And his fear grew great, deep and wide—No such man existed, except him. No other man held the qualities. No other man was everything—only Cinjun was everything. And all would have to submit to everything.

Cinjun—well, he girded his loins.

Push and shove, might be necessary. Invasion and penetration might be necessary.

He was ready and practicing on some of the more beautiful young ladies within the mighty walls of House Crimson. Giving them the gift that would last forever.

Nothing happened.

The season crossed the world.

The sun traveled the sky.

The world stayed in its orbit. And the night sun continued to burn, an inferno in the void. Giving life and love and peace and the gift that would last forever.

He viewed the sun. The world was in his favorite moment of the day . . . when the sun was crimson . . . sending red into the world. The red was traveling across the forest city.

He felt nature; nature filled with purpose. Filled with crimson purpose.

And he bathed in possibilities. All the possibilities.

There was a peace craze in the nation. He turned his thoughts to this.

Some grew violent. Did things to their people. Made nature grow red in tooth and claw. It helped—to stop the dangerous thing that was threatening the nation.

The Peace Craze was taking the nation into its grip, but luckily there were some people who kept their wits about them in the face of threatening peace.

The Love Craze was wreaking havoc. Fortunately some stayed with the traditional way . . . making nature grow red in tooth and claw. They were not seduceable. They were not the tramps and whores of love, and never would be. They maintained the ancient honorable way of nature red in tooth and claw.

In this way crimson purpose survived among the people of right and might. And held out hope for a bright future in which the country would be saved and taken into a House Crimson.

A savior rose among the people . . . a god emperor in form and spirit and power . . . and he was righteous among them. He was righteous among the men. And righteous among the women. Especially the women.

He gave them attention, and the gift that would last forever. He gave them Cinjun Khan Smythe. And he held no part of his body back from the women.

He gave them the bodily gift of the god emperor. He was Cinjun Khan Smythe. The most important man that lived, ever had lived or ever shall live.

And the women—many in number—said, 'Come to my arms. Forevermore stay in my arms.'

He did what he could for their need.

And he gave to them in a mighty way . . . often helping them to experience life change in satin beds among silk sheets. And flowing warmth. Taking them on a ride. Getting on the inside. Getting it on the inside.

He was the god emperor. And most giving of his godhead, of his godhood.

He was warm sensation. And he was warming them.

He was connection. And he was connecting with them.

The Peace Craze loosed itself in the world.

We just have to hold society together until this peace craze dies down, the wise men said. And they girded up their loins. And the people were sore afraid. And there was a great gnashing of teeth.

The Peace Craze crept into reaches of the forest society and exploded itself into being in the most unexpected places.

Soon some people who you might have thought were fine and good people turned out to be peace savages, love brutes, who threw aside all modern manners and joined the Peace Craze.

They threw aside noble anger and softened themselves to this deadly inferno of peace taking shape. Peace taking the changes. Taking over the life changes. Turning good and proper life changes to sordid affairs of peace. And love.

The Love Craze loosed itself in the world.

We just have to hold it together until this love craze dies down, the wise men said. And they girded up their loins. And the people were sore afraid. And there was a great gnashing of teeth.

The Love Craze crept into reaches of the forest society and exploded itself into being in the most unexpected places.

Soon there was even talk of love among assassins and worse yet— among pleasure seekers, sinners—Hell and damnation, was no one safe when love and peace reared its deadly blood ship on the high seas of good living?

And they girded up their loins. And hardened their hearts.

And called for a god emperor to come deliver them. A mighty god emperor who could stand with the people of might and right.

Cinjun Smythe happened to be available. And perfectly presentable. He was the perfect one. And the perfect one moved to seal his perfect destiny.

He would smite any who got crazy. He would deal with the wicked. And the wicked would get dead.

He would put the world in order. And get to any who chose to be crazy—Oh, to be crazy, was a sin. There could be no forgiving the sin of madness.

He would show no mercy. He would produce destiny. And they would get dead.

He would take them to the place beautiful—House Crimson.

He would carry the world that peopled out of orbit and take it to the place beautiful—to the promised realm?—a House Crimson.

He would save them from evil. And he would not be gentle to the evil.

Pity the evil. Cinjun Smythe was come. And the evil would be made nothing.

Cinjun Smythe thought much of evil. Evil filled his thoughts and gave him no rest.

He looked on all the works of evil. And became expert in evil. So that he might reap good with a mighty sword and a stout heart.

Good would be worth the murder.

Paradise would be worth the slaughter.

Paradise was a bloody business. Which he happened to be in.

Happiness for sale. This was his business.

Happiness for sale. Happiness that's fresh and bold. Happiness that's only several days old.

Who would like to sample his supply? Happiness for sale.

Happiness was bloody expensive to produce. This he knew.

He was producing loads and loads of happiness.

For purposes of mass production, he was raising money on the most massive scale in history.

True happiness broke sales records. The proof was in the revenues and receipts.

And this was why he was raising money. Filling a war chest that like some other-world fuel tank seemed incapable of topping off. The more money he put in it, the more there was to get for his war chest.

He raised loads and loads of money. Boatloads of money.

Happiness for sale—He ran a prosperous business.

He found it a prosperous business.

Perfect happiness for sale.

Who would like to sample his supply? How about you?—Might you be able to use some happiness? I'd like to show you some happiness.

His "sell" was particularly effective with women. His happiness operation worked wonders with them. He seemed to be hell with the women . . . Maybe it had something to do with his good looks, his charming smile, his worldly manners . . . Why you could go on . . . Cinjun Smythe was plainly and simply perfect. The most perfect man that lived, ever had lived, or ever shall live.

Ask him yourself, he'll tell you. He's perfect and loaded to bear with happiness.

Who could ask for anything more from a man? What else could there be out there other than the gifts Cinjun Smythe gave?—These gifts that could last forever.

In the weaving flow of the timeslip, *Happiness* made him strong.

The people made him strong.

Everything made him strong.

And every day made him stronger.

Every night made him happier, particularly the nights he spent helping women experience his happiness.

In this way he moved into his full destiny, which he carved one day'night across the night'sun'sky.

He carved his destiny and writ it large—as it is written so shall it be—*Strongman for sale.*

New strongman for sale. A strongman that's fresh and bold, a strongman who would boldly go where no strongman had gone before.

New strongman for sale.

He was perfect. And moved perfectly to a perfect destiny, and everything was perfect around him.

What could possibly disturb his great destiny—nothing. He knew there was no man out there to equal him.

He was a god emperor. He felt his role in the course of human history. Accepted his responsibility to rule humanity. And to rule the world that peopled.

It was a wild world but he would make it tame.

He was a god emperor. And the god emperor would tame the world.

Cinjun Smythe was filled with such humble thoughts. They never left him. He carried his truth everywhere.

He filled the All with his truth. And saw everything through his All.

The All was his to command. And command it he would.

He would make the world . . . His violence would be absolute. He would beat "nothing" into form. And then he would beat the form into shapes that would suit his powerful destiny.

And he would beat any man out there who dared take him from his world beating and happiness ruling.

He was good. That which opposed him was evil.

He would destroy and murder evil. The thoughts filled his head and gave him no peace.

Peace—Ah—Cinjun's thoughts went to—the goddamn Peace Craze that was threatening the world. The Peace Craze—that Cinjun had to smash violently in order to save the world.

He had to take the world into true Peace—the kind of peace that came from bloody slaughter.

The Peace and Paradise you earned and gained through: murder.

The kind they had been searching for throughout all of history. True peace was elusive. But he was about to show them the way to it.

And so he raised his mighty blood sword and strode into the future-flow.

This was the way some people looked at Cinjun Smythe and how he operated—Cinjun saw it as far more beautiful.

Murder worked wonders. Beautiful wonders.

He was off to perform beautiful life-saving miraculous murders.

He had nothing to fear.

Nothing Forming

A MEADOW OF *NOTHING,* in the mist.

A valley green with nothing.

Nothing was in the world. And nothing happened.

Nothing struck. Nothing happened.

The music in the night—faint—nothing. Nothing sang its song and produced nothing making nothing happen.

Nothing was new under the sun.

For a time . . . nothing filled the void . . . and then change came into the world . . .

It came out of nothing at all, you might say.

The Nothing Daze moved, and slipped into Miles Roark, producing an effect.

Nothing Daze, all in my mind. Lately things just don't seem the same—Nothing Daze all in my head, excuse me—

Nothing was happening, and happening in a big way.

And amid nothing, a War Path.

Cinjun carved a War Path.

He beat nothing into form, turned absolutely nothing into form—a beautiful War Path.

Come see the view along the trail, Cinjun Khan Smythe cried, *broken trail so long.*

Leading into distance, a distance that seemed about the size of forever. But probably went beyond.

Come see the Violenceflow River, the Violenceflow Mountains and all the great land of Violence.

The land of the fair and the brave and the stout and the noble, and Cinjun Khan Smythe.

Cinjun On the War Path

CINJUN WAS ON THE *LIGHT*VISION.

"Let's bomb them into the Stone Age," Cinjun said.

"Take out the buildings. Take out everything. It's the only language they understand."

Cinjun was rolling and rolling along. Sorting it all out for the good people. Putting everything into its right and proper place. He seemed unaware of danger to his designs.

But there was danger on the edge of town . . . Miles Roark.

That's where you found Miles, out there . . . To get there, what you did was you rode the highway, to the end of the road, to the edge of the forest society, to the Outskirts of the City.

That's where he was. Just bring your gun, and you would be safe.

You went to the edge, all the damn way, out past everything.

To the outskirts of the city.

In a far recess—in the place Miles knew as home—Miles was watching the *light*vision fascinated, for surely it was the light of the world.

And he did so enjoy watching Cinjun on there. Speaking with such profound wisdom that you found it hard to contain your joy. At the fact that Cinjun Smythe lived in this world. Such a good guy.

Miles spoke to the *light,* and its flickering *Cinjun-bringing.*

"Cinjun, I have got to hand it to you. Let's bomb them into the Stone Age. Wow! What an idea. So fresh, so new.

"Yes, here's a new idea: Let's put large holes in other countries. How about it? What do you think? Let's work these Big Throbbing Missiles and penetrate Mother Earth," Miles said.

"Cinjun Smythe, where do you get these fucking great ideas?

" 'Oh, I just lie in bed, and up come the ideas.'

"Is that so?

" 'Oh, why yes, I just lie in bed thinking of the Mother, and up come the fucking ideas.'

"Well, Cinjun, I'll tell you, you're something else. Hey, you can get other joys out of Mother Earth, you know. There are other delights. How about tasting the sunsweets of the Earth?

"No thanks, I'd rather drop some missiles."

The Sky God Calls for a Healthy Debate

FURTHER IN THE TIMEFLOW—at a tavern, The Caveman's Grotto and Grill—Miles was watching Cinjun on the house *light*vision. As were others, for surely it was the light of the world.

Miles was standing beside a man, who was saying, "That Cinjun sure is a great thing to come along."

The patron had a head like unto a Hammerhead Shark.

Yes, he was standing beside a man, who had a head, oh, such a head—and a wisdom? Like unto a napkin.

The man had understanding, like unto a lowlife, like unto a gathering of stones.

"Hey, keep it down," Miles said. "Let me hear what the great man has to say. Let Cinjun be heard"

Cinjun had threatened to make a major announcement. Of earth shaking importance. And now he moved to spring it on the world.

Cinjun moved into it, in a slow measured tone.

"I feel we are living in a very important time," Cinjun said. "And I feel we are coming into a very important moment. And this is why I have decided to do something revolutionary. It is time for me to step up, and start something altogether new.

"It's time for—A Healthy Debate—" Cinjun said.

—The Hammerhead cut in—"The man makes the most sense of any man I ever heard!"

Miles tried to ignore him—but the Hammerhead was going to talk through Cinjun's words.

Miles turned.

"Hey, shush!" Miles said. "Give the singer some! Is that any way to behave while God is speaking?"

"How about I hammer your teeth into your nose?" the hammerhead man said. The hammerhead man was, possibly—*high strung*. All the signs were there.

On the *light*vision Cinjun said:

"—We must get into a debate of the big questions. I think we need it, which is why I'm calling for a series of debates in which we will look at the issues of the every man.

"A Healthy Debate—" Cinjun said, "not among politicians . . . but among the people on the street.

"Not insiders, we have to let the outsiders get into the ring. It's absolutely essential. I'm a come-from-nowhere guy, and a lot of people dismissed me. But I think I proved that sometimes the come-from-nowhere guy has the most important things to say. The most important questions to ask.

"What I'm saying is: Let's ask The Big Questions—

"Is this the country it should be?

"Do we have the society we need?

"Is the economy fit?

"Is the political system meeting the needs of the people?

"Most say we could do a lot better."

"Yeaaaaahhhh!" Miles exploded. He talked to Cinjun, to the people in the place, to the sheltering sky above.

"I'm calling for—*The People's Showdown!*" Cinjun declared.

People took Cinjun into their interest, and murmured *'The People's Showdown? The People's Showdown?'* A battle was come. A high time would be had by all.

*"The People's Showdown,—*I love it," Miles roared. "That Cinjun S'mythe is such a beautiful man, what a beautiful thing to put into the world—The People's Showdown?" *Yes—it had rightness to it.*

"Yea-agh!" Miles shouted. And held back nothing. "Fortune favors the prepared mind," he said.

"A Fight in the Light Show!" Cinjun said, on the *light*vision, speaking from his home in the City of Gold, with shelter and dream in his eyes. He was going to buy himself a mountain, and build a palace on its peak.

"A Fight in the Light Show!" Miles said. Rolling it over in his mind. He liked it; the shape was pleasing to him.

"He's not talking about you," the Hammerhead said. "You're crazy, you know that?"

"You'll be happy to hear that I do know that," Miles said, "and Cinjun will be happy . . . to hear that he is talking about me . . . it will set his soul on fire."

Nothing was what it seemed.

But Miles saw a path to the Flame. He held his eyes on the path.

Oh, the lightning in his eyes! revealing *Tygers* crouched in jungles, in his dark eyes.

The Night Sun went on shining; the stars stayed in the sky; a river flowed; and a way of knowing formed a path of *'where it goes.'*

Maybe this was where it would go. To where a certain mountain touched the sky, to a place where there was a cold wind blowing.

Ah, where this would go!—no one knew—The people living alone in the city, would know a season of Dreaming. Where in the world would the dream go?

Where it goes! This was where Miles would drive it to. To where in the world the Love did go. To where in the world the Dream chose to hide.

The Fix Is In

THE NIGHT SLIPPED into day . . .

At House Crimson, Cinjun and Skyler were meeting with their committee of advisors.

"Skyler," Cinjun said, "who can we get?"

"Yes, who can we get?" Skyler said.

"He must be a known," Cinjun said. "Mellons and lemons that's what I want to look at— Most battles are won or lost before the first shot is fired—He must be a good sell, but a lemon I can squeeze. Sidney, what are your thoughts?"

"We should go with an unknown," Sidney said. "An outsider."

"Sidney, stick a sandwich in your mouth, and shove it deep. William?" Cinjun broke his contact with Sidney and turned to his son, *William Smythe.*

"Floyd Pernell!" William said.

"Beatable, yet reputable. That's good," Cinjun said. "I want exciting choices like that. Let's think along those lines."

The Land of the Blind

AND NOW—THE DAY IS SLIPPING. And now . . . slipping into night.

And now it is night. Dark, so dark. Cold, so cold.

And here within this sheltering place, within this drinking hall—Miles feels his emotion building as he stands on this platform of this night room. And he speaks to . . . this group of lively people.

"A man walks into the Land of the Blind ————" Miles says to these people, his voice ringing out.

"It's a place where nobody can see. They don't even have a word for seeing. He tells them he can see, and describes what it's like to see.

" *'Can I show you daylight?'*—being this man's desire.

"He's a Sound Chaser. He speaks of things like this; things that he sees. Things he sees that are sad; things he sees that make him hurt so bad; things he sees that make him feel fine.

"He's a Sound Chaser, this man————"

Oh, the breeze blew back his hair as he spoke. The highest power of seeing is to see The Sound Chase. Oh to see forever leading to forever leading to forever—The Sound Chase. Beyond and beyond and beyond. To see forever leading to forever leading to forever. Time slipping—The Sound Chase. The Wãoynde. Cutting through; crossing through; sweeping through. At play in the fields of The Sound Chase. His dreams were not empty. His dreams were filled with life. He was a madman, don't you know. And the mad have a biting imagination that bites hard on their madness . . . The madman's dreams are filled . . . And this madman's dreams were filled. *Oh, the breeze blew back his hair as he spoke.*

"Now," Miles said, "this is the land without Sound Chasers. When this seeing man walks into the land of the blind, how can he speak of sound chasing? ————"

And how can he speak to them of the highest power of seeing?

He tells them what it's like to be a Sound Chaser—they can't see it.

He tells them what it's like to see such a thing—they can't imagine seeing. They can't even think the thought—this thought of seeing is beyond them.

What they decide is that he's crazy—that the Sound Chaser is absolutely insane.

He makes their feelings hurt so bad with his talk. Oh, you cannot take it!

They don't know what he's going through, standing there looking at them with his eyes, his eyes that sit there in slow fire burning . . .

Feeling a slow hot wind.

Seeing a slow hot wind.

This was the thing, he makes it hurt so bad. "Oh, don't make it hurt so bad," they cry out. When he spoke, he made it hurt so bad. "Oh, no! No! No-oo-ooo!"

No, no, no. No! No-ooo-oo! His talk makes them hurt so bad. His talk makes everything hurt so bad.

He tells them what you see when you are a Sound Chaser. He tells them what the view is when you are a Sound Chaser. And they listen. For an instant.

Crack him open! This was the thing to do.

Take him apart! This was the thing to do.

Break him apart! This was the thing to do.

Destroy danger, becomes their concern. *Destroy danger.* And the Sound Chaser describes something very dangerous—an emotion-filled insanity and a tearing apart of the entire order of their world. Oh, their ordered world where everything fits their needs.

"Oh, no! No. No-oo-ooo!"

Hearts burn with it.

Silencing him becomes the step to honorable victory over evil. Silencing the talk of the Sound Chaser becomes a good thing. The most wonderful, marvelous good thing they can do.

"He's out of his mind," they say.

"If we take out his eyes," one says softly, "he'll be fine. Because then he'll be just like us."

And now they reach the great turning point, and the great truth lies before them.

"Yes," they feel it now, "that's what we must do. Why no one likes to do it, when it is not absolutely necessary. But we'll cut out his eyes; it's for his own good."

Why if they cut out his eyes, he'll be fine. He'll stop seeing; stop being a Sound Chaser, and then he'll be just like them. And the madness will be over.

And now The Sound Chaser saw that not one of them knew what it was like to see. Not one of them could be made to see through their blindness. And then coming at him out of a black void, out of black seas . . . he saw danger! Violent, immense danger!—Well, the Sound Chaser has a problem here—you see, they're going to have to kill him before he'll stop seeing what it is to be a Sound Chaser. The only way it will ever be over, is by killing him. Only then will he stop seeing what it is to be a Sound Chaser.

And now the listeners, the saviors, and the wise men carefully, very carefully, but with extreme good feeling joyfully bound across the expanse, and cross through *The Gates of Delirium.*

'Okay,' they decide, 'let's kill him, to save him.'

'Okay,' The Sound Chaser decides, 'I'll keep chasing sounds; stop me. Death may happen—But death not ends it—'

Abruptly—a heckler shouted at Miles from the crowd of people—

Mister Rin Tin Tin interrupted. Mister Rin Tin Tin knew a great many things; and he knew shit when he saw it—

"Oh who the fuck are you!" Mister Rin Tin Tin said. "Who the fuck are you to carry on like this! Who the fuck are you to talk such shit!" Mister Rin Tin Tin was an enlightened gentleman with lots of schooling and book-learning that he liked to parade. He was a spectacular wise man now.

"Who the fuck do you think you are!" Rin Tin Tin said.

Miles let the man shout, and run to a point, to the point of his great cascading wisdom.

"—Who the fuck are you? Who do you think you are to me? That's what I really want to know." Rin Tin Tin said—"Come on, tell me, who the fuck are you!" The man turned from the stage. "Send somebody else on. I don't care if it's Happy the Clown, so long as it's not this guy. "

"You expect us to listen to this shit!" Rin Tin Tin's friend now said to Miles on the stage.

"Why should we listen to this shit!" another singer sang out at the same time.

Miles smiled, and felt their reaction. He took it on the inside. And swept his gaze to Mister Rin Tin Tin.

"There's only," Miles said, "one 'why' that I can think of."

And he spoke calmly and pleasantly. "It was over for you before it began. And I'm telling you about what it's like when it's only just begun—"

"Aw, shit!" Mister Rin Tin Tin said. "Will you quit it! We're here to have a good time—"

"I'll leave with this one little 'what' that is totally free:

"You're living," Miles said, "in The Land of the Blind."

Miles felt his pulse quicken. He was being pushed into a state that he did not want. He knew he should not say what he said next. He couldn't stop himself.

"No, no effect. You don't care in the least, do you? But maybe you'll follow this . . ."

Now Miles pulled himself into a state of calm. He stood on the stage and spoke with total calm.

He spoke in a simple human tone. He was a human being talking to another human being.

He had failed and was pressing deeper into failure.

It was pulling him in and he could not stop himself from wanting to go deeper. From wanting to save it somehow. To pull victory from disaster.

"Let's say I'm a doctor. And I see you. And I see that you have cancer. And it's destroying you. The cancer is killing you.

"Now if I talk to you about your nice eyes, and how nice your teeth look, but I don't tell you that you have a cancer that is destroying you—what am I doing? What kind of sounds am I making?

"Now do you care? No, not in the least. I'm going to join together with the night now. So long," Miles said.

"So long screwball!" the man said.

"So long Mister Whoever-You-Are," Miles said. He crossed the platform. And left the scene with no more interest in it.

Well, well, well, no one was going to steal that act from him—it amounted, Miles thought, *to a fairly marvelous failure.* But learning came from such difficulties. He was close to something. And this thing could be made to work. He absolutely had to figure out how to do it. He would make it work.

And so Miles enjoyed this particular failing, for a very sensible reason. If you want to learn to ski, you don't just go down easy slopes. One of these days, Miles was going to ski down the face of a cliff, and he wanted to be ready.

This thing could be made to work, he felt certainty building in him. A force building, building to an explosion.

His next move would be stronger. And the move after that, stronger still.

There was a fire in his belly. He could sense it. And the fire was growing.

The only question was, what would he do when they came for him; when he collided with them. At that point, he would have to have enough might in him to win. Or he would get dead.

He stepped forward, and kept going.

Traveling. The Seeker moving into tomorrow. The Seeker hurtling into forever.

Probing. Seeking and hunting all the many means and tricks of *survival*.

Loading himself with all the might there was to find.

Acquiring every form of might that anybody in this place could ever find.

Hoping that his growing might would . . . maybe, just maybe . . . give him the soaring force . . . power enough to beat back the dangers, when they came. The dangers of this forest society, that were coming for him . . . The dangers that in time would work to end him.

He did not want his life to end beneath the force of this coming stone cold assault, he did not want his life to end badly.

He was picking up this *might* . . . this power—this thing streaming wild, wild as can be—this power that might, just might save him when he came to his encounter with *Cinjun Smythe.*

Act Two

Wild in the Wilderness

The Wilderness

MILES WAS ON THE STAGE. His eyes were closed. The audience didn't know what to make of him. Miles was doing nothing immediate.

His voice was drifting . . . his eyes remaining closed.

"People take a deep breath," Miles said. "And I'll try to do something good to your head.

"Listen, listen, listen people. Let's go back, way back, to stone and bronze. Back to, back to, back to————"

Miles felt an alerting sensation throughout his body.

He sensed the touch of an uncompleted thing, awakening, rising. Something crouched within him. It was like a coiled spring waiting for release.

He traveled deep within himself and found an area of crashing waves. He entered it and suddenly felt the flow all around him . . . and it was rising. It exploded in waves of red, orange and yellow.

He opened his eyes. And it came out of him. Radiating to the audience. He struck like fire.

He told the tale.

"A Young Lion walks into the wilderness————"

On the far hill, he sees *An Old Lion.*

Down below, *The Others,* listening.

And The Old Lion cries,

Clothed in the colors of old lies,

'We are all equal,' the Old Lion says

'Justice is blind,' the Old Lion says

'You have nothing to fear but fear itself,' the Old Lion says.

And the lies come down,

Like a warm rain,

On the ones below.

All the other lions saying, "Ah-hungh!"

Not one lion questioning.

The Old Lion draws a figure, . . . *outlines* how to *think* and *act.*

While . . . The Young Lion . . . in his lonely height . . . realizes that in back of this old lion's lies is a voice that whispers, *'Don't be yourself, be us. Become a part of us.'*

This is while in glowing features up front, the beautiful, charming Old Lion promises them everything, . . . every wish is there, waiting for his command.

He promises the moon and the stars, the sun and the sky, he promises everything . . . *Sunlight streaming in his hair.*

He promises everything they're dreaming of . . . *Sunlight streaming in his hair.*

Well, they have a lot of dreams, and he can make them all come true. He promises them anything they're dreaming of . . . *Sunlight streaming in his hair.*

He promises them everything.

Roll, roll, roll, *he fills their soul.*

'Hear my song,' he cries.

'Can you feel it, now—that spring is come?

'We're standing on the long lonely lie of freedom's shore, waiting. The first flashing of Eden Estates is striding in cool ascendance here before us. Can you feel it? It's time to emerge from wintery recess; it's time to live in the sun. A strange life. A bold life beneath a warm, glowing sun. A sun touched with red. A sun favoring Crimson. And a House bathing warm in Crimson possibility.'

At that moment, . . .

The Young Lion recognizes the true *danger* in the wilderness, sees its full form and pressure—*The Old Lion is his enemy.*

Oh, the mighty Soft Bull-Mud Parade has now begun. And you could listen to its mighty engines hum.

Miles says:

"The Old Lion is playing the 'In Group' trick. He's selling them on tribal thinking————"

'The wilderness is a dangerous place. To live here, we have to live together. We must make a group, we must make a tribe.'

It's a good thing. The danger is that it always goes too far. You always reach the same point, *'We have to tell The Story of Us.'*

And the story always ends up being: *We're great!*

Now, if we're an In Group, suddenly you need an Out Group. We have to feel we're right. For that we need people who are wrong.

Now here's the question, at which point did this game get dangerous?

At the bar, one drunk turns to another. "What the hell kind of act is this?"—

"Our tribe versus them," Miles said. "Our tribe is good. Their tribe is evil ————"

It always crosses the threshold into *The Bullyashat*.

The Bullyashat is a belief. It is the true belief, of *Us*. Of the In Group.

What would you have to do to set up a country run by group-think gurus? You would need *The Official Story*. They would all have to work off of the same script.

You would need the Official Bull Mud Story. When the old lion comes to you, he comes to you as your friend. He brings a bucket of mud. Hard, bitter mud. He presents it on a velvet cloth. And he says, "This is the finest, richest, and rarest mud in all the world."

This is the Official Bull Mud Story, my friend.

Now to run the Bull Mud thru the changes, you do this: all along the way you drive people into a state of grace, a state of warming *We*-feeling, *The Bullyashat*. *The Bull Satori*—Satori is a state of enlightenment. A state of knowing, and feeling what you know to be *it,* to be The All. *The Bull Satori* is a state in which what you believe is total bull mud. It allows you to become a hippopotamus. And to feel this is the highest form of life you can attain.

It allows you to accept rubbish as knowledge. *Balderdash.* To accept Balderdash as the highest form of knowledge you can reach. Balderdash is a punchy, powerful mode of bull-mudding. Balderdash is the highest level of Bull Satori. Of Bull S'tori.

When the young bull meets the old bull in Eden Estates, that's what the old bull tells him, by way of advice—*the Bull S'tori.*

On the sidelines, two comedians rate Miles's show. They talk over each other's lines.

"What kind of act is this?—"

"—Lame—"

"—All the who's down in whoville are supposed to eat this up?—"

"—Not even one dick joke to help it along—"

"—Before you take on the world, learn to tell a decent dick joke—"

"—Alright, that's not your style. How about a pussy joke—"

"—You don't have to take it all on. A tit joke—"

"—Something—"

"—Where's the art in what he's doing?"

The Platform

IN THE COMMITTEE ROOM OF HOUSE CRIMSON, Cinjun wrote his platform with a committee of people.

That was not how Miles wrote his platform . . .

Miles whipped out a sheet of paper, grabbed a pencil and carved a message.

He posted it on his wall. There was nothing on his walls in the bare apartment. It was as if he didn't live there. This sign lived there.

It said:

one   *"I"* versus *"We"*
two   "I" seems to be a verb
three   Be bright, be brief and be gone

While Cinjun operated in the warmth of his inner core—
Miles erected this at his place in the wilderness.
On the outskirts of the settlements.
He lived in the wilderness manor,
At the crossroads
On the edge of town,
The outskirts of the city.
If you go there, just bring your gun
and you'll be safe.

The Official Bull Mud Story

MILES WAS ON THE STAGE:

"The Bull Mud is a fun ride, with thrills and chills————"

Some people have been on the Bull Mud for a long time. And they forget it's just Bull Mud. A Bull Satori.

Then there are those people who come to us and say, 'It's just a ride.

'Don't be afraid, ever. Be yourself. Love yourself, and love one another.'

And we . . . kill those people.

Shut him up! We have a lot invested in this ride. We've got to stop that boy. He's gone too far out. He's gone wild.

'It's just a ride.'

We always kill those good guys who tell us that. You ever notice that? And let the demons run amok.

What's going on?

What is the moment that must never come?

A Young Lion would step up to the Old-Lion Leader and ask: "Mister Old-Lion Leader, perhaps you are seeing things wrong?"

The leader would get all hot and say, "Are you questioning my judgement!"

And The Young Lion would say, "Is your judgement so perfect that it can never be questioned? Mister Old Lion Leader, I have a question. It's a very old question, maybe you've heard it asked before. *Quis custodiet ipsos custodiet?*

"Who shall guard the guardians?

"Who shall see that the guardians commit no offenses?

"How may we know that they rule rightly?"

"How May We Know That You Would Rule Rightly?"

MILES APPROACHED the lobby desk, where he said, "I'd like to see Mister Cinjun Smythe."

A moment later, Miles was sitting in the lobby. And a House Crimson senior fellow stepped from the lift—it was Skyler, striding across the expanse with a smile.

"Miles, always a pleasure to talk with you," Skyler said, "How can we help you?"

"Well, hello Skyler," Miles said. "You work with Cinjun Smythe now? . . . Congratulations. I'm sure it's more your speed than the old job, huh? I'd like to speak with Mister Smythe, and I'll tell you why—"

"I'm his strategist," Skyler said. "I can likely help."

"I'd like to have a minute with him," Miles said, "and I'll tell you why—"

"—I'm afraid that's going to be impossible," Skyler said.

"I see," said Miles. "Perhaps we could go to your office—"

"I'm sorry Miles," Skyler said, "but it's a busy day. Perhaps you could tell me what it is."

"The Healthy Debate," Miles said, "I have an idea for how to make it a great show."

"With who?"

"Listen, Skyler, I have a way to serve Cinjun's purpose, and make it a brilliant show—"

"With who!"

"Skyler, I'm getting to your answer—"

"With who?"

"Myself. You're asking for a come-from-nowhere guy—"

"—True," Skyler said.

"You're asking for an *'every man' to step forward!"*

"—True," Skyler said.

"You're asking all over the place, true? So, all I'm saying is hear me out. Hey, look, I'll make my pitch brief, as brief as hell. It won't cost you anything to listen."

Skyler cast a gaze at Miles . . . of such penetrating force . . . and said, "Fee, fi, fo, fum, I see a Sound Chaser. Say it isn't so."

Miles held his look.

"You're a Sound Chaser," Skyler said. "Say it isn't so."

"I'm a Sound Chaser," Miles said. "And I can be a great help to you, if you'll hear me out—"

Skyler started walking away. The meeting was over. *Crackpots!* Skyler thought. *Everywhere I turn, crackpots.*

Skyler then asked Miles a question—in an incidental way—he tossed it to Miles over his shoulder as he moved away, and didn't even turn to catch Miles's reaction:

"What organization are you with now?"

"I'll tell you," Miles said, "a little bit about where I'm at—"

"What do you have?" Skyler asked.

"The full offices of Miles Roark International."

"Your affiliation—" Skyler was heading for the lift.

"The human race, it's filling the world. Our folks are everywhere."

"You're very amusing," Skyler said with no trace of mirth, "maybe I could work up a laugh and send it to you."

"If you're going to the trouble, make it a big one," Miles said. "Now honestly, Sky—I truly do have a powerful idea for you; will you hear what I have to say—"

Skyler signaled for the lift. "How would you draw a crowd?"

"By saying interesting things—"

"I understand," Skyler said. "Thank you for coming by—"

"—Please don't understand me so fast—"

"—The security guard can escort you out—" Skyler stepped into the lift.

"—Thank you for listening—" Miles said.

Skyler spoke from the lift, "—My pleasure."

The Spark, Sparks . . . Sparks to Flame

AS MILES WALKED AWAY, he looked around, studying the territory. He looked up at the tower.

It was a fortress, surrounded by a chasm. Well, there was nothing else for it—it was time to build a bridge!

Inside the tower, Skyler was briefing Cinjun.

"I've got a guy here who's yacking off about you. That's his act. The country's full of bull mud and you're leading the soft parade."

"What's his name?"

"Miles Roark."

"I never heard of him," Cinjun said. "Is anybody backing him?"

"No, he's a lone gasbag. I know him from my agency days."

"I'll have someone look into it," Cinjun said.

Cutting

HOUSE CRIMSON, . . . the gymnasium, . . . and everyone was in white karate outfits sitting on mats.

Cinjun was striding among them.

Off to the side, loomed *Brutus,* a fellow with the coiled killer look, and the poise of a methodic man, who does his dirty work with gloves on. He was Cinjun's muscle and head of security.

He was also a very charming guy . . . that was how he got away with a little murder now and again.

"Cutting," Cinjun said, "is a scientific process in which members separate themselves from a source of evil energy—whether a friend, lover, parent, husband or wife.

"You visualize cords stretching from your heart to the heart of the other person. Then at my instruction, you cut the cords."

And the image was upon the water.

"In some cases, we have to surgically go a step further and 'burn the image,' visualizing the person being consumed by flames."

And the image roiled along the choppy surf.

Abruptly, a boy spoke.

"Cinjun, . . . I . . . well, . . . I . . . have some doubts . . ."

Immediately, and with great urgency, he was whisked into a distant alcove.

Where, presently, Cinjun gave the boy: *the treatment.* Cinjun wrapped his arm around the boy's shoulder.

The boy's *doubts,* his feelings, posed a physical test to Cinjun's will. *There would have to be no hesitation.* As always, Cinjun would have to prove invincible. No assault could be allowed to get through. *Press on. Move forward.* This was how Cinjun operated. This was the way to greatness.

Cinjun turned his eyes to the boy.

"I don't feel I can help you anymore," Cinjun said.

That was all. And now he was finished with the boy. That was the entire conversation. The be-all-and-end-all of the exchange.

Cinjun turned to Brutus, and advised him how to proceed with the boy.

"Take that thing out of here!" Cinjun glared at the boy. "Right away! Far away! Take that thing right out of here."

Brutus showed the boy out, and he was not gentle unto him, nor sporting.

Cinjun returned to the gymnasium.

Where he spoke, with grace and lamentation in his voice:

"He was and is against us; he sets himself above us! And so, corrections have to be made. They are being made right now."

The boy's girlfriend was still in the fold.

Cinjun turned to her. She was pretty, a flowing voluptuous figure.

Cinjun saw great potential in her, to serve his needs.

First, she would require domination. Which happened to be Cinjun's specialty, cultivated through long labors.

Cinjun gave her a command to speed the flow of their growing closer. He said, "You must cut the boy! I want you to free yourself. I want to teach you about freeing yourself, would you like that?"

She glowed.

She and Cinjun would presently grow closer, and warmer.

Sharing

A LAVISH FEAST WAS HELD at House Crimson.

Amelia and William were at the center of the gathering.

They were reading from Cinjun's book. They pledged their joint devotion and fealty, and read aloud a passage from the book, "House Crimson."

When Cinjun stood to congratulate them, he did not put an arm around William; rather, he stared into William's eyes as he put his arm around Amelia, around her waist. He gave the pleasure of nearness to his new daughter.

Evening Life

Amelia

Cinjun was having sex with Amelia—his son's young lady—all over the living room furniture.

Vanity of vanities, all was vanity. Oh Cinjun Khan Smythe. His all was fierce. Fierceness leading to fierceness, all was fierce. Tortured. Sin leading on to sin, all was sin. Sin leading to form, sin leading to visitation, all was sin. All was carnality. And fun.

His passions were enormous. His passions needed to stroll. Ooh Shoo Be Doo Be Ooh, Ooh. Shoo Be Doo Be. Ooh. Whoo.

Ooh, her sighs were so pleasure-filled.

Ooh, her glow.

It was at the point of greatest involvement—a moment that called out to and reflected images of other affairs, of bondages and couplings—that very abruptly—*the son entered.*

Enter the son. And for the son, a great beholding. And there was amazement. He stood in the wild breeze. Gazing, beholding Amelia, object of a ravishing.

His senses, were thrown into disorder. *Father, how is it I find you ravishing my girl? Being the viking with my girl.*

Lately, William had begun suspecting things—One things leads to another. And before you know it you're confronted with a great beholding. A great coupling.

William moved into the room. He took a position and stared.

He was shaming Cinjun.

Such were the tests of Cinjun's dignity.

Cinjun held himself still and poised.

Now Cinjun rose. Cinjun moved to the center of the room, stood large, and enlarged his presence to fill the room.

Cinjun stood naked in the room. He was a moment restoring ordered calm to the room.

Now Cinjun removed some objects that had been involved in their affair. He took these, and hurled them across the room.

Then he returned to a state of calm, taking control, entirely, of the center of the room.

This is bizarre, William thought. A chill ran down his spine. He stiffened in fear. His father was dangerous.

Cinjun clothed himself . . . in a robe . . . a kingly robe.

He wrote his personality large . . . as he said . . .

"Apparently, mistakes were made."

And Cinjun would get to the bottom of this. As he had gotten to the bottom of Amelia.

Then he would enter, as he always did. It was all one to him. He was a viking, ruler, lord.

Quinn "Flintstone" Martin

It was the darndest house you ever saw. The front lawn—well, you could squeeze that—just barely—into a great lake, if you packed it tight. And that was the least noticeable part of this house. Everything about this place was immense.

Cinjun approached the front door. The huge double doors that stood strong enough to keep out an army. He heard the strains of muffled sounds that seemed to end in a loud abrupt sound. Then silence descended in folds.

Cinjun took hold of the big brass knocker latched to a lion's head and knocked.

The door came open, in a quick sweep.

The man who appeared at the door was smiling. He was filled with good cheer. Expansive . . . Enjoying the high life, in the full blossom of wealth, health, and I-don't-give-a-darn means.

Step right up, ladies and gentleman:

Meet Quinn 'Flintstone' Martin!

He owns the world, and its gold.

While Quinn was in the washroom, Cinjun surveyed the house.

Scouting expeditions in Quinn's manor often turned up interesting discoveries.

He glimpsed something bizarre . . . He saw a young woman tied to a bed, and blindfolded.

Cinjun didn't seem at all surprised. Quinn too had passions that were enormous; passions that needed to stroll. They knew this about each other. They were large. And their lives were large. And their passions were built to scale.

He continued down the hall.

"Do you want to have a seat?" Quinn said.

"No," Cinjun said, "I have to get going."

In the parlor room, Quinn was providing Cinjun with certain things for his operation—such portables as could be stuffed into a suitcase.

He was giving Cinjun a bronze case that—when it was opened— shone with gold and silver and the startling colors of a thousand and one portables. Gold wafers. Soostones. The little stuff that could buy a small planet.

Cinjun walked out the mammoth double doors of the manor. He stepped out into the night and went away.

Quinn led himself back into the manor and now aimed himself towards the bedroom, toward the woman. He walked down the long lushly carpeted corridor that stretched into the distance, for only about a horizon or two. Quinn spoke to the walls as he traveled.

"I suffer from boredom," Quinn said. "I am prey to the deadly lethargy that envelopes those who are sated, those who have no more desires."

Life-drag. You see, he was fighting life-drag—And what a drag it can be.

He may be king; he may possess the world and its gold. But gold won't bring you happiness when—you limit its abilities . . . Quinn opened up the bounds of his gold, to let it find him somebody to love. And then another. And another. Until his life was filled with great tender cares.

The world was still the same. But now it shone for him.

He had found himself: *Time well-spent.*

From gold well-spent.

The big fat world was his. And for him this world *happied.* It produced happiness leading to happiness, to an all of happiness. He was well settled in the happiness at the moment.

He entered the red bedroom, with the beautiful woman tied to the bed. He freed her with great tenderness. And the couple now proceeded to do something special. He continued speaking—now to the woman—as he mounted the bed:

"I am absolutely preeminent in my chosen profession. I have no more worlds to conquer within my chosen orbit—"

A woman walked through the double door dressed in a negligee—and nothing. She was stunning. Where the woman on the bed was blonde, this young lady was a brunette and filled with independent motion; she glided onto the bed, joining Quinn and the blonde.

"Alas," Quinn said, "it is too late in my life to change my orbit for another one."

A red-headed woman came through the door, glowing with sexuality. She came onto the bed.

"And," Quinn said, "since power is the goal of all ambition it is unlikely that I could possibly acquire more power in another sphere than I already possess in this one."

Other women appeared at the door, floated in, and joined their young bodies to the satin bed.

"I take pleasure now only in artistry, in the polish and finesse, which I can bring to my operations. It has become almost a mania with me to impart an absolute rightness, a high elegance, to the execution of my affairs."

The room expanded. Became intumescent, engorged.

Woman leading on to woman, all is woman.
And Quinn "Flintstone" Martin.
Happiness leading on to happiness, all is happiness.
Something special leading to something special, all is something special.
And Quinn "Flintstone" Martin.
He owns the world, and its gold.

"I believe," Quinn said, "that the approach to perfection which I am steadily achieving in my operations will ultimately win recognition in the history of our times.

"Each day, I try and set myself still higher standards of subtlety and polish so that each of my proceedings may be a work of art."

Red-filled, orange-splashed walls watched as Quinn rose and descended on the bed flanked by a redhead, a brunette, and a blonde.

Meet Quinn "Flintstone" Martin.
His crystal ship is being filled, a thousand girls, a thousand thrills.
Such is life for Quinn "Flintstone" Martin.
He owns the world, and its gold.

When Quinn gained the world, and its gold, he said onto the world: "Please, just good deals. Nothing pretentious. I haven't changed. A pool, a column, and a deal on the vine."

Grace
Princess in the Pale Moon Light

Grace Dor'ythy Park'r K'lly—Cinjun's wife—was seated at the table in a strange way. She was sitting upright in the chair, staring straight ahead.

She was not doing anything. Not touching anything.

Her breathing reflected huge emotion. There was a great driving thing within her.

She had been sitting alone in the mansion, darkly silhouetted against her vast picture window.

She was quietly being assaulted.

. . . the memories were intruding on her awareness, assaulting her present life . . .

. . . the young self of the Grace-being was calling to her in song and fury . . .

A glow that came and went across the years.

Haunting here, thrilling there . . .

In Years Gone By . . .

They say falling in love is wonderful. She had never known wonderful before. He was wonderful.

This was what a very young, clear-eyed Grace thought as she sat on her bed, smiling.

This had been years and years ago, and she had known what she wanted, very exactly.

"Not feeling so well?" she said then.

"Eh . . . hum . . . hrmpgh." Now this man on the bed with her was searching far and wide for his—voice. Where had he put it?

This man, was the young Scofield Morefield—and he was now rising to a sitting position on this bed, holding himself up with the aid of the furniture. He was about seven kisses' length away from her, she noticed.

At his end, he was merely trying to recall—last night. How he had met—Grace. And how he had come to this—place.

This young Scofield Morefield, had gotten soused, boiled . . . He had tasted of strong drink. Not very much more than usual. Just barely enough to give his head that wonderful boiled-in-oil feeling, that it now enjoyed.

Grace sat clear-eyed and smiling.

Young Scofield looked at her. "Oh dear," he said, "oh dear, . . . oh dear, . . ."

He was concerned for her. She was a sweet young lady. And she seemed to have been seduced by a scoundrel, a rogue—himself.

She thought he was a dream. He was out-and-out cosmic.

Scofield's tongue came out of his mouth. Yes, he had definitely been chewing dish rags. Or chomping through used butcher's paper. He didn't know the particulars, he just tasted the lingering delicate flavor.

Grace was sitting on a cloud. She took his hand, which was like a touch of heaven to her. Life was no longer lonely. Now everything was sure.

Scofield's tongue was now back in his mouth. He drove his hangover into—talk. "Uhm," Scofield said, lifting his voice from under the carpet, ". . . how was I last night."

"Oh, you were fine," she said.

"Was I terrible last night?"

"Everybody was feeling high. You were all right. You just happened to be feeling it a little more—actually—than us."

"Perhaps. Well, I tend to run higher than most. Is everybody sore at me? If I ran at my usual high form, I have some apologies to get out this morning? Does everybody hate me?"

"Good gosh, no. Everyone thought you were funny."

"Funny?"

"Of course. Well, now, Jimbo Garrison got stuffy at dinner. But people held him back. It only took three people to get him back in his chair. He calmed down with no problem because people kept *you* away from *him*."

"Oh my, what did I do?"

"Nothing. You were perfectly fine."

"Good, so I wasn't making a pass at his girlfriend or anything."

"You were only kissing her."

Scofield's hand went to his jaw, and rubbed it something awful.

"You were only fooling. You kissed her like she was your sister, except for the tongue part of it."

Scofield's hand fell to his leg, and so did his jaw.

"My God!"

"Just send them some flowers—and she's not his girlfriend, silly—their marriage is still in very good shape."

"I'll buy them a botanical garden. Yes, that's what I must do. Good God!"

"You were fine. Don't be so foolish about it. Everybody was crazy about you. You were very funny—the way you were singing."

"I can't sing."

"Now you would never know that by the way you carried on—what a marvelous performance of lung power."

"In the restaurant?"

"Of course. Where else? You wanted everybody to enjoy it."

"They enjoyed it?"

"Yes, and did a damn fine job of hiding their enjoyment. So that it wouldn't go to your head. They kept you humble. Why the way they yelled at you and carried on, they were such charming foils for your singing."

"How long did I sing?"

"It couldn't have been too much longer than an hour."

"No stopping to eat dinner?"

"A liquid dinner, on the go, I noticed. You go a long way on very little. It's very charming. I love that about you. You're so hearty and full of manly energy, where do you keep it all when you're not using it."

"What happened then?"

"You were overwhelming. They asked you to share your singing with the rest of the world. They insisted that you not keep it confined to the restaurant. And they introduced you to the great outside."

"We went outside."

"With a full escort."

"Then what?"

"You sat down hard, on the sidewalk."

"Then?"

"Now you can't tell me you don't remember what you did then?"

"Help me make the memory a little more vivid."

"I helped you to your feet, and we walked arm-in-arm. Do you recall the lovely things you said—as we took our long, lovely walk? You said such lovely, lovely things."

Laughing eyes, he remembered laughing eyes. And something in him snapping—it had probably been his mind.

He remembered the trees, the breeze—and his heart going whack!

All at once it had seemed nice—and they hurried to this spot.

He wondered how it all came about, but it was too late now. Trapped, he was, trapped!

Something had grown erect—it had probably been his destiny. It certainly hadn't been his mind that took action then. And he remembered laughing eyes making it wonderful.

It had been a starry night and she had made him tingle.

"Forgive me for being taken by the drink. I should have made love to you—I should have made love to you as a gentleman."

"You crazy idiot," she said, "you were perfectly fine."

He noticed her eyes then. Eyes like rolling green mountain fields. Oh, it was damn unfair to use eyes like that on a man. They were too lovely. You really ought to give a man a warning before you hit him with eyes like that.

"I did think," she said, "you were a little tight at dinner—oh, you were perfectly fine; I felt your feelings. I knew exactly what you were feeling."

"Uhm—heh-hmm," he was forced to clear his throat because he wanted to use his voice again and he had to exhume it from its burial ground. "How was I feeling?"

She smiled, the most beautiful smile you ever saw. "You were feeling fine."

She was glowing, a glow that time would never fade.

Scofield noticed this about her. She was a summer serenade; this was what she made him think of.

"You said you had never felt your real self before," she said.

"Did I mention why?" he said.

"Because you had never been with me before," she said, smiling that smile again, "silly." He went weak from that smile. It was very unfair of her to spring that smile on a man, he thought. It made him forget all the ordinary things, sent him into a daydream, made him happy as a kind of king. Foolish as hell. Filled him with high-minded crap. And longing. He sat in slow fire, burning with the mere idea of her.

He looked at her face. She was the tender trap. Bang! it had sprung. He was trapped. This was the end of him. It was cruel; cruel of her to show him a face like hers.

He noticed then that her face had wiped out all the other faces, all the other women, all those other sweet women that he had such beautiful plans for; she wiped them all out. Cruel—life was terribly cruel this morning.

He smiled. "Well, it's a pleasure to know you Grace."

He determined that he would rid himself of the rogue and the scoundrel, and never do wrong by her. Something was taking hold of him—and he feared greatly—that he might be falling in love with Grace. Life seemed to lose its loneliness with her.

As he sat there, seven kisses' length away from her, this was what he thought. And he noticed that the distance was now growing smaller, as she brought her lips to his.

She was too marvelous for words, he thought. *And I'll be a fool for her beauty any day or night she asks.*

He was glad there was her.

A Lounge, Years Ago—Once Upon a Summer's Eve

A young Grace and a *Young Cinjun* were getting to know each other.

"A drink?" offered Cinjun.

"I'll have a highball, but please, tell him to make mine a little one; make it awfully weak."

Later in the evening, after the drinks had come, Grace was questioning him, "Do you really know people that say she's good looking? You must have a wide acquaintance among people with lens troubles."

"Another drink?" offered Cinjun.

"If you're going to have one. I shouldn't like to see you drinking all by yourself."

She finished the drink she had.

"I feel great.," Grace said. "You do too, don't you? Because you look better."

Later, after the next round of drinks . . . she was saying . . .

"I'm not being any way at all. To me she looks like something that would eat her young."

"Another drink?" offered Cinjun.

She was delighted. "Just a tiny little bit of a one."

And later still . . . she was saying . . .

"Dresses well?" She gave it some thought. "Hmm, you mean those clothes of hers are intentional? My heavens, I always thought she was on her way out of a burning building. Live and learn."

"Another drink?" offered Cinjun.

Now Grace refrained. And then thought better of it—all moderation taken in moderation—or some such proverb—or perhaps no such proverb had ever existed and she was creating the beautiful thought on the spot. "Just a little one," Grace said.

"You've got a beautiful heart." Grace leaned in, taking over Cinjun's attention easily, charmingly, and entirely. Cinjun drifted into her beautiful eyes.

"You are one of the best friends I have in the world.," she said in a softy, sexy voice, "but I worry about you . . ."

Her beautiful eyes floated away, gazed to the side, glided across the entire room, and took it effortlessly into her lovely, laughing eyes.

"I don't think you take good care of yourself . . ." Her eyes came back to him now, and he was glad.

"You oughtn't," she said, "drink all this terrible stuff that's around; you owe it to your friends to be careful."

"We *are* friends," Cinjun said, and felt a surrender, to her beauty. He was being swept into it. Just as all the room could be; just as every man who ever saw her could be; just as every man she would ever meet could be.

She had a very special quality—she had eyes, and a face, and lips that you could write your dreams on. The human eye adored her. She had a face that made you envision a lovely background of gardens and seas.

"Yes, friends," Grace said, "aren't friends the most lovely things in the world."

"Yes, friends," Cinjun smiled, "dear friends."

Grace smiled. And it was such an extremely sexy smile. She was so feminine and lovely, thought Cinjun. He longed to kiss her mouth.

"Dear friends," Grace said, with her lovely bite-red lips.

Cinjun's senses were now swimming in her lovely, laughing eyes and red lips. She looked at him with eyes like green rolling hills and bright spring days. He found himself suddenly in a lake of blue-green waters, floating in the emerald eyes.

He felt himself longing . . . to journey . . . with those eyes.

Yes he would take those eyes on a brave, bold journey. Whatever had existed in her life before Cinjun came along did not matter in the least now. She would be his now.

Cinjun smiled at Grace—and it was the most charming smile she had ever seen. Filled with such promise.

The Polar Cap Lounge, Years Ago—Once Upon a Summer's Eve

Everybody who was "in," was there.

This was some nights later . . .

A party made high-society-being in this forest-city place.

The high-society party came into whirling motions, vortexing within the forest city.

Within the whirlpool of body forms, . . .

Within the whirlpool of the night form . . .

A young Scofield and a young Cinjun shared a private moment.

The night was vortexing and shimmering around them . . . and a sea of faces was spread wide before and around them . . .

They were watching young Grace, who was chatting with a friend in the distance.

"I want to tell you," Cinjun said, "about my greatness as a playboy. I keep a list of girls I want to screw . . .

"When I date a girl, I give her a small gift, perhaps with an emerald embedded in it . . .

"When I sleep with her, I give her a bracelet, perhaps—*a bracelet of emeralds.*

"And I cross her name off the list."

"Why are you telling me this?" Scofield said.

"Because Grace is on my list." Cinjun said.

Scofield wished he was in a karate tournament and that Cinjun was his next opponent.

Grace's Flat, Years Ago—Once Upon a Summer's Eve

Scofield and Grace were in bed together.

She said, "Do you want to see some lovely things?"

She put on a fashion show in the moonlight; modeling expensive gowns for Scofield.

Then she came out stark naked wearing nothing but a gold bracelet that had *several emeralds around it.*

Scofield slowly, ever so slowly sat up in the bed. Then he rose. She handed him the bracelet. He looked at the emeralds.

He tossed the bracelet into a fish tank.

In the Caveman's Grotto & Grill, The Present Time—
On a Summer's Eve

Scofield was now telling Miles how the love affair had ended.

"When he fucked her, he gave her the bracelet," Scofield said . . .

"Well, that was it. I was heartbroken. I put my clothes on and said that I was leaving. I just didn't want to see her anymore. She asked me if the bracelet had anything to do with it, and I said it had everything to do with it.

"She had become a career carnivore.

"She was rapacious about getting famous and being important. She'd already talked to me about some of the men she'd been dating, how they helped her to make social contacts, and were teaching her things she needed to know.

"I decided I had had enough of it."

The memory of their separation assailed Scofield.

As Scofield left . . . Grace was still naked and beautiful. She was not reaching for him with outstretched arms . . . she was moving elsewhere.

"Her hand was in the water," Scofield said. "I'll never forget that sight."

For Scofield the old experience had long ago become seasoned and mellowed with a marvelous color, fury, and pageantry. It was toward that sensibility that he now moved.

His words were, "I wonder how things have played out for her. I hear she hits the bottle pretty hard now."

He did not say it with any malice. He spoke it as one in love.

"Friends"—Cinjun's Mansion, Present Time

Cinjun entered his home and was confronted with something extreme.

Grace, was sitting in the house she now shared with Cinjun, this beautiful luxuriant mansion—She was entirely still.

She was startling in a quiet way.

Cinjun stared at her. She sat in a shadow. Silhouetted against the vast picture window. Her feelings were exploding. Her breathing was rapid. But her face was entirely still. The muscles in her face did not seem to be connected to the emotions engulfing her.

"The . . . pain . . ." . . . she said . . . ". . . is . . . unbearable." She shot these words at him out of this face.

Cinjun didn't get too close to her. Much of her was in the shadow. He felt she could get up and cut his throat; she was wound with emotion.

"Did you think it could go on?" she said; or rather things emerged out of her, out of that dark shadow. She tried to talk through enormous difficulty.

"I did. I was wrong." At first he felt he would say yes to anything; he was a man dealing with a woman who was now in an extreme state. She had a lot of spirit; he always gave her that. She was showing it in a macabre way. She was showing it all over the place.

"Why didn't you stop yourself?" She let this loose. "You should have stopped yourself when it first began."

She came out of her stillness. She rushed to him. And began beating him on the chest. Pounding him. Pummeling him.

He did not react. He allowed her to beat him. It was his turn to step up and take it; show that he had the guts to hang on, until he made it.

She had wifely duties. She had her part to play.

They would go on. His arms remained at his sides. He began to feel a tingling delight. *Woman must obey her master's voice; standing up, or laying down, a woman has to work,* Cinjun remembered someone once having said that. It was not absolutely marvelously put, but it had a truth to it that was striking to him now. This was the tenor of Cinjun's thinking.

As for her—she wanted to tear his face to pieces. Wanted to kill him. To expel him. Because he was beyond having sinned. He was into something so unworthy that it overwhelmed her, something had to be cut from her life. Something had to be ripped from her being.

She wrenched. Howled. Twisted. Careened. Came to rest.

She was on her knees. This produced in Cinjun another tingling delight. He moved toward her.

It was important that they be friends.

This was a rough patch, but it only extended so far; beyond was a beautiful horizon.

The moment he tried to touch her, she threw his arm wide; she took herself away from him, took herself to a position against the wall.

He looked at her—He wanted very much to do something special with her in the pale moon light. But it would take time, he would have to bring her into it, slowly. Through slow sensations. To the midnight. He loved her, loved her tonight. This was the heat of the jungle, the heat of the night. He felt slow sensation, ooh, ah . . .

He let his love glow in a tender way. To let her know that she was not wandering alone. To let her know there was a welcome place for her under the stars.

Her breathing became very important to him—he studied her breathing.

"Perhaps . . . we'll have . . . a drink," he said softly. A soft drink would settle her breathing.

Silence took the place. They remained entirely still for a time.

She drew in a breath. "Maybe just a little one," she said.

He went away and returned with a drink.

A strong drink . . . This would settle her breathing. Take some of the cares away.

He placed it down.

She lifted the glass.

She up-ended the glass, and finished the drink. He had poured her a shot that should send her floating over a wall.

He studied her, and what effect the drink was having on her breathing. *Better,* he thought, *better.*

"How . . . about . . . another one?" he said.

She drew in a deep breath and let it slowly. "I don't want a rotten, stinking—maybe just a little one," she said. Presently, he returned with another strong drink. She drank it down.

"Well, well, well," she said, "this liquor has been keeping the right company." It went down smooth, burning as it went.

She finished the drink.

She looked at Cinjun. With her beautiful blue-green eyes.

She looked away.

She threw the glass against a brick façade.

"I care too much," she said. "I haven't got a friend in the world. Do you know that? Not one single friend in the world."

Cinjun was gentle yet firm. "The sky turns dark sometimes, but keep your head together. It's good to know things will get better—when it gets cold, it's good to know things will get better."

"You were with a girl who was going to be our . . ." She broke off.

"Let's not get into . . ." Cinjun said, ". . . the thing—I made a mistake." He didn't like saying it, it wasn't true, but it was necessary. A mistake had been made, and since he was in charge, he would accept responsibility for what happened on his watch, but he did nothing wrong. He had made love to his future daughter-in-law. And he said a number of things to the girl that he need not have . . . upon further reflection. But he had belief, he had his belief to sustain him. He would pull through, pull through fine. No need to worry about him. He knew where to take it and where to go.

Grace was pulling herself together, as well. Pulling through, she was a strong, marvelous lady.

"Don't let this drag you down so far," he said. "Don't let this shatter you. Grace, sweetheart, let's look to the . . . let's look to the good things . . . to better things . . . and better days . . . there will be better days . . ." He studied her.

He was taking it into the heart, and slow sensation. It was a pretty place he saw. And Grace, in a lovely pose.

She said, "You'd cry too if you didn't have a friend in the world. Life's too sad. Isn't life terrible? Isn't life awful?"

He studied her breathing.

"Another drink?" he said.

"I don't want a drink. It won't make me feel any better. I don't want to feel any better. What's the sense in feeling good, when life is so terrible?—" She let out a breath. "All right, just a little one . . . We'll get past this . . . We ought to have a drink on account of us being friends. Just a little one. After all aren't friends the greatest thing in the world."

A Little Rich Girl

Time wondered . . . and slipped . . .

Time said, "A little rich girl we knew was *falling apart*.

"She was hurt to hell by loving art. Hey, little girl . . . No one touches all you are. Strip to show us all you are . . .

"She had it all, lost her dreams . . . She lost her dreams to find a piece of his heart. Now she's on her own, and it's not the same. There is no one here who will take the blame. She just needs some time to figure it out.

"All day, all night. *Your way—this is your life. Take a look inside yourself, and you'll find, you still can win.*"

"No one touches all you are," Time said. "Strip to show us all you are . . .

"A little rich girl we knew was falling apart.

"Hey little rich girl, let me show you how you make me feel.

"Let me show you how you make me feel.

"Argh, remember. Let me show you how make me feel . . ."

On your *love,* . . . intoxicated . . .

Intoxicated by the possibilities, all the possibilities.

Summer night, and possibilities.

Hearts are broken.

Hearts bleeding and breaking.

And people lying through their teeth.

"Let me tell you girl, how you make me feel.

"All day, all night, it's your life.

"C'mon little girl, only you can make the change."

Let me tell you how you make me feel.

Hmmm, little girl . . . oh yeah little girl . . .

Let me tell you how you make me feel . . . And about things that are meant to be.

Nothing's perfect. Nothing's free.

C'mon little girl, only you can make the change.

Let me tell you how you make me feel.

All her life she had been waiting, waiting for someone to come to her side.

Dangling sun, taking her to a world. With no more alone. So strange, a place filled with life-change. A world deep and great. A world so wide. Filled with possibilities. All the possibilities.

Filled with bright sunrays. Sun with a hint of red. Sin with a touch of red. In a House hinting at Crimson.

"I will show you," Time said. "Nothing's free. I can take you. To where worth is—And the way it's meant to be.

"And this old boy, hmm, he was just a-lying through his teeth.

"You heard a story. Sounded easy. Got into your skin.

"And this old boy, he was lying about the possibilities. All the possibilities.

"You lost your dreams to find a piece of his heart.

"Streets turned from Blue to Red . . . Probably will stay that way . . .

"Argh!

"Look for a view. Take a ride. Start moving out from the inside.

"Look for a view. Take a ride. Take a ride. Oh take a ride. On the outside."

Aw, now, all the people around her, talking lonely, talking rides in all the wrong places.

"Oh, take a ride little girl. Let me show you how you make me feel."

She felt alone with the situation.

"But you can kiss the night, oh, little rich girl.

"Oh, Grace. Oh, Grace Dor'ythy Park'r K'lly.

"Let's ride. Let's run. Let wild color light up your face. Only you little girl, can make up your mind. Don't you worry, about these days that have passed. You've still got a chance. You're looking good little girl so don't feel so bad.

"All day, all night, your way, this is your life."

Oh, a little rich girl was coming around—

"Keep looking up little girl, and don't you look down. All day, all night, your way, this is your life.

"Oh, sweet princess, oh, you princess sitting in the pale moon light . . . We love you, good night!"

Lori Kelly—
Skyler meets a girl who swims in mystery

IN THIS TAVERN, Skyler was search and squeeze—he wanted to make her, the lovely Blonde.

He listened to the walls, listened to her skin, listened to everything about and around her. Story to story, he would have to find a way.

He had to have her, he thought.

He cast a probing gaze at the beautiful blonde sitting alone at the bar. He drew up to her side.

"I have a feeling about you," Skyler said, "I think you and I are going to get along famously."

He tossed her this line, almost as a throwaway, as he took hold of the stool next to her. He had never met her before.

She turned to him. She broke in every direction with *very cool*. She remained in every way *very poised*.

"How," she yelled with great penetrating force at him, "do you *speak such good English!"* She yelled this as though she were dealing with a man who was hard of hearing, and had only now come to this country.

Her voice cut through the noise of the barroom. It disturbed everyone in the place.

Skyler noticed people turn around.

He turned back to her.

She had behaved one way. Now, abruptly, she became something else entirely.

She flew away from him. All the way the hell out to the other end of the bar.

Dark clouds rolled in. Skyler was left out stranded in the rain. It was flooding in his part of town. Flood waters were rolling in. He was trying to reach out to his baby. But standing out here in the rain, in the flood, he could not get a single sound. Oh, flood waters kept rolling in. Ooh, they could drive him insane.

From his place deep in the cold, he could stare at her, which he absolutely loved doing . . . Her blonde hair was flowing down in long silky waves.

She was so fine. He decided that it was high time to lose his mind; to check it in a room by the front door and get it later, on his way out of this place . . . with her beside him. *It would be.* And it would be sweet. Oh, lucky her!

No doubt she was a natural, he thought. Her look was rolling and tumbling all over the place—He felt his need for her. *Hey, blonde gal. Hey, shaking and a-singing. Reeling and a-rocking, yelling out for more. I'm going to do you.* Rich would be the comforts once he got inside.

Skyler closed the distance between them. Now, they were in a corner of the bar—it was very cozy. "I'm Skyler Malloy. What's your name?"

"Lori Kelly."

"Lori, what brings you here?"

"I'm here for the dance lessons," she said.

"There are no dance lessons," Skyler said, "this is a bar."

"Then I was misinformed," she said. She tossed her drink into the air, it went down her throat, with just a little, light, easy help from her practiced hand. "Go to hell, will you please. I'm tired."

It was good scotch, she thought, in fact it was perfect.

He held himself still. Calling for her attention.

She turned to him.

She said, "You're very impressive, not important enough that I would write you into my diary, but very overwhelming."

Skyler held his gaze on her. She could cut and bite, Skyler thought. She can slay men. She is a killer—Toss it right back at her.

"Did you kill anybody tonight?" Skyler said.

"I don't remember. I'd have to check my notebook."

How do you like that? Skyler thought. *She's perfect.*

"Lori, I have a good story for you. I wouldn't be talking to you unless I had a good story."

"Speak!"

"I want to tell you about House Crimson."

She didn't seem opposed to hearing about it.

"It's changed a lot of lives." Skyler swung in. "I think it can change your life. How would you like to meet a group of people that are changing the world!"

Lori did nothing at first.

Then she put a wide wave of her hair in front of her face. And kept it there.

She talked to him through this face full of hair.

"You're sitting on my peanut stool."

Skyler held himself still. His love screamed out, into her world, he let his want do his talking for him. He wanted her down on her knees. Rendering. Drawing his essence in warm motions. He let his love scream, penetrate her world, speak of a thing that knew no limits. He wanted her on a pedestal, so he could do her on the pedestal. Her breasts, her —————— There was nothing he wouldn't do. This was where to place your bet.

She felt his blood-filled longing.

"Up!" she said. "Off my stool!"

Again, she disturbed the hell out of the place. And again, all the people turned around. Skyler swept his gaze across the room. A couple of these bystanders wanted to get up and belt Lori. Their rage said, 'Would she shut the hell up already. If not, I'll go over there and shut her up.' Skyler turned back to Lori.

He said, "Why don't these goddamn people mind their own business."

He rose and gave her control of the stool. *Let's see where she goes with it,* he thought.

She took the trail bowl off the bar counter and put it on the lonesome stool. With her long sensuous fingers she made a show of lifting an imaginary thing.

Her empty caress traveled the velvet air. She brought her fingers through her sensuous curtain of blonde hair. She put a finger on her lower lip and licked it. And allowed the finger to enter her red mouth.

Skyler descended into a wet night of heat. *She is absolutely it.*

He crossed to the other side of her.

He opened his mouth to speak—

She went first. "—I'm going to ask you a question so shut up for a minute. Are you talking to me like I'm an idiot? I couldn't give less of a fuck about House Crimson."

Lori brushed the hair away from her face. "What do you have that I might want?"

"Power."

"You remind me of my daddy."

"He must be a giant among men. Is he powerful?"

"He's rich." Lori looked at Skyler. "Stay away from me. My daddy will squash you. You'll regret this—Maybe not today, maybe not tomorrow, but soon and for the rest of your life."

"How do you feel about daddy?"

"I love him."

"And you say I remind you of him—So what you're saying is you love me—You speak well."

The Bolt from the Blue

IN ANOTHER TAVERN, Miles and Daphne applied themselves seriously to strong drinks.

Daphne turned to Miles. "You want to get on a stage and debate Cinjun Smythe? You want to debate Cinjun Smythe!"

"Clobber him," Miles said. "I'm going to show him god himself?"

"You mean herself. You're going to fight Cinjun Smythe?"

"I am fighting him."

"From a distance."

"I'm about to move in for the kill."

"Level with me, this is a put-on. Where are you going with this?"

"To topple Cinjun Smythe."

"What's your plan?"

"I win, he loses."

"You need a helluva bigger box to stand on."

"I have to get onto the Newsfeeds."

She laughed.

"The Newsfeeds!" She rolled it over in her mind.

Then she laughed again.

"We have to get you onto the Newsfeeds!"

She clapped her hands, and rubbed them together—what an act of mischief that would be! She was a prankster who saw a prank worthy of her talents.

The Swell Old Boys

MILES WAS AT A ROADHOUSE, "The Watering Hole"—the layout was horses, a trough and a desert, cactuses and a sawdust floor, booths shaped like adobe huts.

Miles was in the "Hugs and Honeys" room.

It had a mechanical bull. A hell of a broad animal. On a red mat, which caught the people who fell off the bull, and they fell off all the time. The rest of the place did justice to the bull.

On a far platform, Miles stood. As he had entered he had swept his gaze along the seated people, and walkers about. This place had atmosphere, he noticed. If you had a sharp knife, you could cut off a good chunk of it and take it with you for your memory book.

Miles had taken the stage.

And presently gathered a thick fold of silence around him.

And now Miles went about telling a tale . . . A little thing he was throwing together off the top of his head . . .

"The Swell Old Boys———"

The men from the syndicate.

The men from the cartel.

The men from the outfit.

The Old Boys.

Every once in a while The Old Boys put out an ad:

'Sheriff Leader wanted. Complexion shall not be unseemly.'

Up to the door, steps Mr. Whiter-Than-White.

And the image of the thing rolled across the frontier.

Cinjun Smythe comes to the door. He wants to rule Eden Estates. To let loose the dogs of Bullyashat—'I will take you to this old Eden Estates, that's deep in the wild frontier state of Paradise. And we will seize the main ranch house, we will seize the Hyacinth House'—this being the feel and pretty love song of this old boy.

The money man is Quinn Martin.

Cinjun Smythe says, "I want to be your Sheriff Leader."

Quinn says, "Boy, do you know what we do! Do you know what you have to do, as one of us? Here's how the system goes . . ."

Education—The way they teach is nothing but a fraud. They teach with books—they test you, not the books. Let's say you didn't read one of their books the way they wanted you to read it, you fail the test.

Your school record—nothing but a fraud. They test you, not the need for why they have to record and grade every moving part of your schooling.

Now some images rolled and a-rolled across this old frontier.

The work history—nothing but a fraud. They test you, not the idea of why they have to own and run all the moving parts of your work history.

Titles—nothing but a fraud. They test you, not the ideas behind why they have to own and run all the moving parts of you and all your friend's titles.

Healthy Debates—the Healthy Debates they throw at you—nothing but a fraud. They own the moving parts. And they lay the fix in. We're talking nothing but a fraud.

Quinn says to Cinjun, 'Boy, we're full of our own bull mud, and how do you like that?'

Cinjun says, 'Oh, I like it plenty. See if I take your ideas, work with them a little, I could pound you out the best Sheriff Leader you ever did see.'

Quinn says, 'Boy, you're going to go far.'

Cinjun Smythe—we're talking nothing but a fraud.

I want to debate him; I'm going to debate him; and I'm going to give him a healthy battle.

Into the Newsroom

DAPHNE WAS PURSUING Ripkin Kabob, the decisionmaker at the Flash Newsfeed. She wanted to get on the Newsfeed. It was a conduit onto the mainline Associated Feed.

Getting to Ripkin was tough. He would not respond to inquiries.

The only way to reach him was in the flesh.

So, Daphne called a *light*man and got into the newsroom that way. She stood by the *light*man until the news director walked by. Ripkin was charmed by her. She took him to a restaurant to work her wiles on him, and to exploit Ripkin's fatal flaw—Ripkin was a hopeless drunkard.

Soon, Ripkin reached the point where he was losing control and he became very delicate, . . . and here and there deliberate.

"Missus Fox, I don't care what you have! He has no following, no sponsors, no value."

"You can't blame me for trying," she said, as she gave him another glass. "Cheers!" She clinked her glass to his. She was now getting him thoroughly plowed, . . . as much booze poured down his shirt as did go down his throat. Ripkin caught himself, and made an immediate recovery.

As she drank down her own glass, she lifted a hand and helped Ripkin tip his glass back so that he swallowed every bit. They finished their drinks and put them down.

"Ahh . . .," Daphne said, "formidable, yet refreshing."

Ripkin was blotto, his eyes crossed, speech slurred, body slumped. The perfect condition for her pitch.

Now, came "the treatment"—

She put her arms on his shoulders; brought her forehead to his forehead; and talked to him in this way.

"I have a good idea. I wouldn't be talking to you unless this was the best goddamn idea you ever heard."

. . . More drinks were tossed down as they went . . .

Now she sold him on her goods.

And what she laid on him, were: glimpses of fleeting purposes.

She used some words and called them by name.

And goodness the feelings. Ah, the feelings.

This young lady, she worked him in slow, slow style.

She talked to him about the changes that life arranges, nothing but changes, of phase.

He felt himself bleeding and feeling, and coming to a tenderness, there. Very near, yet very far. Very clear. The soft strains of a tenderness there.

So strange, talk of life-change.

He felt himself shook up. Intoxicated

Dangling in possibilities. So many possibilities. All the possibilities.

Too strange.

Mmm, yeah-ah!

He licked his chops. Began to pant. His tongue hung out. His breath began to quicken. He wanted a bone. She rubbed his belly. And patted his head.

She gave him a story. It sounded easy. Got into his skin. She was lying through her teeth.

She was telling him of a sun touched with red.

A sun leaning to Crimson.

And a House swathed in Crimson possibility.

She took him out into the streets, and the Bill Bailey on the Street. And the effect on him.

The ride. The Bill Bailey on the Street.

The talk around the campfire. The Bill Bailey on the Street.

She took him. To get it on into the inside.

Wow! What a story, he thought. He had to have it.

His tongue hung out. His breath came in pants. He growled. He wanted the bone. He had to have it. It had to be his now.

Before anybody else came to take it from him.

He took her ride.

He had to get it on into the inside. Thoughts of inside, filled his mind, and elsewhere regions of his bodily form.

He wanted to take a ride. And get it on into the inside.

Oh, yeah-ah! Ah-huh, yeah-ah!

"I'm going to write out the proposal on this napkin," Daphne now told him. "And we'll sign it."

She worked her charms on him as she wrote out a contract on a napkin. "It's got everything you could want. A roundup like you never had before. And a Bill Bailey on the Street, for your viewers. We want to drive up those ratings. And we will. Believe me we know how to arouse excitement."

His tongue wa hanging loose. He was practically passed out. But his eyes were opened wide. Eating her. Every morsel of her. This beautiful—what was her name again—Daphne Fox. What a newswoman! He had to have her on his team. And her story. Put it on the newsfeed, it would work well. He wished she would rub his belly. And then drift downward. Where was his bowl of drink? Oh, there it was. Mmm, good drink. Lppp, liipp, lip, lip.

She had the restaurateur and a doctor witness the agreement. "Gentlemen, you are witnessing a historic moment."

Ripkin signed it. He started to crumple forward.

She subtly pulled him upright by his shirt.

"Salute them." He did. "Gentlemen . . ." She gave them the pen to sign as witnesses.

They signed it and went away.

She let go of Ripkin's shirt. He folded forward, and put a dent into the table, with his chin.

She folded the napkin neatly and left.

The next day, at the television station, Daphne reviewed the terms of the napkin agreement with a now sober Ripkin.

"I what!" He was defiant.

"You signed it," she told him, as if it were a deed to be congratulated, praised, and cherished.

Ripkin wanted, mainly, to spit.

"It's a napkin!" he countered, and looked into her eyes, wondering which one to spit into.

"It's a contract," she extended the substance of the napkin.

And fastened herself to its purpose, readying herself to advance under its heavy obligation. ". . . And according to this napkin, you are going to pay us to produce a block for the Newsfeed!

"And we will accept the money. Further, you will not pay us cheaply, but rather to the upward extent of your ways and means. And we will accept the small fortune, . . . that is our burden."

Miles interrupted, "Wait Daphne, what idiot told us we had the skill and could produce a block for the Newsfeed!"

"He did!"

"Then that's what we're going to do!" Miles said.

Miles was resolved to fulfill the promises clearly set forth in the napkin.

Fathead Willy Meets The Black Form

MILES WAS DOING HIS ACT at a cocktail lounge called "The Polar Cap." The place was run by the impresario Chilly "Fathead" Willy, who was hovering in the rear of the establishment's big room, 'The Chilly Willy Room.'

Miles was telling a tale.

Cinjun Smythe is a black train, coming down the track.
Coming round the bend.
Mean old rotten train coming down the track.

Cinjun Smythe is a black storm, coming round the bend.
Black storm, sixteen skies across.
Black end, sixteen dreams long.

Sun going down!
Way out on the sea!
Here she comes, little girl going to set me free.

Train arrives. Sixteen coaches long.
Black train arrives. Sixteen coaches long.
Big black train gonna get my baby.

Black storm, sixteen skies long.
Black doom, sixteen worlds wide.
Black void, sixteen centuries long.

Going to get my baby.
Going to take my baby,
Going to get my friend.
Black doom coming round the bend.

My wild love.
My wild love.
My wild love,
Going to get my wild love.

Black destroyer, sixteen fields long.
Black forest, sixteen darknesses deep.
Black crime, sixteen scenes long.
Black night, sixteen worlds wide.

Black sea, sixteen harbors long.
Black devastation, sixteen roads across.
Black carnage, sixteen lands all told.

Black river, sixteen trenches long
Black train, sixteen realms of pain long.
Black train, sixteen lands all told.
Black cold, sixteen winds coming down the line.

"This black train is gonna take my baby," Miles said.
"She'll be gone. This mean old train is coming around the bend. This mean old evil train is gonna take my one and only friend.

"Now, mean old rotten black train—
"Do you think I'm going to let you get away with it?"

A guy in the back of the room turned to the bartender. "Hey, Miles Roark?" he said. "Who is Miles Roark?"

Chilly "Fathead" Willy was watching and listening and catching everything. He was not pleased. He was in an inferno of rage. He was on the edge of a violent explosion. He was smoldering away as Miles continued to say and do things that disturbed him all the more.

"I want to debate Cinjun Smythe," Miles said. "He won't face me. Cinjun's call for a healthy debate is a trick . . . It's fixed.
"There can't be a championship fight without me.
"I'm here to tell you all; you think I'm just talking, running at the mouth, he's above my class, but you can't have a heavyweight debate without me?
"Cinjun Smythe will dodge me. He'll dismiss me, saying I'm a Sound Chaser.
"But there can be no fight without me."

Chilly "Fathead" Willy took Miles and Daphne to his office.

"What is this!" he said, "About Cinjun Smythe being a black train! Is that supposed to be an act!"

"You don't like that?"

"Why does he have to be sixteen of anything?"

"Seventeen, you think?"

"Why does he have to be sixteen rotten lengths of anything?"

"Seventeen is rough. You don't want to make him a monster . . . You don't like it do you Willy?"

"No, I do not like it, son! I do not like it at all!"

"Hmm," Miles felt out the moment. "You don't like it at all?"

Miles gave it thought.

Why damn it all, he realized, *Fathead Willy was right.*

"Willy, . . ." Miles said. He directed a steady gaze and took the moment into slip, into time slip.

Time slipping away.

His purpose was to search for truth.

He would let time slip.

He would go into free range.

He would feel the moment, when it came.

Willy stared at Miles.

Miles dropped back into human to human.

He slipped into no strain, no anger, no harshness.

He stood before him.

Now he spoke to him in simple human to human terms.

Now he connected in a moment of honesty.

Willy stared at Miles.

"Do you know that you're right?" Miles said plainly. "I'm hitting it too hard. You're right. How about we let the audience get it for themselves? How about I make him a magesterial form with a dark secret?"

"A what?" Willy said.

"I'll make him," Miles said, "a black magesterial form, just a plain, simple black magesterial form comin' round the bend. With one or two features, as hints.

"What the hell," Willy said, "are you talking about! A black magic form, what the hell is that? No I don't like that.

"Not a black magic, no, a black magesterial form . . . Right, well done Willy. You cut through again. Hell, let's make it a black form. A black barren form, like a fun black dirge.

"Black door, black dirge.

"Dark hearts dirge, no flowers.

"Opening on black forever.

"Black dirge, comin' round the bend."

"A black what?" Willy said. "Dirge? Isn't that for funerals?"
Willy stared at Miles.

"Black fury, sixteen cries loud," Miles said.

"And we could keep some of the really good parts from the black train.

"Black form, comin' round the bend.

"Black form.

"Black crime, sixteen scenes long.

"Black destruction, sixteen deaths across.

"Black end, sixteen universes deep.

"Art begets art," Miles said. "Form begets form. They'll get it for themselves."

Willy stared at Miles.
It was a cold hard gaze. There was no aid and comfort for the enemy in that stare.

"What the hell are you talking about!" Willy said.
Willy continued to stare at Miles.

"For your next set," Willy said, "here are some things that I'm going to need to hear come out of your mouth. You're going to say, *'We are blessed.'* You're going to say, *'Cinjun Smythe really knows what we're about.'* "

"Yes, there's always that," Miles said.
Now Miles stared at Willy.

"It's your club," Miles said, "I'll say goodbye now."
Miles and Daphne walked out leaving Fathead Willy huffing and puffing with no house to blow down.

The scene was like no other in Willy's life.

Fathead Willy had met The Black Form.

Screwing with the Primal Forces of Nature

RIPKIN STORMED into the newsroom, where he collided with Miles and Daphne.

"You can't say those things," Ripkin barked. "Here's what you're going to say—"

"—Rip," Miles said, "it's your company—"

"—You have to make it normal."

"No—we'll leave."

Ripkin went stark, raving mad. "Why are you here? Who sent you?"

"Take it easy. We were just going to do a piece on Cinjun Smythe's Healthy Debate."

"What do you mean do? What are you up to? Who put you up to this? What kind of footage were you going to shoot? I want answers! You're fired."

As they passed Ripkin, he jumped back with a shriek. "I'm not scared of you. What are you trying to hide! Who are you with?"

"We're on our own. We're leaving."

They were dangerous people. They might have weapons, bombs, Lord only knows what. Ripkin backed away from them as they cleared out of the newsroom.

Then, courageous Ripkin shouted at their retreating backs:

"You're screwing with the primal forces of nature!"

Brutus and the Twins

NOW WHEN DAPHNE AND MILES REACHED Daphne's apartment—they found it occupied by *three professionals*.

One was pointing a gun.

Daphne didn't give a damn.

"You're going to hold a gun to me," Daphne said, "in my flat. I don't have time for your bull mud."

She charged at him.

She ducked under his gun arm. Attacked him in a rapid up-from-under maneuver.

The other two leapt into action. One pointed a gun at Miles. One pulled Daphne off. Slammed her against the wall.

She wouldn't go down.

So he held her while the other gave her a good stiff belt.

Miles had a gun pointed to his head.

Things settled into place. Silence descended in thick folds.

The lead one stepped up to Daphne. "Well, you must be the pride and joy of your little lover boy."

Heart full of darkness, spotlight on his face, he turned to Miles.

This one in charge, Brutus, was very calm. "Now let us get down to business . . ."

"How soon we're finished," Brutus said, "depends on you . . ."

Brutus approached Miles. "My dear boy, the game of red Indians is over, quite over. You stumbled by mischance into a game for grownups. You're not equipped to play games with adults.

"It was very foolish to come out here with your spade and buckets—"

Brutus turned to Daphne. She was mounting a hell of a struggle now. Daphne was kicking and biting; scratching and punching.

She was on the floor. Brutus directed the others to step back.

They cleared a space around her.

Brutus pointed his gun.

He fired a bullet into her right thigh.

She stopped moving; looked at the leg. In a flash, she determined the entry and exit were clean. The shot went clear through.

"Now you shot me," Daphne said, "are you happy? Now get the hell out of my place." She enjoyed talking like a gun moll. This was interesting. She wanted to be a credit to women everywhere.

Now Brutus held the gun on her. The other two grabbed her by her arms.

"You goddamn coward," Daphne said, "get out of here before I send you out on a stretcher."

Brutus had his partners stand her up.

He approached her slowly. Then, abruptly, he belted her across the jaw.

She hit the floor hard; then turned toward Brutus slowly.

He gestured to her with a 'come here darling' motion.

She rose, put up her fists and staggered over. He belted her and she went flying.

She came up again.

Brutus was fascinated. "I wonder."

He pointed a gun at Miles. She went completely quiet and still.

Brutus looked at her. "I see."

He turned to Miles. "We must stop joking. Follow me in developing a cautionary tale.

"Should you continue, our next session will be a torture session.

"I will attack the sensitive parts of your body. And her body.

"I am without mercy, there will be no relenting. No one will stage a last minute rescue. There will be no possibility of escape. This is not a romantic adventure story in which the villain is finally routed. The hero is given a medal and marries the girl. Unfortunately, these things don't happen in real life. If you continue, you will be tortured into madness.

"The girl will be brought in and we will set about her in front of you. If that is not enough, you will be killed. I will reluctantly leave your bodies. Make my way to a comfortable house that is waiting for me.

"There I shall continue my profitable career, and live in the bosom of the family I shall create.

"I stand to lose nothing. You will quit, and live. If not, the young lady and I will get together and we will have a very good time indeed."

Exit Brutus and the twins.

Miles and Daphne were now alone.

"How are you?" he asked.

"No damage that a little hospital won't fix."

"Daphne, darling, it might be a good idea for me to take it from here all by my lonesome."

"We're just getting started."

"There is no way I'm going to take a chance with your life."

"They won't be back."

"You have a fascinating way of reading a beating," Miles said.

"They were just trying to scare the hell out of us," she said. "What are they going to do kill me? I could put them in prison for that. Ignore them. They didn't have anything interesting to say."

Foolish people are always trying to bring me down, she thought.

Looks like they tried to tame me; next time they try, they'll learn.

I was nice and chatty with them because they were just visiting. But these boys better watch out when I come undone. I'll shove these boys back into their narrow world.

She was wild with the power. Eternally wild with the power.

Lori's Bed

IN LORI'S BEDROOM, Skyler was taking charge of Lori's territory, filling it with his lifeforce. Lori was fascinated.

Skyler was saying, "I throw it at them in bursts of passion. It's all about the phrasing."

"Show me," she said silkily.

"Knowing the facts is not the job of a politician."

"You're the vision."

"You work with words," he said. "You have to have lists on the tip of your tongue. What we are is: *good*. When you vote for us you vote for change, opportunity, truth, liberty, help, vision, freedom, peace and pride."

"Wow, that's great," she said. "What about when you vote for them?"

"They're evil. You use words like decay, failure, collapse, destruction, sick, criminal and corrupt. You get it? Isn't that the greatest trick?"

"That's amazing," she said. "So you mean if I say Jesus Christ was a slick, corrupt, selfish traitor whose destructive, shallow self-serving conduct was a disgrace . . . people might start thinking Jesus was a bastard?"

"It can't miss," he said. "Kiss me!"

Lori stopped the show right there and then. "You're married."

"You're going to bring up what I did last month." Skyler was shocked. "It can't compare to what we have together. It's nothing like this. I always knew it could become this. Kiss me!"

"What are you going to do about the marriage?" She was not one to be turned easily.

"That's a tough thing to get out of!" he said. "You'll have to give me a few hours."

"You remind me of daddy," she said proudly.

At a restaurant

Skyler gave Mimi a look filled with sincerity and caring. And then he put his feelings into words:

"It's time for a divorce."

"Oh my God!" Mimi burst seven and a half blood vessels.

Then, she put her hand to her mouth.

"Oh come on now," Skyler said. "Are you going to make this difficult on yourself? Make it easy on yourself. Tonight, let's call it a day. Let it go. This life is illusion. You're clinging too tightly. If you cling to the water too tightly you'll drown. Learn to float."

"Oh, you are so full of . . .," Mimi said, ". . . beauty. I love you."

"Yeah, well. It's time to put that love behind you. Let's get on with it. I'll cut you a good deal. Let's talk cash."

"Where do I go from here?" she ventured. "You said you'd take me through the years. Where do I go from here?"

Skyler could not believe where she was taking this; how she was laying all of the burden on him. "You want me to give you all the answers?"

"I need you."

This was too much for Skyler. "This could go on all night."

"I'm getting nauseous," Mimi explained.

"Quit trying to change the subject. Let's go over the terms of the divorce."

"I want to cry; it's killing me."

"Really?" There was only so much Skyler could be expected to take. "Why don't you let it win, then? I'll have my lawyer call you. I tried to be nice, now I'm finished with you! You're not getting anything! And I hope you have some cash on you, because you're going to pay for this dinner. It's only right—*You eat like there's no tomorrow*—So long screwball!"

She didn't know what to say. He was standing now. Moving away. Walking to the door.

And she was heartbroken. Crying with everything she had. Bawling. 'Ahhh, oooohh, egghhhh.' It hurt so bad.

He was not affected. He was king of the world. This was nothing. She was nothing. These people around him were nothing. They had some nerve to be staring at him. Why didn't these people mind their own goddamn business?

He came in here to have a nice meal. These people had some goddamn nerve to be looking at him. He was not doing anything wrong. He was just divorcing a girl he married last month.

It's all too much for her. It hurt so bad. *Oh-oh, it hurts so bad. Don't make it hurt so bad.*

The people squirmed. 'This is the cruelest thing I've ever seen in my life'—'He's the worst human being you've ever seen in your life'—'Why is he feeling so much pleasure from it?'—The guys wanted to fight him. The girls wanted to fight him—'Have you ever seen anything like this in your life?'

In a flash, the people got so incensed at this that it was like—they took turns: *Who's going to kill him?* The girls wanted to kill him. The guys wanted to kill him.

All this flashed in the time it took for him to cross the room, headed for the door.

At the door, Skyler turned to the people. "Everybody here has their whole life ahead of them!" he said.

And Skyler, walked out the door, a hero!

Lori's apartment

Skyler said: "I'm free."

He hugged Lori.

"How did she take it?"

"Very well." Skyler was pleased, boundlessly so, but was able to word it succinctly and beautifully: "Very well, indeed. Lord, she's a trooper. A survivor. You know the type. What more needs to be said?"

"You remind me of daddy."

Next, they would make love.

Her lips were delicious, that was his professional opinion.

Daddy's house at night

Skyler, at long last, was meeting daddy, the banking impresario.

"This is daddy," Lori said.

Skyler stepped forward. "A pleasure to know you."

Daddy went along with a handshake, and as he held his look, he raised his chin into the air.

Lori moved the proceedings along: "And this is my brother Biff, and his friends from the football team."

Skyler looked up at Biff the football player and his two monstrous friends who were the sizes of some small states.

Lori explained, "Daddy invited them to join us for dinner."

Daddy, again, raised his chin into the air.

Lori said, "I'll get mom."

She left them alone.

Daddy said, "Would you like a drink?"

Skyler said, "Certainly."

The three football players stood there, quiet, cold marble statues.

Daddy withdrew a key, unlocked the liquor cabinet. He gave Skyler a drink. And then immediately, locked the cabinet. No one else was drinking. No one was speaking.

As Lori returned with the mother, Skyler looked at the bourbon and water he was holding. Everyone else—each standing there empty-handed—also shot a look at Skyler's glass of bourbon.

The mother decided he must be some sort of alcoholic.

The dinner table

Daddy finished his meal and wiped the corners of his mouth with his napkin. Skyler was talking to the mother and Lori.

"I think House Crimson is going to be the most important idea of our time."

And now Daddy got up from the table. "I'd like to talk with the boys."

Daddy's den

Daddy and the three football players entered. Skyler followed them in.

The father had the three football players sit in the back.

Now . . . Skyler walked in . . . like this was a happy occasion. It was wonderful to be alone with her father, and the boys. It was very interesting. The father was a nice man. Everything was going beautifully.

The father would love to strangle him, right there and then.

Skyler walked in like the happiest priest in the Pacific islands. He took his time walking in, looked at the room, yes, more proof that this was a very nice home indeed.

The father would love to throw the table at him, would love to belt him with the chair.

No matter how disturbed the father seemed to get, Skyler just looked at him with perfect serenity. He kept his constant, . . . uh . . . sense of everything was going to be all right, and while everybody was a little crazy because they were all full of normal emotions—which he didn't have—he kept—he kept smiling.

Skyler confessed, "This is the loveliest night of my life."

The father was direct. "Have a seat."

Skyler was floating in warm waters. "It was a good dinner, healthy food."

The father wasn't listening—as he proceeded to sit at his business desk. So Skyler continued to talk to himself.

"And now Skyler's having a little cozy meeting with dad."

Skyler glanced at the football players. He was in good cheer as he lifted his arms lightly into the air, and turned back to daddy.

"It's wonderful to get to spend some time with you, dad."

"You don't know me."

"I've fallen in love with Lori."

"I hear there's a complication."

"Not a one."

"Your wife."

"My wife—I did make that mistake last month—that's true. She was a nice girl. Not my type. It's been fixed. Now in all candor, how do you feel about me marrying your daughter? We'd like your approval."

The father's fists clenched.

"I'm going to give you cash to leave and never see her again."

"So that's the kind of talk it's going to be. Man-to-man. I can go there if you want. What a body on her. I enjoy getting inside of her."

The father's fists went white from violent constriction of blood. "Let's talk amounts. How much is it going to take to get rid of you?"

"All kidding aside, I'm going to marry her. We'd like your approval."

"Not if you tied me to a horse and pulled me across town by my cock," Daddy said.

"You've put a lot of thought into it," Skyler said.

"Not if you hung me upside down from a tree and shoved a stick of dynamite in my ass," Daddy said.

"Keep thinking about it, I wouldn't want to discourage your creativity. But I work a little simpler than that."

The father was so filled with rage that he was rising out of his chair, with his fists clenched. He was struggling mightily to check his rage; to not strangle Skyler. He dug his fists into the desk instead of Skyler.

No matter how incensed the father got, Skyler stayed perfectly calm and smiling. And even sympathetic toward him.

Skyler said, "Why torture yourself in this way? There's no point to it. Everything is going beautifully. Isn't it? You'll see. She's going to join House Crimson. And we're going to become very important people."

The Story that Sounded Easy

CINJUN AND SKYLER ENTERED the building, and goodness were they ever having fun thinking about the scare they put into Miles and Daphne.

Skyler liked the idea of doing damage to that bitch Daphne.

Cinjun was imagining the effect Brutus must have had on Miles.

"Ah," Cinjun said. "If he disappeared suddenly, it couldn't happen to a nicer guy."

A security guard appeared.

"Mister Smythe," he said, "there's a man in the courtyard."

"A man?" Cinjun said.

"Making trouble, all kinds of noise, and saying things about you. Weird things. And saying you're going to call the police. Saying you're going to have him arrested."

"Well, how interesting," Cinjun said . . . Something to disturb the routine.

The men strode to the outer expanse of the lobby.

Outside, through the enormous picture windows, Cinjun could see: *Miles and Daphne.*

Standing there in the courtyard. Not doing much. Not doing much at all. No movement, as far as he could detect. They were holding still, in a position dead center in the plaza.

Now Cinjun began to hear the strains of Miles's voice, traveling the distance of the plaza.

Miles wasn't speaking loud. Not speaking loud at all.

He was just talking to his friend Cinjun.

"I heard a story," Miles said. "It sounded easy. But the man was lying through his teeth. This old boy was lying through his teeth."

Miles stood there.

Paused.

Then took a ride on the groove—taking it on the inside. Lending it another moment's color.

"I heard a story," Miles said.—"It sounded easy. *But the man was lying through his teeth.*"

Miles stood there. Talking—to get his thoughts—and to carry them deep into Cinjun's heart.

"Let me show you," Miles said, "how you make me feel. Miles held Cinjun in his look. "And the people that you touch."

Miles stood in the summer sun . . . dangling possibilities. All the possibilities.

He did not move at all.

"I heard a story," Miles said. "It sounded easy—But the man—was lying through his teeth."

Towering Figure

CINJUN HEARD MILES. Felt the possibilities. All the possibilities. And the way it was going to be.

He swept his gaze . . .

Cinjun saw Miles standing there. And a little way's back, a bowshot's throw away, a ravishing woman—Cinjun knew who he was meeting there—that was the Daphne bitch. Past this he saw some people turning, looking at Miles with interest. And that was all there was—There was nothing more to it.

Cinjun held his look for an instant, taking full measure of this scene.

"Leave him," Cinjun said. "Make sure no one disturbs him. I want him to keep talking. I want him to talk himself a blue streak. And then when he's finished let him leave."

Cinjun strode from the scene, comfortable with the possibilities.

"Leave him be. We let that kind of stuff wash from the streets with the rain. I don't want to hear anymore about him. When it comes time for him to leave, let him. He's not worth our time. Let him work himself ragged. And then let him leave. What we have here gentleman is a son of a bitch. No need to play with the bastard. Let him play with himself. He seems to be doing such a good job of it. Who would want to stop such a natural display?"

The guard smiled. It was a laugh. He laughed. The other guards laughed.

Cinjun Smythe was something else.

Working for him was the best.

"Now nobody bring him any sandwiches, if he gets hungry," Cinjun said. "And if he gets tired, nobody rubs his back—And I don't want to see anybody helping him answer his fan mail—Now, I'll trust you gentleman with the remaining executive choices to be made in this."

They laughed. Cinjun was the best; this was what they considered . . . as Cinjun made away from the scene in his trademark elegant, powerful strides.

He was a heap of class. It was hard to determine how a man—how one mortal man—had the strength to carry so much class. And to make it look so easy.

Perhaps, this was the thing to notice about Cinjun Smythe . . . He told stories . . . They sounded easy—Yes, it seemed someone had said that about him . . . Who said it?—Who can remember—it was so long ago and so far away. And—the man who said it—well, hell, he was probably amounting to a whole heap of nothing by now.

Let's Bring It Out in the Open

HE WAS MAKING HIS WAY into the port of Sans Souci.

Go boat, go, go. They have no room here for someone like me.

Sail, sail into these waters. Enter this port. Where they have no room for someone like me.

They are gathering to hunt him down. He comes into this place. And he's not supposed to do that. He's the hunted. Doesn't he know? He knows.

He's sailing in. Go boat, go, go.

Tried to tell me I was evil. Tried to trample on my soul. Go boat, go, go. Oh, oh-woah.

Sans Souci. I'm walking, and it ain't no dream. Go boat, go, go.

And I'll fill my sails with all the laughter and talk that makes it entirely me.

Sans Souci. *Go boat, go, go—they have no room here for someone like me,* Miles thought, as he stood in The Sans Souci Plaza.

The Sans Souci Plaza.

It was a mood plaza, reflecting mood in the world that peopled.

The plaza told a story of the world that peopled . . . a story of the Hunter and the Hunted. Out there—in the world—the story ruled. The story of the Hunter and the Hunted.

Sans Souci. *Go boat, go, go—they have no room here for someone like me,* Miles thought, as he stood in Sans Souci Plaza.

He was out there in the Plaza of the Night'Sun'Sky'Sea. The Plaza of Mood Swings. Dancing the mood swing. Watch it, watch it now.

They have no room here for someone like me. Unwanted and unforgiven. He was prey for the hunt, and a young man who must not reach for greater being.

The Hunter and the Hunted—Now he was young and stood a chance against the hunter—This was why the hunted stood before the hunter . . . This was why the hunted stood wide and open before the hunter and his forces. The hunted called for the hunt. Bring the hunt on him. *Let's bring it out in the open.*

This was the way it was meant to be. The way it had to be . . . Now he stood a chance in hell . . . And now he stood there with deep longing in his heart. With the longing, and a will to survive as entirely himself. He stood there, making moments come alive.

To be young . . . oh, to be fit for battle . . . He must act now. He was revealing—*need.* A silly need to survive.

He moved into the urgency with relaxed motion.

Relaxed motion, making it tender.

Miles moved with relaxed motion in the plaza outside House Crimson.

Miles stood alone with the situation—Telling Cinjun . . . who wasn't far from the scene . . . who was out there, close enough to feel it even if he didn't hear it . . . telling him something, the man ought to know. About troubles.

The subject of this day's lecture was rhythm. Soft rhythm. Soft now. So soft. You wanted to cuddle up and lie in it for days. That soft.

It should be gentle and extended, soft and lovely, Miles thought.

Miles stood there—Giving the moments a soft, laid back quality.

This is soft life, Miles determined. Not throbbing, pounding. This is pulsing, mild motion. Give it subtlety? Yes. Give it relaxed motion. Sensual, flowing, but relaxed motion.

It doesn't have to be wrenching, Miles thought, *or forcefully wrought.* It can ease. What's happening is big enough. It doesn't need extra pushing.

Silky.

Tenuous.

Not rampaging, but rather a mellow tone. Simple, elegant. Contained energy. Poised, reserved—He would give it those kinds of qualities.

Give it a switch up, a twist up. Release the mood into softness.

It gave Miles relaxed motion. Pulsing tender motion. He was a sensualist.

Making himself smooth in confrontation . . . In this thing, now, he was not a molding force of character. He was light. He was flowing. He was relaxed motion . . . He was poise. He was wild grace . . . He floated. He danced. And his moves, were like the wind.

In the courtyard, he just went into a sensible, relaxed talk. He was not trying hard. He was not forcing anything. He was just there and talking to Cinjun. He got emotionally involved in what he was saying and let that color his tone. But it was a light and easy and tender talk. He wanted Cinjun to understand. Miles was not a jabbering lunatic.

He was talking to Cinjun—mind to mind.

Miles was present and he stood for something. And he let that work for him. Let his mere presence work in his favor. To give him force. He didn't push. He let the story of who he was, and why he was there work for him.

And he explained. That's all. No madness involved. No strain.

It was conversation. It was talk. It was free form expression.

No one else needed listen. He was making his way by force of reason.

He was not compelling people. He was appealing to their thinking, to reason with him. They could come to their own conclusions. He only offered some starting points. He was not drafting anyone; he was not inducting anyone; there was nothing compulsory in any of what he was doing.

It was free expression. That came out of a great deal of thought and conviction. It carried its own force into the world. It existed on its own. He was not inventing or discovering anything; he was just allowing the flow, from him to them.

He was moving through the changes. Making his way through the changes.

"Let me show you how you make me feel, Cinjun," Miles said.

"You're asking people to give it away to you, Cinjun. Well—you've asked for feeling—let me show you how you make me feel.

"Let me show you the people that you touch————"

You talk of taking me through life change. Of taking my life into your possibilities. Let me show you how you make me feel.

I'm here to show you. I could show you. Would you like to see . . . what is meant to be? Where your too-strange talk of life change will take you to be.

And the people that you touch.

You told a story. It sounded easy. You were lying through your teeth.

"Mm-hmmm mmm. Ooh, ooh, yeah," he said softly, in a warm cushioned tone.

Let me show you where you will take the world with your life change. Cinjun had put out a story.

They heard the story, the people. It sounded easy. Got into their skin.

But he was lying through his teeth.

"Now bring it out from the tight spot and into the glare of daylight. Your story about a fight; how you would bring a fight, a great fight, that would be tall and handsome and would speak loud and strong.

"Well, the fight is here. The fight you asked for is here.

"And it's a capoeira. A dancing, burning fight————"

And it doesn't belong to you. It doesn't belong to anyone.

It is. And it has arrived. Hear the song. The song confirms it. The capoeira is here. The dancing fight is here. Step onto the dance floor.

What's in back of the sky?

I heard the story. It sounded easy. But there was more to it.

"Don't you know—it's pain—that I'm feeling?" Miles said.

The Hunter and the Hunted—Bring the hunt out. Take it out of doors. Open your doors and call me yours.

"Animal inside—leads me to the conclusion—" Miles said.

If Cinjun was going to take over, to rule the world, then Miles was going to show him that—oh baby, baby . . . *it's a wild world*— Everybody wants to rule the world, . . . well, in this room, it won't be so easy.

Miles was being hunted. Now he wanted to bring it out in the open.

Let's bring it out in the open!

The confrontation came from being hunted—Somebody wants to take you over and destroy you . . . How do you deal with it . . . how do you cope with the danger . . . where is the grace in the way?

Miles won't let it remain hidden behind screens.

"You've got to give it away . . . *Let's bring it out in the open.* You want to take people over, try it, but try it in the open. Cope with doing it in the glare of sunlight—in a plain and apparent setting. You want to attack—make it that. No tricks!

"No more tricks, Cinjun Smythe. Let's bring it out and have a hard look at it.

"You've got to give it away or else you don't reveal what it's worth. If you don't show how it works, you don't show what it's worth. Don't hold on like it's your last night on Earth. The more you take the less you

feel. You've got to give it away. The less you know, the more you believe. You've got to give it away.

"If you win, you lose—don't you know the spin you're in. You've got
to give it away.

"Slipping away, Cinjun. Slip sliding. The world turning; making you
feel dizzy?—It's slipping away. You've got to give it away."

Do you feel that wave coming closer to you every day—you've got to
give it away.

What you thought you had—you've got to give it away.

Let's dive into the swimming pool blue—you've got to give it away.

"Strip to show us all you are," Miles said.

"Let me show how you make me feel.

"Give it up. Give in. No one touches all you are. Strip to show us all
you are. And let me show you how you make me feel."

So strange your talk of life change. I hear your story. Sounding easy.
All the possibilities. Summer nights. Everything easy . . . The aim sure
and fast . . . Everything perfect. Everything coming to be.

I could show you the way it's truly going to be.

Let's take a look at the life change. Let's hold it in the open. Let's
take the life change into the open.

And I will show you what it's worth. And the way that it's going to
be. What is meant to be.

He didn't have any idea from one moment to the next what was happening, what he was saying, what would happen, where this was leading.
What would work, what wouldn't work. He would try things.

He was breathing, and pulsing.

Miles did not know where he was going. He was attempting things.

Let it roll, baby, roll—was the feeling.

Some rolls go.

Some rolls stop.

Some pick themselves up, dust themselves off, start all over again.

"Come out of your stronghold. Ancient shapes all around you. You're
making love among empty sermons. You hate to leave your sacred lay.
But it's time. The fight you asked for is here————"

You're sitting in your safehouse, saying I want a fight. Well, the fight
is here.

You're saying bring it on. Well, the battle is here.

Can you feel it? Watching you, touching you. Can you feel it? In the darkness, touching you. Feel it taking control. The beachhead is the street.

The wild thing is out there Cinjun. The wild thing. The wild swing. Is going to whoop you. That wild swing, oh, watch it, watch it.

"Can you feel it?

"Can you feel it?

"Can you feel it?

"Can you feel it!"

"Bring it out in the open—give it to Lady Day.

"Let's bring this into the light———"

Let's bring it before the *light*vision. Into the realm of worldlight, and society spotlight. Into forest city sunstreaks. Let's bring it into the light.

Don't go breaking my heart. Cinjun, must you hide? Don't go breaking my heart. Don't throw love away. One sad goodbye doesn't mean we can't begin again.

Let's bring it into day. You remain in my heart. Come. Join the day. And forever more stay in day.

You've got to give it away, Cinjun. Give it to Lady Day. You've got to give it away.

Miles had to do it now!

Because now he was young—He could make mad dashes. Try the impossible. Do the things you're not supposed to do. He could do them now, but his strengths would wane. He had to hit them now, while he was at his most powerful. Later, he could only do less than now—Now was the time.

He had to break on through now!

He had to will his way through now!

Now was the time! There was no other time.

Nothing lasts but the Earth and sky. It slips away, and another minute you cannot buy. Dust in the wind.

Soon the summer would be over. The summer was almost gone; it was all tumbling away; escaping in the wind, escaping on the winds of life, leaving on winds streaming in cool rapidity—fall serenade would soon be in the air; and winter would not be far behind.

His powers would fade, and he would fall into the winter. Now, while summer was in the world, he stood at his fighting best, feeling the coursing ability. He stood and looked around . . . and wondered where he was going.

Above—the sky trembled.

The High Window

THE TOWER OF HOUSE CRIMSON ROSE into day.

And now shooting upward through the structure, a steel liftchamber rose into enormous heights.

Within the steel liftchamber, Cinjun stood tall. Skyler stood beside him.

Cinjun settled into the center of the lift. He owned the place. He owned whatever place he happened to be in.

"I have a number of important things in front of me today," Cinjun said.

He spoke to Skyler, who stood ready, as they hurtled upward into the mighty tower to work their mighty engines.

"Several important moments," Cinjun said, "and this Roark thinks he can come along and take up my time. Take me away from the important matters. The secret, Skyler, is to keep your focus."

He cannot win if he is unable to feed off my fire, Cinjun thought. *And I am not going to blaze in his direction.* He will not steal any sparks off Cinjun's flame—This was where to place your bet.

Miles got nothing unless you took him on the inside. If you gave him nothing, he got nothing.

He had nothing himself. And nothing comes of nothing.

Cinjun observed this, as he traveled higher into the tower.

Now high in the structure, rode The Octagon Office—the domain of warrior might. A beautiful place, of streaming daylight, auburn woods, strong oaks and shorewalls. Escaping through a vast picture window, a patio terraced its way into distance.

Cinjun entered with Skyler. They came to the office. And a high view of the situation. In this place, they came to The Command Chamber—and a Command View, at their mighty High Window. This was *The Octagon Office.*

"I'll keep an eye on him," Skyler said.

"If you like," Cinjun said.

"I'm not going to let him produce any trouble," Skyler said.

"He's no trouble," Cinjun said.

"How do you mean?" Skyler said.

Cinjun crossed to his command desk. He passed his patio door—from his high patio you could observe Miles down below. Cinjun did not pay any attention to Miles out there at all. No sight seduced Cinjun, he had seen all before. You did not take him by storm. It was not possible.

He was moving, a man in total control of his destiny.

Cinjun observed the sky out there. His destiny burned across that sky—this was the only beauty worth pause. *Beautiful today*—Cinjun thought—*yes, it was quite lovely today*. A fine day for moving, gliding, along the upward slope of his great and high destiny.

"You're making him important," Cinjun said. "He's not important. He's nothing. He's a tramp madman shouting in the middle of the street. I mean, what are we talking here."

"We're not going to have him arrested?" Skyler said.

"The threat is a phantom. There's no substance to it. It's all show. Marvelous. Excellent show. That seems to be a dangerous advance—But when you look at it closely—it isn't that at all. It can't be. It is nothing. And left to itself, it has to go away. There is nowhere to take it—You understand, Skyler?" Cinjun said.

"Hmm, of course. I see what you mean.," Skyler said.

"I had thought he was smarter than the average bear. He's a man shouting in the middle of the street. Now is that any way to achieve stature?"

Skyler rolled it around in his mind. It was laughable when you thought about it, when you put in the right light.

"I'm following you," Skyler said. But Skyler didn't laugh.

Cinjun smiled, he produced his golden charming smile, but you noticed there was no laugh anywhere in that smile.

"He's making a mistake," Cinjun said. "And I wish him to go on making mistakes."

Into the Changes

"DID YOU EVER THINK ABOUT IT, Cinjun?" Miles said. "It could make you cry about it.

"Could you ever live without it, Cinjun? You've got to give it away. You're holding on so tightly."

Miles spoke to Cinjun up there in the tower as passing people took Miles into their attention. And searched his talk for answers to war and pain.

Did the people think about it? They would try the changes. Taste them.

"You've got to give it away, Cinjun." Miles turned from the tower to the people. "What kind of champion hides in bed all morning?"

He took a picture of it for their children. They might have a look. There was a lot to see here.

Miles took it into the changes. He was the changeling. See him change.

Miles was laid back, as he spoke to the people in the plaza.

He was traveling the changes. Trying things.

He was the changeling. See him change.

He was attempting things. Trying this, trying that. Fitting changes. Taking on dimensions.

What caught the changes, he kept. The rest let slip, he let it drift away in the timeslip continuum.

He moved through the changes. He was the changeling. See him change.

He was experimenting. Some of his experiments were startling.

He did not know where he was going. If you asked him what he had just said . . . what he just did . . . he would not have the slightest idea.

He was experiencing the changes.

The people followed the changes. Tasting them. Trying them.

This is a capoeira, Miles thought.

He had to find the strange in the sense.

He was there attempting things. You had to give it to him—he was attempting things.

Trying them on—feats of strength. Trying them, taking a look at where they would go, where they might take him. He crashed more than he flew; he burned more than he grew.

But he stayed there—attempting things.

Experiencing forces. And hearts broken and bleeding. And the way it was meant to be.

He was experiencing. He was being experienced. And some of the experiences were startling. Filled with *to live* and *to die.*

He was moving thru experience. Moving into startling ways, heading for strange days. Strange days had found him. Strange days were dragging him in. He was being experienced by Strange Days.

He was trying different things under the sun. Reaching, probing, extending, searching, trying, moving, whirling, turning. Wearing some things out, turning to other frontiers. He was attempting things.

He heard stories . . . That got into his skin. He got shook up . . . drove, through the possibilities. Through the changes.

In the Sans Souci Plaza, Miles said, "Miles Roark is in town."

And he stood next to a fire. He stood in a fire. He stood surrounded by fire. And his heart? Burned with feeling.

He spoke to the who's in whoville. Sparking some slight interest. *Who the bloody piss-besotted hell was Miles Roark?*

The field peopled. And grew, and grew. And got on with it. And took it to the place where the people could really get it on.

He was starting a party. Splish Splash. He was taking them into the bath.

Miles built it. He built the field of Strange Days. And then the Strangers came.

Miles built it; and then the strangers came.

Streaming.

A *He,* stepped up. Then, a *She,* stepped up. Soon all the Who's in Whoville were stepping up to listen to his engine hum.

And he got on with it. Yeah.

And his heart? Burned with feeling.

See shining changes. Be experienced.

"Are you experienced? Have you ever been experienced?" the Strange Days said, calling the people to journey.

You see, he lived today.

He was alive today. And that made it a good day, a very good day indeed.

You see, he lived today.

Oh his mind was damned messed up! His mind was messed up, going round and round. Colors, all these colors.

Oh, but his heart burned with feeling. You see, he lived today.

He reeled in confusion, experiencing living. He was alive today.

Oh, pounding. Oh, going round and round. Colors, all these colors.

And a heart burning with feeling.

And the wind cried, all around him.

He was experiencing the changes.

He was the Changeling—see him change.

See shining changes. Experiences. Try this, try that. On this third stone from this sun. On this world that happened to people. Stay with what catches changes. He was the changeling. See him change.

If you asked him what he was doing, he would not have the least idea. He would have no idea at all.

He sank into the changes.

He didn't give them any more than they had.

He spoke softly, casually. No differently than if he was sitting in your living room.

His approach was laid back. *Underplay the changes,* Miles thought. *Experience. Add nothing that stretches the changes.* Experience. Try coming at it from different directions. Looking for better views.

Never satisfied.

Roads ahead.

Choices to be made.

No special way.

Flying. Never rest, never be satisfied. Move into future dreams. Leave the past. Keep moving, looking for the way. Abandon reason. Know hope. And know the changes. They are come. He was being—experienced.

The seeker moved in forever. Carved its way through the changes. Leaving no story untold; denying no turbulence.

If winter took summer, that was the change. If summer tossed in storm, that was the change. The changes were being experienced.

He experienced the changes. Careful with nothing. He was lost and got more lost. The trick of it was—to lose your sanity.

A tough trick to will into the world. It took him vast effort—to lose his mind. Now he never lost control; that was always the danger—the trick was to lose your senses without losing control. He worked the trick.

Tricking existence.

You would have thought he was absolutely crazy if you didn't know better. Some took an interest.

He skipped a light fandango, turned cartwheels across the floor; he did the best he could—the crowd called out for more.

They called to each other. Miles to the people, the people to Miles.

He told them tales. And they told him his worth. Some did not use kind terms. Some cuts were most unkind; they would not let him be. He moved into the next impossibility. To struggle and to hold form . . . Taking it further into distance, lonely distance. He danced by.

Hang on! This was where the ride got—strange.

Miles drove on down the road. Until he came to—a fork—chose—and kept shooting down the byway to parts unknown.

Breaking thru to *strange sensation.* To strange days. To strange rains. To strange being. He was making it all—strange. They looked at this stranger—He was the changeling. See him change.

His mind tore free.

The people came. He built his big generator, and they came to listen to its engine hum.

His mind is gone, they noticed.

He tore a hole in space; burned across the sky. Catching a fall. Flying. His mind tore free . . . of *sanity.* Tore free—and his mind shouted out loud. Tearing across the night sun sky of pained tender love dreams. Sailing on the winds of life. Leaving sanity behind for others to play with.

His was not a small mind to be held by reality. How he came to his escape? It began with rhythm. The subject of this day's lecture was rhythm. Ground rhythm. And moving through the changes of harmonies fast and furious, slow and sensual, vast and near. To . . . *strange sensation.*

Soft Insanity

TEARING INTO UNREALITY.

Not this reality. He was tearing into the one that should be. A crazy reality filled with love dreams and winds of life that swept and swept and swept on through an *All* of cool rapidity and warm slow sensation.

An *All* of sunstreaks. Leading to sunbursts. And explosions of color.

In a void—a black void—a black that was great and vast and deep and wide.

Where a seeker sailed in forever.

A dancing burning fighter—a capoeira—exploding through green into summer and hurtling through blue into winter. Sailing through yellow into orange and red nebulas.

Sailing on the winds of life that swept and swept and swept into forever.

Giving gifts that would last forever. Wild with the power, wild as can be.

'There is a fine madness. A far finer madness than this one.'

Travel with me there. Run with me. Sail with me. Into the further forever. And the realms beyond forever.

He takes himself into soft insanity here.

All Ride. It's all ride.

Skyler

SKYLER—HAD STEPPED from the command floors, and found himself . . . needing to be in the lobby, and looking out the big window at Miles.

Skyler had heard a piece of something Miles had said in the Sans Souci Plaza.

"If you're marketing shit," Miles said, "then you talk about the packaging and the things it comes with, the nice texture and color and you give it a nice sounding brand name like *Eulodia.*

"And you talk about how elephants have been eating it for centuries. Because they know intuitively that it's full of nutritious bacteria that build up you're body's immune system. If you're selling a diamond, you just say I'm selling a diamond. It sparkles."

For some reason, Skyler couldn't work on the campaign after that.

It made him angry. He could not put his mind to the work.

A burly guard was at Skyler's side. The guard turned his gaze from Miles to Skyler.

"Just say when," the guard said.

Skyler did not answer. The guard turned his hard gaze back to Miles.

Skyler looked at the guard. Strange, Skyler had used the same words himself once making love to a woman. *'Just say when'*—Pull yourself *together,* Skyler thought. *Just say when and you'll never have to see him again. That was what the guard meant.* Something was shooting Skyler's mind all to hell.

Something was making Skyler angry. He was getting angrier and angrier and angrier. And he didn't see any outlet for it. He held his anger. Tried to work through it. Forced himself to think clearly through the anger.

Cinjun knew what he was doing. Skyler felt certain. Cinjun was a master strongman. And knew where to throw his weight.

There was nothing to having Miles stand out there and talk. What could come of it? Nothing. Still something about it disturbed Skyler. He decided to not let it disturb him.

He was determined to put Miles in his place. The loser box.

Penthouse Patio Planning

CINJUN STOOD ON HIS PENTHOUSE BALCONY, and looked down at Miles.

The thoughts of the Crimson King were elsewhere. He turned to the sky. His thoughts took him into distance.

Cinjun was weighing the ways to deliver himself into his proper place in history, to reach his rightful position, his proper place in the course of human events.

Much was coming together. It was all so lovely.

His mood was very lovely indeed. As he enjoyed this skyview before him. And this world that he would soon own.

And he did not look down at all—to the man down below—Miles Roark—the man talking, voicing some thoughts that came in no particular order.

Drawing a course that was evidently going every which way but straight. He was a sidewinder this man below. And of no importance. No importance at all.

It seemed to be talk tinged with a touch of crazy—and that spoiled it.

This man was of no importance. His talk—was talk of no importance at all.

Cinjun's thoughts were—far away, far beyond. Having traveled on to higher ground and taken full flight into the beyond. Boldly, into the wild blue beyond.

'Can you imagine the hole in the world?'

IN THE SANS SOUCI PLAZA—
The Changeling and the People of the Changes.
They called out for another trick. Try something else.
Interest us, you bastard! Let's see what you can do, bastard.
Each moment demanded a new impossibility. It was like the problem a juggler faced when he had to interest an audience by juggling with nothing whatsoever in his hands. No balls, no objects. Nothing to toss into the air. Except the ride itself. He made it all ride. Miles made it all ride.
And loaded the ride with bright color.
The brightest colors he could find. He put what he had into it. And he moved.

He was floating stone free on this third stone from this sun.
As he rode this breeze of cool rapidity, turning his ride loose, he braced his being—in the now—for opposition.
And now, in this burning now, this man whose heart was burning with feeling, in this now you just know what has to be . . . he encounters opposition. People who *will* him to stop!
Listen to this. They will have no more of him. Listen, baby it's time to put him in a cage.
You see the people, taking their attention to it now. Setting up boundaries for him. Feeding him dead stops.
They had ways that surrounded them, filled with demands for Miles to cease. And come to sanity.
They loathed insanity. And they hated this man.
He rubbed them the wrong way. His attitude disturbed them. He would have to stop. There was nothing else for it. He must not be allowed to be this way. He must be stopped.
Terrible, for a man, to be this way. Insane. Completely and totally insane. If only somebody would shoot him.
Now that would be interesting.
Somebody should really stop him. He was too much. Far too full of himself. Arrogant. Not humble like themselves. They had the good sense

to keep their hatred and rage and murderous thoughts closed off and reigned tight. You really had to be civil about it. That was the thing that this monster didn't understand. He only cared to seize. To seize the day; seize the night; seize on some tricks of the tongue that made him sound as if he made sense. But he made no sense at all. None. Somebody really ought to kill him.

They began to talk of ways to end him. And people like him—The Know It All's. Who were not like them; they were humble and kept to themselves. Yes, he was not like them; they were nice people. And only performed nice murders.

This Miles spoke of nice beautiful things that could be gotten now without delay. It was absurd. Absolutely absurd. Everybody knew that the only paths to true beauty were through the detours of murder, carnage, bombing, slaughter, executions, military operations, invasion forces, assault squads, and other civilized practices.

They didn't come easy. They didn't come the way he said, just by letting them be. If it was that easy, why weren't people happy now. Here and now. Hear it now. Near and now. It was nonsense.

If that were possible, there would be a lot of happy people in the world. Where are all the happy people? Show them to me.

They don't exist. I prove my point. Case closed. I don't think I need to say another word, but I will . . . And so it goes.

The ticket was red and bloodied from loving arts.

. . . And the tank was flooding with love sense.

He didn't make any sense at all; he was not *of people,* people made sense.

Sense was tricky business. Not as obvious as you would think. In fact it took a lot of tricks of thought to make sense.

These people made sense. Miles—he was crazy.

And he looked like the type that was going to stay crazy.

Which Miles did; he made sure to stay crazy, once he was there.

You don't give up the feeling when you've finally got it down. You keep it hot and squeeling when you take her on the town.

You don't give up that crazy when you're up against the wall—you keep it hot and squeeling when you have yourself a ball. Yeah. Keep. It. Hot. And squeeling!

Miles kept it hot and squeeling. The feeling that is.

His delivery was laid back.

He spoke softly and carried large truths.

Carried them on his back—like Atlas, who only carried the world on his back, incidentally. Miles proceeded to carry the All on his back.

He was crazy you know. Ask all the best people, they'll tell you.

He's crazy that boy; stay away from him. He'll wipe your mind out and fill it with obscene talk of good, clean living.

There was no way to that—without good, clean violence. Miles would learn; in time he would learn.

The learning process would begin. The ancient ceremonial phrase for it was: *a beating*—The learning process would come. Somebody would give it to him; and give it to him good.

The good people hoped Miles would die soon. Now, however long the learning process would eventually take, it was too long. He really should get dead today. They wished somebody would go over and help the boy get dead. Then he would be quiet. And that was where he should go more than anywhere else—that was more important than anything—taking Miles to silence.

He was not too obliging on that score. He kept talking.

Experiencing, trying things, breathing life into the changes.

Those god-awful changes. You could gag on them. They just kept coming.

He was the changeling. See him change.

If he kept talking, the way he was talking, he would get a beating.

And then if he kept mouthing off, he would get dead.

That was the way it had always gone. It was beautiful. Beauty being truth, and truth being beauty as someone once noticed. Discovered. And made known. Beauty would get him. Kill him, something beautiful. Beauty would come and end him. Something beautiful always came along.

Generally in the form of a beautiful man—like Cinjun Khan S'mythe. An ancient spirit moved in Cinjun Smythe. The people saw it, and it made them feel tender. They dreamed of Cinjun Smythe! And in the dreams, darling, they were never lonely. They loved Cinjun whenever he was inside them. They loved him for sentimental reasons. They gave him their hearts—Hey, wasn't this place House Crimson? Well, what do you know—how about that?

Yes, the word around the campfire was that Cinjun Smythe would take care of this man—what was his name again? Miles Roark, huh. A forgettable name if ever there was one.

He would never go places. Not like Cinjun Smythe. That Cinjun Smythe was something else. Now there was a beautiful person. With beautiful crimson talk of murder and carnage and other civilized practices.

If Cinjun ever went away, can you imagine the hole in the world?

Look at this Miles Roark, will you.

He was the changeling. See him change.

Love filled with murder. This was the pulse of the world life—Not empty love like Miles proposed . . . Plain love, no taste to it at all, really—No, give me strange love over that any day, thank you.

In An Empire of The Hunter

THE COURTYARD OF THE CRIMSON KING WAS FILLED with people and an engine that hummed, sending its vibrations, its rippling waves of energy into the people.

Somebody screamed. It was a crazy scream. There was something crazy in this air, you could feel it. But you could not hone in on it by the talk. As a matter of fact, the talk was quite tame.

In the Sans Souci Plaza, Miles said, "In an empire, a court reporter can't blast the Emperor, it would mean never working again. So when the Emperor shreds a good treaty, he says, 'The Breach in the Treaty Is Well Timed.'

"Now that doesn't sound bad at all—to shred a treaty—when you put it like that. Why if you shred some human rights and some justices with the other well timed activity, it almost sounds like you're a helluva good chap for being a son of a bitch bastard devil. You timed it well.

"What do you say when he murders someone? It was well committed.

"Now that doesn't sound like a bad murder at all.

"It gets tough to make it sound good sometimes, but you will be amazed how good you can make the worst thing sound when you give it a try."

"Who the hell wants that kind of act!" Burt Higgins said. He had stopped. Looked at Miles. Looked with open eyes. And listened with ears that took in everything. Looked at Miles. And concluded. "He won't stand," Burt Higgins said. "He won't last."

But Miles would not come down. He was gone. Felt that wave, and rode it. Taking steps, higher and higher. Learning to go as he went. Experiencing freedom, life in the Sans Souci Plaza.

He was holding on to nothing.

"The Emperor says the Earth is flat," Miles said.

"The headline becomes, 'The Shape of the Earth Is in Question.' It appears to be even-handed.

"If he says, 'Up is Down,' the headline is, 'Some Leaders Have Seen Upness in Downess! Some say up is actually down.' "

A pair of reporters were taking themselves away from the scene in a slow walk.

"It's fucking boring," reporter Karl Wentworth said, "there are no strippers. No games. You know what I mean, there's nothing there."

"Nothing interesting," reporter Morty Wallace said. "All he gives you . . . are these principles."

"Fuck him. And the horse he rode in on. And his ancestors. And the ship that brought his ancestors."

"What is he? The guy with the secret of the world?"

"He's on a power trip. What are we, his stooges?" he said, with a tone like he had broken bones for less.

"I could tell you," Karl said, "things that would work. Strippers, games, tricks, something. You've got to have a little bit of something to it."

"True, very true." Morty said. He wasn't afraid to call the shot.

"Ah, he upsets me," Karl said.

"It's bullshit," Morty explained.

He liked to be precise. The whole thing was terribly upsetting, made you just want to beat the uppitiness out of that Miles Roark. Cut his roses down.

"It is . . . bullshit." Karl killed it there, with his tone that brought the matter to ground, deadly stilled.

Karl was leaving the scene with no interest in what he was leaving behind. "The hell with him! The hell with his speeches, the hell with his mother, the hell with the horse he rode in on! The hell with everything that brought his family to this great country!" Karl was much impressed with his strong ability to damn things to hell this day, and suffer the consequences without fear.

"Yep," Morty said. As they started to travel away from each other.

"Strippers," Karl said, impressed by his keen sense of the possibilities, all the possibilities.

"That would work."

"Games," Karl said, tossing in something for the kids.

"That would work," Morty said, in the same high-minded professional excited tone.

"Principles and Rules—" Karl said.

"That don't work," Morty said. "No day, no how."

They were parting entirely now.

"See you later partner," Karl said.

"Later partner," Morty said.

They moved from the scene, taking their massive brains with them.

Pivotflow

PIVOT, MILES THOUGHT.

Suddenly, experiencing pivotflow.

Everything wheeled in pivots.

Separate yourself from sense. Take a ride, get it on the inside.

Crazy for sale.

Bold—like no crazy you ever saw.

Who would like to sample his supply?

Crazy for sale.

This crazy told of *world*—the crazy breathed through a crazy dream—like the kind that spooks you in the night. Faint as will of the wisp. But clear—and the animal was sadly serenading the moon. The C'mon Serenade, under the worklight.

C'mon.

C'mon.

C'mon now touch the world.

Cinjun tells a sane reasonable accepted completely allowable story of: He, that is—*god* man.

Now the animal breathed in the dream and what it said was:

'I wish to tell a story. The story of: He, that is good man.'

Crazy for sale. Crazy story for sale. He, That is Good Man.

He, That Is Good Man

"CINJUN, I'M CALLING YOU out to a Capoeira. A dancing fight. C'mon! A dancing fight. Whoo-yeah! That's what I'm talking about! C'mon———"

That which will be, will be.

That which is, is.

He that tries, does not do it.

Let the fight rule. Let the fight take us over. Let go to the fight, Cinjun old boy.

My old friend, Cinjun. Capoeira!—Dancing fight. Let's go. Let's roll.

The fight doesn't follow your rules. The fight is here. The fight will be.

C'mon, baby.

Cinjun Khan Smythe—c'mon!

He who is good man, does not try.

The love that wants to be, well, it is.

Who says much that goes, does not go—As well as it does not go, it does not come.

You cannot fight this fight from behind soft lies, you cannot march behind a soft parade. You cannot hold on to anything. The fight that is, will be. The fight speaks. The fight that is good does not fall, and if one day it falls, it falls well.

Sadness walks away from this fight. This fight is a Capoeira!

This fight is not rules. This fight is not deals. This fight is not ceremonies. This fight is me. I am the fight. C'mon Cinjun. The fight that is, let it be. The fight that has come, let it come. The fight that will, is good. And if it falls, it will fall well.

Capoeira! Cinjun.

"He that is good man, *is,* " Miles said.

"He who is good, does not try.

"He who is there, does not reach.

"That which is, will be.

"Sadness walks, away.

"It is. And when it falls, it falls well.

"See, does not less. Suffer, does not let. Strive, does not need.

"It is. It will be.
"That which will be, is."

He who is good, does not try.
    He who loves, does not try.
    That which goes, goes.
    He who says much, does not go.
    He that tries, does not go.
    As he does not go, he does not come.
    He that seeks, has not found.
    He that preaches, does not know.
    He that moves strong, does not know strength.
    The capoeira that will be, is.
    He that tells much of love, does not know.
    He that forces love, does not love.
    He that is a good man, does not try.
    He that is good, does not fall.
    If one day he falls, he falls well.
    Capoeira speaks! Sadness walks away.
    Hey, hey, sadness walk away.
    Hey, hey, sadness walks from this place.

He who is peace, *is.*
    He who *is,* does not praise.
    He who wars, praises peace.
    He who wars, searches.
    He who searches, has not found.
    He who has not found, does not know where to look.
    He who has found, knows Peace.
    He who is Peace, knows finding without search.
    He who knows Peace, has no need to speak of peace.
    He who knows Peace, knows how high Peace can grow.
    He who cuts it down, will never know.
    Hear it now.
    Here and now.
    Near and now.
    Peace is now.
    Capoeira speaks! Sadness walks away.
    Hey, hey, sadness walk away.
    Hey, hey, sadness walks from this place.

He who does not know Peace, speaks of *Honor*.

He that is this man speaks of Peace with Honor, this is *Victory* . . . he that lusts for victory, does not know honor.

He that is this man, who does not know honor, speaks of *Mission*.

He, that is this man speaks of Peace Mission, this is *War* . . . he that makes his mission war, has not made it peace.

Capoeira speaks! Sadness walks away.

Hey, hey, sadness walk away.

Hey, hey, sadness walks from this place.

He, that is this man speaks of Dynamic Entry; this is *Invasion*—he that invades does not know welcome.

He that is not welcome, is not well come.

He that is not well come, does not rightly go.

He that does not rightly go, does not know love.

He that does not know love cannot save.

He that is this man speaks of Save; this is Destroy—He that destroys, does not build. He that does not build, does not win.

That which is the name, is little. That which is, is much.

What is done, *is*. What is named, *is*.

"Save," you say, when you destroy.

"Own," you say, when you visit.

"Listen," you say, when you ask for silence.

Do what is good, when you say it is done.

He that says much, does not do.

He that is, does.

What is done, is.

What is, is named.

"Capoeira speaks! Sadness walks away from this place," Miles said.

Hey, hey, sadness walk away.

Hey, hey, sadness walks from this place.

"He that is good man, *is*, " Miles said.

He who is good, does not try.

He who loves, does not try.

That which goes, goes.

He who says much, does not go.

He that tries, does not go.

As he does not go, he does not come.

He that seeks, has not found.
He that preaches, does not know.
He that moves strong, does not know strength.
The capoeira that will be, is.
He that tells much of love, does not know.
He that forces love, does not love.
He that is a good man, does not try.
He that is good, does not fall.
If one day he falls, he falls well.
Hey, hey, sadness walks away . . .
Hey, hey, sadness walks from this place . . .
Hey, hey, sadness walks away . . .
Hey, hey . . .

The soft strains fading.
Time slipping, time slipping.
Miles now, taking the moment into silence.
The silence looming.
Time slipping, time slipping.

The silence stood and felt itself assaulted.
By other moments. Calls to other worlds.
And the battles of other times.
The silence felt the world taken—to the desert, to distant desert sands.
To white dunes and slipfaces. Among this sand-splashed place, the world peopled. This world stretched before these people and called them to journey—to experience pursuit of desires. Riches—and to search out the possibilities. To take moments. To search for glory. And high purpose. And know life among the desert sands.
'The Sultan' spoke:
The sultan said to the old horse trader:
"Old horse trader, I wish you to bring me a black stallion that runs so swiftly that it leaves no tracks. Buy this horse for me. I wish it so."
The old horse trader said, "My sultan, I am an old man, I no longer do this work. But I know a fish monger who has a very good eye for horses. He will find your horse for you."
The next season, the sultan brought the old horse trader before him, and said:
"Old horse trader, why did you tell me the fish monger has a good eye for horses? I asked him to bring me a black stallion that runs so swiftly

that it leaves no tracks, he brought me a brown mare. It is an ugly horse. A horrible horse."

"But your majesty, may I ask, does the horse run so swiftly that it leaves no tracks?"

"Yes, it runs so swiftly that it leaves no tracks."

"Then the fish monger has better eyes than I, for he sees beyond appearances."

Capoeira speaks! Sadness walks away.

Hey, hey, sadness walk away.

Hey, hey, sadness walks from this place.

The Rundown

SUCH A LOVELY . . . loving . . . loveable grip—*the Hunter.*

And his grip reaching for the Hunted . . . and you . . . and you . . . and you . . . and you . . . and you . . .

An ancient spirit moved within Cinjun. Everyone could see it.

The Hunter in the Red Vest

INTRODUCING THE HUNTER IN THE RED VEST. Swaying side to side, with movements like a god. There's no one like the Hunter in the Red Vest. You may meet him, you may see him—The Hunter in the Red Vest.

Oh, the wonder of the thing—the Hunter in the Red Vest. There's no one like the Hunter in the Red Vest. There never was. There never will be.

The Hunter in the Red Vest is here.

And he's telling the story. That sounds easy. Gets into your skin.

The burgundy god emperor—The strongman in the red vest.

New strongman for sale—

The Hunter in the Red Vest.

He's putting the pieces together, every movement, every moment.

The Hunter in the Red Vest speaks—

The Burgundy Parade. Care to take a sip of burgundy brew? Intoxicating burgundy brew?

The Parade—He writes it with his eyes. His eyes take everything. Take hold of everything.

He puts a spell on you . . . because you're his.

The Hunter in the Red Vest.

Breathing.

Among forest shapes.

Coming alive.

The Parade

COME SEE THE PARADE. The parade of purposes and the parading possibilities.

Feel free to swoon when your purpose comes up.

The Puff Parade, Miles thought. *Puff! Puff! Puff those rings away.*

A Smoke Parade, Miles thought. *Puff! Puff! Puff those rings away. Those smoke rings I love. Rings I know so well.*

"Strip to show us all you are, oh, parade.

"The Puff Parade—Puff! Puff! Puff it away.

"The Smoke Parade—smoky little rings. Puff! Puff! Puff those rings away.

"A phantom parade of love. Puff! Puff! Puff the parade away."

Blow, blow them through the air—Silky little lies. Those little smoke rings of lies that I love . . . taking away.

Puff! Puff! Puff your cares away. Leaving Night and Day.

Blow, blow them through the air, silky little rings, those smoke rings I love.

Leaving—A night sun, a capoeira, and a chance to die.

Sultan See Beyond

"STRIP AWAY BONES AND SKIN," Miles said.

Strip away the soft parade. Strip away the eminence front.

Strip away all.

Walk the elemental parade. Walk nature.

Now you are outside. Walk the forest wilderness. Walk all of the days. Walk all of the nights.

Walk all the pain and pleasure. Without the hunter in the red vest.

Show me what lies within. Won't you be—

One.

I am—one. Seeming one, be one. Being one, be one.

Be Wãone.

I am Wãone.

Be Wãone and enter the Wãoynde.

Be Wãone who enters the Whirlwind Wãoynde. The Wild Whirlwind Wãoynding Wild. Screaming Wild! Wild with the power. Wild as can be.

Be Wãone.

Hey, hey, sadness walk away.

Hey, hey, sadness walks from this place.

Oh good fellow Soft Parade . . . Let's knock out the eminence front, and pound these things into some raw shapes.

Raw shapes—Showing them raw shapes and all the love in your heart. Raw, elemental beauty.

Beauty, creating the Elemental Parade, right before your eyes.

How much of this does Miles know as he takes the plaza, as he enters the port of Sans Souci? None of it. He does not know what he's going to do. He moves in experience, being experienced by his experience. At times, he moves in startling directions. To find dimensions.

To show them elemental beauty. This is all he knows.

"The lies, the lies, the lies, oh, are they dressed to kill. Dressed nice. Dressed pretty. Dressed so fine.

"They shop for clothing in all the best places.

"The lies have to be dressed perfectly so all you will see is the dress.

"But when they come to you with that pretty lie, see nothing but the lie."

See merely the lie.

Lie Shapes.

"Let's pound some pretty lie shapes into raw shapes, into elemental shapes.

"Strip to show us all you are. Strip away bones and skin, strip away hide, strip away cover, strip away eminence front, strip away put-on. Let's go to what you are.

"Let's have a good look. Have a real good look.

"Not all looking is seeing, but when they come to you, . . . you see."

Wild in the Wilderness

"OH TO BE WILD IN THE WILDERNESS."

That's what he wants, great weddings of garden forms, producing beautiful soaring people shapes.

"Oh, let it people!" Miles said. "Let's have ways . . . And the next thing you know we'll be closing down the town; going way across town, wondering what can go flying between the moon and the forest city."

Splish Splash, he was taking them into the bath!

"Now is the time. Let's go! We'll go a-reeling with the feeling! How high can the people shapes grow? If you cut them down, you'll never know."

"I'm here to have a good time," Miles said.

"They don't want a good time at their party; nothing wild. Their party is all business. They're working some deals, that's all. Everything else stays out.

"I say, 'I want to see my people have a good time!'

"I'm driving this thing; and I'm going to drive it all over town."

The memory started then. He stood in the memory.

Memories are assaultive things, or birds taking wing. Or things returning suddenly. They're very active things when they're hell-bent on being this. Memories haunt, memories sting, memories comfort, memories reveal. Memories do a whole hell of a lot.

His mind was assaulted then by an image of Scofield, and Miles's thoughts rolled back to a moment he had had with the old man.

"He's asking for a nice, healthy fight," Scofield said. Now Scofield asked Miles very nicely. "Give the man what he's asking for. Oppose him . . . Then see where your act leads you . . ."

Miles's thoughts rolled through it, searching the work and the way. It was night-driving, he could only see a little bit at a time, but he could probably make the whole trip that way.

"Work," Scofield said, "more than one dimension. Give them the impossible."

Miles gave Scofield a look. "That's an enormous idea."

"I packed it tight and marked it fragile for you," Scofield said. "By the way," Scofield drew a breath, "where is this plaza you're playing? I happen to have some time on my hands to go sightseeing."

"I'm not talking about no revolution," Miles said in the plaza.

"I'm talking about having a good time.

"I'm talking about dancing.

"I'm talking about my people getting wicked and feeling nice.

"You know Cinjun doesn't like the way I do my thing. He doesn't get with that thing.

"C'mon, people! Let's show him what it's about!

"I'm talking about dancing. Splishing and a-splashing, a-rolling and a-strolling. I'm talking about a-reeling with the feeling. I'm talking about dancing on the living room rug. Laughing in the rain, dancing in the snow, having a good time————"

I'm talking about seeing my people have some fun. Tonight, let's have some fun, let's run. Let the wild color light up the night!

I want to feel good, I want to feel nice, that's what I'm talking about.

Oh, to be wild in the wilderness! I want to see my people have some fun.

People, people, people, I'm talking about having some fun.

How high can the people shapes grow? If you cut them down, you'll never know.

Oh, wicked fun. Be you bright, be you light, and let it fun. Oh, let it fun. Now let the world fun itself.

And oh, let it people!

The world is big now, and all grown, it can fun itself!

Oh, let it fun!

Hey, Pachuco!

"I DON'T LIKE WHAT HE'S SAYING," Pachuco said, "it's so vicious."

He had nothing against fun, he was just opposed to it on moral grounds.

As a matter of fact, this was actually the main reason he had been hired for his job—he was an objective reporter. This was his profession. A reporter for the *light*vision.

He's against, Daphne thought, *the fun? He's right it could lead to funning in the streets—and cocktail hours?* Immediately, Daphne grew much opposed to strong drink. Except sometimes. After meals was still good. Before meals was also good. And during meals was good. In the morning, was fine. Afternoons, were fine. Evenings, were fine. But no other time. This talk of rampant fun had to be viewed through that prism.

"Yes, horrible, horribly vicious," Daphne said. It was a wonder she could still look on this man Roark, but look at Miles she did, as she soothed Pachuco's sensitive nature. They stood in a distant expanse of the plaza.

Pachuco was a chief Barker—a very famous face—with an enormous show and an enormous following on the *light*vision. Or so he hoped.

Or so it would be—Daphne assured him. No one knew him now. But he had the stuff of legend. He was only a young reporter for a *light*vision station. He was hardly known in his own power station. But he would become a legend—Daphne made him feel his importance.

She gave him the treatment . . .

Her treatment . . . She operated in a familiar way. She put her hands on his shoulders; brought her forehead to his forehead and locked it there.

"Listen," Daphne said, "we want your stock to go up . . ."

Now she took her head back . . . slowly pulling from Pachuco's forehead . . . the effect was intense—on Pachuco. He drew a breath.

"The next time your contract comes up," Daphne said, "we want you to be in a position to bargain. You have to get known. Here's what I would do if I were you . . . I would shoot a nice-sized segment about Miles Roark . . . I would take it back to the newsroom . . . and tell them you stumbled onto this thing that's blowing up into more than local news, it's going national; and this belongs on the national newsfeed—Of course, you would shoot it in such a way that—if they put it on the feed—they would also want to show you reporting from the scene . . . Shoot yourself interviewing Miles Roark."

"Hmmm," Pachuco said.

"See this way you go national," Daphne said.

"Hmmm," Pachuco said.

"You ought to make a pattern of that. You ought to be going national all the time. It'll put you in a much better position for your contract. And take you to possibilities beyond your contract," Daphne said. And paused.

"Hmmm," Pachuco said, filling the pause, "hmmm." He was definitely breathing . . . all the signs were there.

"That's why—if I were you . . . I would shoot as much of Miles Roark as I could . . . until I had a nice big fat story . . . and then I would take it to the bank and draw some cash against it." That was what Daphne would do, but she made it clear that was only because she was ambitious and ready to achieve worldly success. Such things were not for everyone.

"Why should I help him?" Pachuco said. "I don't like what he's saying."

"Don't help him at all. Help yourself. Nobody likes what he's saying . . . it's not going to get him anywhere."

"Myself, huh? Our news program goes to housewives and retirees. We're not a tabloid.'"

"A lot of people don't like what he's saying—there's value in that— are you following me?"

"Maybe. Would he work with us? Maybe work a little at it, if I rolled him in front of the *light*vision?" Pachuco asked. " I mean can he say some more—*stuff,* you know what I mean, can he come up with off-the-wall material on his feet . . . to make the damn thing a little more *newsy?"*

"Oh, I don't know he's terribly shy," Daphne said. "But maybe we could get him to say one or two things of color—why, yes, he just might give off some color, under the worklight, that is."

"Let's roll, then," Pachuco motioned for his crew to move.

"If I were you," Daphne said, "I would find reasons to space out the 'live from the scene' coverage over a few days. You might be able to work two or three national bumps off this one thing if you play it right. You could 'own' the story nationally."

"Hmmm," Pachuco said. She was right—this was a good idea indeed—he was glad he had thought of it. You could depend on him to be a free thinker. He moved into the plaza and took—somehow dragged— his massive brain with him, as he moved closer toward: Miles Roark.

Miles was ready. The subject of this day's lecture would be rhythm.

As luck would have it, Miles was ready.

That evening, Cinjun noticed that Miles Roark somehow made his way onto a national program. You couldn't help but notice a thing like that.

Cinjun laughed. Maybe because he didn't find it funny. This Miles Roark had gotten his fleeting touch of fame, after all. And that would end it. That would be that. There was nothing else—nowhere else to take an act like Miles Roark's.

Cinjun then went ahead and enjoyed his dinner, untroubled by any thought of Miles Roark . . . The man didn't matter at all. Not at all . . . The dinner was delicious.

On the following days, when Cinjun observed Miles making another appearance on the *light*vision and then—somehow—yet another, he drew himself to attention—three national hits based on nothing—how was it possible?

Cinjun felt himself grow angry. He let the anger grow.

For some reason, the dinner wasn't absolutely delicious that third time he saw Miles Roark.

Mounting Pressures

GRACE WAS ON HER WAY to visit Cinjun. She was traveling through the crowd gathered in the plaza, a most curious gathering.

Suddenly, she recognized Scofield sitting to the side. It came as a shock to her.

"You're part of this?" she said.

"He's a friend." Scofield smiled. "It's nice to see you Grace."

The Jesus incident

Scofield and Grace were interrupted by a missionary who came on the scene.

The missionary was a fervent man living in fervent years, who had smelled converts—There is a predator for everything under the sun.

There was a harvester for every field. And the field was rich with open people.

He was rude with intrusion.

"Will you accept Jesus as your savior?" the missionary said.

"No, I don't need to do that," Scofield said, gazing steadily at the man; his eyes locking on the man, taking him into a powerful hold.

"I am Jesus." Scofield said, firmly. Scofield forgave him seventy times seven, for his intrusion.

The man blinked; Scofield did not.

The man said, "You oughtn't be fooling like that!"

"I'm not. I am Jesus." Scofield said. Again, Scofield forgave him seventy times seven.

The man turned to Grace. "He says he's Jesus?" the man asked.

"Perhaps," Grace said, "in a way he is, look into his soul. It reaches back that far."

The man looked. Searching deep into Scofield's soul. Scofield did not shift in form or feel. He breathed easily, and exuded the ages of man. Scofield had let his soul reach back to the ancient world, and let the feeling of centuries pulse calmly within him.

Scofield was springing the Jesus capoeira on him.

Scofield was giving him the Jesus capoeira.

He who is good, does not try.

He who loves, does not try.

That which goes, goes.

He who says much, does not go.

He that tries, does not go.

As he does not go, he does not come.

He that seeks, has not found.

He that preaches, does not know.

He that moves strong, does not know strength.

The capoeira that will be, is.

He that tells much of love, does not know.

He that forces love, does not love.

He that is a good man, does not try.

He that is good, does not fall.

If one day he falls, he falls well.

Scofield breathed easily . . .

He let the religious man's mind do the convincing. Do his work for him.

The hunter was being hunted. The converter was being converted.

Turnabout was fair play.

Turn, turn, turn.

The hunter was being hunted.

Scofield stayed in his Jesus-being. The missionary tried to get his footing back to a reality he could understand.

The missionary was sore perplexed. He thought:

Jesus wouldn't try to be Jesus, he would just be Jesus . . . Scofield was just being. Just being the Jesus-being. The love, the compassion, all there. The religious man began to doubt his sanity. And then it collapsed altogether. "Can I show you to my wife?" the missionary said.

"Certainly," Scofield said.

The man brought his wife to stand before Scofield and Grace. "This man says he's Jesus."

"Shalom!" Scofield said.

They stood still—breathless—in this great moment.

"That's from my native tongue," Scofield said. "It means hello, peace, . . . and goodbye." Scofield remained in his state of being, of certain living being. Giving them the goodbye feeling.

"Shalom," they said.

They didn't know what to do with Scofield. They walked away, in a kind of walking daze, dreaming of a thing that could be. Yes, a thing that very well could be.

"Grace walk with me awhile," Scofield said. "And tell me, how you're doing? I want to hear all about—you."

Grace smiled.

. . . And a little rich girl, was finding her way . . .

Cinjun and Grace in the tower

Grace was jolly sunny when she at last came to Cinjun in the tower.

"Wow! What a scene going on down there! Splishing and a-splashing, and people just a-reeling with a-feeling."

This was how Grace entered Cinjun's thinking parlor—his Octagon Office at House Crimson.

She was in full flight now. "Oh, they were rolling and tumbling."

She swung round on Cinjun. "How was I to know, there was a party going on! Goodness, people just a-reeling with the feeling!"

Cinjun was in a mood. Deep in brooding thoughts.

He was coiled. In this state, he was dangerous. He sat in his chair, and did nothing. Something was happening inside him. His being was flooding with sheer and intense rages, terrible sensations that were taking him deeper into his dangerous state. He did nothing.

He did not move. He did not turn. He sat, far back and deep in his chair; his muscles sat in release but his emotions and all the sensations running through his body were wired and at full charge.

He was winding and winding and winding deeper into extreme, almost uncontrollable rage.

This was what Grace encountered when she entered his Octagon Office. She recognized it.

Grace smiled.

"Scofield Morefield is down there." She said it plainly, and then held herself still.

"Scofield," Cinjun said, lifting his gaze. "Is he still alive?"

"This Miles Roark is a friend of his."

Cinjun took a breath and extended his back along the line of his cushioned high-backed chair.

After a while, Cinjun took his eyes away from Grace. He directed his stare and his attention away from her. "He's nothing, Grace," Cinjun said.

Grace reacted. "You never show an appreciation for my taste in men."

Cinjun turned slowly, and looked at her.

She gave him presence. Gave him a look. And a sexy grin. A sultry grin.

She said, very carefully and precisely, giving full value to her words:

"This Miles seems like a handsome and virile man. If I weren't married, I'd like to meet and spend some time with him."

Cinjun's features took on a firm alertness. He allowed his energies to gather and quicken.

Grace held herself completely still.

Cinjun rose from his chair.

He was holding her in a steady, hard look.

He stood poised, graceful, handsome, in control of his massive frame. At his side his hand rose into the air, the palm open; he held his hand, suspended down and back. He was allowing energy to flow into the hand. He was allowing his rage to grow and take him over. And now he moved forward, slowly very slowly. He was going to slap her, and slap her hard. But he would not allow the moment to pass hurried; he would play out the full value of her physical punishment.

He stared her directly in the eye as he neared her. He was going to slap her good and hard. She knew this. He had never hit her before, and she knew this too, but now she had brought herself to this moment. She must submit. Now, she was all. And all must submit. This was for her own god-damned good. She had brought herself to this punishment.

As he traveled slowly, ever so slowly across the room, his rage grew and grew. And it was as if the slap that was coming had started far, far away and was crossing a room to punish her face.

Grace remained entirely still. And her face remained beautiful to see. She was a ravishing, beautiful woman. And she was showing him presence.

Now, he was close to her. He gathered enormous energy into his hand. And pulled the hand back, ready for hard release.

He stared at her hard. With mayhem in his heart. He was going to enjoy punishing her face.

She looked at him. She paid no attention to the hand that was going to slap her.

Cinjun's features took on heated tightness. His brows and eyes gave out concentrated beams of pure rage.

And then opened. He was still staring hard at her.

He held himself in this moment.

And then smiled at her. Charmingly.

"Excellent," Cinjun said. "Excellent."

He relaxed his hand.

They stood there a long moment. Cinjun was filled with rage, but so charming. He allowed his smile to take his handsome features.

Grace betrayed nothing.

Cinjun took her hand. Not the one that was on the mirror side of his slapping hand, but rather the one across. He took her into this crossed-hand hold, and then led her to a seat.

He sat her down. And he sat directly across from her, still holding her hand in the cross-body way.

A lamp lit at her side, filled in highlights and colors on her sensual face, the face that was already bright and beautiful from the sunlight entering the room. Her features were soft and womanly. They called out for touching. Everything about her beauty spoke of bedrooms, and of making love.

Cinjun held her in his look.

He stayed in this moment. He gathered his energies.

He was holding her hand very tightly now. She was feeling pain in the forceful grip. He held her fast this way, and held her attention entirely. Through the grip, it was as if he was reaching into her belly, and holding her by her guts.

He allowed his rage to grow within him; to take him over again. She must submit. He grew angrier and angrier and took himself to the edge of violence. It was only then that he took control of his energies, and held them fast.

In this state of extreme anger, he said to Grace:

"Open your heart!"

She was still. She was feeling pain in her hand, but she let the pain hurt her. She didn't do anything to resist. She looked at him. She was the center of his reality in this moment. And she felt his being.

He gripped her harder.

She was crying now.

"Will you open your heart!" Cinjun said.

She was crying. But there were no tears. There was just her beautiful face.

"Yes," Grace said.

The Swat Pow-Wow

Quinn was visiting House Crimson for a pow-wow. And when Cinjun greeted him, Quinn was direct: "What's happening down there?"

The question traveled the space of the Octagon Office.

Cinjun sensed the full dimensions of the moment.

Quinn Martin doesn't just question, he tests. Quinn was implying a greater question, of Cinjun's tactical approach. Cinjun was aware of chatter and muttering in the group around them and among the staffers standing out in the corridor.

There was a question in the air.

"Hold it down everybody," Cinjun said.

Quinn looked around and observed the room go to silence. The voices in the outer corridor also went to silence.

The air was still. Now they were entirely in a thick silence. The chamber was proofed against sound, and held away all except the sunlight streaming in through the high windows.

Cinjun took in a deep breath. "Good."

He returned his attention to Quinn. "Go ahead, Quinn."

Quinn was aware that Cinjun was taller and broader than himself. But he also seemed to have expanded beyond his body's dimensions. It was an odd sensation. But Quinn rose past the troubling sensation to take control; he owned his man Cinjun and he did not let his startling posture trouble him. Quinn said, with great charm: "What's happening down there?"

Cinjun reacted also with great charm. They were two leaders talking.

"Don't worry about Miles Roark." And now how does he reassure Quinn? Quite simply. With no effort involved at all. It's all quite simple. "He's not getting anywhere," Cinjun said. "Nobody's paying attention to him. That kind of act only appeals to a small lunatic fringe. He's a madman. He's not worth our time."

"Still," Quinn said, "I would take some care with this."

"He's a fool shouting in the middle of the street. I mean what are we talking here?" Cinjun said. "People get tired of that. They get tired of it awfully fast. The only way he can sustain it is if we react. Why would we react? There's nothing behind him. There's nothing holding him up. If we leave him be, he'll collapse. There's nowhere else he can take this."

Quinn considered it and reached a judgement. "I agree."

"Good."

They proceeded into the meeting.

Cinjun went into "The Swat Pow-Wow" as an act of dismissing Miles Roark.

He would go about his business. And have none of Miles Roark. He was rude with intrusion. And Miles would only win, if he got your attention. The way to beat Miles was to ignore him; the way to defeat Miles was not by fighting him but rather by walking on past Miles; by just walking right on by. And going about the business that mattered.

The executive committee commenced its activity quickly; Cinjun carried them into much pressing business.

Cinjun was drawing their attention to a grid on the board. Quinn and the quorum of the executive committee were seated around the broad horseshoe table.

SWAT

"Swat!—Strengths, weaknesses, attacks, threats." Cinjun was calling out the quadrants of the grid. "Let's examine them."

This was the Swat! Session.

They would look at their *strengths,* to be cherished; *weaknesses,* to be ended—*attacks,* that was where they might attack—and, *threats,* that was where they were under threat.

It was a see-all system, so that they might be all. To be employed, used, cherished. So that they might be all, and, end all ungood things, under the sun.

Everything must move forward. This was how Cinjun operated. Everything must operate without friction. Smooth and efficient.

In the Swat session, Cinjun talked of their enemy as being "behind." Not able to keep up. Having trouble. House Crimson was in a winning position. Had the whole machine together. Everyone else was struggling.

Cinjun's talk was achieving an effect. They were starting to feel very secure. To feel flush with power. To feel a swelling sense of victory. They had it all. They were making history. They were on top and bulletproof.

No one could reach them. No one could touch them. No one could stop them.

He was taking them back on course. They were moving without friction. Good; this was good. They were moving smoothly, efficiently. A first-rate operation. Cinjun felt his strength and the burning of his muscles in strenuous activity.

He was taking them into the rapids. Taking them to higher ground.

Abruptly, Cinjun heard a sound.

Distance intruded.

Cinjun saw their attention seized.

They were being assaulted by a wave of sound, from outside. They were being disturbed. They looked to the windows . . . there was a kind of screeching, squeeling hum out there.

And now they were interrupted by a greater wave of sound coming from outside. They ran to the window.

The commotion intruding was so great, that they were forced to the patio. To step out on the edge of the aerie. And take in the scene from the high patio.

Now, they stepped onto the patio, streamed out to the aerial courtyard, and lined up by the parapet. Cinjun cut through them and had a look for himself.

Earlier Cinjun stood on his patio, his aerie, and looked at Miles standing below in the courtyard. Miles was no longer down below. Now, he was directly across from them. He was mounting a skyscraper.

The Scraper in the Sky

WHAT CINJUN SAW WERE: the canyons of the city, skyscrapers streaming up . . .

And on the mountaintop across from House Crimson . . . Miles Roark!

What he saw was Miles's look. A still, steady, relaxed gaze. Everything else swirled around the gaze. The look told what he was doing.

He was taking it into: mountaintop capoeira.

The flow of the buildings, realized itself.

Form follows function. Beautiful forms to house beautiful people shapes. At the peak of the form—Miles Roark.

From the canyons, Miles arose. Striding. Taking the forest city.

This was more than a human being, Cinjun thought, this was an idiot. This boy didn't know enough to come in out of the rain.

The crowd was cheering, not because he had climbed a mountain and had become the scraper in the sky. They were cheering for what took him to this moment. An intense passion.

Each in his way, wanted that intense passion. The passion of youth. The passion of purpose, and force. Where had it gone, each thought; many had it, and many saw it slide away.

Before them was a young man who had it, still. And for this, they cheered. Watched. And wondered.

It was an inspiration to the crowd, that was what made it disturbing to Cinjun; it was more than the theatrics, the trouble with it was—It was emotional.

People wanted to be up there.

To feel the being of being Astride the Colossus.

Oh, to do it in daylight, and even in company. It must have felt rich.

He made the crowd aware of the soaring forms, of rising, sweeping gold and purple into pale blue.

Behind the pose of the forest society—*the eminence front*—. . . People forgot sometimes that the skyscrapers were merely *mountains.* That was what they amounted to. They were heaps of ore and rock taken from far mountains; brought to the city, and used to erect *man mountains.* And the thing to do with a mountain was to climb it.

Hell, just because no one did it, that didn't make it any the less sensible.

They didn't rise by themselves, the man mountains rose by the work of *mountain climbers.* Now why should men stop climbing it the moment the scraper hit the sky? Silly, wasn't it? A beautiful sky form just sitting there, and nobody was supposed to climb it. Silly, really.

Miles would have none of it—he climbed the man mountain.

And when he came to the sky, to one of his truest friends, he spoke to it. Man to sky.

The moment came, and was not designed by Miles, but by what stood below the moment. Made by the ground on which the moment stood.

Trained not to intrude, they were all trained not to intrude. All their lives, taught not to intrude.

Taught that the world did not belong to them. That the rock and ore of the world that peopled did not belong to the world. It was 'owned,' by specialists in owning. Taught that much was forbidden, that ways of walking, and ways of being, and places of going were forbidden—to all but these certain people—the people of the eminence front.

Miles would have none of it—it was not a system of order, it was a system of control.

Nature was chaos, and curves, and sloping forms. Man—was the creature that straightened everything out. Nature did not make straight lines. Nature saw no value to straight lines.—Wiggles and twists and great sidewinding. Twists and swirls and great sidewinding, this was the natural way.

Miles moved in the natural way.

He climbed the scraper in the sky; he was moving to become the scraper in the sky.

It was an act of emergence—And all who sought to stop him, be damned.

He was about to intrude . . . on Cinjun Smythe.

Be strictly correct.

Hold on to everything, so tightly. Be strictly correct. Be a clenched fist, for all your days.

Do not come down from the heights of "stricly correct"; the heady altitudes of "proper" and "getting somewhere properly."

They don't talk about what you leave behind.

Goodbye, Miles would say, you can keep your suit of lies. I'm not coming down to the depths of your heights. To your griefs of joy.

I like to take steps that make you feel dizzy. That take you into a frontier swirl, a wild whirlwind, wãoynding wild. Oooohhh, yes. Sunrays, speedrays and boundless skies. And a frontier swirl. That was the way to live.

Miles threw his head up, for a flash of a second, to look at Cinjun Smythe. It was a reintroduction. All that was needed.

Cinjun locked eyes with Miles, and in the flash Cinjun saw the startling thing that was in Miles's eyes: he saw sunbeams. And *Tygers* crouched in jungles in his dark eyes.

Miles broke away.

Miles went on, following the form, the form following the function.

He felt, he felt, he felt, Love!

It felt like the rain. It felt like heavy weather taking over. It felt like a man and woman sticking together.

And he felt, . . . Love!

Love like the sun, that felt like rain, with heat, piercing through the rains.

Sun Rains!
And a wild whirlwind wãoynding wild. Screaming wild.
Oooh, sister! Ooooh, brother! Yeah, yeaaaaah!
He did not say a word.

The eyes of the *light*vision were able to come in close on Miles when he looked down. And the *light*vision crew hovering in the air was able to come in close on Miles's eyes when he looked up.

He had a face lit with wild color, and in his eyes, that thing: *Tygers* crouched in jungles in his dark eyes.

This child, this goddamn child, Cinjun thought. Where were his parents?

Where were the adults to come take him away before he forced a man to drown the child.

Miles did not say a word.

Lady Day

The Steel Hulk, rose into the blue sky.

Summer stretching on the grass.

Resonant drops of sound rolling in the sunny clarity of the summer air.

He stood on the summit, his legs planted wide apart, leaning back against space.

Staring, staring, staring.

In this moment, life was good.

Oh, sweet lady of love. Sweet lady of the All. Lady Day!

She was his love, Lady Day. Her presence was here, she charged the air.

The form of the moment breathed life, and sang sweetly to the lady that swam in mystery. Sang with full-throated ease. Of summer, and spring, and springing ease.

Oh, sweet woman, he reached for her, a true friend of his.

He put his hands out to touch her.

"That guy can't stop himself! He's in love with her!" He could not keep his hands off Lady Day.

Could you call on Lady Day?
'Cause she'll wash your troubles,
Your troubles, your troubles away!

He stood on the steel cliff, astride the structure, and looked out to the countryside, out to the long reaches of trails twisting out to shores and horizons, and beyond.

Everywhere, jumbles of bright fluttering winds.

Streaks.

And Miles forgot. Forgot everything.

There was just him and the wild whirlwind wãoynding wild. Screaming wild.

And a mad love affair with lady day.

In the summer evening . . .

Darkness mounted slowly up the beams of the scrapers in the sky. The last sunrays retreated.

Time slipped, time slipped.

Summer was almost gone.

Miles was able to summon the full force gale; but the waning of his powers, the end of his heaven, was ever near.

The End was chasing him. Hounding him in the time slipstream.

It was dark.

There was a strong wind. The feel of cold; whistling pressure.

Flow ripping the air. Nothing moving in stone corridors. In this realm, not a tree to stir. Only naked masses of stone. This was the feeling of the moment.

Miles held a news conference, a Moonlight Sonata in this.

The Moonlight Sonata

MILES HELD A NEWS CONFERENCE, to give power to his punch. He had to show the world all the love that was in his heart. And show them a heart drowning in love dreams.

Time slipping, time slipping.

In the now . . . He has to let it rip, for all to see. He steps up, concentrates. Builds up, builds up. He has to bring them into slow sensation. Into a heart drowning in love dreams.

Time slipping, time slipping.

Take it into the now of the moment. He steps into the light. The beams are on him.

Nobody else here, baby. This wave was all his. Just him and the *light-vision.* It was his to do. He had to take them into slow sensation.

Shake them out of their rut, and take them into slow sensation.

He would will them to take a good strong look at this child.

It was time for soundshape. *But first, must come the feeling,* Miles thought.

He seized upon the fury of the moment, and formed a big generator. A mighty engine. And he let the engine hum.

Feeling, stretching out—past the shades of willow trees—shattered the night—attacked masses of stone. And cascaded on. Rending. Throbbing. Resounding. A heatwave tearing loose.

Moving.

Time slipping, time rending.

This was aimed straight for the Night Sun, the Cosmic All, and sweet Lady Day.

He threw himself into it.

Astral fields come away!

The boy took them into it, into slow sensation.

Heatwave, white lightning, when he moved, he moved everything.

He formed a big generator. Such a strange generator. Striking.

The Big Generator, cruising through the night.

Miles, moving up from under, he took it up high, until it began to crack apart, and let rip, in slow, slow style:

The Double Lung Scream.

This was the beginning, an exploding *double lung scream;* white lightning, bound to drive you wild. And a heart drowning in love dreams. Drowning, dying, in slow, slow style. Dying, dying, dying.

And the double lung scream—

Extending, extending, extending.

On and on it goes. On and on. Stretching, stretching, extending.

Reaching. In slow, slow style.

He was screaming, screaming, screaming, . . . screaming, . . . screaming . . . screaming wild.

A song of longing for.

The twilight washed off the buildings.

They rose, thin shafts of blue—and the colors of evening and dis-tance. They rose in bare outlines, breaking upward, taking existence into a world without curves.

The single shafts, stood tall, broke out of the earth. They were of their own, and held up to the sky a statement of what people could conceive and bring into the world. The people had come so far—and could go far-ther. The forest city on the edge of the sky held out a question—and a promise.

A will to beauty, a raw presence.

Into this, Miles hurled the force of his being.

The people of the *light*vision caught the extending.

On this street, where time had died, he let it fly.

The street was cold, dark had won.

Miles let it fly.

A heatwave, white lightning.

And there it was. Growing, growing, growing.

Tearing loose.

Out and away.

Argh, remember! The feeling had come. Slow sensation exploding in slow, slow style. Up. Up. Up.

A sound sunburst flowering. Emerging. Rising.

Argh, remember! Come on home. Your place is here, it sang.

The winds of life were coming back. Sweeping in. Taking the mo-ment into cool rapidity. Rending through flowering slow sensation.

And they were there, the people who watched, they were suddenly in the station. A place of . . . a power station, . . . and shockwaves. Of heat-waves, and white lightning.

And in the station, the boy. And this boy could move, everything.

When he moved, it was a sin, so sweet and true.

A song . . . deep and rich and blue.

A song, . . . deep, and rich, and true.

They lay in it for days, *A Pacifica Love Dream Experience.*

The audience, they were, well, being experienced.

Argh, remember! Come on home. Your place is here, it sang.

And grew.

C'mon home. You got to come on home. Ooh, c'mon home.

C'mon, Bring it on home.

Argh, don't forget, no! Come home. Come along, and come home.

The howl.

Going, going, going. A fire. Ascending the brightest heaven of invention. In slow, slow style.

The city moving away. In the vast emptiness of sky and ocean, the city was only a small, jagged solid. It seemed condensed, pressed tight together, not a place of streets and separate buildings, but a single sculptured form. A form of irregular steps that rose and dropped without ordered continuity, long ascensions and sudden drops, like the planes and realizations of a stubborn struggle. But it went on mounting—toward a few points, toward the triumphant masts of skyscrapers raised out of the struggle.

He saw it.

He felt it.

He let it rip.

The way he moved, it was a sin, so sweet and true. In slow, slow style.

He knew how to move, everything.

Always wanting more, he'd leave you longing for, slow, slow style.

Heatwave, white lightning, bound to drive you wild.

The way he moved, always wanting more, he'd leaving you longing for slow, slow style.

Every word of the song that he sang was . . . for *you.* In a flash it was gone.

A slow, slow style. Springing wild. Screaming wild. It was here, and then it was gone.

And coming out of the shockwave: *Miles Roark.*

In a slow, slow style.

Can you feel it?

Can you beat it?

It was an impressive display of insanity.

Let's keep the crazy train rolling, the world screamed.

The *light*vision bounced back to the anchor desk:

"Have you seen this before?"

Bryan J'nnings—turned from the *omniscio* to a fellow barker, Mister Linus Gravitas—His eyes held little interest. But, Linus played it up.

"Oh, no, this definitely is a first on a certain level, yes, yes, oh yes. Yes. Yes. On a visual, and I would say on a sound level."

Bryan ate up the analysis as if it were a seven-course meal, and then he turned to the show's leading expert on human affairs and the world stage.

Anchor Bryan J'nnings was now turning to their most absolutely expert barker—Mister Gennarino Kar'Uhnckio. Who was being beamed in on an omniscio. "What's your view Gennarino?" He tossed an aside to the audience . . . "We all know that Mister Kar'Uhnckio has seen just about every kind of twist and turn."

"Well, what he's saying is obvious," Gennarino Kar'Uhnckio offered, generously. "I'm afraid what he's saying is very obvious. And I'm afraid it's nothing we haven't heard before. Just the sounds are different this time." Their expert on human affairs and the world stage had spoken. So let it be said, so let it be written. Let the word go forth, Kar'Uhnckio had—determined.

The anchor nodded, and reacted like this was the most goddamn insightful thing he had ever heard in his life—

Kar'Uhnckio held his gaze steady in the *light*vision. He might have cleared his throat.

Kar'Uhnckio had determined what was obvious using expert methods.

He let his wisdom go shining on. Generously embalming it in the substance of fire.

But such subtleties may have been left for the more captivated observers . . . left . . . for the more . . .—oh, something was happening—

Bryan broke off, taking it back to Miles Roark . . . "Let's go back to the conference, Roark appears to be wrapping it up."

They cut back to Miles—Miles was standing on a riser. *I put a spell on you, I put a spell on you, because you're mine.* This was the feeling he was casting into a thick silence. He was waiting for the sky to fall down. Once it settled to a nice, quiet still repose of dead silence, he tore the silence softly. And what he said was:

"There's a hell of a good universe, next door.
"What do you say we take a trip over, and have a look?"

Then Miles smiled. Or at least it seemed like he smiled. But as a matter of fact, he did nothing that he hadn't been doing already. And the son of a bitch didn't do another thing for a good long time. He stood there and smiled. If you could call it a smile.

THE SEEKER IN FOREVER

Cinjun Smythe—Come Out Of Your Cave

"SET IT FREE, CINJUN! Set it free." He said it plainly. He didn't add anything to the words except their plain, and apparent color.

"Why do you keep holding on so tightly? Set it free, Cinjun, set it free. Let it be, Cinjun, why don't you?————"

You can't talk to a man with a shotgun in his hand. He thinks he knows how everything is going to be.

C'mon, Cinjun, come out of your cave.

Hear this Shotgun Man: C'mon out of your clubhouse. C'mon out of your warm bed, and step into the arena.

Cinjun, let my people see you.

Come out of your fortress, come out of your tank. Come out of your safehouse. Come out of your stronghold.

Come out of your warm bed. Come out of your house. Come out from behind your gate, and guards. And see the world. Come see the world Cinjun Smythe, it's out here waiting for you.

It's your turn to step up and take it.

Awake, Cinjun Smythe. Shake dreams from your head. Enter the world. Enter the hot landscape.

I know you're comfortable in your bed. It's nice and warm and soft. But you say you're a champion and a champion does not stay in bed all morning.

All your ways, . . . but lead to bed. Up and out and back to bed again.

Though you go in pride and strength, you come back to bed at length.

Though you shout in mighty woe, back to bed you're bound to go.

High, you toss your head, but all your days but lead to bed.

Up and out and then back to bed again.

Let's go to the ledge, let's go to the precipice. Come my nemesis, let's go to the edge.

C'mon Cinjun, step up. It's your turn to step up and take it.

It was an impressive display of insanity, and it didn't matter in the least—It got covered like all the other world happenings out there.

The Barkers spoke of it in the same terms and degrees of heat as everything else. Everything was equated to everything else in value for attention. And through this means of treatment, none could gain enough velocity and power to hold the reveal of true meaning—thus none of it had the reveal of true meaning because contrast was lost. They covered it in the way they covered all things—with 'some say this' and 'some say that.' Everything was held in equal value; it did not matter if one side came to you with truth and the other side with the unreal; it didn't matter if one side came to you with the stuff of cosmic matters and the other side with the stuff of velvet-lined buckets of bull mud. And in this way they ensured that nothing got said.

The Barkers had no other way of operating in how they covered this world's unfolding events. They believed they had been trained in *reporting,* but only the very few good ones had made themselves into Sound Chasers; most had only received their training in *repeating.*

"I don't understand what he's saying," one Barker said.

"He's very unclear in his message," another Barker said.

It didn't matter who did the talking—It followed the ancient patterns—and the safe, allowed pattern search—

'He doesn't explain what he wants, and once he gets what he wants, what is he going to do?'—'You can only go on screaming for so long— It's nice—But what is he about? I think that's what he has to discuss'—'I think the scream has to be the beginning—He has to prove that he's about more than the scream'—

'I agree. I feel the scream was nothing.'

Cinjun Makes a Move

CINJUN WAS NOT A THICK-HEADED MAN. He was one of the rarer forms of man—he was a genius. A true genius. And he applied himself.

He did not allow the talk of the Barkers to make events mush. In his way, he saw clearly. And knew when to produce changes.

Cinjun turned to Skyler and said, "Let's send the come-from-nowhere guy back to nowhere."

To perfect nowhere. To winning nowhere. To absolutely, beautiful, tastefully decorated nowhere. To Nothingsville. To Nobody Town.

Now Skyler descended to the courtyard, and brought himself to a point a pace away from Miles.

Miles turned and looked at Skyler with some passing interest.

"You're on, Miles!" Skyler said.

And waited for a reaction.

He didn't get anything.

This Miles was made of something dense, Skyler thought.

Miles looked at Skyler. Skyler drew a breath.

"Cinjun wants you," Skyler said, "to drink your orange juice, eat your vegetables and keep your mouth shut—for now, if you have any control over that thing wasting space on your chin—Hold yourself together and if you can do that you'll get a chance to debate him—"

Skyler held his look on Miles. Miles did nothing.

"We'll get it on . . ." Skyler said. "You follow?"

Miles did nothing.

"Good," Skyler said. "Now are we clear? We'll get it on. And then he's going to ram his fist so far down your throat it will take you a week to get it out."

Miles looked at him.

Skyler prepared to leave.

"Do you want to say anything?" Skyler said. "Before we end this social."

"Yes, did you ever think you'd see a day," Miles said, "when you had so much trouble trying to say something clever in plain English?"

That was all Miles said.

It got to Skyler. Got to him something fierce. Miles didn't have to do anything else. He looked at Skyler and waited for him to leave.

Skyler might have said a few other things. Or he might not have. Skyler was mad as hell. He might have said something. Don't ask Miles. Miles wasn't paying attention.

Miles was wondering if it was time to take this trip to the next phase.

At the pace Skyler was setting, nothing would get done fast. And probably nothing of import would happen after that, if Miles followed the trail they were carving for him.

Cinjun was taking control. And if Cinjun was taking control that could only mean one thing: This was now going to go where Cinjun wanted to take it.

Peace Pose

CINJUN UNDERSTOOD the Peace Craze that was killing the country. It would blow over.

The Peace Craze was nothing. The Love Craze was nothing. They would pass.

Love is like a cigarette . . . Has your heart aglow, burns to ashes. Ashes of regret. So much for love—it held the value of ashes, when you priced it high. Cinjun laughed. Love was for master criminals, a pose to defy the law. Defy order. Order was everything. Cinjun knew how to put the world in order.

It needed a good strongman in charge.

New strongman for sale. Strength that's new and fresh and bold. He would boldly go where no strongman had gone before. To god emperor and an era of peace. The kind of peace that remained stable, at the point of a gun.

Cinjun laughed again. It was amusing how fools might fall for love dreams.

Cinjun was proofed against it. Pharaoh's heart was hardened.

He would rule the known world. So let it be written, so let it be done.

He would employ master builders, and build a world. Naysayers could go live outside. He would send them to the black void.

It would all be easy, part of his moving on.

They would get gone for good. They would get dead. He saw the battlefield then. A beautiful battlefield, the most beautiful the world would ever see. And above—a Crimson Sun.

He was the most important man that had ever lived or ever shall live.

And he strode forward under a Crimson Sun to a House Crimson.

Love took you to hands and knees on the floor. Some majesty it offered. Ugly and small.

Revenge is a dish best served cold.

It was time to trap Miles Roark.

He was conspiring a trap for Miles Roark. He was moving with care, allowing it to take shape in the fullness of time. And when the time was ripe, he would stop Miles Roark, softly.

Softly.

He would proceed in steps. And then he would stop Miles Roark.

Softly.

Cinjun would move in deliberate, driving steps. Wise, strong, cunning steps.

Cinjun deliberate—

Miles was striking on impulse, where he might. That was evidence of enormous weakness. Cinjun would use it to stop Miles. Miles's talk was scattered, random. That evidenced weakness, he left open many strike points.

Cinjun saw the many ways to manipulate Miles Roark.

To take all the force out of his assault.

Miles's arrows went wide. Cinjun would hit the mark, again and again. There would be no relenting, no missing, and no mercy given to his enemy.

This would end with Miles stopped and Cinjun victorious, stronger.

Battles go to the strong, races go to the swift. Speed kills your opponent, dead. Explosive power kills your opponent, dead.

Miles would get dead.

Blows had a cumulative effect. Blood would be taken, and taken, and taken. Cunning move after cunning move, it would add up.

Cinjun knew these smells. He knew these signs of battle. Now they were in his game. Playing on his field. This Miles was fighting out of his weight class. He would make Miles cry like a baby. Nothing less would do . . . This was good versus evil. And Cinjun's belief sustained him. He would triumph. And destroy, so that he might build. He was fighting for peace . . . and nothing less.

But Peace was a bloody business, full of death and destruction. That was Peace. But to live in peace, that was a great thing. A great gun.

Cinjun fought on the side of peace.

Peace was slaughter.

It had to be. He wished it could be different. But he had tried it, it didn't work.

Now, he would reap peace with blood and sword, and, . . . uhm, . . . gold. Peace was expensive.

Peace was written in slaughter and beauty, beauty with a fist.

He loved exacting peace with a good strong violent blow.

He loved breaking a nose for peace. God, he loved Peace!

Peace costs lives. Everyone knew that this Miles had crazy ideas. Dangerous ideas.

He had to silence Miles . . . stop him . . . in order for peace to sing its song of love and glory. Glory was the thing he sought, this Cinjun Smythe being. He would smite the wicked, and that was his glory. That was why he was the most important man in the world. The most important man that had ever lived, or ever shall live.

His peace would go marching on.

Slaughter leading on to slaughter. Bringing peace leading on to peace, in this way all would be peace.

That was the idea. Brilliant? Cinjun knew it was.

Slaughter, sad, but necessary. If only there were another way! But the ends would justify the means. Bringing peace leading on to peace, all would be peace.

That was the idea. Brilliant?
Cinjun knew it was.

Cinjun, Speaking for the Record
Talking fight and right and might

"HE'S A NOWHERE MAN." Cinjun held himself poised, holding a *light*vision interview in his Octagon Office.

"He's heading to nowhere fast. You can keep adding zero to zero for a long time and still end up with zero."

Cinjun was determined to be orderly about it. This was about putting Miles in his place. Putting him in his box. And naming him, the nowhere man.

"I just hope he keeps well and I sure hope he shows up."

Abruptly, noise came from the corridor.

The double door came open.

Miles appeared at the door.

Cinjun came on alert.

Miles stepped into the Octagon Office, and with him Cinjun saw a flow of people. People entering. *Light*vision crews making themselves known in the throng.

Cinjun held himself in readiness.

Miles stepped into the office. One step. And this amounted to a tremendous disturbance. The mere fact that he had entered Cinjun's office was huge. Miles let that work for him. He didn't do anything more for a good long while.

People flowed in around Miles. Presently, the walls of the Octagon Office became lined with a perimeter of people.

The people moved their attention to Cinjun.

And now—

Cinjun does nothing. Cinjun does a lot of nothing. He's coiled. He's on the verge of doing many things, but he holds himself. He does nothing, nothing immediate.

And the people wonder, what's coming?

Cinjun lifts a glass from the table and has a taste of tea.

They are moving to a full-scale confrontation. He's aware of the showdown and what that means. He's aware of what moments are coming. He's going to move in deliberate steps, with great care, assurance, poise and dignity. There is no need for him to do anything. In fact, he's more powerful if he stays still. To not get heated, that's what he's working at. To not spring recklessly. To not waste movement. To not waste effort. To not kill Miles Roark. Cinjun is solid. That's his pose.

"You want to feel like the big man." Miles said, giving him plain, laid back talk. "Come on big man. Let's debate. It's all over. Let's get it on.

"Cinjun," Miles said, "let's get it on now. You throw in yours; I'll throw in mine. Only one makes it out alive. C'mon, make it. C'mon!"

Cinjun burned, in a controlled inferno of rage.

"No," Cinjun said. Cinjun took another taste of tea. He would allow Miles the moment, because it would serve Cinjun's designs. This made it more of a grudge match. Fine. This made the battle more necessary. For those who understood little of what was truly going on, it made it more of a grudge match. Fine.

"You want to feel like the big man. Come on big man. Let's get it on now. No more playing around."

"I'm not fond of your manner," Cinjun said.

"I've had complaints about it," Miles said, "but nothing seems to help."

"Some prefer it more honorable," Cinjun said.

Miles smiled. "Oh, is that what it's called nowadays?"

"Don't let everyone know what a fool you are. Hide it a while longer. Your springing-in-the-sun days are almost over; night is drawing near."

"Hell, Cinjun, what's the point in waiting? Let's get it on. Let's hit it right here and now. C'mon let's go."

And in the primal flow of the now—

The house guard enter the arena and carefully approach Miles.

Cinjun holds up a hand. The house guard cease their movements. He motions for them to withdraw. They pull back, into the mountains. Miles stands as he was; he hasn't moved at all.

The house guard stand back—ready, but away from Miles.

Cinjun rises from his chair; comes to full attention, standing tall and straight, chest out, chin high, full command stance.

Something about Cinjun's approach seems to be saying, 'Look at this upstart. Isn't he horrible? I'll show you how I deal with this kind of traitor, homegrown traitor.'

Cinjun reacts with deadly seriousness. He smiles. He's charming. But he is deadly. Someone could get hurt. Cinjun will restore order through the force of his will alone.

Cinjun crosses to Miles, and stops, holding Miles in a locked gaze.

"Now Miles, listen to me. We will fight at the event. Do you understand me?"

Cinjun talks to Miles now as if Miles had burst in brandishing a gun.

'Watch out Cinjun, stay away from him,' they murmur. Cinjun waves them to silence. "You made your point Roark. Is there anything else you wanted?"

Miles smiles. He's finished. "Excellent, Cinjun. You handled that very well."

Leaving The Sans Souci Plaza

"WHAT WAS THAT ABOUT?" His friend asked him about the changes . . . *What is going on? What are you doing?* . . . "Why did you do that?" the friend asked Miles.

"Cinjun has been boasting," Miles said, "that he's afraid of no man alive. And, everybody is scared of him—He goes into every fight feeling strong, feeling sure.

"I figured if I act crazy on him, that would scare him, because you never know what an insane man is going to do. You have to fear an insane man—*he doesn't care what you do to him.*"

"We want it to be everything it can be," Miles said. "That's what Cinjun will make it now. When he comes at me, he'll come at me with everything he's got. He'll spare nothing."

"You mean," the friend asked, "you want him to give you trouble?"

"I want him to give me his best. If I can stand up to his best, then I'm really standing."

He was the changeling. See him change. Change taking place. Root yourself to the ground. Taking the song to keen rhythm. Taking the song into harmonic changes.

"He has everything going for him," Miles said. "I want him to feel it might not be enough." Miles was striding. "I want him to come at me with his best. I want him to throw everything he has at me. I want his full might, his full force gale, I want to match wits with a maelstrom, a whirlwind, a tornado. I want Cinjun to go after me with everything he's got . . .

"So I get in his face," Miles said. "I keep coming at him. I do not relent . . .

"And he steps up his game. I get him at the top of his form." Miles was striding and his friend was striding at his side. They were leaving The Sans Souci Plaza. "That's a battle," Miles said.

He was the changeling. See him change. Change taking place. Root yourself to the ground.

Fortune and fate and marshall forces—took to the changes, and drove them into distance. Into long, lonely distance.

Movements formed, created traps. Loaded the dangers. And took the world into the unknown. Into mystery. Into sidewinding.

Some who witnessed the wild breeze, gave Miles a name. They called him *the sidewinder*. They did not fill their tone with kindness.

They ached for Cinjun Smythe to show the sidewinder the wages of sin.

Cinjun Smythe took himself to readiness. He produced a smile. Quickened his energy, and allowed his strong life force to become a House Crimson.

The sidewinder was destined to get dead in House Crimson, Cinjun thought. And Cinjun's eyes took on great life. He was about to enjoy himself. Enjoy himself indeed.

You could depend on Cinjun Smythe to enjoy himself.

He was the god emperor savior. He was their god—And he reached into the life of god. He would enjoy himself indeed.

He got into his god car, and drove into distance, into long distance.

Which he crossed with great speed. Growing in strength as he traveled. Into distance, into long distance.

He was the god emperor of the world that peopled.

Time stretched out before him, and called him to journey.

Murder by the roadside, would speak of his progress as he sowed a brave new world.

He was the god emperor of the world that peopled. And he moved into distance, into long distance.

And he moved with the sweetest movement the world had ever seen.

Act Three

His Scandalous Sidewinding

Windsprinting

"THIS IS WHERE it comes together; this determines all that will follow."

Miles was running down the country road. Running fast. Beside him, a friend, Grimaldi, kept pace. And a few paces behind them, proceeding steadily, was Scofield.

Miles was running, and tasting forever in his run. "Yes sir, this is where it all starts. Right here in training. What happens here determines all that is going to happen after."

It was early morning. Sunrise was carving through the air. Running on the air with flair. Traveling true. Settling. Then again passing through, leaving, leading down the trail.

The trail stretched out before them, carving, streaming into the country. Traveling. Broken trail so long. Into country vastness.

Now pounding rhythm coming down the open road, heading out, stepping on out. Miles was running. Running fast. Grimaldi was holding his pace at a matching, burning clip.

Miles was finding the place, with the aim of staying sure and fast, pounding out a rhythm, leading down the trail.

Driving it to performance level. Only pressure can take it to where it needs to go.

It has to be about carrying the train off the track. Carrying the world out of orbit. It's heavy duty work. It takes tremendous will and ability.

Don't give it up. Don't give in. No one touches all you are. Let me show you how you make me feel! Whoa, rhythm is his business.

Don't give it up. Don't give in. A sidewinder windsprinting.

Miles Roark—there—showing all he is. Grimaldi—there—working it, showing all he is.

Windsprinting is the heart and soul of the business, Miles thought. That's what you have to be able to do. You need to be able to burst. To be a sunburst. To explode. To tear loose and go far.

Rhythm is his business.

He's got to learn how to sprint.

How to burst. How to explode through the changes.

Rhythm is his business.

Laughing, oh how the wind was laughing. Roaring. This uncommon breeze—the kind that does with hearts whatever it pleases.

Now pounding rhythm coming down the open road, heading out, stepping on out.

Wind changing, rearranging lives.

A sidewinder's windsprinting.

Wind sprints.

You have to train your body to recover under stress.

Miles was there, fixing up some rhythm cocktails.

Rhythm is his business. No more sleepy head. Take care of everything.

'Don't look for me. I'll be shooting ahead.' Remember, darling, rhythm is his business. Don't look for him. He'll be shooting ahead. Racing. Remember, darling, rhythm is his business.

Grimaldi was also finding the place. But finding that he could not make it last. "I'm going to cut out for a minute or two." Grimaldi said. "My doctor says it's okay to push yourself; but when it becomes a strain, you better quit."

"Your doctor doesn't know what he's talking about," Miles said.

Miles is running. Rhythm is his business. Rhythm that can make you go insane. Upside, inside, out. A fine devil crazy.

Got to.

Got to.

Got to.

Rhythm is his business.

Got to.

Got to.

Got to.

C'mon.

Sprinting to wild rhythm. Exploding. Rhythm is his business.

"The doctor told me to cut out when it becomes a strain."

"Some do—but your doctor doesn't know what the hell he's talking about. Life is a strain. You have to train your body to recover under strain. You follow?"

"No—"

"That's what you want to do, is strain. You want to run until your heart is bleeding and breaking, and no good at all. You want to run until it pains."

Miles was running. Tasting the run. Tasting the pain. Grimaldi was keeping up with him, seeing what the trip was all about.

"You want to keep running until your legs are in absolute pain. That's the way that it's meant to be."

Miles was tasting the run. Tasting all the pain. Grimaldi was getting the trip.

"Hear the story; that's the way it has to be. The run has to get into your inside—You have to go—you got to get it on the inside. You have to strain. Until you're going to die, until you're killing everything; until you're going to fall out. Run until you stumble."

They were both running. Both at their limits. Both in agony. Now Grimaldi knew where Miles was going with this. Grimaldi was getting it on the inside—Some called it a heart attack.

"Until your heart starts coming apart; feels like you can't go another pace, can't go another step. Keep going. Feels like you're going to fall down in your tracks, then after that, you've only gotten started; that's when you've got to create the rhythm grooves. That's when you have to go to work. That's when it begins."

Grimaldi—to his horror—suddenly saw where this was all leading. Against his will he was suddenly thrown into a course straight there—

Abruptly he was stumbling and stumbling forward—

He was tumbling to the ground—

Rolling uncontrollably—

Until he crashed into a tree.

And settled comfortably into ground agony.

. . . The tree wasn't hurt too bad.

"Come . . . on . . . man," Miles said . . . between gasps.

Miles danced around his fallen friend.

"Come . . . on, . . . mumbles! Don't you taste it? Aren't you starting to taste it? . . ."

"Ah . . . ah . . . .." Grimaldi is now empty of breath. He can't spare enough breath to speak.

"Ah, rest easy," Miles said. "You're off to a good start. Tomorrow we'll really see what you can do. No more fooling around. Tomorrow we really do it."

And in the now—

Miles turns away. *Rhythm is his business.* He moves, whirls, cuts, runs.

Ah, yeah. Got to take a ride. Get on the inside. Get it on the inside.

Rhythm is his business. Got to get it on the inside.

Miles takes his run to Scofield. "Come on, Sco. Let's hit it." He runs a ring around Scofield. Scofield just keeps running along at exactly the same pace. And gives Miles a look. Miles races ahead, leaving Scofield behind, far behind.

A few horizons down the road, Miles begins to really appreciate the scenery—there is nothing else he can do!—Miles is collapsed against a tree, completely out of breath.

Now Scofield runs by—cool, steady and solid. Scofield gives Miles the same look again.

"Pace yourself kid," Scofield says. "You'll go longer"—*Rhythm is his business* too.

He leaves Miles there.

Miles holds his gaze on Scofield's departing figure—You can't "burst" like that. That was no way to "burst" through the changes. It's too planned. Ah, Sco is a show-off. A rotten show-off who runs a lot. That's not a fine devil crazy. That's not sprinting to wild rhythm. That's not it at all.

Now Miles yelled a little something to Scofield who was whipping into the distance at a steady clip, floating away with uncommon velocity. "I don't go longer!" Miles said. "I go to a finish line! And call it a day! I'm not going to spend my whole life out here! Running like a fool! Like some old bastard that hasn't got anything better to do!"

Then to himself, he says, "Damn him, damn, that old man really knows—nothing to it—but, damn, he knows—"

Miles falls over, onto a pile of leaves. He has spent the last of his breath.

Miles lies there, alone with the situation.

Cinjun Forming

"EVERYTHING IS SET. You watch," Cinjun says.

Now Cinjun turns it over in his mind; does a lot of holding still. His manipulations are paying off. It's *harvest time.* He's plucking the fruits of his labors. Of *their* labors.

"Just you watch." Cinjun does a lot of nothing. "They will come and do everything we want. Watch. You'll see. I know them. I know what they're about." Cinjun knows that when he shows up, they will all be on his side. "Yes, we will do very well."

All his difficulties were behind him. That is how Cinjun feels.

He's throwing a party and everything is coming together. He's getting the best barkers money can buy.

God emperor is his business.

And it's an easy business for him. It suits him. All is going right. Breezy.

Now he would underplay it; that was what was left for Cinjun to do. The whole operation was in place; the wheels were turning smoothly; the big generator was humming along. He was being proclaimed a god emperor. Now he would underplay it. He would let it work all around him and play humbly within it.

Life was perfect; absolutely goddamn perfect.

Cinjun is feeling comfortable. Feeling "right." Everything is nice. Ah, yeah. Oh, so nice. He's giving Miles some space. We'll make it a big, fantastic show—and then he'll beat Miles down to size. It appears Miles is not as weak as you would imagine—so much the better. Cinjun is feeling a thrill. It's aim your rifle; lock target; fire! He's getting Miles in his scope. Setting his sights. Going to shoot him. It's a nice thrilling hunt. A fox hunt and Cinjun is the lord of the manor.

"I'll tell you how we'll handle this . . ." He knows how to do this work. He has trained his body and mind. He is ready. All is right.

He's mounting a great show. It's going to be a blockbuster. Spectacular. Brilliant. Altogether excellent!

Cinjun described how they would move into the ceremony and how they would produce their effect.

Creating god feelings, god being that radiates feelings . . . that produces reverence . . . that leads to sanctity.

Keening ceremony. Sharp, brave ceremony. Keen sensations everywhere.

Part of the ceremony is setting light to Cinjun while burning Miles to ashes. Cinjun will make ash of Miles in the *after spin.*

In his training, Cinjun acts as if the battle is over. Because he *knows* the battle is over. The lessons of war history—tell the tale. Most battles are won or lost before the first shot is fired. —The setup is everything.

He's going to kill. He always kills. What he works on, is the effect, the after spin, the after battle. Victory being another word for the process—Where should it go, once he takes care of the victory. What's next? Who's next? He sends his energies into the pattern search and the prime projections.

The ceremony is already shaping itself as he wants it.

He wants a panel of top newscasters. He's getting them. He wants to bring out crews and reporters. He's getting them.

He's getting some true heavy hitters for the Barkers.

It's going to be a big, large, mammoth thing.

He's in demand. Very popular. He has built it, and now they will come.

He's going to fill the biggest arena in town.

They're coming for him. Miles doesn't matter at all. Cinjun just hopes Miles can go the distance.

The difficulty for Cinjun now is to hold back. To let the forces work for him. *Don't look like you're working,* Cinjun thought. Don't look like you're in any difficulty whatsoever. Now let the forces work and be loose of muscle within it all. Stay loose. Stay sporting.

Let the audience do the work; let the people do the work of building him up. Of enlarging his image. Let the reporters do the work; let his minions do the work. Now his job was to hold back; to underplay; to be at ease within the seat of power.

God emperor is his business. And he knows how to play it.

Now everything is aligned around him; he has to hold himself back.

The way to play the god emperor is to underplay being the god emperor.

At House Crimson, the executive committee was meeting to decide how to build up the great debate.

Sidney said, "Let's make Miles sound big—an immense danger—so that when you cut him down, you can play up the victory."

Now when Sidney proposes this thing, of making Miles an immense danger—Cinjun is immediately driven to the edge of violence—it can't go that way at all! It would make no sense whatsoever. He's the god emperor and he's supposed to make this nothing, this Miles Roark, a possible danger. Cinjun with all his powers and Miles with nothing and he's supposed to make Miles into a danger?

He wants to do violence to Sidney. He becomes so goddamn enraged. But he holds it. He controls himself. He speaks softly. And plays things on a small scale. He knows how it has to go now. He must be the underplaying god emperor.

He just puts Sidney in his place.

"I'm not going to make a mouse into a lion."

In the evening, Cinjun makes a *light*vision appearance.

And when he is asked about Miles by a reporter, he must be certain and godlike but play it small. Play it simple. Play it plain.

He says, "He's new. If your memory only extends back to breakfast. He's a showman. He's going to use a lot of bright lights and opening acts. Tricks. That's what they are. I'm going to arrive as myself and demolish him with rightness. Right is might."

Cinjun was as charming as could be.

The Sex Between Skyler and Lori . . .

IN THE MORNING, LORI STROLLED BY SKYLER, as he emerged from the washroom. He had just prettied himself up for an important business day.

"You look," she said, "like something heavy and flat hit you in the face."

She was searching for something this morning. Could she ever live without naughtiness? No.

Her days were drifting.

Her nights coasting.

She noticed that Skyler was a busy boy. A very busy boy. He was constant business, and aspiration, and ambition. Very admirable. In the evening, Skyler told her of coming glory. He was moving into a winning streak. He hoped to move her. To arouse her—

"Business is dull—" Lori said, "besides, I hear you're going to lose. Don't spend so much time on it."

"We're going to destroy him," Skyler said.

"Really, have you got something on him—a scandal?"

"No, a slap."

"Watch out for his looks," she said.

"Why should I care about his looks?"

"Because he looks like he slaps back."

Skyler held her look.

"Why don't you go rest your sex appeal?" Lori said. "Before you hurt me." She shook his tree. If you looked fast, you would see it go limp.

She didn't believe in winning streaks; she didn't believe in working streaks—oh, get her out of there! Take her straight to a fun streak!

Skyler was working. Let him. He was an industrious boy, out to prove himself in this big old world.

Lori—was out to dig for soul, and sex, and sin, and all the other good things in crime.

She kissed the warm night. Dug for her soul there in the corner of a fine restaurant, there in the balcony of a fine theater, there among her friends. They dug for soul among society changes.

Among fashions.

Among styles.

Among men and women, spouses and playboys, lovers and contenders.

Among rascals, scoundrels, and strong drink.

Into this realm, entered a certain party hound. A playboy. He was a walking show. When he talked, he played to a gallery. His name was Francisco.

"I've come to town for two important reasons," Francisco told Lori, "a coat check girl at the Cub Club and the sandwiches—I'm a meat eater."

She instantly became slow sensation. Lori found him interesting—enough to slap. She brought blood to his lip. And pain he would not soon forget.

Presently, Francisco was pulling up to a seated Lori. In one of the dark corners, of one of the fine dark restaurants.

As he took over a seat, he looked at her. As he would look at precious art, that he would like to acquire.

She slapped him again. Almost. He stopped her as she moved into the motion. And he slapped himself. Then smiled.

She did nothing. Revealed nothing.

He spoke to her and her friends of day trips to strange forbidden places. And he lured the group of friends out to one spot.

He didn't tell them where they were going. She discovered that the trip was to: a nudist colony.

On a sun-splashed beach filled with naked people, Lori was sitting when Francisco appeared in the corner of her vision. She didn't look at him. He made a motion. She glanced at where his hand had been and now there was a picture there. She turned it over. It was a tongue.

"This is a poor move," Lori said, "who's tongue is this?"

"Mine."

"I hate it."

He drew near. Met her eyes.

"Little Red Riding Hood goes out into the forest," Francisco said, "but this time she's hiding a gun in her package of goodies, ready for action. The wolf follows her into the woods and grabs her from behind. *'Now that I've got you I'm going to fuck you until dawn,'* he growls. But Little Red Riding Hood pulls out the gun, holds it to his head and says, *'No, you're not. You're going to eat me like the story said.' "*

Lori looked at Franscisco with a level gaze. She revealed nothing.

Nearby, her friends laughed. They were some nice young ladies who had been listening to the story.

"You," Lori said, "remind me of my daddy." She revealed nothing more.

Nothing

AS OFTEN HAPPENS, NOTHING HAPPENED . . . for a while.

The autumn leaves were coming.

The autumn leaves were coming into the world.

Dancing to the Midnight Whirlpool

LATELY, DAPHNE HAD LOOKED AROUND.

Got to seeing, wondering.

Lately, the look in *his eyes* disturbed her. Disturbed Daphne all to hell.

Something in his eyes. Shimmered with blue skies and the wings of her fate.

She wondered what she was seeing.

In Miles Roark.

Lately.

Daphne was thinking, got to feeling.

Her thoughts turned to Miles. She chased the thoughts away.

Desire developed an edge.

He was a monster, she thought. She was a princess, queen of the by-ways, she told herself. It did nothing.

Desire developed an edge.

It could not continue, she said. It did.

Desire developed an edge.

Someone else might make love almost as sharply.

She, might meet him some summer. And he might whisper in her ear. She told herself—it did nothing.

Miles, remained.

Somewhere in his look—a madness was clear—And somewhere—All the feelings you could find, all the lies that came in hot moments, all that you could see chasing you in loving moments, . . . all the love that you could find in all your life. All that could rise and fall.

She was the kind of girl who knew what she wanted. And where to go. She wanted Miles Roark.

In pieces rough and tumble. She wanted his feet upon her stage. It was elemental. Pull. Push and pull. A force so fine. A gift to last forever.

But she was not going to get weepy and willowy on him.

When she stood before him, she stood with arms thrown back. She was—defiance. And devil mirth.

Loving arms?

No, she threw him across a table when he came.

She lit the torch and burned the table night.

Oh, well, he smiled and came again.

He, turned to her.

She, turned to him.

They danced around each other, similar prowls.

They were friendly with sounds you would never know.

Changes falling out of the blue.

I want to make love to you!

Fascination.

I want to make love to you!

Moments running through their heads.

The world is crazy. Only one thing I want to do. I want to make love to you! I can't stand to be here without you!

It moved.

I can't stand to be without you, baby. You—who's got a feeling for me.

It moved.

The world stood crazy. Howled and wailed.

Insanity's horse adorned the night. They tumbled into an endless roll.

On the bed, deeper and deeper.

Touch!

Sense and skin!

Release and swelling seas!

Driving dreams through the changes.

Fascination for limits of love. Taking them deeper and deeper, and deeper into her. She was intoxication.

The bed beneath them.

Silk, satin, sheets, a frontier swirl. And dancing into the midnight whirlpool, the two most beautiful people in the world.

They kissed the changes that shaped their lives!

All around, rise and fall—all the lies you find, all that you can see, all was rise and fall.

They were traveling deeper and deeper.

They went.

Deeper and deeper.

Further and further.

Nearer and nearer.

Run run run.

Burn burn burn.

Soon soon soon.

They were drifting and drifting.

Farther and farther.

Nearer and nearer.

A swinging sway. Force and swirl. A force to find, a triumph to tear your mind. All deep down the river.

Care to fall in love with Daphne Fox?

Miles had.

His world was on fire, and nothing was on fire except her, she was the world, and there were no people.

No sailors on ships. Only her.

Mmhm, oohhh.

No generals on fields. Only her.

Mmhm, oohoohh.

No ground amid ocean; only sky, and her.
No pilots in the sky. Only her.
The world was stripped of people.
She was stripped of clothes.
There was only her, naked.
And shining sea motion.
Care to fall in love with Her?
She is thrill.
She is now.
She is sun.
She is moan.
She is wild love.
And his wild love, was screaming.

Uh, uh, uh, uh!
They had the world to themselves.

Nothing Strikes Again

NOTHING HAPPENED FOR A TIME.
   Time slipped. Slipped some more.
   Went right on slipping.

Probing—

BLUE NIGHT SLIPPED into blue night. Night slipped into day and day
slipped into night. Time slipped. Time slipped.
   The battle drew near. The fight approached.

Rhythm is his business—
   Miles, is here now, getting ready for the fight.
   Probing, probing, until he's feeling it.
   Rhythm.
   Probing rhythm.
   He was searching, seeking the way.
   The fight drew near.
   The showdown was here.

And what would be the rhythm and the form, the shape and the motion. He was probing.

As for Cinjun . . . the effect, was his main concern.

Soon would come the battle, which Cinjun knew he would win. But what concerned him was the effect. Putting the right effect into play. Cutting how you thought about it. Cinjun was making his plans for how to make them think the right way. To see the battle the way they should.

He was working over the points he should drive home with his victory.

The collision course.

The day drew near.

And then it came. It was upon them. Combat.

What was this rhythm and this motion? Miles wondered.

Capoeira Nebula! Ah, it was a capoeira nebula.

He sensed it. Probed it.

Misty colors, vapors. A yellow capoeira, that was where they were heading. A yellow capoeira with red and orange relief . . . and exploding forms.

The Stately Pleasuredome

IN THE FOREST CITY, amid forest field, did they a stately Pleasuredome decree. Where might you and me, see, fight on fight, fair and brave and free.

Here were people come.

And here were pleasures of Sultans and Kings, Kings and Khans—

Boundless and bare.

Lone and level, the ground stretched to far away. To city and buildings and avenues and night and light.

Here were people come from alien worlds. From strange journeys in strange nights of sin and stone.

They came, from round and round.

And here were rivers come. Here—were rivers running.

The river British. River Rome. River Ottoman. The river Egypt. The river Greek. In mysterious union, here did meet.

A stately Pleasuredome for one and all! *"Step right, step right up!"* the Barker cried. Here were the passions and the tatters of the world that peopled. Such battles! as knew no equals.

And here was a savage place.

A stately Pleasuredome here stood. With many pleasures to share. A million ways to spend your time. A million ways to fun most fine.

And here they came:

The team of Mahoney and McSmithers.

Pachuco Cabeza.

And the Fair Fathead Willy.

And here they came:

Cinjun Kubla the Khan Smythe.

Skyler the Larkin Malloy.

Fine and larking malicious.

And here they came: the streaming people floating in waves from all around. To the Stately Pleasuredome. Boy and girl; and friend and enemy; oh, on, they came . . . to a fight-in-the-light show. To know and grow.

To smell the blood and the cool clean country air. Of battles raging in forest city.

Step right up! Step right up! the Barker cried. "A battle of truth!" he lied. But he knew not, "For in truth it would be truth that fought tonight," they cried.

And here, was a stately Pleasuredome! *Step right up! Step right up!* the Barker cried.

And oh! the deep romantic chasm which slanted down the green hills to a savage arena, beneath demon moon haunted by woman wailing for her demon-lover—or, perhaps the other.

And here, was a stately Pleasuredome!

Step right up! Step right up! the Barker cried.

In this place did the people a stately Pleasuredome decree

Step right up! the Barker cried. Come and see; this was, and is, and well will be, the lone and only place. Oh, lone and only: The only place to be. Great shows and changes of face—that come—and race—and rend with eerie grace—startling and sad face—with sad and startling and rapid pace. Changes, and changes and changes of face.

Oh, lone and only: The only place to be. Where you can be you, wild and free. Yes, wild and free, here you can be. For in this place, did they a stately Pleasuredome decree.

And here did they revive color and splendor

Vapors leading on to vapors. Oh! the splendor!
Oh! Such splendor!
Oh! the splendor!
Hear and now.
Near and now.
Voices, hear them now.
Oh! the splendor! And the cheer! So fast and so near.

The works of man and woman fair. Beautous and sexy wear. Suits and gowns. A place in color. Bust lines and lace. Fabulous and outrageous. Looking and clothing.

They were here.
They drew near.
They were here.
Well, for combat, dear.

To see combat. Giants fair and tall rend each other in the hall. A battle royal, grown in a stately Pleasuredome; grown immense in a measure Rome.

They came to sit and watch, and live! in a stately Pleasuredome. And know lightning life, and strife of life, and death of life, and mighty being. All was here for joy-splashed seeing.

The seeing was started.
The lights grew brighter.
The sounds were moaning.
And here the Barker cried:
"Is everybody in?
"The show—is about to begin."

Dancing Barefoot

THE INSIDE OF THE PLEASUREDOME was an immense cavern.

In wait, among the crowd, lay: Brutus and his two associates.

Skyler was striding, leading Daphne and Miles through the throng of people. Rattle and hum all round. Skyler was leading them—in the direction of Brutus and his crew.

Daphne cast her gaze into the crowd, and her attention was caught— She fixed her stare on Brutus.

Brutus smirked. Actually, his smile was quite charming. Not really any menace in him at all. Except that he revealed a concealed gun.

Daphne's gaze stayed level as she flicked it to Skyler. She studied his reaction. He had seen the exchange. And seemed pleased.

Brutus smiled. He came forward. "Make sure you lose tonight," Brutus said. He was now a few paces from Daphne.

Skyler was much closer. She felt him breathing. Daphne turned to Skyler and saw a satisfied gleam in his eyes.

"Skyler," Daphne said, "in the time it would take you to kill one guy, I could get three guys to the morgue."

Immediately, her fist went to Skyler's nose, smashing it something awful, drawing blood.

She pivoted toward Brutus and moved into his space.

"You're going to threaten us!" Daphne said. "You're going to come here and threaten us!"

Now, everyone in the immediate area stopped. Their attention was seized, pulled fully to Daphne and Brutus and the two men. They froze, riveted, with charged alertness.

Brutus and the two guys held still, staying ready.

Miles was standing at Daphne's back. Readying himself to protect her.

Time stood still. Each player stood ready, waiting for the slightest motion in the other—except Daphne—she allowed her life force to quicken. And then moved.

Daphne flew at Brutus. As he started to react, her foot pounded a course through his jaw.

She was connection. And she was connecting with him.

Now she was spinning ceaselessly. Taking over.

She was dancing barefoot.

The other two thugs were nearby. She knocked them into positions that better suited her needs, as she went back at Brutus.

Some strange music drove her, made her come on blithely. A kick through a granite jaw there. Dancing barefoot. A fist through a man's chest here. She was dancing barefoot.

Spinning, outside of gravity.

She took over. She brought it on.

And they reaped: a full force gale.

And now—

She is whirlwind. She is stinging force. She is deadly. You see, her father had mated with a tigress, a temptress and an assassin to produce her—She sends Brutus to the floor in a hard crash—She breaks bone, rips flesh in the two associates—

She was showing them what lay within her.

It was part of her moving on.

Great effort, vast effort.

Training of years.

Sprung swiftly in her moving on.

Done, in a flow fierce and natural.

Her training, her work, work measured out in years.

She relieved Brutus of his gun.

Now she pointed the gun at the other two. One held still; the other seemed to be a little more restless—he just might show her a little more life than she expected; and teach her a lesson in violence.

"Down with the hand—" Daphne said quickly.

The man was fast, moving cunningly, weaving, making himself a shifting target, impossible to hit with precision; he was drawing a pistol and moving efficiently into a kill shot, using the faces and bodies in the crowd for cover.

Daphne fired. A sure shot as it turned out: the man's gun flew back and crashed against the wall. Miles grabbed the gun. While she took care of the third man's gun.

Then she returned to Brutus. Who was working successfully at his recovery.

"Up," she said encouraging his powerful recuperative ability.

He rose and readied himself for action. She took a crack at his face; delivered a series of blows in lightning succession.

Bam, whack, thrak, b'boom!

He might as well have been frozen in ice for all the resistance he was able to mount. He went down, harder than before. But she wouldn't stop!

Bam, whack, thrak, b'boom!

People gasped! She pounded and broke his body.

"Up," she said. "Come on, are you going to leave it there?"

But his lights were out. He was in a total bringdown. She was talking to an unconscious body.

"Up," she said. "Now is that all the fight you're going to give me? Up! Up! You're going to go to bed this early?"

Now she stopped. She looked around, scanning the crowd.

"You saw him," she said. "He had a gun."

They didn't seem to be getting it.

"Did I have a gun?" she said. "No. He had me at his mercy. Luckily I can get by on my wits."

The Show Is About to Begin

INSIDE THE GREAT STADIUM, the seeing was about to get started.

The lights grew brighter.

The sounds were moaning.

"Is everybody in?

"The show—is about to begin."

The Barker cried, "The curtains will soon be parted! The seeing will be started!—Bright with sin—sound and fury—and its kin—Is everybody in? The show is about to begin!

"Sinning sound and sinning fury.

"All sin and all its kin, perhaps might win.

"Or would truth slip in? And truth in end, to sear and win? And truth in end, so sear as to win?

"Drawing fast and mighty and near, and in this way to win?"

The Barker spoke above the din—"Come in and sit," until the battle is writ, . . . all fin.

With fast and certain reason, we were about to go to heaven, fast, so fast and in season. Go fast, so fast, and get there in season.

The truth seemed this day, not far away.

"Is everybody in?" the Barker said.

"The show, is about to begin."

Capoeira! The Dancing Fight

THIS WAS A YELLOW CAPOEIRA, with red and orange relief. Red and orange waves, emergences.

As Miles moved, this was what he was seeing.

You sailed in yellow . . . hunting for orange. And red! Worlds. Exploding worlds.

They were sailing deep in the yellow capoeira.

All around, swirling vapors of yellow mist.

Capoeira Nebula!

Sailing in misty colors.

All this—as Miles took his journey into: The Arena.

Miles would take the night into mystery. To take it into the mystery, was to take it into the nebula.

Miles had to take the night into the winding way. Warp and shift the form into its fullness. Into its raw existence and reach. Into the nebula.

Miles had to take them into the Wãoynde. Shift and warp the form of the moment, until they went into the Winding Way.

Miles would make the fight big. Much bigger. He pursued a fight that radiated. That formed a whirlpool Wãoynde. A worldwind, whirlwind Wãoynde.

This was a capoeira!

Miles, felt it.

And saw that Cinjun moved the night to a more formal arrangement.

No, they were into capoeira.

He that is good man, will be.

But no planning, no ceremony, Capoeira!

Floating force.

Charging.

"Che-gung-ging!" Miles said.

He would take it into its raw shape. No soft lies, no soft parade, Elemental Capoeira!

"Kai-bing!" Miles said.

Cinjun observed this. He considered what Miles was speaking into the night. As if they were words.

He turned from Miles and swept his gaze across the people. They had not picked up on it. It had just been a passing piece of bizarre behavior. Cinjun put it out of his mind. It was nothing.

Miles too was sensing the people all around, their energy filling the place, the form of the thing.

He, Miles came for a capoeira, a dancing fight—a Wild Whirlwind Wãoynding Wild, screaming Wild!

He put everything out of his mind, except the moment, and the moment was Capoeira! Let's dance and battle in the Night Sun, my enemy, Cinjun Smythe and I. My enemy, the Dark King, and I. Capoeira! And a chance to die.

The Capoeira that dances, will be!

All that was left to Miles, was the becoming. How that would happen? He had no idea, and it didn't worry him a bit. He had wit.

In the other corner, Cinjun moved to seal the covenant set long ago between himself and the powers that sprang him. He was here to collect the world.

The men and women of the world that peopled. His mighty forces. His weapon that peopled. His military majesty.

He was here and he was about to win. He was here to write history— He had charted it on the way here—And now all that was left for him was to breathe victory in the form that had been set long ago.

Miles felt a shape and a becoming. He didn't know from form. He knew flux and change and sun streaked looks. And soaring Capoeira. A wild whirlwind wãoynding wild.

Miles drew a deep breath. He let it out ever so slowly. Drew his next, deep breath. And braced himself.

Miles would have to carry this night, carry this train, off the track. Hmmm, crash to the other shore. Fly across the sky, into the nebula. Let the nebula wash all over them.

Yes, time to carry this night away.

Carry it to where it belonged—outside of time and place.

Enter the nebula.

Enter the scape.

Enter the escape.

Enter the dream.

Enter the dreamscape.

Enter the bender.

Enter the mind bender.

Enter.

The night resisted. Everything in the place resisted. And fought, and would fight him.

He moved.

C'mon.

C'mon.

C'mon.

C'mon Miles. No stopping. Move damn it move! Miles's thoughts grew furious. *You saw the Capoeira Nebula. Now take the night off the track. Damn it, take this train off the track!*

Pa doo dum . . . Pa deem doo . . . da doo dum.

Listen to the wind and the mystery comes alive.

Pa doo dum . . . Pa dee doo da doo dum . . . Da de Doom. Doom. Doom. Doo doo de doom . . . de doo doop. doop. doop. De doo dooop doop dum—

Pa de dum! . . . Pa dee doo da de dum! . . .

Cinjun was training his eyes on Miles—he felt there was something very strange going on inside that boy.

Miles—He knew the important impulse, it was: Don't save me from myself. Don't hold on to anything. Let it go.

Into the mindbending nebula.

Into the Wãoynde. Into the mindbender. Into the dream.

To the far horizon. To the far reaches.

Into the further forever.

Take it into the beyond.

Into the wild blue yonder.

Into cool rapidity.

Miles could see that Cinjun was moving the night into a formal arrangement. A ceremony of soft strokes and fightless fighting. No, Miles would have to find a way to carry this night off the track. He must not let it grow cold—stone cold—he must not let it move into the stone cold black hold.

That is where Cinjun will take it. Where ancient and forest city forces will control it; hold it down.

Time to breathe life into it; and life was a simple form, a form of: Anything Goes.

Collision course, . . . and connection!

Battle joined.

The people wanting, wanting, wanting more. More and more and more.

Yes, the fight was moving to "on"!

Cutting loose.

Into the storm.

The voyage had begun.

The people lent force to the movement.

War, put on your faces! Miles's mind wanted to shout out loud.

Tonight we have—a battle of: Anything Goes. Miles's mind wanted to shout out loud.

Welcome one and all, gentle all. Tonight we present a muse of fire. A battle of fire. Within this O, we have packed two mighty forces, the Barker cried.

On one side, we have . . . Miles Roark.

On the other side, Cinjun Khan S'mythe.

Tonight, we have . . .

Miles walked away and did about the looniest thing you could do in a debate . . . He sat down and closed his eyes.

He was probing.

Probing the night. Getting a feel for it.

As the Barker opened it up . . . Miles quietly sat down.

Cinjun turned.

The Barker glanced down at Miles.

The audience grew more alert.

For Miles, it was the experience of diving into cold water, and exploring. Feeling alive. Feeling life within him, and around him. Feeling the flow, and going with the flow. Tonight, he would swim with the currents of mood . . . This was Miles's way of beginning the fight.

For Cinjun . . . this was like nothing he had ever encountered before. It made him mad.

The Barker stopped speaking, he was unprepared for anything random to happen.

Miles spoke, picking it up where the Barker had dropped it:

"My friends, tonight, we present a fight for the heavyweight title! In olden days, debates were about words and prose, tonight *anything goes!* Tonight is about making changes go round, everything changing, everything shifting: *Anything Goes!*"

The crowd goes with it. That'll work. Jolly good. Good show!

That's what they wanted: a good show.

Cinjun didn't like this one lick. What was this grandstanding? He jumped into it.

Miles seated on the floor? This boy had no respect.

Cinjun would play to the crowd's sentimentality. And to its dignity. Here was a major encounter of historical importance—and the boy was sitting on the god-damned floor. Disgraceful. Cinjun would use it to play to the audience.

Cinjun moved in and took charge of the moment.

"I called this—" Cinjun said "—so that we could get into the big questions of our lives. I say to my respected opponent—I disagree with you but tonight I want to hear your thoughts. But you must understand respect, there is a way to do things—"

"No!" Miles said.

Cinjun turned. "That's not the way to do things, Mister Roark—cutting people off—"

"No!" Miles said.

Miles was sitting on the ground, eyes closed.

Out of those closed eyes, he seemed to be seeing things. He said, "There is not a way to do things. Doing, is the way."

Time to breathe life into this, and in life: Anything Goes.

Anything Goes. There is not a way to do things. Doing is the way.

Anything goes. Of course. Form follows function. How you do it, is the way. Miles was sitting on the floor, his eyes closed.

Cinjun turned to him.

"There is not a way to do things," Miles remarked.

"Show some respect."

"Respect?"

"That's where we have to begin," Cinjun said.

"Respect?" Miles said.

Cinjun was like the strongman—who had the army, the navy, the air force, all those guns—he was the strongman—pointing, all those guns at you, and saying: Let's not . . . use force.

Cinjun is steady, taking the higher ground. "Yes, respect for rules of order."

Miles opens his eyes.

"Cinjun," Miles says, "there's a small patch of common ground you and I can share as we pass each other by—

"People are flawed; people are savages and a whole lot of trouble. We have a streak of barbarism in us. Rules hold that barbarity back. Rules are necessary. They take care of a lot of the trouble . . . they take away a whole sweep of trouble—The federation constitution. The articles of human rights—I like those rules. They're helpful. Your rules, I can do without.

"I'm here to build a new house. I don't need rules, and rulers, I need wood."

Miles rises to his feet.

Miles swings from the audience to Cinjun. "I may respect you, but I have to hit you to win the fight.

Where is he going with this? Cinjun came on guard and moved into burning feeling.

"Therefore," Miles said. "I apologize for what I'm going to do." Miles shifted and moved.

"Cinjun," Miles said, "you were right when you tried to skip this session, this dance lesson. You never should have come here . . . but I'm glad to see you made it."

"Miles," Cinjun said, "speak in our language—it'll be so much easier to understand you—it's hard to follow a blathering mumbling fool, so please speak clearly." Cinjun smiled, so nicely, and politely, but with a look whose handle should have stuck out a few stone lengths out of Miles's back.

"Cinjun," Miles said, "here's where I'm going, . . . here's what I want to know: Will you and your friend get on down? Or are you and your friend going to let me down?"

Now in a hush, Miles traveled. Where was he going?

"Cinjun, are you and your friend gonna get on down—or are you and your friend going to let me down." Miles spread his arms and opened himself to the audience. "When he and his friend come around, let him know. Tell him and his friend how to get on down. Cinjun! Are you and your friend going to get on down? Or are you and your friend going to let me down?"

Miles started into the audience. The hush grew vast. Miles walked over to Quinn Martin, who was seated deep in the mass.

"I apologize," Miles said to Quinn. "I know you've spent a lot of money on him, but I'm going to have to take him apart. You bet on the wrong horse."

The crowd and barkers reacted with interest.

"You want a tough fight?" Cinjun said. "Fine. Let's play games. Let's play horse—we'll each take an end . . . I'll be the front, you be yourself."

Miles turned to Cinjun.

Miles would let Cinjun have that one. It wasn't worth topping. Miles revealed nothing. Miles saw a sign, a physical sign. What he saw in Cinjun was, rage. Wonderful, beautiful rage, Miles thought.

He wondered if he had ever seen anything so beautiful. Beauty being truth, and truth being beauty, as someone once observed.

Ceremony

THE BARKER LAUNCHED IT with questioning, fine questioning, hurling—the open question—to Cinjun . . . Now, the question, was made tame by Cinjun.

Just close your eyes and feel the wave.

Cinjun making all questions tame. All attacks into womanly openings, which he would penetrate with His Destiny. At least this was how *Unumbatai* saw it.

Cinjun Khan *Unumbatai* S'mythe rose to *Sky God*.

And in this way spoke Unumbatai—

Cinjun Khan *Unumbatai* S'mythe. This, incidentally, was his true full
name. Everything about it was true.

Vrooom, thrak, b'boom, went the engine.

Vrooom, vrooom, vrooom, went the feel.

Thump, thump, thump, went their heart strings.

Swing, swing, swing, went their feel.

Zing, zing, zing, went their mood.

And when he smiled they went into a universal reel.

And in this way spoke Unumbatai—

The Barker had kicked off the debate with an open question. *Well,*
Miles thought, *isn't that the way of it?* Handing it to Cinjun, to run with
as he may. This was the way of modern civilization. The powerful were
privileged to fight in fightless fighting.

The question, Miles thought, was very sporting.

Very gentlemanly.

Very softball.

Very nothing.

The barker had said something that amounted to the cutting force and
controversy of a stage cue. He may as well have said: "Mister Smythe,
can you tell us anything you damn well feel like telling us?"

Cinjun reacted. The themes flowed. The big wheel went into a spin.
People fell in.

And in this way spoke Unumbatai—

We're talking a united red front, think what that means—a Song of
Unity. A beautiful song of unity. United we stand.

Like a fiery sun—a sun rising—together—we are House Crimson.

The Song of Unity. It was a crowd pleaser.

The cannon of unity.

The fighter plane of unity.

The citadel and weapons and great works of unity.

The firepower of unity.

Just think what we can build with the sword of unity.

What strokes of love, when we wield the sword of unity.

Of red—crimson—purpose—fighting for Peace.

This was Cinjun's Moonlight Sonata.

Miles studied the ceremonial hosts.

A pack of Barkers.

His judgement spoke of them, as a pack of dogs, a pack of wolves. Just there to eat the carcass. Not helpful. Not adding life—*They're devouring. They're feeding*—but this is not a supper.

The Hosting Barkers—were a pack of common barkers, who sought to be important by packing other people's moments.

Miles saw them in their own themes. Saw them deep in it. It was up to their knees.

Life and Time
A box of thunderbolts

THE HERO WITH A THOUSAND FACES. That's what Cinjun is. When you count the faces modestly.

The powers of life, and their inflection through man and woman.

No empty spaces, for the imagination to struggle for myths.

We have a whole new realm.

And in this way spoke Unumbatai—

New Unumbatai for sale. Unumbatai that's fresh and bold. Unumbatai that's only a few days old. Who would like to sample his supply?

And in this way spoke Unumbatai—

The Hunter in the Red Vest become a Swordmaster—A stranger can show up and help you. We're talking not only a physical force, but a center.

Wielding this strange weapon . . . This too strange talk of life-change . . . A story, sounding easy. Getting into your skin. This thing communicates. *It is in a language that is talking to young people today,* the wise man says.

The Hero goes for something—everyone knew—he is not just along for the ride, not a mere adventurer.

Now the Hero in the true sense. Are you ready for it? For the themes.

The achievements? Of the hero? Are you ready for? Manifestation. The landscape. The conditions. The environment . . . Can you match the readiness of the hero?

He begins as mere mortal, ends as hero. Evoking a quality of higher character.

This man, functioning beautiful in the world, *a something* pushing it.

Bringing favorite themes, true purposes, and big wheels—where you are is—on the edge—about to embark on outlying spaces—real adventure—this is the jumping off place. You haven't been there. I have. Now I take you. To the atmosphere.

Use space.

The walls were closing in on them.

Now they were descending into the dark place.

Going in, to come out again.

Down into the depths, many fathoms deep in the Black Sea of Dreams.

He was taking them deeper and deeper into The Black Sea.

The Black Sea.

The Black Sea of Black Dreams.

C'mon.

C'mon.

C'mon.

Miles held himself still, taking in the view.

Cinjun stood strong before the people now, and spoke to the multitude.

And in this way spoke Unumbatai—

Water. Being. The unconscious. Darkness.

First stage in *hero adventure.* Leaving realm of light, moving to threshold. Monster comes to meet him. Will the Hero be cut to pieces? No, he may kill the dragon power. Take the power. Take the song of nature, the powers of nature, unity, the Song of Unity.

And come upon the land, bringing the Song of Unity.

Know you Unity?

'This thing up here'—Cinjun directed their attention to his beautiful charming, shining head and face and those eyes of his, those eyes, them darn eyes, wow—'this thing up here removes us from Unity. Unity is the total human being.'

This thing up here must not put itself in control. It must submit to its humanity.

We're talking about living in terms of a system.

Systems of Unity and Might. Cinjun pulled a clever, most clever stop then. Turned into Systems of Unity and Might.

We operate in our society in relation to a system.

Will the system eat you up? Or will you use the system to serve a high purpose? We don't need to change the system, we will help you to live in the system. Not make it impersonal.

Be a scholar. This is what happens in your spiritual life. Listen to its demands. Do not insist on your own program. Do not put yourself off center. This is not what your body is interested in, because you have stopped listening to yourself.

Commit yourself to a system. Obey it. The creative spirit ranges strongest within the support of a great and mighty system.

System—great and deep and wide—creating Establishment, and The Man. Listen to The Man, y'all.

The Man is a Hero.

And The Hero lurks within each one of us. The system evokes more and more and more of us.

Now let us evoke our higher nature, rather than our lower.

A terrific darkness came over them then. A strange darkness of strange sensation. Darkness—made by some magician at work some-where.

Let's gather. Collect wood for a fire and spend the night here.

I have come to save you, I await your reply.

I'm serious about all this.

Mere human beings are not good enough. Another domain, is where we go. The adventure is marvelous.

In His Lodge, the people greet you, you feel comfortable.

The next day, you go off to—*hunt.*

Strange sounds, strange days. Evenings come.

You hear strange sounds again.

The Hunt is where you need to be. Follow your bliss. Follow The Hunter in the Red Vest—Unumbatai.

And in this way Unumbatai speaks—

Hear the voice of The Man. Pulling you out of the water. You have moved from hard ground, solid earth . . . and you are in, caught in the abyss. You are rescued now by the elevated powers.

We're talking something smashingly brilliant, my dear friends, we're talking forces out of the local field, higher powers!

If you are not eligible to join, it's going to be a demon wedding for you. It's going to be a mess.

This is a story of expressing a truth.

The edge of what can be done and the mystery transcendent of all human search. The source of life. Knowledge of mystery. Balance and harmony.

We're talking: Thinking, in terms that help people.

We're talking: Ask not what you can do for yourself, ask what you can do for others.

See positive values.

Organ*ization* raised to high art.

Organ*izing* raised to high power.

Cinjun felt His Destiny, surge.

His Destiny rose, driving to climax—

And in this way spoke Unumbatai—

Miles applauded.

Cinjun turned—interrupted—damn—it was a kind of interrupted sex—

Miles relaxed his arms, relaxed his hands and relaxed in the moment.

"Oh," Miles said softly, "I'm sorry. I thought you were finished. I'm terribly sorry." And he looked it.

Where could this be going, Miles wondered, and how far?

Miles motioned for Cinjun to take it away again.

Cinjun drew a breath, and let this one pass. He turned to the people. Cinjun returned to the bed of the fair and strong for some more . . . involvement. He felt His Destiny surge anew.

The whole world is conscious.

Plant and animal life.

Is Consciousness something peculiar to the head? Well, it isn't. It's an organ that inflicts consciousness. There is a consciousness here in the body.

Energy is the same thing. Where you see energy is consciousness.

We come out of energy.

Now observe, a form, an aspect of the energy.

The eyes of the earth are a Force Red. The voice of the earth is a Force Red.

Okay, y'all, you raise your consciousness. That's what meditation is for.

Levels of meditation, is what we're talking now. All right y'all.

Concern for family, and nation. Important concerns. And physical conditions.

Communicate now.

How do you get that?

Now—What this too strange talk of life-change is for, is to bring us to a level of consciousness that is spiritual.

Mystery. Everything speaks to us of mystery and atmosphere.

Bring your consciousness to a higher level. Then when you come back to this one. Associate it.

Hold it on that level. Don't let it drop down.

This is simply a lower level of that.

Express *relationship.*

Anyone who has spent any time fully awake, has felt it.

Look at every single figure in the museum, in the history of our people. Be there—so much so—that . . . you climb . . . to the great bell. Go up and up. Up there. And ring the great bell.

Bong! Bong! Bong!

Brilliant, adventure, lord.

Miles wanted to show them where this room was.

Presently, he would act presently . . . for now he let time slip.

Time slipped, time slipped . . . and Miles considered where Cinjun was going. Why was this so important to Cinjun? Miles considered it. Rolling the pattern search through his mind.

Ripeness was not now. Not yet. It was near. Miles put his ear to the ground—and heard a gentle sound. A sound of revealing, revealing what he was witnessing in the wild breeze this night.

A very moving beautiful thing, Cinjun was saying. I want to go there time and time again.

Take me to informed principles. You can tell their importance by the size of the principles. They're the tallest in the city. Wow! Such dwellings.

The history of civilization, was all he was talking about.

And who can build the tallest building.

Magnificent building. Architectural triumph.

A statement—We are a power center!

Here is what you will dream tonight.

Symbolic forms. A planet of moneyflow and violenceflow.

Beautiful.

Maturation. Adulthood of the world. And how to do it.

And relating it to the cosmos.

And—oh my goodness—what a society he was talking about! It could take the planet.

Oh, to see this thing from space. A force very small, but growing very grand.

New world to come. And the people. To be one with it. Surrender yourself to it. To the journey.

Expand your view of the world.

These are the things Cinjun is saying and has been saying. This was where it was all going.

This night Cinjun would take it there. He was on his way—such a way—all through the night.

The journey formed around him . . . a journey to a House Crimson.

The promised realm. The big view. The breathtaking landscape.

Cinjun was in full form, at the top of his game. And he played.

Now he took them on a journey in the form of a story.

The world was without form. Darkness was upon the face of the deep.

The song of the deep.

Violence—Gathered thick in places. Violence—Crowding, then separating.

Violence—The spirit was moving. Violence—The ancient spirit.

In the beginning was Reflecting. This am I.

Cinjun—Takes them to the field.

The ultimate word for what was transcendant, divine: god being.

Took them to god being. The universe is divine.

Mask of Eternity, expressed. Now—move into the god emperor savior, moving in the field, coming forth in male being, Cinjun Khan Smythe.

Who has eaten of the fruits of knowledge, good and evil, man and woman, future and past. He knew everything.

Being and non being.

Realization. And the promised center. House Crimson.

Emerging from this great zone, *Cinjun Khan Smythe.*

In the full cool of evening.

Man and nature in one man, beautiful, with big fists.

An ancient spirit moved in Cinjun Khan Smythe. Everyone could see it.

A totally different way of living. Full of revelation.

Passing between god being and the world. Between the moon and the forest city.

In the full cool of the evening.

No one knew where nature ended, and this man began.

Introducing the Hunter in the Red Vest.

Open up the world! He was coming in from outside.

He had taken them out of this world. And now brought them back.

To run with him.

The Visiting Deity, at least this was the way they made him feel. With their recognition of his identity.

And with Deity always came: *The One Forbidden Thing.*

The forbidden fruit which . . . you very well know you will eat.

Knowing *The One Forbidden Thing*—was being *One*. Miles was *One*. He was Wãone. And looked the type to stay Wãone—And would not be forgiven for it.

And—now—in this night, emerging—Unumbatai—the great god being, oh sky god—came down from the sky, and said, 'Who told you that you could be *One?*'

"I did," Miles said to Unumbatai.

"How dare you be *One!*" Unumbatai thundered.

"Because I feel like it," Miles said to Unumbatai.

He spoke thus with his presence—Miles Roark—was what he said. Being and becoming was his end of the talk.

He remained One. And studied. Readied himself for when he would make moments come alive. He remained One, wild with the power, wild as can be.

Now—Life was throwing off the past, and continuing to live. The moon shed its shadow.

Unumbatai was now the next thing to the Buddha in the field of time. Throwing off death.

In this moment, being eternally alive.

A fantastic thing.

Fantastic Things for Sale

IF YOU DON'T GET IT HERE, you don't get it anywhere.

Heroism requires you to take a journey and share it.

Now—he gives them a Crimson Teaching on the go.

Takes their interest into a Teaching on the go.

Keep it strong, keep it pure. And get serious. About belief. This being the lesson.

It's important to have; it's an important thing to people. People live by this.

Here's the offer. Move through the night.

Values—found. From study. So fresh.

New values for sales.

Values that are fresh and strong. New values for sale.

He was a great teacher of values, raising money, keeping the teaching going. *Appreciate it.* Please, we need your help—It was about more than just Peace and Love and Fun. It was about something far higher— *Murder.* In modern language.

Belief systems. *New belief systems for sale.*

Varieties of belief. Gain them. Let them act upon you on the journey to maturity.

What he invented now, was—A good way to talk about killing— When you kill—You come away with a few things that are wonderful, and make wonderful things possible.

Now it was time for you to make your contribution and get the entire set of powers.

New powers for sale.

Powers that are fresh and bold. Powers that are only slightly old.

New powers for sale.

No better time to join. A convenient time. Support the program, right here, and join us. Be proud of the part you play.

We're in Prime Time.

Are you willing? Can you feel it? Let's see the real you!

Join us. It takes only a moment, and the change we will make will last for generations. For a long stretch of time, reaching—oh, for about the size of forever.

Illumination—Realize—In time.

Don't withdraw from the world. Horror is the foreground of wonder. Come. All life is sorrowful, it wouldn't be life if loss were not involved.

This is the way it is. Nobody intended it. This is the way it is.

History is a nightmare from which I am trying to awake.

Do not be afraid. Recognize.

All of this, is as it is, is as it has to be.

The ultimate conclusion is beautiful.

Know philosophy. Know wisdom.

Participate. *I will go to War!*—Is this a private fight or can anybody get into it?

The Hero is the one who comes to participate in it.

Feel the sense of wonder. Try to understand this existence.

Feel universal being.

Don't go out there, come in here.

Resurrection. You too can feel god being.

We're talking a thing, beyond the concept of reality. This goes beyond all thought.

A line connecting you to mystery.

Buddha—was the one who woke.

Wake up to what is within us.

Heaven—that desired goal—Heaven—and Hell—are within us. All the gods are within us. All heavens, all worlds are within us. Magnified dreams. Dream manifestations of energy—forms in conflict with each other.

Energies within us, in conflict with each other.

The ground of being.

Inward we are the source. We are mystical teaching.

Let me show you a Fixed Star by which to chart your course through the spaceways.

A Myth forming life instruction. Gives you—life models.

Listen—Time—changes, and continues to change, so fast. Virtues of the past are vices today.

Godphrodite, for the women. How to be a goddess of beauty.

Godeus, for the men. God with a lot of rules and no mercy. Give me some of that old time god.

Signals.

He went up to the mountain of the world and built a palace.

He filled it with what you yearned for—Bigger Ideas. He was marvelous; there was no end to his desires. He was caught for life in life.

He was sitting on a lotus of divine energy.

Telling his story. The story that sounded easy. Got into your skin. Shook you up.

Fixed you right; fixed you nice; made you feel nice all over.

And Unumbatai spoke in this way—

"Welcome!" Unumbatai said.

The thunder was rolling on the horizon.

. . . and Unumbatai took your thoughts, to far away, to a galaxy far far away . . .

Go there now!

Think of the galaxies beyond the galaxies in infinite space.

This was the Highest Illumination—drop your thunderbolt in it.

Sit on the throne. Go ahead try it on for size. God being for sale. Beautiful new god being for sale.

God being that's fresh and bold and only a few days old.

Enter the God Palace.

Oh, the beauty of this Palace.

He touches them with his Crimson Myth.

They experience it.

'Have as much as you can of this experience,' Unumbatai says. 'Have a marvelous time. Here is the place to have it.'

Join your thoughts to these actions . . . details to follow.

Sign on below. Genesis for sale.

He was explaining the universe through story.

A coat of many colors.

With a red vest.

Touching people, making impact. Citadel forming.

And the companion book to the power of this myth—was a book called *House Crimson*—To touch you personally. With insights and the universal story. Put life into your life. Please join us.

We're pleased to welcome you.

We have the pleasure to have you be part of our world. Thank you.

He was: A marvelous teacher.

Listen, we all search for meaning; this we know.

He makes meaning. Makes it with his character. He is the meaning. Striking chords. Distributing meaning.

Is there anyone better? Anywhere? People responded. Recognized their own appetites.

Now they will back Cinjun with their bodies and of course their money.

Oh the Power, they thought. *Yes—Do the walk of life.*

You can depend on him for quality power. Go to him now and get yourself some power.

New Power for Sale. Power that's fresh and bold, and only a few days old.

New Power for Sale.

Goodness, Miles realized what this all was.

The showdown was nothing more than a sideshow to this; the showdown was meant to be nothing.

This was an enfolding drive. This was one long extended unseen vast enfolding drive.

He was picking up people. He was sweeping up people.

That's what this was all about.

Cinjun Khan Unumbatai Smythe was far more brilliant than Miles had appreciated.

Whirling around this fireball of a star, on this orbiting form . . . rode great meanings . . . and great structures.

Cinjun was creating a great structure and pulling in people to pleasure themselves in the great painted cave.

He was offering light for inward darkness, and nightly visits of well being.

He was enfolding. This goddamned thing was one massive enfolding drive.

Space blazing crystal ship burning across the spaceways. Soaring into distance. Powering, from its massive enfolding drive.

Power springing from its internal combustion reactor, from its massive enfolding drive.

Enfolding

HE WAS THE STAR ATTRACTION. And the night was a Ceremony Capoeira.

He was enfolding people.

He was taking people in.

Power Ordeal.

Enfolding people.

Ceremony Capoeira.

This was the mix. Seasoned with fine talk.

This was about enfolding people! This had been clear from the start, but now the full form of Cinjun's dreambird was taking wing.

Cinjun was proving to be, not only a smooth, but also, a grand operator. So much the better, thought Miles, the bigger the size of the evil, the greater the victory if you are able to bring it down.

Cinjun's ploys and maneuvers were fascinating. Miles held fast, and wondered what Cinjun would do as he traveled in his ascent.

This was a capoeira, a dancing fight. They were in the Roman Arena.

All this, and for Cinjun, more—Cinjun was forming *A Crystal Ship.*

Cinjun was playing the teachings of power. He wasn't going to show his power. He was past that stage. He had sealed up his power. He didn't have to prove his power. He had to get people to believe in him and join him, that was what was absolutely necessary for Cinjun now.

He was moving to seize immortality and great being.

He was seizing the world.

Violently seizing the world.

Oh, The Beauties of violence. Thoughts to help you go with the violence. Traditions that helped. Names that helped. Stages that helped.

All this working toward—the violent. Charming, beautiful, enjoyable violence.

Relaxing in the wonder of violence.

The body reaching for power over others.

A vehicle to take control of you and you . . . and you . . . and you . . . and you . . .

Watch this thing go.

Gradually, the whole thing becomes violent environment.

Violent consciousness.

Violent being.

Murdering without effort.

What a beautiful future Murder would have under Cinjun Smythe rule.

Cinjun would turn it to the image of death.

And laying the image on some people, on some troublemakers. On some men and women that did not see life right. Did not see it through your experience.

Make them *not there.*

Get them lying down, and turning cold, and rotting. And making themselves *not there.*

Help them get *not there.*

Beautiful burials. Beautiful burying. Of burying people *Alive!* While he held up the sky.

Sacrifices for noble purposes. Noble anger leading to noble murder to save life and save the world. All being saved under this sky.

And this was were Cinjun was pulling it all. To save the world by murdering *you.*

It will all be better if we get rid of *you.*

Miles remembered now the story of the Land of the Blind he had placed on a plane of energy.

This Land of the Blind will be great once we get rid of you, because you can see. Seeing is preventing you from knowing joy filled life in blindness.

Circling round, it was circling round—to Homegrown Traitors.

Murdering the Homegrown Traitors.

Strip to Show

MILES APPLAUDS.

"More! More! Bueno! Bravisimo! You didn't get to the part where we turn on the people—on our own people. Where we silence the artists. The people who won't play along, the Homegrown 'Traitors'. That's the best part of the trip. The part of the trip I really like. The best part, that's where you can be proud to be a part of this number."

The Barker moved in, to draw the proceedings to order. "Mister Roark, you'll have a chance to respond, once Mister Smythe has used his time."

Miles casually emerged from behind his wooden stand, moving between Cinjun and the protective Barker.

This was very stilted for a Capoeira. This wouldn't do. What was the Barker to the Capoeira or the Capoeira to the Barker? Old friend, Cinjun my old friend, what is the Barker to the Capoeira or the Capoeira to the Barker. Away, sweet Barker! Adieu.

"Cinjun, are you sure the things you say are right?"

"Yes," Cinjun said.

"Then," Miles said, "you would want the questions presented to you to be the most penetrating they can be. So that you will have a chance to get right to the root of things. And speak exactly the truth? Correct? And the truth can do no harm to you?

"Correct," Cinjun said.

"Now who will ask," Miles said, "the most penetrating questions, your friend or your adversary? Who will ask the most dangerous questions, your friend or your enemy?—You make peace with your enemy, not with your friend."

"You want to trip me up, Miles," Cinjun said.

"But you said you're right," Miles said, "so you're not afraid of being tripped up. If you speak the truth, how can the truth trip you up? Now this esteemed gentleman is your friend. I am your opponent. Whose questions are more dangerous? Mine, correct?"

"I agree." Cinjun paused a beat for effect. "Your questions are off the wall, offbeat and off the mark. I suppose that's what you mean by dangerous. Yes, Miles I'm willing to let you ask me off—err, excuse me dangerous questions. Yes Miles let's call them 'dangerous' questions. Dangerous to which one of us we shall see."

Now the audience ate it up. A lot of them loved Cinjun Smythe, loved him so.

"Who should ask you questions?" Miles said. "I should . . . That's why we won't need a barker today."

He dismisses the pack of—err, panel of barkers—He makes the lead Barker a feather in the wind, and sends him on his way.

Now Miles saw that the trail he was carving was taking on colored dimensions.

The Lead Barker happened to be a fellow by the name of *Profumo Moraz.* Oh you've heard of him. Yes, he was the great legendary Mister

Profumo Moraz. The most trusted, beloved, popular man of the *light*vision. He was *that* Profumo Moraz.

Oh he was known the world over. A very famous Barker indeed. Mister Profumo Moraz. Highly respected. Highly powerful. Highly revered—Miles didn't give a damn. He couldn't have given less of a damn if he tried.

The soft strokes of Mister Profumo Moraz held nothing for Miles. Nothing of any interest at all.

But when he sends Profumo Moraz away—oh my God, what a scandal! Cinjun and everyone, the people close to Cinjun most especially, are immediately outraged. Doesn't he know how difficult and what a high honor it was to have Profumo Moraz put in an appearance, attend to a debate himself? How dare Miles send Profumo Moraz from the scene in a kind of disgrace? This was damnable stuff. Mister Profumo Moraz was a legend among Barkers. This would turn many people against Miles—You did not just treat the great Mister Profumo Moraz like a cherry pit; chew him up and toss him away. Oh no.

Miles couldn't have given less of a damn if he tried.

Profumo Moraz held nothing for the capoeira. And a capoeira was come, into this place. Miles knew what to want and where to go.

Ah, better, freer, more open, Miles thought. *More possibilities for wheels of fire.*

Now, Cinjun was behind a wooden stand, Miles saw. Well, what was the wooden stand to the Capoeira? Or the Capoeira to the stand? The furniture made it very neat, very sporting . . . This was not a place for furniture, Miles thought.

"Do you want to be completely open?"

"I am open," Cinjun said. He spread his hands wide.

"Do you need to hide behind things? Are you completely confident? Or do you need to hold onto things that comfort you such as the furniture? Do you need a stand?"

Cinjun's hands were still held wide. And open. "No, I don't," Cinjun said, smiling. With great charm.

"That's why today we will argue without any stands. Let's remove everything that gets between you and me."

He made the wooden stand a branch and sent the branch a-tumbling, to the woodpile.

Better.

For wheels of fire to carve through the Sun Night.

Miles was pleased.

For an instant they were eye to eye.

Then Cinjun turned toward the audience.

"Stunts are the name of his game," Cinjun said. "Let's not be fooled. I am so certain that I'm right, I'm willing to continue in this way and win on any playing field he chooses. Any proving ground will do."

Now, Cinjun was directing his look to the audience.

What was the audience to the Capoeira or the Capoeira to—now wait a moment, the audience was fitting, was handsomely becoming to the shape. The world of people lent force to its seasons. The audience was a goodness. But Cinjun was sore astray.

Miles would help him see the path. See the wheel of fire between them.

Miles said, "Don't talk to them, talk to me. You want to talk to them, go ahead. When you're finished, talk to me."

Rip Currents

AH, BETTER, FREER, MORE OPEN.

It could breathe now.

All was right.

And then, . . . moves.

Needs, . . . beginning.

Battle, joined.

Flying, to where shadows ran from themselves under the night sun in the place of *light*vision.

Cinjun turned, looking into Miles's eyes, he saw *Tygers* crouched in jungles in Miles's dark eyes. Cinjun saw them and then they sprang. And Miles laughed.

Chilling and weird; it rubbed Cinjun the wrong way. Launched him into a blood rage. Bloodlust!

Blood in the streets. Bloody red sun of House Crimson rising.

Cinjun charged deep into the blood rage. He was in a fight to the finish with a madman. He would fell him. It would come in necessary, certain steps. It had to be a progression. He would win the audience with his war art.

Miles—he recognized the night. It was deep and rich and blue. It was deep and rich and true.

And a yellow Capoeira soared across the blue.

Now The Wonderland Band plays in the background to lend force to the seasons, to lend force to the capoeira. As in the long tradition of capoeiras, the berimbau begins the rhythm—the bass beats, sets the ground rhythm of cool rapidity, and then the drums kick . . . and the Wonderland Band is swinging away. Moving phase by phase. Lending some wild swing, some booming bass, and kicking rhythm to the substance of fire.

The audience sways with it, feeling it, going with it—yes, they like it. What the hmmm—it's a good time—This works for them—They ache for more. More and more and more. They'd like to see some more of that wild swing.

"Capoeira—Cinjun! . . ." Miles said. "Capoeira is come, capoeira is here, the berimbau confirms it."

Enter the bender.

Enter the mindbender.

Enter the fantastic voyage.

Enter fantasia.

Ah, Cinjun thought, *the games grow a little wilder.* Cinjun knows where to take this—to his home territory—to his mighty territory. The field of armed forces and might.

Cinjun turns to the audience. And smiles.

They love it. He's still in control. The old boy is really something—yes, that Cinjun is really something, he'll show Miles "the way of might."

Cinjun's presence fills the pleasuredome . . . he stands in silence for a breath, and then—taking the territory—he strides.

"Bring it on Mister Roark! Put on your traveling shoes we're going to take a trip. Run and dance as much as you like. And when you're finished let's get down to business like true men, let's get down to the people's business."

The Wonderland Band played a tropic rhythm, setting up a tropic corridor, a tropic splendor—and a wave, of oceans calling. Of salty air, and of going on down to cool rapidity—of taking it on down, oh yes, a rhythm that would take it on down and keep keeping it down—You know it just might fly on down to Rio, swoop into an upward glide, fly round the world, in a big old plane—fly round the world, round and round and round again—The Wonderland Band and the blue night called.

Miles smiled. "Yes, let's take a trip. A big trip. A trip the size of the world, what do you say? Shall we go. I'm ready when you are?"

"Let's take a world trip," Cinjun said. "Let's take a tour of what you're doing . . ."

The World Trip

"WHAT YOU STAND FOR," Cinjun said, "is sneering at systems. Tearing down beliefs. You're not sure that the earth is here and men walk upon it. Beware of him. Do not let him make the worse appear the better.

"He's about tearing down everyone," Cinjun said. "Tearing down is an easy game to play. In this day and age, when our might is so important, we need somebody who understands how to work within a group and to move that group forward! To be the leader of a group!"

Miles said, "You deliver all the colors of a monotone."

"Tearing down," Cinjun said, "throwing things off balance, shaking things up is easy. Stirring. That's all an easy game to play. Chaos is easy. Order is the hard part. Setting up order Mister Roark. What do you have in the way of order?"

"Seems to me we had some pretty good systems lying around the house. Somewhere, I came across a few I liked. Yes, somewhere I read about . . . ————"

Somewhere I read of the freedom of assembly.

Somewhere I read of the freedom of speech.

Somewhere I read of the freedom of the press.

Somewhere I read that greatness is the right to protest for right.

Somewhere, I read it. It was written on something small, so I guess it's easy to miss.

The ideas behind it, were good.

You pool together.

You don't become a group thinking thug.

You bring together a sea of different people.

You don't make every person into the same person.

We don't live under one strongman rule. We shouldn't. We should be free to be you and me.

That's what I read somewhere. It was a pretty good thought, so it stayed with me.

I'm talking about nourishment.

I'm talking about having fun.

I'm talking about my people getting down, having some fun.

Dancing on the living room rug.

"How you talk Mister Roark," Cinjun said. "I don't hear how to run a country in anything that you're saying. My book has a plan for saving our country. What do you have?"

"What do you have," Miles said, "in that book for people who don't want to be part of your system?"

"Don't dodge the question—what's your plan?" Cinjun demanded.

"Majority rule, minority rights," Miles said. "Freedom of speech, freedom of expression. And decadent frills like public education and health care."

"I believe in the same," Cinjun said. "Not free preaching. We're not required to broadcast sneering. We're not required to listen . . . to be subjected to a jabberjaw."

"Oh, free speech," Miles said, "as long as no one hears it. Perfect."

"I'll cut to the chase," Miles said. "I'll tell you what I'm all about. I'm about freedom of character. With me, everybody gets to become a character. With you, everybody gets to become a humanoid, a machine, a cog in the system of machines, if they're lucky; some people only get to be a piece of a machine, a piece of a people-shape. You want an assembly line. I want a kaleidoscope. What you're missing in your picture, is people who don't want to be part of your plan."

Cinjun relished the moment, the fool had handed Cinjun a winning hand. "Drop out, get high. We've gone down this road before. We've heard this story before."

"Just once," Miles said, "I'd like to hear a positive drop-out story. To hear what it's all about. ———"

The Drop-Out Story

"TODAY, A YOUNG MAN ENTERED a state of relaxation in which he shut everything off.

"He realized that all matter is merely energy condensed.

"He realized we are all one.

"He lay in a field of green grass for four hours going, 'My God, I love . . . everything.'

"The heavens parted and the sun shone through.

"He realized it doesn't always have to be about going on towards going on towards going on.

"Rest, is when your body does all the good things; it builds up everything you need for motion.

"If you're sprinting all the time, you get achy and can't sprint. If you stop sprinting once in a while to rest, you can sprint all the better.

"If you want to improve your 'on,'—you don't keep going more and more on. To improve your on, you have to shut off.

"To get really cool, you have to chill out. To get really groovy, you have to get laid back. To get really sexy, you have to release your load.

"That's what I think you have to do Cinjun is release your load. And I'm going to help you do that.

"To be a truly good warrior, you have to be a lover. Love is the answer.

"If I could melt your heart, we'd never be apart. You're frozen when your heart's not open."

Taking It to Mighty Territory
People Shapes and People Force

STRENGTH, seemed now supremely important . . . This is Cinjun's great message. This is his battle cry . . . And that's where Cinjun angles *it*— and to *all that jazz*—He wants to take it into muscle and strength. That's his territory. He's sure to win there. To smack dab in the middle of *Mighty Town.*

Miles goes with it—He'll beat Cinjun where it's hardest to do it— smack dab in the middle of Mighty Town.

Plop me smack dab in the middle. You can drop me smack dab in the middle. And I'll swing.

Get hit in your soul. You've got to.

Give him some of that ole' wild swing, Miles thought. See what it does? Yeah, smack dab in the middle. Here we go. Hit it! Warrior, samurai, capoeira. Cool! Let's run with it.

Miles saw the battlefield landscape spread before them now.

Ledges and rolling landscape, like a wilderness.

Natural forms for the playing field.

Turning absolutely nothing into form.

"That's what it's about," Miles said, "turning absolutely nothing into form. The secret, is that form emerges. Form follows function, and emerges. People emerge."

"You'd make," Cinjun said, "a fine fourth-rate poet." Cinjun favored Miles with a smile. "Let's stop talking about nothingness and things you can't touch. That—again—is an easy game to play. Let's talk about strength and healthy might, a force for goodness, now when it is so important, now when we are under attack by so much evil. It's a nasty world. Leading us into dreamland is an easy game. *It's a nasty world;* we have to do nasty things to protect ourselves. I'm talking about protection. I'm talking about protecting you."

"For my protection?" Miles said. "Who's going to protect me from you? That's my question for your suggestion box."

"I'm talking about fighting for peace," Cinjun said. "I'm here to show the way to peace."

"Your mind is fled and gone," Miles said, "there is no way to peace, peace is the way."

Cinjun felt good. Miles had lost, and he didn't know it yet. But it would be made clear to him.

"Tricks, Mister Roark," Cinjun said, "no more tricks. Are you here to talk the people's business, or not? You're back to tearing down, and sneering at people who lead. And now, we need leadership, we need someone who knows how to lead a group and move them forward."

"I'm talking about people shapes," Miles said. "And nature. Nature shapes. Elemental shapes. There's nothing more important in the whole wide world, not a thing more important in the whole wide world."

Cinjun shot a look at Miles. "Your plan for evil nations, for the enemies that hate us?"

"Books," Miles said.

"Books?" Cinjun said.

"Poets—" Miles said.

"Hah—" Cinjun explained.

"Jazz. Rock and roll," Miles said.

"That's your plan?" Cinjun said. "To fight dictators with books and poetry?"

"That's what they're afraid of," Miles said.

"That's the best you can do?" Cinjun said.

"That the best there is," Miles said. "That's what they always try to shut down. That's what they're afraid of. That's who they try to hold down. Haven't you ever noticed that? And that's what you're trying to hold down—"

"Now," Miles said, "I do wonder—why are you so obsessed with giving people big, mighty shafts . . .

"You know Cinjun," Miles said, "anyone who is so obsessed with guns, missiles and sticks is compensating. I think you're thinking about what you're missing. A hungry man thinks about steaks. A lonely girl thinks about men. Why are you thinking about giving people big shafts? I wonder."

"You can't see a belt," Cinjun said, "without hitting below it."

"I think you're frightened."

"Frightened of what?"

"Of what you're missing."

"I'll ask the President to pardon you, for being a jackass."

Cinjun was starting to lose it in ferocity—that was more like it—and the audience surged with the ferocity of the moment. The delightful savagery.

Good show! Bravo! Intense Savage Night.

"This is too much," Cinjun said.

Now Miles put a hand out, swept it across the audience. "Look, Cinjun. It's just right."

The people were leaping out of their seats, lunging into the air. Cheering.

Cinjun felt the people urging him. The crowd wanted to see a man get eaten by a lion.

They were screaming, and howling.

They seemed to be saying, *'Fight! Fight! Fight!'* Telling Cinjun: *'It's time—Put him out in the rain; hammer him down to size; show him who you are! Show him. Show him.'* The crowd ached—for moments of high stakes; and it sided—oh, you know, the crowd sides with the guy who takes—oh, they love a rake.

The audience was aching for savagery.

Cinjun was fighting to stay in control. To not kill him.

And the crowd wanted it, so bad. Wanted a fight in the light.

Good Show! Bravo!

CINJUN FELT HIS IMPORTANCE.

Cinjun was an important being. So important. A being of high value. A marquee being—in headlines. A man written in headlines. A man of headlines. A man made of headlines and epic being. Conquistador, khan, mighty general. The soul of triumph—this was an important man. And this was his time.

Back slapping. Good show man. A leader. A ruler. An important man, much glory being given unto him and much to be taken, in the way of great men.

Statuesque being—Giant who walks the Earth—Striding—A Colossus. Great and grand and good and a general. Distinguished extinguisher of evil, ungood, untrue things under the battlefield sun.

Cinjun was tall bravado.

Staggering bluster.

Keen cuthroat-ery.

Miles felt *intensity*. And moving.

Into intensity and currents and storms.

The winding way. Taking it deeper and deeper, farther and farther, higher and higher, away and away. Out! To outer reaches. Into distance. Distance! To the size of forever.

Driving into long distance, taking the size of the road to the size of forever.

Forever, . . . give or take a few steps.

To immense feelings, whose time had come.

How slow the moments did go—Time had died.

The world stopped spinning.

And now, into cool rapidity.

The winds of life came sweeping through.

Wildfire feeling, letting slip, letting slip . . . letting a lifetime slip away.

Slipping and slipping and slipping.

Time flow, river currents,

A wild whirlwind winding wild. Screaming wild.

And now—Cinjun thinking, *"What a goddamn bastard!"*
And now—Cinjun, feeling the train coming.
Miles now taking the night off the track, away—past all, to the nebula.
Let's go into the Capoeira Nebula.
Deeper and deeper, we sail. Into the yellow mist. Into the sun mist. Into the heart of the sunrise.
Sail past the nasty world, past war and peace, and might. Past us and them. Past control.
Nebula all around. Vapors all around. Misty life.
The Capoeira Nebula.
Miles was deep in the nebula now. Cinjun saw Miles emerging from yellow vapors, orange and red explosions—coming at Cinjun, a full force gale, radiating.
And it was affecting the audience, taking them into the sweep.
Danger! Cinjun thought. The man was a danger.

Mighty Grind and the Battle Brew

HOW'S IT GO? Not too slow. A maddening pace.
Dirty and lowdown.
They kept it low, low as can be.

So they go, at a maddening pace.
Keeping it low, low as can be.
You don't want to say a little too much.
You don't want to do a little too much.
When it's all going at a maddening pace.
You've got to take the place, at the maddening pace. Take it tenderly.

So many roads to choose. And it's all just begun.
So many horizons to choose. And it's only just begun.
Watching for signs, working way by way.
As the evening came, and smiled. So much ahead. So much to choose. And it's only just begun.

Getting savage. Getting intense. This was where the feelings were going.

Time to make it tricky. Time to make it a little tricky. Oh, yeah, Trick It Out!

Each man held himself still now, revealing little, just letting the feelings slip, and slide, across the timeflow.

The crowd sensed the feelings; saw the physical signs of the feelings.

What the feelings might have said was myriad.

But the fighters held the feelings in control. Guided them. Guided their energies.

A capoeira was come, here and now, hear it now, near and now, A-Whack and Pow!

What they actually said to each other was simple.

Things might have been said; things were possible now.

Some of them might have gotten said.

They moved quickly now. Collision course realized!

Course realizing collision . . . details to follow.

The night moved fast now.

Tempo in time, time in tempo.

Pictures forming.

Make elegant choices, even in a fight.

It was about the choices you made. How you attacked the thing. All in how you attacked. *Choose wisely.*

This they knew. Each chose wisely and moved with skill.

Collision realizing itself.

Defining moments; define the moments; do not let the moments define you. Do not let your enemy press you into the wrong choices, into wrong action—This was victory for your enemy—No, you had to choose wisely; at times very quickly. This was the nature of the thing. The nature of deadly combat.

Choices weighed heavily.

In free form combat.

How you pressed your advantage was important.

You had to think not just one move ahead, but many moves ahead. You had to determine a strategy, based on the difficulties. And the difficulties were shifting under your feet.

Choose wisely. *Oh, choose wisely.*

Impulse had to be directed toward a plan, and the plan had to be made up as you went.

This was the most difficult part of free form combat—the great thinking involved, the rapid thinking. Making choices on very little visibility, with damn little time. With no recovery time to be had if you slipped in your choices.

Now it moved.

The ground shifted under their feet, and the walls closed in, the ceiling came down, and the shifting ground rose in eruptions beneath them, exploding here and there in dangerous, startling ways.

This was the playing ground. This was the arena in which they fought.

In this arena, think fast. Sense everything. Be ready to react to anything—You did not know what was coming.

This was the way the crowd liked it—now seemed it rich to die; rich for someone to die.

The deadly blows will come from unexpected places; this they know.

Every moment is a moment of testing. As the hustle roamed deeper and deeper into this thing.

Cinjun's strategy—To go to the mighty.

Miles—He will go again to the land of the fair and strong. He wants to fight Cinjun where Cinjun is strongest, where Cinjun has every advantage.

Mighty Sideswipes

CINJUN WAS THE MASTER OF HIS DESTINY. He would not kill him. To not kill him. To not kill him.

"You can stretch the truth," Cinjun said. "And you do."

"Use caution in your tone," Cinjun said. "I'm a fair guy. But you're moving out of bounds; you're using up my entire stock of patience."

"What's fair got to do with this?" Miles said.

"You're a champion repeater; repeat it and repeat it," Cinjun said, "until it sounds important. Because it sure isn't. Bend your mind to the problem. You ran out of things to say, but want to keep talking. So come up with anything. Then go fry your brain in it.

"Put your pieces together," Cinjun said, "create a great big work of nothing."

Then glue it to your rear; I don't know what else it would be good for. Maybe you can sit on it for the hell of it. I'm not going to sit on it.

I won't say it! I won't do that! He can take it from there to some moves that will put me in jeopardy. He avoided the clear traps, moved with skill. This, I must not do . . . you had to know the limits. You were expected to know limits. He bounced up against the limits like ropes.

Choices looming.

No! *Downfall,* lay along that path.

Diverging paths presented themselves. Cinjun chose.

"Put the pieces of your mind back together," Cinjun said. "Maybe you could still end up with something that works."

Or maybe you could steal a better one from a donkey. I don't know if you want to risk working with a brain that advanced for you. Let others do the thinking, you don't have the equipment.

Choose, in the heat of it, in the hottest point of it.

"Be careful," Cinjun said. "Don't preach. And don't pretend that you can teach."

"I'm not preaching," Miles said, "because I'm full of sin."

"Would you like," Cinjun said to the people, "to live in a lion's roar out in the world? Or sleep in a corner, and belong to a dying nation? That's the choice. That's the only choice there has ever been. Now—" he swung round on Miles, "don't pretend that you can think, Mister Roark."

Cinjun turned to the people—

"It all belongs to you out there. Not to this man standing in front of me."

"I make an impression, don't I?" Miles said. "I've tried to fix it. Nothing helps. I mourn for my impression over long winter evenings." Miles shrugged. "My only gift is that I can see—*Comedown is calling.* I can see, what will be—*Comedown is calling.*"

"I'm beginning," Cinjun said, "to think you write your own dialogue. I notice it's a little thin on plot. But don't let that stop you from giving us some more. And we'll put it in an appropriate place."

Rip this place apart. You're the boss.

Cinjun felt his bosshood surge.

"Comedown is calling," Miles was saying. "Cinjun is taking it on the inside—*Comedown is calling.*"

Miles, the nowhere man, was naming Cinjun the Go Scared Man. He was holding the repeating rifle of *Fear;* aiming it sure and fast at Cinjun; and firing off rounds of *'You are scared.'*

And now—the people turned to observe—

Cinjun easing the bite of it, smiling in spite of it . . . forgetting Miles while he was still burning inside his brain.

"So you're going to beat me, huh?" Cinjun said. "Remind me to get scared. I'll write it into my calendar. Leave a note on the door on your way out," Cinjun said, turning to the people, "and I'll have somebody write it into my schedule. 'Get scared of Miles Roark.' " Cinjun heard his engine. It was cooking. And now Cinjun turned his shooting looks towards Miles. And shot a look at him. "I'll see what I can do. But don't look for it too fast. I'm going to have to do a hell of a lot of work to get scared of you . . . to work up to getting scared of you . . . I don't see a way to do it quite yet. But maybe you'll yell *'boo'* some time, that should startle the hell out of me—"

"Boo," Miles said, stifling a god emperor that strove to make him rot, in a life lonely.

Cinjun held his rage in silence.

"It worked—you look scared," Miles said.

"It'll scare me for days and days," Cinjun said. He was about the farthest thing from scared you ever saw.

He was about as scared as an atom bomb.

"Straighten up and fly right," Cinjun said. "Flatten out, and do right!"

"Sit there and count the beatings," Miles said. "Go on take it easy, if you're afraid to lead."

"Do right, Miles Roark. It's time for you to do right, Miles Roark. We want to count on you. Do right!"

"Your hope is getting slender," Miles said. "Cheer on."

The world is still young. There is lots of world left to experience. Does your ending need mending? Let your end take wing. The world is full of possibilities. Sweeping wind-tossed possibilities. Oh so many possibilities.

The Road Less Traveled

"YOU'RE AFRAID," MILES SAID.

"Now why suppose such a thing?" Cinjun said, charmingly—he was the most civilized, charming man you ever saw. And he was forcing caution to be the better part of valor.

"Because," Miles said, "you're not coming to get me. You stand there. And stand there. And stand there. You're going wrong, Cinjun. You're doing it all wrong. You're making a lot of noise. I don't see anything. Take away your noises, and what do you have. Nothing. You're going wrong, Cinjun. You're doing it all wrong."

"Use caution in your tone, I'm a fair man but—" Cinjun said.

"The talk of a coward." Miles swung round. "Is there anything to you? Is there anything to you at all? I want to see the real you. Can you see the real me, Cinjun! Can you? Whoa, can you! Can you see the real me, Cinjun?"

The audience—the people—looked on Miles with interest. They wondered if they might see the real him? They looked at him. They looked at Cinjun.

"I seem," Miles said, "to scare you a little, Cinjun. I'm going to show you to the Golden Gate. This is the *end of days,* Cinjun."

"You make me laugh—" Cinjun said.

"Do you betray what you think?" Miles said.

Cinjun looked sharp. He saw Miles's trick. He felt the turning of the world. Cinjun held himself, and thought coolly, *to not kill him.* To not kill the son of a bitch. Outside he remained smooth, a smooth ocean under the moon.

"Can we see the real you, Cinjun?" Miles said. "Come on, show us the real you, Cinjun. You can't be this scared man, can you? Strange person you are—maybe that's you—a coward living in a yellow house. Doesn't want to know trouble. Is afraid of trouble. I am true trouble Cinjun and I'm here for you. Can you see the real me, Cinjun! Can you! I'm full of life and I can't wait to show it to you. Come on, Cinjun. We want to see the real you. Will you show us the real you, Cinjun? Will you? Will you!

"I'm coming at you." Miles said. "I'm crazy god help me. But I'm all here. Can you see the real me, Cinjun! Can you see the real me!"

Miles was swirling his upper body with the flow of the emotions. Hovering, floating, lightly, easily. Swirling.

Cinjun was still. Entirely still. Breathing deep and strong. And holding his look on Miles. Holding Miles's eyes. With great force.

Miles was taking Cinjun into full force winds. He would not let it be. I am the master of all destiny, Cinjun thought. I will not kill him. To not kill him. To not kill him.

"You declared you would be taller," Miles said, "you only become what I make you. You thought you were chasing a destiny calling. You only become what I make you.

"Look here now Cinjun," Miles said, "what do you see? Can you see the real me?

"You thought force could make the changes go round? What do you see now? Where have you ended up? You're coming up against something. Let's see how your force stands against it.

"What is there to your force? Nothing. What is there to you? Nothing. I'm looking at the real you Cinjun.

"You're framed large. I'm framed larger.

"You're something. I'm something more.

"Can you see the real me, Cinjun? I'm wildfire. And I'm taking over. What are you going to do about? What are you going to do? How long are you going to let it go on? How long are you going to let it go on?"

"I'm trying to speak between lines of your oration," Cinjun said.

"It's hard," Miles said. "I'm saying a lot."

"You're saying nothing—at great length."

"Yes, I'm talking about nothing. I'm talking about you."

"Be careful," Cinjun said. "Don't pretend you can teach."

"We're on the dance floor, Cinjun. This is a capoeira. We're in a dancing fight. The fight is dancing around you. And you're afraid to take a step. Cower. Quake. Run, if you're scared. Flee if you quake. Goodbye Cinjun—if you can't take it."

"I am *One,*" Miles said. "You are nothing—without your people. I am *One.*

"Where do you get your talk of force, Cinjun?" Miles was provoking a reaction. "You're a goddamn coward. You're nothing.

"While I —am *One.*"

A soft sound came at them, from a distance.

Cinjun turned. He saw a marvelous, beautiful woman now standing in the crowd of *his*—of Cinjun's—people. He recognized her. This was the girl Miles loved.

She was a scorching beauty, Cinjun observed. And she was smooth. And she was hot. And she was standing by a burning sun. She was fire. And she was the turning of a world. Turning round and round. And her emotion was hitting. And her heart? Was *burning* with feeling.

And now she was emerging from her flaming world, and she was saying, "He is one." And she laughed. "He is one." And she laughed again. "He is one." And she saw her cosmic kiss taking on dimensions—and she saw a wheel of fire carving into the Sun Night. And the wheel of fire was heading for Cinjun Khan Smythe. "Goodness gracious," she said, "great balls of fire! He is one."—No, it was not going to catch her now— she was not going to let sanity catch her now. No more sanity for her, she was her reason for reason. She stepped into her cool, and lifted the place up to better suit her mood—"He is one!" she said. She swept it into the audience now. She shot her gaze—and the look of love in her beautiful, radiant eyes, and her scorching beauty—at a fellow in the crowd—just for the hell of it. "He is one!" she said to the fellow. It did a few things to the man. One thing it did was—it startled him out of his senses.

The audience reacted with interest.

The fellow felt the turning of the world. This life wasn't good enough. He would change his life. Enter her cool. He had to enter her groove. He wanted to feel the turning of her world. In her body, he saw the kind of loving that could be so smooth. The fellow opened his jacket. Took a deep breath, and reached for her cosmic kiss. He joined into a kind of *'dance'* with this pretty girl. "He's the one!" he said. Oh, how he wanted her cosmic kiss.

A laugh nearby.

Daphne shot her gaze and shot her scorching beauty at the people behind her. "He is one," she said. And burned in a wide sweep with the look of love in her beautiful radiant eyes. Her heart was *burning* with feeling, they saw and it took their breath from them. As they felt the turning of her world, they couldn't breath.

The look in her eyes startled the hell out of the people who fell under her gaze. None of them had ever seen a look like that. And they felt it was the damndest look they would ever see come out of a beautiful woman's eyes.

She's crazy, god help her! They could see the real Daphne. And from her eyes they could see rivers of flowing rain and lunging flames.

It brought some of the other tickets into a lunge; they felt the turning of her world; tickets along the sweep of her gaze, lunged from their cushioned reclines, and began to say, "He is one." They jumped into her groove.

And it was the real them!

Daphne returned her gaze to the man. She looked at this strange man who knew her now, and would long for her for the rest of his life. She flashed him the real her. "He's the face!" Daphne said to the stranger in the jacket, giving him a sultry look that always spoke to men, to the deepest part of men, to somewhere dead in their middle. And that place in this man became flushed, and flooded with blood. And yearned to bursting for her cosmic kiss. This thing in this man saw The Golden Gate. And in her body, the turning of a world so smooth, and he saw scorching beauty, and he was bursting with desire. And he had to jump into her groove. And Oh God! He couldn't take it anymore! He couldn't live if he couldn't fuck her right now!

"He's the face!" the man in the jacket said—and made it real. Having no idea at all of what he was talking about. He felt the turning of her world. And with her look, he would yell out anything she damn well tossed over to him. And make it real.

A laugh nearby. A grunt. Strange sounds. People in strange worlds reacting to strange actions along strange territory.

Daphne danced deeper into the ballroom.

"He is *One!*" she said. And they all felt it, the chill divine. The men felt bursting yearning. The men looked at her. She didn't own the clothes she was wearing.

She tossed it back to Miles.

Miles turned to Cinjun.

"You're running a helluva unit!" Cinjun said. "What do you want to discuss now? What kind of color you are? What kind of flower you feel yourself to be? How do you feel about geraniums? What's next of great consequence and meaning for us here?"

Emotion was taking Cinjun. The night was spinning.

Cinjun remained in control; he remained—high up there; high up in a towering world. He would not dive down and kill Miles in the ocean. He would stay high, above the storm. Let the tide wash and wash below. He would take it in slow control.

"I'm flying through the sky," Cinjun said, "that makes me an easy target for snipers." Cinjun began flowing across the sky. "For idiotic, do nothing, moronic snipers—now you wouldn't happen to be one of those would you Miles? I'm here to help you Miles; you do believe I'm here to help you don't you; we have to help fools. Especially ones rippling in stupidity, boiling in assinineness—who forget where the truth is. Now if you're a jackass, just say again 'you are one.' "

"I am *One,*" Miles said.

"I'll believe you. You look like one."

"Underneath your great show," Miles said, "is a frightened man. Are you a mighty warrior or a blowhard? It comes down to the dare. You're a fighter or not—I am *One.* What are you?

"You're piling it high and deep tonight, aren't you Miles?"

"And you've been laying in it for days Cinjun. My force is bigger—"

"I could shove this fist—" Cinjun said.

"—My force shoots farther—" Miles said.

"—so far down your throat—" Cinjun said.

"—My gun is more dangerous—" Miles said.

"—even your missus will think you're a hole in the ground," Cinjun said.

"—More powerful—" Miles said. "That's why you're scared and I've won."

"You haven't won."

"The last man standing is the winner."

Whoa . . . everyone is with it. It's a show-stopper moment. Bloody excellent.

"I know I'm a man," Cinjun said. "What are you?"

"The word you're looking for is, winner. You do know what that is when you're looking at one, don't you?"

"You're nothing; you seem to be able to talk a whole lot of it."

"Well, I know what nothing is, Cinjun. I'm looking at it—Run, if you're scared. Go on. Git. Go home Cinjun. If you stay you might get hurt. And I don't want to see you cry."

Cinjun produced a smile. "Very good Miles. Excellent."

The smile grew fierce. Rage carried the expression.

"Use force Cinjun," Miles said. "Use force. Let's see what you have."

Cinjun held himself still. To not kill him. To not kill him. To not lose control. To not lose control of his senses. To not let Miles carry him off the track—of sanity. Cinjun held himself. To not go mad. To not go mad.

He was the god emperor. And the god emperor had responsibilities. He could not unleash himself. The rage had to be controlled. He must not go mad. He was insane when he went berserk. He would not let himself enjoy this. He must not allow the pleasure—of killing this man.

"Lone and only you stand there Cinjun," Miles said. "Your people are wondering if there's anything to you. If there ever was anything to you. I'm wondering myself. You look like such a lost soul. Oh, you poor thing. Standing there all by your lonesome."

Miles begins to feel it now. "It's so—it moves me deeply Cinjun."

Miles starts to show him love. Shower him with love and compassion.

"You poor thing Cinjun. Oh how the night has gone for you. All your streets have turned from red to blue. Now you're looking for a better view. I feel terrible for you. You look so sad and lonely standing over there. Would you like some love Cinjun. How about it? Do you feel love. Do you feel loved—do you feel luh-uhved? Do you feel loved?

"Would that help you to be strong? We want you to be strong. We wouldn't want you to go off and kill yourself after this. And go to bed and cry with the lights out.

"We're looking at the real you now, Cinjun.

"Tell you what. I'll show you something to take your mind off your troubles. I'll show you the real me."

What had he been saying? Miles wondered. What on earth had he been saying? Suddenly, he couldn't remember for the life of him? Suddenly he felt himself elsewhere.

Perhaps the wise thing to do was pull himself together. Get himself back on track. It would have been mighty smart to take a deep breath and make it back to where "it" was—where sense and logic was. That would be what everyone else in the world would have done. That's why Miles didn't do it.

Two roads diverged in a yellow wood. He took the one less traveled.

Abruptly, everything came awake. Miles crackled with energy.

He felt it coursing through him—he was suddenly capable of anything. His entire being, crackled and produced a kind of energy. His arms and body shot it into the air—the surge cut through the atmosphere, taking it over. It filled the world.

It flowed and flooded, filling the world.

Miles crackled with energy—The energy taking shape. The feeling deep within him growing, evolving. Taking on greater and greater form. Surging outward in an explosion that took him over.

Miles crackled with energy. He felt it from the ground rising and surging through all his being and then shooting into the air. Slow sensation—taking over.

"Oh, Let Me—Show You—How You—Make Me Feel!" Miles said. In a voice that may have been a little too loud. "Argh! How You—Make Me Feel!" And in the background, maybe The Wonderland Band played the moment a little too strong, maybe too many trumpets blared. But he was One. And he saw things. Now he was the face, and he was dressed up better than anyone.

He saw things along this road. It reached into the Capoeira Nebula.

This was an extending of the fight, into something. He put out— *probing sensation.* He was taking in *wide sweeps.* Wildfire slipped from him. Sweeping feelings and cosmic winds swept in. The winds of life came sweeping through.

The currents grew strong.

Miles was on his way—such a way.

Love had exploded into the form.

He would use it; work its colors in among the green and fold; among the azure; against the orange and red backdrop, splashed across the yellow Capoeira.

A love Capoeira? He would see where it led. And he promptly lost his mind. The world disappeared. And for Miles, there was only the love capoeira.

Miles lost himself in the love capoeira.

The currents grew strong.

Run with the currents? Will you?

Miles was—Miles was on his way.

Some like it hot.

Some like it storming.

Some like it wild.

Miles was on his way.

He would show Cinjun the way to the storm. To wind swept, rumbling, thunderous being—There were men and women high in the forest society who had seen everything, who had seen quite enough of the world, but they had never seen anything like this. A man standing calm, and traveling the world in sweeping orbits around him.

The lights made stars shine on his smile.

Miles wasn't paying attention to anyone. He wasn't aware of anything. His time had come. The only thing he cared about was: Did he like what he saw?

He stood in this place, calm.

Using his imagination to start a fire. And making some sounds that made changes go round. Who gave a damn about the sounds!

It was just thunder.

But the feelings, oh, the feelings!

Immense feelings whose time had come. He was using his imagination to start a fire.

The feelings swept through the streets.

In this place where time had died—the winds of life came sweeping through.

The Pacifica Love Dream Experience.

The audience was being experienced.

Cinjun felt it. Spreading wildfire. Swooping energy fields, emerging stars—an energy field—an emotional nebula.

Miles was making the little world—big! Making "your" little world bigger and bigger.

Cinjun had to match it.

He would not let the devil take the night. As if he was doing no wrong.

It was taking the audience into its sweep.

Madness.

Feeling.

The energy coming off Miles—goddamn him! Damn him to hell! Cinjun thought.

And Miles made it look like mere living. Miles seemed to be standing in a state of perfect calm. Framed in a state of perfect grace. And all these feelings—were flowing, and flowing. Outward. Onward. And roundward. Conspiring an armor, and flowing out again. Moving outward into the outer reaches of forever. Remembering distant memories, recalling other worlds. Flowing under. And traveling down. Sweeping up. And rising over. Rippling over canyons. And flying through the skies. Flowing into the oceans, and flowing through the skies. This was stormy. And this was calm. This was the actor. And this was the scene. He was in this water. And this water was outstreaming out as far as you could see.

This was the actor. And this was the scene.

Now one of the girls Miles loved was a perfect dresser. And this girl had a scorching beauty that danced across the ballroom with a face that looked quite a lot like Daphne's. But this lady was a flow of day energy. Of energy, pure and easy. She was the day trip. And she went by the name of Lady Day. And now heaven above tried to match her for perfect pure and easy grace. Miles saw her dance across the ballroom, the lights making stars shine on her smile.

Miles was the face, and she knew him.

What the hell kinds of feelings, Cinjun thought, were these he was throwing into the mix—that he was mounting? Child's feelings.

The boy was becoming a child.

He wanted to drown Miles in cold water.

The boy was growing younger before him. These were the timeslip feelings, of youth—No wisdom, no sense of the world, no order. Feelings of—*Got to, . . . got to, . . . got to get away.* Feelings of—*Got to, . . . got to, . . . got to Go.* Feelings of—*Oooh, turn me loose!*

Feelings of he can't sleep, and he lays and he thinks.

Of—Love rain on him! Rain on him. Over him. Under him. Over him, under him. Love rain on him.

Of—There's a stranger inside him some where, who stays up all night. A stranger. Who never dies.

Of—Can you see the real him? Whoa, can you! Can you! Can you! Can you see, can you see, can you see the real him!

Primitive feelings and tricks, of not being held down, of riding the breeze.

Life and play. Turning loose.

Running wild, screaming wild.

Careening wild. Stone free.

Winding wild. Stone free.

Miles was on the road to dreams.

He was on his way.

His heart drowning in love dreams. Radiating feelings, sweeping feelings across the ocean, the people ocean.

His heart was drowning in love dreams.

Whipping tails and swirling vapors, of feeling, and a young man, drowning in love dreams.

Cinjun saw the danger.

This stripling was the worst kind of bastard.

Playing to every rank stupidity he could grasp.

Leaving the world behind, Cinjun thought,—same old story,—drop out—as if to drop out was a glory.

And shouting to Cinjun out of yellow vapors that a fight was come! That a fight was here—a blood ship upon them.

Cinjun saw *Tygers* springing all around.

Miles was firing shots directly at him. Cinjun was under fire. Exploding shells of yellow dust. Collisions and tumults.

Cinjun was under total attack.

This wildman was a wolf. This wildman was a villain. What he was playing to—

Cinjun was alone with the situation.

"Do you like what you see?" Miles said. "Crazy. Isn't it?"

He was radiating love.

Cinjun's reaction was *hatred*. Raging hatred. He didn't complicate it; it was not a mixed drink; it was pure raging hatred, every fluid ounce of it.

He didn't look on the emotion coming off Miles as a kind of beauty. He saw it for what it was. *An opiate for the masses.*

He was taking them into love. A man drowning in love dreams.

He was showing them a kind of peace. A swirling vaporous feeling of peace.

Cinjun recognized this thing. It was the peace used by the enemy. The thing used to lower their guard. To take them into a dreamy lull. Ripe for slaughter.

There were fools out there falling for it. It was taking them into its sweep. They were walking on the trail he was carving.

A road of dreams. A road of love dreams.

Miles was experiencing it. Sending it into the audience.

The audience was being experienced.

Goddamn him! Cinjun thought. Goddamn him. Damn him to hell. This stripling was the worst kind of bastard.

Taking them by their feelers into slave existence. Into losing being. Into weak chambers of languid sins. Strange nights of sins and satin sheets. Of pliant women and tender men. Weak striplings.

It would lead to bloody faces—Victory would belong to the enemy— This was where he was taking them—The goddamn bastard. Goddamn him to hell!

Cinjun would be damned if he was going to let this son of a bitch get away with it.

"Do you feel loved, Cinjun? Miles had said. *"Do you feel luh-uhved?"*

This fucking son of a bitch! Cinjun thought. Taking shots at Cinjun, like he could do no wrong. Where does he get his balls packed so tight? His walk so swaggered? His bullshit so thick? Where does he get that done? Cinjun saw him. Saw the real him. Studied him.

Miles had no idea what was going on, where he was, he wasn't thinking—Was Miles's voice screaming too loud? speaking too soft?—Where was he? what was he saying? what was coming?—he had no idea in hell what was going on anywhere in the world—he was feeling—he was bleeding feelings into the world.

The Pacifica Love Dream Experience. And a man drowning in love dreams.

The audience was being experienced. They were dancing across the ballroom with him. Lights shining from the stars across their faces. And Miles was *the face.* This was what they knew. They hoped he would take them deeper into cool rapidity. Please, oh, please take us to where you're going. Heaven above laughed, trying to match this thing.

The Pacifica Love Dream Experience. And a man drowning in love dreams.

Bring it on! Cinjun thought. He watched Miles's feelings dance across the ballroom. He was the face. Fuck him.

Cinjun would blow his mind.

Anywhere you want to take it—Cinjun thought—*I'll take you apart.*

Cinjun towered.

He would destroy Miles. Shatter him. Leave nothing.

Cinjun was high up there. Whoo! He took the world into his sweep. Now—*His Feeling*—he produced a feeling that grew immense—taking the world, taking the night. He would flow further and wider, deeper and vaster than Miles Roark. Miles was just a tear in a baby's eye. Cinjun was the ocean—an ocean boiling with rage; a sky storming with rage. A world on fire. Cinjun was the actor; this was his scene; he was coming into powerful form.

Cinjun was passion. Great, flowing, passion. A rage. A red rage.

He was a House Crimson. He was one.

Ruling—that was what this was about—and warring for Peace. Miles knew nothing of how to rule a world. A world where people could be. This Miles was an absolute disgrace. And a lot of fools were falling for it.

Miles was an opiate for the masses. Dressed up better than anyone for the trick. Peace—but not true Peace—no, Miles was selling the slogan created by the enemy—the many enemies—to get people of right and might to drop their guard. Drop their all. And give this world away. Render the great systems to dust—render them lifeless, grind the great systems to dust, pulverize the great systems to inert powder. To smash and destroy and bring down the beautiful world order. And all that destruction would be done in the name of love and peace—this Miles Roark was indeed the worst kind of bastard. The worst bastard in the world. Cinjun could see it now. He had to be stopped. The most dangerous kind of enemy. One who pretended to come in friendship. Cinjun saw right through him. And knew what was necessary. Destruction. War for Peace. To destroy Miles, to smash him.

But with war art. Cinjun recovered his senses.

He would hold back, be sporting, show that he—Cinjun—was in control.

Exploding Form

ONLY LOVE can make the rain, Miles thought.

Love.

Love exploded into the form.

Only love can make the storm. Only love can bring the doom that falls—in tears—from on high.

Only love could take the fight into tender sensation.

Only love could take the fight into utter madness.

Only love could set light to the Capoeira Nebula.

Only love.

The night grew hot.

Only love.

And now—

Love Explodes on the Scene!

Pow!

Pow! Cinjun holding back, watching the dance floor.

Pow! Miles moving into prowling, and rocking.

Pow! Miles winking at Cinjun, "Hey, lover boy . . ."

Pow! Miles moving into tigerish strut. And crowd feel.

A ship in the night on a lonely sea, a man leaping off a mountain into cold canyons. Feelings and waves of motion filling the expanse.

Love Explodes on the Scene!

Pow!

"Hey, here's the thing," Miles said, "she's wishing for someone to come and sweep her away.

"Here's the thing, she's got the world on a string.

"And my baby only cares for me. Hey lover boy, you ain't got nothing she needs.

"We're a ship in the night on a lonely sea. My baby only cares for me.

"Love, something to sweep her away. What can I say? It could happen. The Lady of Love. She's wishing for someone to sweep her away! What can I say? It could happen."

Miles prowling.

"Come as you are Cinjun. Here's the thing, she's got the world on a string. And here's the thing, you ain't got nothing she needs. My baby only cares for me."

"She does what she feels, as the crowd roars, she doesn't care what anyone else thinks of her."

Miles, dancing and prowling, circling Cinjun.

Miles, floating and drifting, circling Cinjun.

Shaman dance, bringing spirits on the scene, bringing the lady—

Love explodes on the scene!

Miles, taking him into the dance.

Showing him how to bring it on the scene.

Bringing the lady, bringing the rain, ooh, the cool, cool rains—

Love explodes on the scene!

It's cool all around the pool.

Miles, singing the song of the insane. Bringing it on, with the charm, of the insane.

A poet's thing for drama, the charm of the insane. Bringing it on down. Bringing it right on down—love rains—Love exploding on the scene! Whoo, yeah!

Columns of fire, vines of naked senses. Love. Watch out! Watch it, watch it now, wild swing. That wild swing gonna whoop him—. Knock him on his—. My! Oh, my! Watch your senses, baby!

And the lady waiting for something to sweep her away. The sweet lady, only caring for Miles. That other one, he ain't got nothing she needs.

A brand of loving, sets her soul on fire.

A brand of loving that drives her wild.

She doesn't want no other lovers, no other loving.

She wants his love, got to have his love, got to have all of his love.

The audience feeling it.

Feeling sense waves, and something lovely beyond the sea. Waiting there. Waiting for them on golden sands. Ships sailing, and somewhere beyond . . . a little something for them, each and every one of them.

Yeah, they're into it now—It's shaping into a helluva night—

Flying, like birds on high. They're all sailing into the nebula.

Into this strange night of strange dreaming.

And in the heart of a nightfall sunrise, a young man with a strange brand of loving—Miles Roark—screaming wild and slipping across time, taking them to forever. The wild blue forever.

Sailing, sailing, everyone sailing.

And now Cinjun was holding tightly to a thought—his lifeline to sanity. Insanity's horse adorned the night. It threatened to take Cinjun's mind. He held the thought strong. The simple thought, that was saving him. The thought was: To not kill this son of a bitch.

Cheap but lovely tricks—Cinjun thought—where is the true force in his hustle . . . taking them to a city where the night runs deep . . . into an unwelcome sleep, into cotton wooly living . . . dreams of being hip and sunset strips . . . taking them to one side of the town, to bright shiny lies.

They don't see the pimps, pushers, the boulevard of broken dreams and shattered forces, of corpses in fields, and blood soaked slaughter.

He was taking them into a disastrous, dirty sleep of cheap tricks.

And Cinjun was thinking, to not kill the son of a bitch, stay sporting, let his hustle roam, and then take him into endings, into shattered doom-filled endings.

Cinjun was going to stop the wild swing. Watch it, watch it now.

He had to stop him now.

The young have problems, many problems, they need an understanding heart, not this monstrous deranged eager pitiful thinking.

"How you talk!" Cinjun said.

"How you hear!" Miles said. "Listen, here's the thing . . . Take away the noises coming out of your mouth and what do you do? Nothing. You're frozen, because you're afraid. Let all the hurt inside of you die. Love is the answer, baby. Peace."

"Don't be seduced," Cinjun said. "Don't let him make the worse appear the better."

"There's no point in placing the blame," Miles said, "I suffer the same. If I lose you, my heart would be broken. Let all the hurt inside of you die. Love."

"That's where your kind always leads—" Cinjun said.

"Love," Miles said, "hides in strange places."

"To an imaginary—" Cinjun said.

"Love," Miles said, "hides in narrow corners."

"Will you stop cutting me off—" Cinjun said.

"Love," Miles said, "comes to those who seek it. The men don't know what the little girls understand—love."

"I don't like what you're saying," Cinjun said. "There's nothing in it to like."

"Then forgive me," Miles said.

"Lewd and low-down—" Cinjun said.

"Just when I thought you couldn't feel it," Miles said. "Love *comes*— when you least expect it."

"—What was that about coming?—" Cinjun said.

"Love—" Miles said "—Is the answer. La, la, la, love." Miles sailed on. "If I could melt your heart, we'd never be apart. Give yourself to me. You're frozen, when you're heart's not open. The road to peace is peace."

"How dare you!—" Cinjun said.

"—Love one another—" Miles said.

"—Why you obscene son of a bitch!—" Cinjun said.

"—Wine, love and song!" Miles said. "Love yourself! Love free or die!"

"You better straighten out and fly right," Cinjun said. "You have right now to pull yourself together."

"Okay. Let's teach people to stop fighting, . . . by beating them up."

"I'm warning you."

"Oh, I'm sorry. I'll go with your message, as the preacher said, 'Let's flock!' Nah, nah-nah-nah nah. You're a scaredy cat. Scaredy cat, scaredy cat!"

Miles puts up his dukes, starts dancing around.

"You want to go to heaven," Miles said, "you'll be there in seven."

"Love the planet," Miles said, "love your neighbor, love is the answer. La, la . . . la, la, la. La, la . . . la, la."

Now—Cinjun Holding Back

To not kill him! Stay in control, old boy. Stay, be sporting, let him work with that.

Way was leading on to way. Cinjun fought to bring the ship back to port, out of the storm.

To not kill him! To not kill this son of a bitch. Stay sporting.

Turn It Loose

"WHOA, I'M COOKING TONIGHT," Miles said plainly and softly. "I'm on my way, such a way, all through the night, whoo! Come on Cinjun, put me out, or I'm going to burn you up.

"It feels pretty good to win," Miles said.

Cinjun held himself in an upward surge. His eyes held still in a down from over look.

His eyes were something else, Miles observed. Commanding eyes. The devil must have given him those eyes. They seemed like they could control a world. No wonder he was who he was. No wonder so many people followed him. Those were some eyes.

"Go home," Miles said.

Cinjun leaned his gaze—in.

"Walk away," Miles said.

Cinjun scowled something fierce, kept his look loose. "You couldn't handle me if I came at you," Cinjun said.

A trace of a sneer. The eyes lost nothing. They stayed in command.

His brow tightened.

"You snotty bastard!" Cinjun said.

"Turn around. If you're done," Miles said. "If you're frightened to keep going."

"I save lives," Cinjun said, "I don't take them."

His eyes narrowed, staying in control, staying in command.

His expression widened. The eyes burned. His gaze took on flaming existence.

He leaned further forward. And the eyes took on an up from under look. A look that was fierce. Those eyes commanded everything; missed nothing.

Miles felt the eyes. They locked in on him and took him over.

Holding Miles with his eyes, Cinjun shifted his weight back. His head pressed back, letting loose a wave of rage-splashed emotion.

"One drop of rain doesn't make the sun run away," Miles said. "Don't go away. Don't go breaking my heart."

Heated battle! The crowd roared. Good show! Bloody excellent! Yeah!

This had been worth the trip, this had definitely been worth the trip.

Blood, battle, shaking and rolling, bam bam, yeah! Rumble, ringside seats. Rumble tonight. The pounding was here. Go cat, go!

There's a rumble tonight, ain't a damn thing anyone can do! Rumble tonight. Yeah! Who will be the last man standing? Who will be the last man standing!

The Wonderland Band kicked up a storm, this was the heat, this was where it all got—wicked!

Ah, dirty boogie! Let's live it up! Stomping on a hot roof! Shaking loose! Out on the town! Head spinning! Shaking loose! This was not too clean. This was lowdown. The forest city, singing, you ought to slow down.

But when the wicked night gets low down you don't slow down.

You don't give it up, you keep it hot and squeeling when you take the feeling on the town, when you take her on the town!

"Give it up," Miles said. "Let me show you all you are."

Cinjun's eyes held the world in their grip. The eyes swept from side to side, taking control.

The eyes held still. Looked.

Miles felt a chill travel his spine. Those eyes could make you lose your mind. Miles could have sworn that the eyes were on fire. They had to be flames—they couldn't just be eyes. They were burning, blazing. Miles never thought he would see such blazing.

Miles turned to the audience—Good God! They were all lunging into the air. Screaming. In the outer extremities of madness. The crowd was absolutely berserk. Violence charged the air.

It wasn't Miles that had taken them to blazing emotion. It was those eyes.

He turned back to Cinjun's eyes.

Cinjun was doing nothing, absolutely nothing, but his eyes were taking over the world.

Miles stopped breathing for an instant. Those eyes were getting to him. Shaking him something awful.

What the hell was Cinjun doing? He had never seen anything like this in his whole goddamn life. Miles wasn't driving this anymore. Something was taking over.

Miles stepped back then, startled. It was as if an animal were taking over Cinjun. There was something like a wolf there. If Cinjun wasn't a wolf—then he didn't have far to go. Nature red in tooth and claw slipped into Cinjun's eyes and that too began to blaze.

And now—Cinjun moved—to dance across the ballroom.

Now Cinjun was—the face.

He was the night. He was everything. He was these people's world. They knew nothing except Cinjun being. And the Cinjun being was a flame the size of a world. An inferno the size of the whole goddamn world.

Cinjun stepped onto the dance floor.

Miles smiled.

Miles danced around him. Then stopped in front of Cinjun.

Cinjun was startling the hell out of Miles. There was a lot to notice about Cinjun now—Cinjun was fit. Hellishly fit. Steely muscles.

Rippling sinewy muscles. And the frame nature had used in making him was massive. And everything about him was developed to scale.

And now—Miles is standing here—is here, understanding what Cinjun is—

Cinjun is a mountain of power. A man who can throw "anywhere" punches—anywhere they hit a person, they break something.

He can pound an opponent to dust. He has arms, made to break other men's ribs.

And now—he is approaching Miles.

Scream and shout! The trip.

Cinjun heard the trumpets blare.

He heard the waves crash.

He heard the beasts roar.

He heard the moment forming all around, the canyons creating corridors, wind canyons. Way leading on to way.

Cinjun, coming into it, giving the audience what they wanted.

You only go around once on this big spinning planet.

This was his ride.

He came into it, came into it fully, he was now fully his own—Cinjun Khan Smythe.

And he struck.

The Prizefight

FROM THE DISTANCE you could see—Swing and rip, and whipping vapors.

They were in the nebula, coming at each other.

A fight to the finish.

The end of days.

One will be left standing.

The music was hot, the lights were low.

Beneath the sun night, beneath the demon night that had heard one thousand voices and seen one thousand murders, they entered the feverish nocturne.

A fight to the finish.

Cinjun moved in—a mountain of force. Skilled to a peak. Rich with the possibilities of animal force.

Cinjun stood before the people, and the people observed—an *Iron Man*. Hard as steel. Strong as the mountains. Loaded with anywhere punches. Rough and tumble. Heavy weather taking over.

As they stepped out onto the floor, they forgot all other troubles. They had the world to themselves. They stepped lightly. They heard the hot music. They let themselves go. Cinjun let himself go first—he launched a shot that traveled with great speed, and landing with great force, crossed Miles's face. Within this, Miles let himself go, stepping lightly, moving in time with the blow, moving into a counterpunch, which landed hard on Cinjun's face. The men were locked in battle. And took the measure of each other. Searching for answers to war and pain . . . They lay in it for days . . .

Among the observers, some hearts were broken.

It was clear—uhm, that punching Cinjun—was about as effective as punching a mountain. He was a man not meant to be bothered by little things like punches. If you hit him with a steel bat, you just might get him to itch. But don't bother with less.

"Oh oh." Miles, Daphne and a few others got that 'oh, oh' feeling. Yes, Miles felt the feeling. It came with the chill that traveled his spine.

Miles had taken himself into something. The dimensions of his problem quickly became clear.

Miles took a few shots, proving to himself *that he was never going to win this fight.* Cinjun was solid steel. That was the nature and feel of him. Not agreeable at all to Miles's designs of surviving into old age.

Cinjun was steely death in the shape of hammering arms that had all the softness and give of steel girders.

Cinjun would fold this up—Cinjun moved in the way. Animal inside—leading him to ripe conclusions. Cinjun—listened to the wind and the mystery came alive. Delicious night. Nothing would turn him off. Animal inside—led him to the conclusion—The animal took hold. The training, the cunning, the skill, the abilities, they were all there in Cinjun's form. He felt it in his body. And more. He felt the animal taking control—leading him to ripe conclusion. He was coming to the party with all the tricks he could want.

And now—Cinjun punched Miles. It did a little something to him. Miles hurt on the inside. He felt that if Cinjun spoke harshly to him now he might burst out crying. Oh dearest hell and damnation—that hurt! He had never imagined that Cinjun could pack that kind of strength. It was a fascinating surprise.

Cinjun surprised Miles in yet another way—he favored Miles with a smile. Now, since hell and heaven were siding with Cinjun—each moving under Cinjun's guiding fists, he could afford to be generous—he gave Miles an opening.

Miles moved in. Miles counterpunched. Miles gave it a lot—aiming to rip away skin and bone.

The blow did nothing to Cinjun. Except maybe to make him smile.

Cinjun knew fist fighting—as it turned out.

Well schooled in combat—he was. He hadn't made it too well known until now . . .

Well schooled in martial arts—he was. He hadn't made that too well known until now . . .

A master of hand to hand combat—he was. And he was revealing this now. Why not let the world know?

Miles had asked to see the real him. Did he like what he saw?

Cinjun was in his element. He was comfortable working with his fists. This was almost relaxing to him. A nice change of pace.

And now—

Cinjun took total command of the ring, of the arena.

His eyes took command; locked on Miles. He would stay eye to eye until Miles lay beaten and bloodied underfoot. Cinjun understood combat. He knew everything there was to know about working with fists.

Miles moved in to test his ability.

He didn't get far. With startling swiftness, Cinjun delivered a shot to Miles—a nice solid body blow. Very clean. As smooth as good Scotch. You did not want to be on the receiving end of that—While, Cinjun did not even feel the effort of it. He could deliver a few more before the effort would even make him blink.

Miles countered. He took a shot at Cinjun. Miles was certain it was the closest thing to hitting a wall he could experience in hand to hand combat. Miles's shot rolled off Cinjun. Miles had hoped to get a blink out of Cinjun—He hadn't delivered enough to earn that.

On the sidelines, Daphne commented on the situation: "Oh, oh—Oh, dear, oh, dear, oh, dear."

Miles had to fall back—*How to go at it? How to do it? How?* His thoughts raced.

Miles was assailed by a memory. He was in an outdoor gym. He was with Scofield. It was one of their *conditioning* sessions. Scofield said, "Pace yourself, kid—Pace yourself, has many meanings. There's a science to how you wear down an opponent that's stronger than you— *heavyweight fighters usually burn down when you set a wide open opportunity to punch and punch in front of them."*

Hmmm, Miles wondered. There was something there. Some great secret. What form of capoeira was this?

He riffled through looming passages. Hmmm. Ah, it was to be a *bait capoeira.* The plan frightened Miles. Frightened Miles all too hell. Could you pull a thing like that off? Would Cinjun take the bait? Ah, you never know until you try. He played bait capoeira—hidden capoeira. He hid it in the guise of defeat, and taunted, with what appeared to be final stings.

He went with it, loose and flowing capoeira.

The plan called for Miles to tire Cinjun out by getting Cinjun to beat the life out of Miles, while Miles called out for more punishment. Brilliant, wasn't it? Well, it was the best Miles could do.

He drove Cinjun mad—until Cinjun was applying himself seriously to the work of ripping Miles's head off his body!

Miles sheltered his head . . . Gave his ribs to Cinjun.

Blow after blow. Shot after shot. The punishing beating developed.

Time slipped.

And now—Miles—was *enjoying himself!* Well, he had never been in bait capoeira before—this was entirely an experience that few ever knew. That few ever imagined.

Time slipped.

He gave Cinjun a lot of his body to beat.

He danced a lot to escape Cinjun's blows. He escaped a lot of them. Eventually Miles's dance lapsed—

Cinjun fanned his fist across Miles's jaw—

Vrooom, thrak, b'boom!

Ah! This was trouble! Miles noticed. He was in deep shit!

His legs were—

He hit the floor hard. *Ah, this was pain capoeira!—Agony capoeira!* Miles felt an alerting sensation. He was in the mysterious room of agony.

Suddenly, his legs were gone. Where had he put them?

He was—spilling over, down, everything falling away, all he could feel was pain.

He had to come back from this. He had to make it back from this! He had to get up! He had to bring it together! He had to make his legs work! He had to make his body work! Everything was—*pain.* Agony! Waves and waves of pain.

Miles willed his way through it.

Forced himself to function. Forced his body to work.

He got his body to work, moved back into the dance.

They danced around each other.

Miles was not going to let it end.

And now—Miles—

Here he comes—the people thought. *Here he comes.*

Miles broke through, this was walking agony. But he moved, forward. Walked his way out of the mysterious room of agony.

He circled around Cinjun getting his energy back. He just kept breathing. Kept breathing. Escaping blows. Ducking and weaving when he could. Learning to bruise and bleed on the other occasions.

They exchanged blows.

Time slipped.

Cinjun was turning Miles's body to dark colors.

Showing Miles how he made him feel. Through the twilight . . . oh, how Cinjun tried to make his feelings clear to Miles.

Pounding away turning Miles black and blue and bruised and bloody and not feeling so talkative.

Cinjun's fists were speaking, saying, 'Let me show you how you make me feel.'—'Can you see the real me?'—'Can you?'

His fists were revealing their secrets. They didn't want to hold anything back from Miles. The fists were showing Miles all they had; they didn't want him to feel he was getting less than their best. The fists spoke clearly. *I'll tell you they are very easy to understand,* Miles thought. *It is so nice to have such plain talk presented so cleanly.*

Miles appreciated the privilege. This was everything he had asked for and more. Much more. He had feared death. He didn't even consider mutilation. Torture. Torment. Suffering. Pain. Anguish. And all the other trips Cinjun's fists could take him on. Nice to be surprised. The fists had so much in them. Who knew? Apparently, Cinjun did—but he had kept it to himself.

Cinjun had gone about his business of building and acquiring power without *'acting out'* his power. There had been no need . . . He actually had the power! Rather than flaunting it for all the world, Cinjun had actually been doing a major job of hiding the full extent of his power. This man was superhuman. He truly was an Iron Man.

Now he was showing what he had. Miles just hoped Cinjun didn't have much more in him to show. If this was success for Miles, he didn't know how much more success he could handle before he would get very badly hurt. He would already be several seasons recovering from this encounter.

He wondered when he would know Cinjun's limit. The fists kept coming.

Miles did his best to breathe. And think. And do the other things that he had taken for granted until now.

Cinjun was beating Miles's body to hell sensation. To pain sensation. To agony feeling.

"Thank you," Miles said.

What the hell is this bastard thanking me for? Cinjun wondered at the thank you. Then decided he didn't want to sit on his accomplishments; he would give Miles more to thank. Now Cinjun became iron sweetness; and offered him a new blow. It was marvelous. Of course, Miles accepted it. Nothing was changing at all. Cinjun was delivering blows; Miles was taking their measure with his body.

The people watched Cinjun dance across the ballroom; the lights making stars shine on his smile. *Cinjun was dressed up better than anyone,* the people thought. And the people recalled other memories; recalled so many other beautiful moments in this world that had been so very much like this thing they were seeing now.

Cinjun was moving with great promise. To take off a head here; to remove a few ribs there; to soften that middle with pain; to reshape him.

He didn't stop. He didn't want Miles to get to feeling lonely from neglect.

He took some sweet time on Miles's middle. Making sure the work was coming along just fine, making sure that it met his high artistic standards. Yes, it was growing balanced.

He was sculpting. Doing a fine job when you considered his options.

Miles kissed the warm night. Dug for his soul. There—right at the end of that fist. There was something real about the fist he could appreciate. He was getting a lot of truth. Now he sought—truth change.

Now he was twisting, turning, considering the deal being offered. Maybe he would think about it for a while.

Attention! Miles called to his senses, *back to the fight. Next!*

"Listen . . . Cinjun," Miles said mildly, "if this is the best you can do, I'm afraid it's not enough. I wouldn't hold back so much if I were you."

Cinjun looked at Miles . . . Cinjun was smiling; having his way, having a lovely day.

"Are you," Miles said, "getting tired? Geez, I hope you can last the fight. I'm here to go the distance. Why don't you plan on putting in some more effort on this job. I think you can make an impression if you apply yourself." Bam! Cinjun applied himself, like that. Miles was now bleeding from *that.* "I thought," Miles said, "it was a little weak. To be honest, you've led me to expect more."

"Listen," Cinjun said, softly, mildly, pleasantly, "I'll see what I can do. I'd hate for the deal to collapse when we're both so close to the finish we were asking for."

"Well," Miles said, struggling for breath, "I'm sure if we concentrated we could move this to a grander level—something 'jungle,' does that sound good?"

"My thoughts exactly," Cinjun said. "Here we go; let's take you to the end of your air breathing streak. You seem to have too much to spare. You're doing a whole lot of talking."

Cinjun's strategy had been, and remained, very becoming—To go to the mighty.

Miles was deeply journeyed into the land of the fair and strong. He had wanted to fight Cinjun where Cinjun was strongest, where Cinjun had every advantage.   This beating was the realization of Miles's greatest ambitions—with every blow Miles was getting what he had wanted—Cinjun's best shots.

Cinjun was at his absolute best now. The only thing stealing satisfaction from Miles's perfect joy was that if Miles got much more of what he wanted, Miles would get gone—and Cinjun just kept coming up—for more, with more. There seemed no end to his vast energy reserves.

Get him with talk? Miles asked himself. *Get to him? Get him worked hotter and hotter still?* Or was Cinjun warmed up enough?

Should Miles continue talking to bring out the monster in Cinjun? Should he?

Should he do it? I mean, would you do it? Would you make a choice like that? And where would it lead?

It was all about the choices you made.

The possibilities rolled through his mind, flashing, in lightning patterns.

He wasn't getting tired! Miles observed.

The observation had meaning. That was it! He didn't seem to be tiring at all! That revealed it.

That was the reveal—the reveal was no reveal.

He was hiding what was really happening. Cinjun was a master gamesman. There were no physical signs but Miles recognized—*A Show of Force.* Cinjun had to be getting tired. Miles moved into the proof phase of his theory.

Miles felt certain. Yes, Cinjun was mounting a Show of Force. Behind it—he was weakening. Miles felt certain. He felt cozy and warm with the theory.

And took certain action, based on this. On his gut feeling of the situation.

He was alone with the situation. And chose. It was all about the choices you made.

Now he was taking it through the changes. He was the changeling. See him change. Change taking place. Root yourself to the ground.

Cinjun had not appeared to be tiring at all. There were no physical signs. He was working to—*To scare the life out of you,* Miles thought. He was playing Scare Capoeira, Miles realized. *He's playing scare the shit out of Miles Roark!*

He had been doing a damn fine job, at that.

But think it through, Miles, see beyond appearances—Hey you, strip to show us, all you are.

Now Cinjun, let me show you how you make me feel!

Cinjun played the most solid game Miles had ever seen. It was scary, how good he was.

Bam! Miles moved fully into the fight.

Miles moved into the changes.

And abruptly made clear to Cinjun that he was walking his way out of a *bait capoeira*. There was no more need for it. Now he moved with revived pace. And took the fight into this strange mystery.

Cinjun reacted, with a slight, coolly startled pause. *So, he's not as finished as we were led to believe!* Cinjun realized. *All the better! Let us give the people a show to surpass all shows.*

Cinjun felt all warmed up now. This fellow Miles was nicely readied—yes, there *was* that. Cinjun moved deeper into the feverish nocturne. Picked up the tempo of his symphony.

The two men were taking themselves to the peak of their existence.

Now Miles stepped in with a barrage of punches, finding an opening, and sideswiping Cinjun. Then finding another opening, sideswiping him. Stepping back.

Cinjun charged Miles—who sidestepped—no movements wasted. Miles whirled around.

Cinjun took the long road, wasted shots and momentum. Miles stepped in with another set of punches, finding an opening and connecting a lightning jab to Cinjun's chin—The shot connecting hard.

Cinjun blinked. And stopped. That got him.

Daphne let loose a hurrah.

Miles moved in fast—a hook to Cinjun's face. Just right. Miles felt hope spring strong within him.

Now Cinjun stepped efficiently further into the fight.

Miles wasn't playing around anymore. Bait capoeira was over. That was finished. Phase by phase, he probed the looming passages.

Now Miles was staring Cinjun dead in the eye, and out of the corner of his eye looking for openings or violent possibilities from Cinjun.

Cinjun opened up.

Miles stayed put, blocking and deflecting shot after shot. Keeping his movements minimal.   Taking punishing blows from Cinjun. In this way, the fist fight moved into fullest, richest spectacle.

Cinjun looked into Miles's eyes and he saw *Tygers* crouched in jungles in Miles' dark eyes. This Miles was as stupid as a mule, he didn't know enough to dodge a death blow. Cinjun was in full form and raging peak. Cinjun slid away and brought himself to fuller life . . .

Cinjun considered moving in to mutilate Miles, to end Miles's life. People did die in fighting arenas! Cinjun thought—Cinjun saw a vision of the moment. He could make it be, easily—The audience wanted it. And Cinjun had a responsibility to give them the wings of their fate—They wanted to see a man eaten by a lion.

He would—in a sense—"murder" this man, Miles. He could mutilate his face—Cinjun knew how to do it. And he raged. Cinjun knew how to wreak lasting damage.

Miles was too dangerous. He had to be taken out. The fool had brought it on. Now let him pay the price to grow wise, if a little mutilated. He wouldn't be so pretty in a few minutes.

Cinjun—the strongman—took himself into a moment of readying.

A moment where he gathered himself, gathered his strength, pulled himself together, brought all of his muscles to full alert . . .

He willed himself into a heightened state. Forced his energies to quicken. Brought his pulse to an extreme. His adrenaline to an extreme. He took himself into heated sensation. And then sprang.

This was what he did to take himself into *a kill round.*

Now, he reached the ultimate moment.

And he moved forward, with new purpose.

And they watched. Watched Cinjun dance—across the ballroom—lights making stars shine on his smile. He was the face—they knew it. He was dressed up better than anyone they had seen or imagined.

He was the man they loved—wearing their fashion. Getting it to the tee. Heaven above, tried to match him for *charged being.* Ah, watch him—dance—across the ballroom—lights making stars shine—on his smile.

The strongman glided across time. Slipped across the timeslope. Slid along, fully alive. Primal force. Blazing being. Violence. Violence.

Violence to violence, all was violence.

What Cinjun would now give Miles—no one would ever be able to take away from Miles. This gift would last forever.

Cinjun heard the music—he relaxed—let himself go, to the moment.

Wouldn't it be better for him to move to actually kill Miles? Or just make him ugly?

Rich possibilities expressed themselves in his mind. He liked each idea. Maybe he could have both. He would make Miles ugly now, and he would kill him later!

He would make Miles ugly now. Later—he would kill Miles. He would make it seem an accident. For now—he would just make Miles ugly.

The kill?—Maybe Cinjun would do that himself; he liked the idea of later killing Miles.

No, then . . . no one would know who had done it. He wanted the murder to shine on him. Oh, heaven above—he wanted heaven above to shine on the murder. He didn't want anything taking the shine away from him.

He wanted to kill Miles. Now was his chance. He would kill Miles, make it look like something that just happened of its own. Cinjun would express great sorrow later. He could make a great show of it—oh, how sorry he would be. Yes, it would be marvelous.

Now, he had the murder to enjoy—he was free to Murder Miles Roark!

He was free to murder. Cinjun thrilled at the thought.

It seemed so right. Yes, it was right! Murder, so pure. Murder, so rich. Murder, so shining.

He would make the moment shine.

It had been so long since a strongman had risen to power in this nation on a platform of murder. So long since a man had taken the seat of power backed up by an act of murder. The people wanted it so much. They wanted a murderer in charge.

He was a God Emperor. And now they would feel his power.

He invoked the ancient principle: *Reward, if you follow me; punishment, if you oppose me.*

He would use the power principle; prove his God Worth. Ancient spirits called to him in this ancient arena. And now—he was fully in The Pleasuredome. This was true pleasure that lay before him. He was man enough to take the pleasure. He was the most pleasant man that lived, had ever lived, or ever shall live. He was absolutely *pleasant*—supremely pleasant—in The Pleasuredome.

Now Cinjun stepped forward, *To Prove His Godhood.* And to feel his pleasure surge, along the long mighty shaft of His Destiny.

He was a supreme being. Open up World! He was stepping in form outside! He was stepping into God Emperor being!

And there was pleasure all around. The people felt it—pleasure. For the first time in a good long time, they were going to see a man get eaten by a lion.

Hurray! It had been so long. So goddamn long since pleasure was come to them. Now Cinjun carried pleasure into this place.

Ancient tradition, ancient ceremony—*Oh, what a show! this was about to become!* the people thought.

Gladiators! In a fight to the death! Could it get any better? Could it get any more—*civilized?*

Death in combat for noble purpose—was the mark of a higher order of civilization.

This thing was about to get very civilized indeed.

It had been a long time since a strongman took the seat of power through an act of murder.

He wanted the murder to shine on him. Heaven above—he wanted Heaven above to shine on the murder. How to do it?

The murder danced across the ballroom of his mind. Lights making stars shine on Cinjun's smile.

Could he have the murder! Miles had made it possible. Miles was giving Cinjun everything he needed to perform the murder and to prosper by it. It would be a brave wedding of summer mornings. It would be *good* shining for all the world to see!

It would be so perfect! Oh, he wanted it so badly, so longingly. His being yearned for it: Oh, Murder! He was the actor and this was the scene.

Murder, sweet goodly, pure, righteous, beautiful, helpful life saving Murder! Oh Farewell, My Lovely! Cinjun found the beauty laid out before him now. He saw the landscape of the futureflow.

Beauty is Truth; Truth is Beauty. And this murder had such beauty to it!

Cinjun stopped then—abruptly—in the arena.

All gazes took Cinjun into their interest.

Now Cinjun was The Rage Changeling. See him rage. Rage Change taking place. Root yourself to the ground.

Murder! Murder moment!

Murder! Murder to prosper by.

Murder! Murder to save a nation by.

Murder! Murder to take the seat of power by.

Beautiful Violent Enlightened Murder!

Who could resist?

Only murder could bring the love! Cinjun thought.

Only murder could bring the love that rains—like tears—from on high!

Murder Explodes on the Scene!

Oh, Murder shape taking form.

Only murder can make the *Love Life* that rains—like tears—from on high!

Cinjun felt all the love in his heart—all the love in the world—calling for Murder! In a cool, cool rain.

Cinjun stood on the rim of the hill; felt the chill of the night.

Cinjun stepped forward, taking the night into—higher dimensions of sanity.

New murder for sale!

Murder that's fresh and bold. Murder, that's only a few thoughts old.

New Murder for Sale!

Sanity sang the song, so sensible—and—soon to be so sensual.

Sanity, was most sane when it led to murder. Cinjun invoked the ancient principle now as he moved, and he was perfectly sane. As he moved with all the rage in the world, and a lot of love in his heart. It was about the sanest behavior you could ever observe. And Cinjun was now the most sane man in a very sane world, that peopled.

Kill Strike

MILES—knew the moment—This was finality, this was heated death—It had come, the Black End.

Evasion? Could he escape it? Take it into something else? His mind leapt and darted. Yes, Miles recognized it immediately when it began. He was going to have to stop *a kill capoeira.* He had very little to stop it with, he surmised. He moved with the least movement, the least effort wasted. The timing of this dance was important. Here, speed would tell the tale.

Cinjun moved in for the kill.

Yes, Cinjun moved.

Miles saw passages. He chose.

He danced into an open space.

Cinjun moved in for his kill strike.

Now Cinjun was flinging away a wave of rage-loaded emotion. Rage-splashed color came off him in flowing waves. He was rage now. There was nothing else anywhere in his world. And it felt good to him. Strength flowed from the force of it. It made him intensely dangerous. Supremely dangerous. He was the edge of a blade crafted by some master sword-maker. His every motion could now produce death.

Cinjun had killed men before. His mind rolled back to the alien worlds he had inhabited. He remembered murdering the men. And he remembered how much he liked the feelings that came to him. They came to him now again. Delicious feelings. What do you know—this was turning into fun. Cinjun couldn't have had any more fun if he was coming at Miles with an axe—to hack his body to pieces. There was no need. Cinjun would brutalize him with his hands—his fists—he moved into a fine moment. It might be the finest moment of his existence. It certainly felt that way. He would make the final moment look like an accident—He was tasting the accident.

Cinjun stripped to show Miles all he was.

Cinjun moved in to show Miles how he made him feel.

Moving in the twilight, Cinjun put a thought deep into his mind, tasting it. *Miles wouldn't be so pretty in a moment.* The gift he would give Miles would last forever. The people would see Cinjun's mighty work—and know his kind to be work that stays done.

No one could touch all that Cinjun was. He was going to show Miles all he was. Show him how he made him feel.

Cinjun stepped into the kill strike. He moved to change the shape of Miles's face. Hah!

Cinjun knew he would like the new shape.

Cinjun moved in with life change for Miles.

Cinjun moved in. His *Iron Fist* moved to tell a story. Of possibilities for brutality. And the end of summer nights for Miles.

All this—passing through Cinjun. Flashing through him—as his *Iron Fist* went into motion.

The full weight and force of Cinjun's being in the strike.

And for Cinjun it was easy. Moving so easy. Dancing across the ballroom—lights making stars shine—on his smile. He was the face. His eyes were there. Ruling the world.

He was feeling slow sensation.

Miles was looking up from under. Living in slow sensation.

He saw looming passages. Riffled through motions and chose.

He moved.

The motion took him out of the range of Cinjun's *Iron Fist* for a brief moment, only a moment, it was taking Miles into a more open position.

Cinjun saw Miles opening up and trapped him.

Now Miles had a brief opening at Cinjun—a flashing instant—Miles took a ride. Took the moment on the inside. Got the moment on the inside. Extended the flash into a long moment, filled with slow sensation.

Miles and Cinjun locked eyes. As Miles's fist whipped into the world, and took over.

Cinjun's eyes were there when Miles's fist went through Cinjun's face. Took it on the inside. Got it on the inside. Went through. To a place where Cinjun's face had been.

Cinjun's face was thrown back, taking Cinjun's commanding eyes with it.

You might want to grab your wartime coat, Miles thought, *as you step out into the wind and sleet.* I am the face, Miles thought . . .—Hoping. Trying to be the face.

Now Miles was flowing.

Now Miles was on the inside.

Took the ride

for all it was worth.

His fist whipped into Cinjun's world again.

And now—

Miles's fist hit Cinjun's face.

Square

dead-on

and hard.

Vroom! Thrak! B'Boom!—The fist was forging fearsome being.

The fist was alone with the situation. It owned the ride.

Cinjun's face kissed the warm fist, digging for its soul. For a hard instant, the fist and Cinjun's face remained alone with the situation.

Filled the situation.

Cinjun—at this moment of impact, deep in this hard instant—thought, *I've been stopped—How?*

And now the fist went a-wiping—

wiping across Cinjun's entire world.

Streaming, driving, voyaging—this summer night belonged to this hard instant, and to this streaming hard fist.

The fist continued on its way, leaving Cinjun behind.

The fist was moving away from Cinjun and into tomorrow—the fist was alone with the situation.

Returning home to Miles.

Miles brought it on home.

And Miles stepped on back—

As Cinjun went into—freefall.

He went into falling sensation.

In the flow of it, he determined to *recover.*

Twisting and turning moving into *recovery.*

But suddenly he came to the end of his falling streak—hard instant—hard impact on hard tight ground.

He lay on the floor recovering.

Alone with this situation.

Did you ever think about it Cinjun? Miles thought. *Did you ever think what to do in this kind of situation?* Interesting, wasn't it? A lot to consider. All at once.

Cinjun trusted in his ability—as he took himself into recovery. Into strong recovery.

He lay on the floor recovering.

Alone with the situation.

Take a picture for your children, Cinjun. This is a moment you will remember for more than a season.

Were you coming to the end of a certain conquering streak? No. Of course not.

This was a tight spot—But Cinjun had gotten out of tighter spots.

He felt the recovery taking hold.

He took a straight course through the recovery. Feeling it in every reach of his body.

Ah-huh. Taking away the pain he was feeling. Now he was working again. Coming into the next phase. Fully Cinjun Smythe. Fully a strongman. Moving. Moving. Moving.

He wasn't going to take this lying down—So—uh, now, baby, he was moving into: *all right*. He would make everything *all right*.

Cinjun 'The Vision' Smythe moved. Taking observers with him.

Love, Put On Your Faces

"GET UP CINJUN! They're going to think it's a fake." Miles said.

"You're going to go down from a lovetap! Come on, get up!"

Cinjun would win, of that Cinjun was certain, that was where this was heading. But this difficulty had to be dealt with.

The moment was to be attacked, by Cinjun. The burden was upon him.

The thing had been given to Cinjun, and it was his to do.

The task was his to do.

It spurred Cinjun to defiance. Cinjun operated in his old way with . . . his old strength. Nothing would stop him.

Press on. Move forward.

Step, right, left. Left. Right. Heart attack!

Go to the floor. Fold. Rest a while.

His present difficulty had to be dealt with.

Oh, yes, Cinjun, now contemplate your mixed emotions and inner feelings at this key point in your imperial campaign.

Cinjun proceeded in this way.

It pained Miles to see Cinjun like this, in this sad state. After all he had been to Miles, . . . and it seemed like only moments ago.

And now—Cinjun down, Miles above—Miles rode the whirlwind moment.

All was in a freeze around them, verging on action, intrusion and calls to other moments. But in the moment there was only Cinjun Smythe, the most important man in the world, and his brave visitor, Miles Roark.

Now, Miles carved—Miles carved *inventions* into light, in the depths of this night darkness—now Miles was struggling, searching, probing to make everything all right.

Now Miles was moving in the native way. Every rock, tree and creature had a spirit. What you felled was a spirit gift of the Earth given to you. To be treasured, cherished and enveloped.

Spirits Parting!

Ah, Spirits—you treated spirits with special being. They were to be experienced.

Now Miles was experiencing Cinjun life, Cinjun being. And all the love you could find in summer and winter or anywhere the hell else you looked.

You had to fulfill certain rites at the close of the hunt. A spirit had been felled, and had now to be elevated.

You had to sing the blues!

And Miles knew—that you can't fool the blues! Oh, no.

See, you can fool the world, but you can't fool the blues. When you're making all the moves, it's so hard to lose—but you can't fool the blues. Oh, no.

You *can* fool the *rich*—But you can't fool the blues.

It just laughs at each lie. You can't fool the blues.

The Blues called Miles to journey—

The journey pulled on Miles heavily with its spirit demands.

You see, The Hunter has to fulfill certain passages of feeling. The Hunter has to feel the Blues. He had to actually feel the Blues! And you can't fool the Blues, it just laughs at each lie. You can't fool the Blues, oh no.

Before him—this was the Animal, whose spirit death he had brought about.

And his need of him, had to be made clear with blues-splashed feeling.

You had to show your feeling for the animal spirit that was killed in the hunt. This was Hunting Ceremony. It was very essential. It was more than respect. Miles was standing before a messenger of divine power.

Miles—the Hunter—was killing a God. Wiping him out.

And you must not make it a personal act. You are performing the work of nature.

A bluesy privilege, was being given to you.

It had to do with the power of the animal master. When the ancient ones of the distant lands sat down to a meal, they thanked god. But when moving in this land's ancient native way, there was another spirit force to be considered and felt—a native power to thank. These native people thanked the animal.

The felled animal was a power superior.

Providing relationship.

Lower relationship.

Now the Superior Animal, has powers that human beings don't have—and Cinjun had proved he had Animal Being.

So Miles—as the ancient Native Ones had—moved in one way. Be friendly with the fearsome animals' threats. And then kill some of them.

Then know, feel it in your soul, that the Animal was a giver of . . . purpose and being.

Now the journey called for Miles to carve his invention of light in the dark passage.

Cinjun Khan Unumbatai S'mythe would be many years dead before he could rise again.

Miles would have to leave Cinjun in the Capoeira Nebula.

Love, Put On Your Faces!

"There will be other nights like this," Miles said, "and I'll be standing here with someone new. But there will never be another you.

"There will be other songs to sing, but there will never be another you.

"There may be others, but they won't thrill me like you used to do.

"Tomorrow, I'll have to find a way to live the rest of my life without you.

"You taught me how to live, how to be myself.

"Now you're giving up on giving, baby. You're out of my reach, baby. You're gone.

"And there will never be another one like you.

"Now, it's time to say good night.

"Good night, sleep tight!

"Oh, Love! A world has opened up for me. A world filled with all your love."

Cinjun thought, it was bad enough that he was on the floor, he also had to listen to this talk, about Love! All this bilge, was merely the stuff, rubbish that rhymed with wit. He wasn't going to dignify it by using the word—ah, it was just shit.

The flow of the ride that had taken him here assaulted Cinjun. He was getting it on the inside.

Left, right. Heart tremble! Heart tremor! —Hit the floor.

Now the ticket was to—Hold onto the floor!

There you go! Keep that floor steady, don't let it wobble!

Perfect. Now stay still and stay a while.

You're just time away from standing up, Cinjun.

Lying down for a while could only do you good.

So let it do its good and might works.

Be floor, Cinjun, be floor, my friend.

Oh, Cinjun *The Vision* Smythe.

Gentle soldier, lie and rest.

And scheme of how to take over the world from this abutted place. Think of valor and blood. Rise and murder; slaying and slaughter from this abutted place. The many women you will have; the many men you will rule from this abutted place. Stay in bed all morning and then rise like the giant and wreak your revenge on the world that peoples.

Love has exploded and rent your mighty blood ship. Oh cruel vicious love! Love is a bomb. A vicious bomb, thrown at you by sinners. Hate love! That's the most beautiful thing you can do. Hate love for all the damage it has done. Hate love for the way it weakens men. Hate love for the way it seduces women. And let something die in you, inside.

There, well murdered!

Soon, you will rise   and wreak havoc like a mighty tempest on the world that peoples.

A light and breezy murder. Very well murdered.

Cinjun lay there, alone with the situation.

As a crowd rushed in.

Good night sweet God Emperor, Miles thought. *Another night has passed. Time for me to get moving . . . time to move on.*

Let's slide out the door.

Miles Roark walked against the current of the people to—Daphne Fox. Her love was burning. He could not keep out of the flame. He felt her against him. And then—they were alone with the situation.

Love, Put On Your Faces.

He turned to look at Daphne, and the bunches and bunches of people weren't there. They didn't matter at all.

Honey, let's slide out the door.

Come on, darling, the time we have isn't long.

In a flash he was gone, it happened so soon. He was gone. And she with him.

Nobody saw him. Nobody heard from him. One writer wrote a book about him.

Time to get away from this side of life. Honey, I want you to be by my side. Me and my back-door moves. Let's slide out the door.

Come to me. The time that we have isn't long. Honey, let's take it.

No more, honey. No more of this. Let's get away from this side of life. No more, honey. No more.

Come to me, darling. Come to me, woman! Argh, let's slide out the door.

They slid out the door forgetting painful memories. It was time to move on. No more cold shots. No more, honey. No more.

They were gliding away.

Let's go.

Let's go.

People asked if he was dead. No reply.

He did the craziest thing you can do when you win—He disappeared from the scene.

And he was not to be found.

He couldn't stand the weather.

She went away with him.

She couldn't stand the weather.

The time they had wasn't long.

They were gone.

The time they had wasn't long.

Come to me, darling. Come to me, woman.

Me and my back-door moves. In the morning dawn and night.

Good night, darling. Another night has passed.

The Beat Goes On . . .

WITHIN THE *LIGHT*VISION NETWORK, within the core feeds, within the central feed—in the command center—a call within the body of the works—

At the Associated Feed, a voice called out:

"Big Red is down. Repeat, Big Red is down. Gilligan is still standing."

The Night Holds Sway

DRINKS FLOW. People dance across the night. With the stars shining on their smiles.

The big wheel spins.

And the beat goes on . . .

The beat goes on . . .

The ride goes up and down, and round and round. It has thrills and chills and it's brightly colored. Feathered against the dark night. Against the black reaches of a long dark night. The night is great—deep and wide.

Somewhere, a couple falls in love. Somewhere, a couple breaks up. Drums keep pounding their rhythms. A bass booms.

And the beat goes on . . .

The black night takes Miles. Removing all that came before—Miles is done. If it's not revolutionary, it'll have to do until the real thing comes along.

If it isn't jazz it'll have to do until the real thing comes along.

The black settles. Casting wide. Taking the world.

Time slips, time slips.

And the beat goes on . . .

Out in vast reaches of the black sea . . . jazz comes into the world. Escaping from the core of the world that peopled.

Escaping. Escaping. Escaping. Now.

Sunbursts of Morning

ESCAPES from the black, black ocean of black dreams.

Sunbursts!

Light dreams burst into the blue sky—escaping, tearing loose of the black, black sea! Forming sunbursts.

Erupting, breaking through the strange night of stone.

Sunbursts!—Scorching beauty, your sun has risen, leaving it for all to see, if your warmth can touch your many ones. Mornings made in love understanding.

Into realms of blue and light.

Sunbursts rising from black seas.

It was the morning of the world.

The sunbursts rose from the black seas.

And filled the skies—sunbursts—forming sun dreams. The dreams grew in the air. Watered by rain, nourished by sun, the dreams grew.

Grew wild, and began wãoynding wild.

Wãoynding and wãoynding.

The sunbursts and the sun dreams began to seek, to seek in the river wild. Through the endless reaches of the river all, they sailed. Sailed into eternal realms. Casting their light, . . . their light descending on the day.

Quinn

LIGHT DESCENDING from the sunbursts descended on the realm and manor of Quinn "Flintstone" Martin.

Life was quiet now. Everybody was settling back to business. Cinjun arrived for a meeting, and found Sidney in the parlor.

Quinn sauntered in. Quinn looked at Cinjun.

"We're going to take House Crimson," Quinn said, "away from you. Congratulations. We're going back to the old concept, Foundation House. Sidney will help you make an exit."

Quinn started to leave. Considered the moment. Quinn turned to Cinjun. He wanted Cinjun to be perfectly clear on where this was all going. "You bore me," Quinn said. Quinn turned from Cinjun and walked away.

Now—how would Cinjun live—without all the gifts that Quinn Flintstone Martin gave to him!—Well, that was not Quinn's problem—He would take all the light from out of Smythe, and leave not a beam behind.

Cinjun would remain, not much else would be there to cherish.

Not much would be left that stirred or spoke, or breathed.

And now—moving things along, Quinn put the lid on the tomb, and went out to play golf!

It was a beautiful day outside. Of that he was certain—Every day is beautiful when you own the world, and its gold.

Miles Roark would be ridden from the world, the beautiful world. Of that there could be no doubt. But that was work for another day. Quinn never took his work with him. Today was meant for golf!

Golf, and then after, maybe a square meal of *women!*

Boy, that sun was just bursting out, today. Mm-hmm, it was bright out there! Blazing away out there. It was really cooking.

Quinn Martin, the man from down south, way down south, stepped on out . . . He sailed on out. Ricocheting away.

He was Quinn "Flintstone" Martin! He owned the world, and its gold.

The Twin Whammy!

LIGHT DESCENDING from the sunbursts descended on the realm and doings of Grace Smythe and Lori Kelly.

Cinjun and Skyler were being visited by Grace and Lori together . . . with Lori's father.

They sat here together in House Crimson, comfortably in The Octagon Office.

Grace took a breath. A rather pleasant breath.

Grace turned to Lori. And smiled. Lori smiled. It was the beginning of a beautiful friendship.

Grace turned to Cinjun and Skyler.

"We've decided to break up with you," Grace said. "We thought it would be a hoot to do it together."

Now Cinjun and Skyler looked at the situation—Reacting with a stop. Everything came to a dead stop. The world moved into a dead stop. And held itself there.

"Lori," Skyler said, "what's going on here? I mean, what are you thinking?"

"Love fatigue," Lori said. "It ran its course and now I'm over it. It was a love cancer. It was a phase. I've asked daddy to take care of it."

Skyler turned to Daddy. Daddy produced a smile. It was shaping up to be a memorable day for him.

"Get rid of him, dad." Lori said. "He bores me. I'd like something more interesting."

Skyler looked to Cinjun. Nothing moved. Cinjun was still. Cinjun shifted his weight in the large cushioned high-backed chair, and held his gaze on Grace.

Skyler Larkin Malloy turned to a point between Cinjun and the women. This was a situation. His head hung there—defeat!

The smell would be strong upon him, he thought.

And on this place.

It was time to leave House Crimson. Start his own cult. He could find a virgin. Start a religion. That was the thing. He would leave this place of murder, and limp slaughter. And he would be fine, don't you worry none about him, thank you. He was Skyler Larkin Malloy, and he was on an ascent, momentarily interrupted! He was Skyler Larkin Malloy.

And in the alley behind House Crimson, he would presently beat a fast retreat.

You could consider him gone, on.

To a place further on.

Left for further on.

Later that day, he would pack his trunk and make his getaway. The nightime was the right time, to flee from this place.

This girl had a heart like a rock in the sea.

How dare she do this to me, Skyler thought. She'll pay for this just wait and see, some day.

The Industrialists—
Maybe a great magnet pulls all souls toward truth

THIS MILES WAS of some interest to them now.

They would go to him.

They would ride in on limousines and wide body jets. They would come in with contracts and lobster dinners. They gathered together, forming plans for his talent. They would mold and shape it and work it into the routine.

They would go to him. Yes, they would come to him. As friends. And help him work his act into the routine.

They would find he wasn't home. Miles was with Daphne, and they were away.

Where were they? the industrialists asked.

Off to an island. They were off on holiday.

When would they return?

No one could say.

Well, how do you like that? the industrialists said. Outrageous! Crazy and outrageous!

Now they wanted him all the more.

They had to have him. He was special. And this Daphne, she was something too. Word had traveled 'round the campfire that she had felled three tall men just by dancing barefoot across their smiles.

Well, where was she?

Off to an island.

An island?

Off on holiday.

When would she return?

No one could say.

Oh, damn it! Outrageous!—They wanted her all the more.

Who was she with?

Miles Roark.

Oh, he was special. This Miles Roark was something too . . . word had traveled 'round the campfire that he had . . .

Goodnight Grace

CINJUN'S MANSION WAS QUIET.

Grace was standing on the front steps with packed bags.

Scofield pulled up.

She ran to him, leaped into the air, landed on him and wrapped herself around him, shapely legs and all.

Cinjun was watching from lonely distance.

Grace and Scofield would take a drive back to the old town, back to the place where they met. Back to where they met . . . back to the old way. In a state of go your way, laugh and play. Exploring the joy to be known, in a mellow tone.

Cinjun turned his thoughts from the scene and drove them into distance.

Crash to the Other Shore, Cinjun thought. Cinjun considered age, and basking in darkness. And what it meant to be: Forgotten! He would be many years dead, but then he would rise again. And he would take the world!

He had: future. A lot of blaze. Oh, he would—Crash to the other shore . . . Comet flying across the sky . . . He was going to carry the world away, . . . lead it, to a House Crimson. All, would begin again. He would crash to the other shore. He would carry this train off the tracks. Crash to the other shore. His future loomed! Freedom comes when you learn to let go. Life goes on now—Bring it on—Carry on now! Bring it on! Peace, would be worth the killing.

He was, after all, the most important man in the world. The greatest man that had ever lived, or ever shall live. And other such honors.

Burdens that weighed heavily on him. Many tasks were his to do.

It wasn't easy, but somebody had to be Cinjun Smythe.

Cinjun Khan Smythe. Emperor, regent, lover, philosopher and savior.

Cinjun would act fast, move rapidly, and lethally. His great works, were dying in waves, fainting in coils. There was no time to waste. Every breath would be directed to winning. And the bloody slaughter that need follow. Or preceed. Wherever, the bloodshed lay, he was ready. He was getting a little mixed up these days, but he would pull himself together, and wreak havoc, to build paradise.

Paradise was a bloody business.

He would hunt him down and revenge himself. The revenge would be sweet, the sweetest moment that ever lived or ever shall live. He was losing it a little bit. Not so you would notice, but he would pull himself together. Paradise, was a bloody business.

There would be time enough for love, once the killing was done.

The Beach

MILES AND DAPHNE WERE on a beach.

A surf of sunstreaks.

A sky of blue waves.

Daphne said, "Cheers!"

Daphne and Miles were on holiday . . . Raising drinks into the air.

Stretching out before them . . . white sand, surf, clear blue-green waters.

A gentle breeze.

Palm trees.

And sun.

"I'll race you in," Daphne said.

They raced into the water.

They crossed the surf. They both dove into the blue at the same time.

And crossed into the futureflow—

And—

Oh, the places they will go!

Into Forever

RISE SPEED & AWAY. Time slipping, a-slipping away.

Rise speed & away. Time slipping, a-slipping away.

And the beat sailed on . . .

The sunbursts sailed on . . .

The sun dreams sailed on . . .

And among them, a Seeker moved in Forever.

In the reaches of Forever, the Seeker sailed on . . . its heading, past tomorrow and to Forever.

Meeting other seekers.

In The Wãoynding Dream.

The Relief from nightmare.

Ah, the Wãoynding Way.

Songs. Deep and rich and true. Songs. Deep and rich and blue.

Of people shapes flowing. People flowing across fields; shaping themselves in skies; forming the All into beautiful wild people shapes. Human forms and human giants. He's and She's, stone free. Each song of to be, open and true. Each song, the ancient spiritual, "Do What Is Inside of You."

And the dream sailed on . . .

Ah, the Wonder in a World that Peopled.

Ride the wind. Take to the skies.

"Why, it's *All Right,* it's all right, it's *All Ride.* Move on. In the way, of Life and Play. To See and see and see. To Fire and fire and fire. And rise ever higher."

The river forming people, the Olde Man R'hivyr, the river forming people, rolling, a-rolling along. Forming people song.

Forming The Lady of the All, The Lady of English and The Lady of Love. The All saying, 'Give me a river of people.'

And inside each, a Seeker.

Boldly going and boldly being. Giant in being, open and seeing.

'Oh let it People. Bring me giant people.'

Be they light, be they bright, and . . . oh let it People!

Ah, the Olde Man R'hivyr forming the river of People. Open shore and open way. Opening on Forever.

And in each a Seeker, a Seeker moving in Forever.

Rise speed & away.

Thru sunbursts—

Thru sky—

Thru air and stratosphere—

Thru outer madness—

Thru black and infinite reach—

A Seeker moving in Forever—

Running wild—

Wild with the power, wild as can be.

The End

www.ingramcontent.com/pod-product-compliance
Lightning Source LLC
Chambersburg PA
CBHW072101020726
47501CB00003B/668